Korea 38-Parallels

Hoyle Leigh

Sutro Crest Publishing, San Francisco

ISBN 9780999248409
Library of Congress Control Number: 2017911735
Sutro Crest, San Francisco

Dedicated to Alexander, Vinnie, Carol, Jia, and Gary,

and to the memory of Joongshin and Ok-Hi

CONTENTS

1	Escape	1
2	Smoke Rises in the Distant Mountain	16
3	Father's Sins	19
4	Love, a Hateful Stranger	33
5	A Glorious Dream	38
6	The Thirty-Eighth Parallel	44
7	The Patricidal Society	51
8	The Stick of the People	54
9	In the Land of Our Ancestors	60
10	War!	64
11	A Fateful Night	75
12	A Shattered Dream	80
13	The Match Girl from Kangwha	84
14	Snow, Blood, and Ideals	89
15	An Oath of Great Trust	96
16	Dislocations	103
17	Of Storks and Open Doors	107
18	It All Depends On the Competition!	116
19	The Magic of Chemistry	128
20	Paradoxes	133
21	Of Changing Seasons	137
22	Work Will Set You Free!	147

23 A Home for Every Patriot 160
24 Perry Mason versus Sigmund Freud 164
25 Of Cherry Blossoms and Magnolias 175
26 The Cost of Survival 186
27 A Silent Night 203
28 In God I Distrust 213
29 The White Deer Days 221
30 Lucky Again 225
31 Bo Erectus 230
32 Kiss Me, Kate 240
33 April Is the Cruelest Month 248
34 The House with the Darwinian Garden 263
35 Salt and Tears of the Earth 266
36 The Ice Castle 269
37 The Trophy 275
38 Saving Lives 281
39 Regrets of Dying Young 291
40 Secret Missions 307
41 Of Fathers and Mentors 313
42 The Last Train to America 318
43 Not for Kimchi Alone 326
44 Love Reborn 338
45 A Red Rose for a Virgin Queen 343
46 Not Before the Casket Closes 346
47 A Tokyo Interlude 353
48 Ou Est La Choo-Choo? 359
49 Toward Sunrise 368
50 Epilogue: Parallel Tracks 377

Author Biography 383
Appendix: Background Information 384

This is a work of fiction. Except for historical facts and figures, any resemblance to actual persons or events is purely coincidental.

1

ESCAPE

Overcrowded train from Manchuria to Seoul, South Korea

The train whizzed through the platform that announced, "Sunjin Station." Not an express stop. Then, the train came to a screeching halt. Suk tried to look out the window of the train, straining past the broad shoulders of the man standing in front of him. Suk and his wife, Yunhee, had managed to weave themselves into the front end of the car, and Bo, their three-year-old son, managed to sit on the trunk that Suk had put on the floor against the wall. Yunhee was holding Bo's hand and providing support for the trunk Bo was sitting on. Neither could see out because their views were blocked by the surrounding taller crowd.

There was a palpable tension in the air even before the train came to a complete stop. Suk could see glimpses of brown uniform outside the window. Suddenly, the doors of the train were opened loudly, and they heard shouts coming from outside.

"Every passenger must unboard the train immediately! Hurry! Hurry!" These words were shouted in Korean by a coarse-looking man in a wrinkled greenish-brown uniform, brandishing a pistol in his hand.

Men in similar uniforms were surrounding the train, some on horseback but most on foot. They were of all ages, some in middle age, most in their twenties, and some looking barely in their teens.

Their weapons, rifles with bayonets attached, automatic carbines, and even flamethrowers, were pointed at the train and the people in it. A few feet in front of the spot the locomotive stopped was a large tree trunk, obviously freshly cut and allowed to fall onto the tracks to stop the train.

All the passengers were rounded up in the station's square at gunpoint. There, they noticed tanks on the streets. Heavy black tanks with red stars painted on them and soldiers with pale hairy faces who wore three watches on each wrist.

"Comrades, the People's Army, and our friends, the Army of Occupation of the Soviet Socialist Republics, welcome you to the Democratic People's Republic of Korea. We understand that you are coming back to Korea, trying to escape the cruel, dying tantrum of the Japanese Imperialist Army and their dogs. You will find a welcome home in our People's Republic," addressed a middle-aged, kind-looking man with a red scarf on his neck to the crowd in Korean, using a megaphone.

"You will all be fed and provided shelter and work. But, first, we must process you according to what you need and how you can serve our society. First, we must ask all those who are Japanese to come forward. You shall be repatriated as enemy aliens according to international conventions."

A few Japanese shuffled out into the area indicated by the soldier. Then, a few more.

"By international agreement, all Japanese must be repatriated by our Soviet Occupation Force. If any Japanese are found who have not surrendered to the Occupation Force, they will be treated as active combatants who refuse to surrender and punished severely. All Japanese must step out immediately," the soldier said deliberately, authoritatively, and persuasively.

Now, quite a number of families stepped forward. Suk saw his former boss Ito, his wife, and their two small children step out. "Sayonara, Ito," thought Suk. "Stay well, and take care of your family. I hope to see you someday."

"OK, all the Japanese subjects. Please follow Comrade Soh here, who will lead you to the waiting train on the other side of the platform.

"Now, our society needs leadership resources—intelligentsia, teachers, professors, government officials, writers, poets. Those of you who are, or have experience being, teachers, professors, government officials, writers, poets, and their families, please come to this area," said the man with the red scarf.

Quite a few people were stepping forward. Suk was about to take a step forward when Yunhee grabbed him by the wrist, whispering, "No. No." Suk was confused and torn. He felt rather reassured by the gentle-looking and gentle-sounding man with the red scarf, and he felt he could contribute his expertise in government and education to the People's Republic. After all, he had, at best, a very uncertain future in Seoul as he was practically a fugitive, having disappeared after a scandal. But he also trusted Yunhee's intuition, and she was warning him to stay put.

"We also need expertise in land management. For this reason, those of you who have had experience with land management, as landowners, bankers, or real-estate brokers, please step forward also," continued the man in the red scarf. Again, a sizable number of people stepped forward and joined the intelligentsia. Now the group numbered perhaps 150 people.

The man with the red scarf faced the remaining group, which almost filled the small railroad station square, and said, "Is there anyone else in this group who would like special treatment?"

His tone had changed, and his voice filled with contempt and hate as he said, "The intelligentsia, the teachers—they are the worst enemies of the people, because they poison the minds of children and teach them to aspire to serve and become the bourgeoisie. Then, the officials of the corrupt Japanese government—they are the traitors of the nation and of our glorious class struggle. Landowners, bankers, real-estate brokers—all vampires exploiting the proletarians. We have no room for them in our new country!

"Here in the Democratic People's Republic, we do not have the corrupt judicial system of capitalist lackeys. We, the people, are the court. So, in this people's court, I demand the death penalty for self-confessed enemies of the people standing in front of you. Anyone who is opposed?"

The square, filled with people, was unbearably still. The silence was finally broken by the man with the red scarf, "The people have unanimously convicted the criminals!"

Ta-ta-ta-ta-ta-ta-ta-ta-ta-ta-ta!

Even before his words left his lips, the men in uniform standing in front of the condemned group opened their automatic fire and mowed them down in waves until not a one was standing.

A little girl shrieked as her mother fell on top of her. She crawled from under her mother's body, only to be shot in the head repeatedly until her head burst open like a ripe watermelon dropped on concrete.

Even then, they continued to fire bullets into the dead and dying men, women, children, and infants.

Blood oozed out of the collective heap and formed several little brooks, soaking the feet of many of those who had not stepped forward, who just stood there as in a trance, mute witnesses to a tableau that would be ingrained in their brains forever.

Evening

Smoke and the sweet, sickening smell of blood still hung over the station's square when the remaining group was marched off to a school building consisting of only one large auditorium or classroom with a wooden floor. There was another larger building adjacent to it, with perhaps more classrooms and offices. The desks and chairs were stacked up on one side of the wall. They walked into the building like automatons and ate the cooked rice and barley made into balls handed to them by women in tattered clothes, obviously local peasant women.

The man with the red scarf was again addressing them on the megaphone, standing on a desk.

"Comrades, you are the proletarians, those worthy of our new nation. Rest tonight in this school building, and beginning tomorrow, you will learn about the great deeds of our leader, Comrade Kim Il-Sung. You will learn right thinking and will be comrades in arms in building our proletarian utopia, our Democratic People's Republic of Korea. Long live the Democratic People's Republic of Korea and our leader, Comrade Kim Il-Sung!"

Each was given a blanket and some water. Then, they were told to lie down and sleep. There were two buckets on each side of the room, to be used as toilets. No one dared to use them. The two doors to the auditorium were missing, perhaps taken off the hinges so that the guard could peek in any time. Every man, woman, and child lay down and closed his or her eyes. No sound. No conversation. Even infants did not cry.

When the lights were turned off, everyone fell asleep. Or so it seemed because of the stillness, the silence of the night except for the guards' footsteps. It was a clear but moonless night. The interior was dark; the only light came through the high glass windows from the starry skies. It seemed the red scarf left only two or three guards in the school building. Perhaps he felt secure that the newly declared proletarian comrades would be too scared to move, much less run away. Or, perhaps, he understood that, at least during that night, these people simply did not have the will or the presence of mind to do anything but obey his orders.

Suk opened his eyes with a start as he felt his arm being tugged. "Sh-sh-sh," breathed Yunhee as she gently awoke him by tugging at his arm with her hand. Her other hand was still holding that of Bo, who seemed to be fast asleep.

She whispered, "We must leave here. Tonight."

"But that's impossible. We will be shot!" Suk whispered back, astounded.

"Yes, we can escape. There are only two guards on this side of the building. And one of them fell asleep over there about ten minutes ago. I looked carefully as we came in to determine how we might escape, and I saw a little path between the two buildings that leads into a pumpkin patch. We can sneak into the path, which is invisible unless you stand right in front of it. We can crouch and walk through the path and then into the pumpkin patch. I noticed that the guard makes circles by walking out of here, turning right, and then going around the building, coming from the left. We can get to the path by crouching out of this room and turning left when the guard is walking about halfway in the opposite direction."

"But what about Bo? Do you think..." Suk was not sure.

"Don't worry about Bo. He is good at being quiet when I ask him to," whispered Yunhee.

"OK, Yunhee. Let's pray this works. Tell me when, and we will go," said Suk, squeezing Yunhee's hand hard. Increasingly, Suk felt that Yunhee gave him strength and courage at times of crisis.

Yunhee woke Bo gently by squeezing Bo's hand that she was already holding while he fell asleep.

Bo opened his eyes right into those of Yunhee, who smiled and whispered, "Bo, we will play a game of 'sneak out.' We will all be very quiet, and we will sneak out of here and go into a pumpkin patch. Not a sound. All you need to do is crouch and walk gently and avoiding stepping on people, and then once we get out into a little path, we will walk quietly through it till we reach the pumpkin patch."

Bo winked and whispered, "Yes, Ma. I like to play these games."

The guard peered into the dark classroom. Silence. He turned around, lit a cigarette, and started walking to the right. When his footsteps had become about half as loud as when he started, Yunhee whispered, "Now!"

The two adults and one child crouched up noiselessly and started walking carefully to avoid the limbs, torsos, and heads, in and out of blankets, that lay spread in a random fashion in the classroom, all fast asleep. But no one snored. Only the barely audible sounds of regular, rhythmic breathing that nevertheless was a symphony of muted anguish.

They were now almost at the door. Just a couple more hurdles.

"Oops! Oops! Oops!" Three muted cries. Bo had stumbled on a leg. The leg bent at the knee and then just resumed its previous position. The owner had not awakened!

The three looked out the door, saw no one, came out of the door noiselessly, and tiptoed into the path between the buildings. As they were about halfway along the path, they could hear the footsteps of the guard, initially soft, then louder and louder. Then it stopped! Has he spotted them? Yunhee motioned Suk and Bo to stop, and they held their breaths. If the guard comes into the path, they will surely be caught! Suddenly, in the stillness, they heard a stream of water hitting the ground. Someone opened a faucet? Now, it dawned on them that the guard was urinating near them, probably against the wall of one of the buildings. To the threesome's immense relief, the sound stopped, and the footsteps resumed, now getting softer, away from the path. The threesome resumed their tiptoeing on the path.

They were now in the open pumpkin patch. The pumpkin patch was rather large, and the pumpkin stalks were about waist-high with variously sized ripening pumpkins here and there. Beyond it was an orchard. Suk, Yunhee, and Bo crawled across the pumpkin patch and then into the orchard. Among the trees, they could stand up and walk. Away from the schoolhouse, away from prison guards, away from the smell of blood.

Dawn. They walked for miles and miles through orchards, grain fields, ditches, and hills, trying to avoid any signs of habitation. Yunhee was holding Bo's hand as she walked, the other hand clutching her handbag with Bo's birthday pictures. Suk walked empty-handed as he had left his suitcase in the classroom. They walked in silence. Bo knew that this was not a game.

They were now walking among shrubs, about Suk's height. The sky was definitely lighter now on their left—must be the eastern sky.

"Who goes there?"

They stood still, behind a shrub that did not quite conceal them. They were horrified and tried to stifle the sound of their labored, now-all-too-audible breathing.

A rustle of the leaves, and there appeared the figure of a man dressed in traditional white Korean casual wear.

"Oh, hello there. You must be refugees," said the man in a kindly voice. Now they could see that he was an oldish man, perhaps in his sixties, with a white beard.

"Don't be scared of me. I am just taking my morning walk. I live over there," said the old man, pointing to a house with a thatched roof, about two hundred feet away. There was white smoke coming out of the chimney. He continued, "In case you are wondering, you don't have to be afraid of the Russians and the Communists here—not yet, anyway. They are not here yet. And if you are trying to go south, there is a boat that leaves to Inchon from here. But you look tired and famished. Why don't you come to my house and have some breakfast? We have plenty of barley, and my wife will be happy to give you a meal. We are Christians, and we like to help people who are fleeing the Communists."

Bo did not understand much of what the old man was saying because he did not understand Korean. But he could tell, from his tone of voice, and from what little words he understood of Korean, that he could rest awhile and, perhaps, eat! Bo had walked a truly long distance for a three-year-old boy, and he was famished. He bowed to the old man and blurted out, "*Arigatou gozaimasu!*"

"Ha-ha, young man, you will have to learn to speak Korean from now on. But you are very welcome. You really look tired; come on in," said the old man as he led them to his little house.

"Yes, Bo, you must learn to speak Korean. Right now," thought Suk. He said to Bo as they followed the old man, "See that village in the mountain up there? See the smoke? Say in Korean, like this, 'S-moke rises in the dis-tant mount-ain.'"

"S-moke rises in the dis-tant mount-ain," repeated Yunhee.

"S-moke rises in the dis-tant mount-ain," said Bo.

It was August 24, 1945, 2:00 p.m. One week after Japan's surrender in World War II. Northern Korean Peninsula, 39.6 N Parallel, 126 E Longitude

Nine Days Earlier
August 15, 1945, Noon, Tokyo Time, Daeduk, Manchuria (44 N Parallel, 128 E Longitude)
Suk sat in front of the squeaky radio with his boss, Mayor Ito, and some five or six of their subordinates. This was a special broadcast from Radio Tokyo, relayed by Radio Harbin. The martial music was interrupted, and the announcer said, "Attention, subjects, His Imperial Majesty, Emperor Shōwa!" The voice of the Emperor of Japan, Shōwa, whose given name was Hirohito, came on the radio.

Everyone stood up and bowed toward the radio. The Emperor spoke in a barely audible, shaky voice, made even more difficult to hear because of the static: "...thus I ask you to bear the unbearable, suffer the insufferable. To prevent further bloodshed and ruination of our country, I have decided to accept the Allies' terms and unconditionally surrender..."

World War II was over. So was Manchukuo. So was Suk's career in the new frontier.

There was no panic in that small office following the Emperor's announcement. Only stunned, tense stillness. No one moved for perhaps two minutes. Then, everyone's eyes were fixed on Ito, the mayor, the leader, the former Japanese soldier. Would he commit suicide in the fashion of the old soldier with the loss of the war? Would he ask everyone to kill himself, like a samurai?

Finally, Ito looked around the room. He cleared his throat and said, gently, "Looks like we will go home. Yes, let's all go home."

The war in Europe had ended in May of 1944, with the suicide of Adolph Hitler. Mussolini's fascist Italy had collapsed one year earlier. In February 1945, Roosevelt, Churchill, and Stalin met at Yalta and decided on the division of Germany, and of Korea at the thirty-eighth parallel, the northern part to be administered by the Soviets and the southern part by the United States, until full independence was granted to Korea, "in due course." This division of the Korean peninsula proposed by Stalin was accepted by Roosevelt and Churchill in order to entice the Soviets to enter the war against Japan. The Soviet Union, however, still demurred from actively entering the war against Japan. Meanwhile, General Douglas MacArthur's forces were defeating the Japanese island by island in the Pacific.

On August 6, 1945, the first atom bomb in the history of humankind exploded in Hiroshima, which resulted in some one hundred thousand casualties. Two days later, the Soviet Union finally entered the Pacific War against Japan. The second atom bomb was dropped in Nagasaki three days after the first one. Japan surrendered within one week.

August 20, 1945

The Soviet Red Army was now pouring into Manchuria. Hordes of Cossacks on horseback, old Russian proletarians in uniform, peasants with peasant manners and a thirst for blood. Soldiers who slept on black bread as pillows, sat on them as cushions, and ate them for food. To the "refined" Japanese (including Korean) colonials in Manchuria, the Russians were feared barbarians. Tales of summary executions, rape, torture, and dismemberment were rampant. In one village, the Russian soldiers gathered all the men, Japanese, Korean, Chinese, Manchurian, in the schoolhouse and then locked the doors and set fire to it. They pillaged the village, raped the women, and then shot them all. Then they stole the rings, watches, and any other jewelry they could find from the corpses. They did not hesitate to cut off the finger of a woman, live or dead, to steal a ring off it. Many Russian soldiers were wearing three watches on each wrist.

An orderly transition of power to the Russian Army was what Ito had planned. Now, the tales of atrocities of the invading Red Army made it abundantly clear to Ito that an orderly transition was an impossibility.

"The honorable way would be suicide. But the Emperor asked us to suffer the insufferable. And, perhaps, after suffering the insufferable, our children will see another day of light and sunshine." Ito instructed his secretary to obtain train tickets for all close subordinates—destination, Seoul. Then, from Seoul, he and his family would go back to Tokyo, Japan.

August 22, 1945. 6:30 p.m., Daeduk, Manchuria (46.6 N Parallel, 126 E Longitude)
Train Station
The core officials of the city government and their families, who held the train tickets, arrived at the station in an uncovered old city truck at the end of the day. Ito, the mayor, sat in the front, and all others were in the open back. Late-August evening in Manchuria may be anywhere from comfortable to boiling hot to freezing cold, depending on the direction of the wind. It was freezing that evening, with arctic winds blowing from Siberia. Ito had bought reserved block seats for his entourage in the second-class compartment, and everyone expected to travel together until they reached Seoul. The railroad station was filled with people, Japanese, Korean, Chinese, and Manchurian families with children, and trunks, valises, and all sorts of bags containing whatever possessions they could carry. They were all trying to get on the train south to escape from the Russians.

Suk, the Korean deputy mayor, first got off the truck, lifted Bo out of the truck, and putting him on the ground, helped his wife jump down. While Suk's attention was focused on Yunhee's jumping down, a wave of crowd rushed in, and little Bo was swept by the crowd out of their vision. There were people, including children, everywhere.

"Bo, where are you?" Suk cried as he looked around frantically. "Where is he, where is he?" asked Yunhee, face pale, feeling faint. Too many people all around. In the sea of people, mulling about in waves, they could not find Bo. All they could see were heads and shoulders of people, thousands of people, and above their heads, only the silhouette of the station building and the flagpole with a tattered flag flapping in the punishing, freezing north wind. In the confusion of the crowd, Suk's coworkers and their families just rushed into the station without a second glance at what was happening.

"What were you doing, taking your eyes off Bo?" Yunhee's eyes asked Suk, without words. "He could be crushed by the crowd, and nobody would even notice."

They moved frantically, in random movements, pushing the crowds, being pushed by the crowds, searching for Bo. Time was running out. The train was due in five minutes. And no sign of Bo.

"We will have to take the next train," said Suk dejectedly. "Perhaps we should ask a policeman how to find Bo?"

But there was no uniformed policeman to be found. In fact, there were no uniforms at all among the throngs of people filling the grounds of the railroad station. Even if there had been one on another end of the plaza, they would not have been able to reach him before he moved away. Suk and Yunhee looked at each other, not knowing what to say, and continued to look around calling Bo's name.

"Ma-ma, Da-da, Mommy, Daddy," Yunhee seemed to hear Bo calling. She turned around—no Bo. She turned around again, looking in every direction. "Da-da, Ma-ma, Daddy, Mommy," Suk seemed to hear Bo's cry.

"Bo, Bo, where are you?" cried Suk as he looked around, but there was no sign of Bo.

"Here, Mommy! Here, Daddy!"

This time, there was no mistake!

"Here, under the flag, Mommy, Daddy," cried Bo. Frantically turning toward the flag, they saw first a waving hand and then the top of Bo's head, barely above the thousands of heads of the crowd. He had climbed up the base of the flagpole and was crying out for Mom and Dad.

Yunhee did not know how they finally got on the train. All she remembered was that she finally got Bo back in her arms and vowed that she would never let him get lost again, let him be away from her again. She threw away the valise she was holding (She didn't even remember what she had in it—perhaps clothes? Perhaps jewelry? What does it matter?) and held on to Bo's hand tight. Never again would she let his hand disengage hers. Never!

The Japanese train system is renowned for running on time. Even during the chaotic days of the end of World War II, the Seoul-bound train from Harbin stopped at Daeduk on time. Once the train stopped, a mob scene followed—everyone was climbing onto the train, with or without tickets—in fact, there was no conductor to check. Forget about reserved seats in the second-class compartment. Forget about seats at all. Suk and Yunhee were grateful that they could just get on the train. Yunhee held Bo in her hand, and in her other hand, she just held her handbag that contained some jewelry, money, and Bo's photographs taken at birth, at one hundred days of age, and on the first and second birthdays. Their only other possession was one large suitcase that Suk still held containing some warm clothes. Suk also had, in a hidden pocket inside his pants, a silver knife with a jade handle that his father had given him as he left for Seoul to find his destiny.

They were grateful that they were aboard the train. And they did not know then how grateful they really should have been, because that train was the very last Seoul-bound train to leave Daeduk—the next train never left Harbin, and the Manchurian border was closed to all traffic within twenty-four hours.

The seven-hundred-mile train ride from Daeduk to Seoul was long and tedious even under normal circumstances. A full two-day trip, the train usually had lengthy stopovers at Dongha, Manchuria, then at the border town Kangye, and then at Pyongyang in the northern part of Korea, and finally it would approach Seoul, exactly forty-four hours after departure. Suk's train could not, however, keep the normal schedule.

For one, the train did not make any stops. It could not, because it had absolutely no capacity to add any more passengers. The conductor was warned by telegraph that there were mob scenes in each station in Manchuria and that the train would probably not be able to take off again once it stopped. The train was ordered to proceed without stopping. It made the long and tedious Manchurian crossing in record time, stopping only to replenish its coal supply in a very small out-of-the-way station, the stop of which was unscheduled. So, in eighteen hours' time, the train had crossed the border and was in the northernmost part of Korea. The passengers cheered loudly as they sped into Korean territory after the border crossing, which was remarkably perfunctory as just one guard glanced at the train from the platform and waved it on.

9 Days Later
August 24, 1945, 7:00 a.m., Hwanhung, North Korea, around 39.6 N Parallel, around 125.5 E Longitude
During the chaotic days of the power vacuum, August to September 1945, the Red Army overran some parts of Manchuria and the northern part of Korea, but other parts were left intact. The People's Army of Kim Il-Sung was a ragtag group of partisans that numbered only in the hundreds who loosely served the Red Army.

In some localities, the local Communists took charge of the government in anticipation of the Red Army. In others, the old order or a modification thereof still existed—for example, in some towns, the Japanese mayor invited a reputable local Korean political figure to take over the government as a "provisional mayor." Amazingly, in these localities where the old order had not been demolished, even trains and buses ran.

Suk, Yunhee, and Bo found themselves in Hwanhung, only about ten miles southwest of Sunjin where the train was forced to stop. Hwanhung was a small port town on the west coast of northern Korea, where a non-Communist Korean was running a provisional government and where there were still boats leaving for

Inchon, the gateway to Seoul and South Korea. They were able to buy the last remaining tickets on a fishing boat that was carrying passengers now.

The medium-size boat was filled with refugees. Although not every one of them had witnessed the mass executions and other atrocities, they had seen and heard enough to want to avoid being caught in a Communist state.

So, in three days' sailing, tired, seasick, hungry, nauseated, and smelling like fish, Suk, Yunhee, and Bo touched the ground of South Korea, safe from the Russians and the Communists. For Suk and Yunhee, it was a homecoming of sorts. They cried with joy when they saw the still-familiar landscape of Seoul, the familiar mountains, and the Han River, flowing peacefully just as they had remembered. But they also mourned the loss of their pioneering dreams and their successes—their social position, wealth, power, and acceptance in Manchukuo, which had now all turned to ashes.

When Suk first recalled these events of August 1945, it was like seeing a silent movie at the wrong speed—in slow motion at times and then sped up with jittery pictures, skipping from one place to another. Eventually, though, the speed settled down, and the sound effects came on. Suk added polished, theatrical narration, and played these scenes over and over again for enthralled audiences.

2

SMOKE RISES IN THE DISTANT MOUNTAIN

1946, Seoul (37.5 N Parallel, 127 E Longitude)
Bo

"S-moke rises in the dis-tant mount-ain," said the father intently to the three-year-old son in Korean.

"S-moke rises in the dis-tant mount-ain," repeated the son, trying to please the father. The son spoke fluently beginning at age two—in Japanese, not Korean. The father was trying to teach his three-year-old son Korean in a hurry. It was January 1946. The Japanese had surrendered to the allies the previous year, and the son, who spoke only Japanese, had to learn to speak the language of the new country that was to be his own, Korea. The father had known Korean but had to suppress it and learn Japanese during his childhood when Japan occupied Korea. His son had to unlearn Japanese and learn to speak Korean at age three.

When Bo looks at distant snowcapped mountains, he still hears a voice—a rather high-pitched voice—his father's? his own?—saying in Korean, "Smoke rises in the distant mountain."

There on the distant mountain where the smoke rises, perhaps there is a little house filled with love, where a mom, dad, and baby son live. The smoke rises from the chimney of a woodburning stove in the kitchen, and on the stove is a pot of stew, dinner for the family. Perhaps the mom is rocking the cradle where the baby sleeps. Mom is singing a little Japanese lullaby in a low alto voice: "Sleep well, my baby, nehn-nehn go-ro-ito, sleep well." *Nehn-nehn go-ro-ito*—a nonsense phrase that sounds like Japanese. Why does it always come to my mind?

January 1992, Snowbird Ski Resort, Utah (40.5 N Parallel, 111.5 W Longitude)
"Stop here, Dad, and enjoy the scenery," says Ali, making a neat hockey stop a bit to the right of the soft snowy trail. Ali, age seven, has been skiing already for four years. His face has a healthy red glow, and his eyes sparkle happily in the early-morning sunlight. To the left of the ski trail is a cliff and a striking view of the valley becoming clearer with the rising sun, with misty snowcapped mountains looming in the distance.

My dad was a wonderful storyteller. He used to tell me, when I was around Ali's age and younger, bedtime stories that were so fantastic, so frightening, and so amusing that I would stay up wanting more. Stories of ghosts, egg monsters, love, hate, and revenge. I knew that he made up most of them, and I also knew that they were so good because he made them up. He said he was going to write an autobiography, and I was looking forward to reading it someday. But he never wrote the autobiography. Instead, he drank and told stories. He could not sit down and write what he could so easily tell. (Why didn't he at least tape them?) Stories of his elopement. Stories of his glorious days in Manchuria. Stories of his perilous escape from the Russian Red Army at the end of World War II. They are now fragments of my memories, and I shall give them life.

Where there is smoke, there is fire, it is said. Fire from a now-distant mountain, North Korea, would later engulf the whole Korean peninsula and devastate countless lives.

The Korean peninsula is about the size of Italy and juts out from Manchuria into the Sea of Japan. The bigger powers of East Asia, Japan, China, and Russia, vied for influence in the peninsula, and there have been many invasions and incursions from both China and Japan in Korean history. The end of World War II resulted in the northern half of the peninsula being under Soviet domination, and the southern half was first occupied by the United States and then became, initially, a democracy in name only and then, eventually, a liberal democracy after a number of popular uprisings. North Korea remained a Stalinist hereditary dictatorship of the Kim dynasty even after the collapse of Soviet Union, its only reluctant ally being "Communist" People's Republic of China. North Korea's economy remains stagnant at 1960s levels, while South Korea became a thriving modern state, with the twelfth-largest GDP worldwide. Now one can ride a bullet train from Seoul to Pusan in two and a half hours, compared with the ten or more hours it took for the trains in 1945.

The events I recollect here may shed some light on how the two Koreas diverged so much since the end of World War II.

3

FATHER'S SINS

Bo

In Ali's face, I often see my own dad's face. Dad said my face resembled his own father's. I was proud to hear this, because I knew that Dad respected his father. His father (my grandfather) was an acknowledged genius, who spoke both English and Japanese fluently in addition to Korean, and was a high government official in the diplomatic corps of the old imperial Korean dynasty before Korea's annexation to Japan in 1910.

Ali never knew my dad, his granddad. He died just a few months before Ali was born. Ali is almost like a reincarnation of my dad's personality—carefree, easygoing, sociable, musical, nature loving—very different from me. But I also see my own face in Ali's and for a moment remember the carefree feelings I used to have when I was about Ali's age. No. Before his age. Before I was in the third grade in school, the year the Korean War broke out.

My mom's face, a blur before, becomes vivid with the memories of the war. Her short stature (four feet tall), her granite face, and her strength all come to me vividly when I think of the war. And my thinking then that I would never be able to survive without her, that I would kill myself if she died. Then, I think of the whiff of fragrance I smelled when she came home and the joy I felt that she was home.

Uncle Chang

Uncle Chang was visiting. He was a bear of a man but very playful. Whenever he visited, he would either lift me up on his shoulders and run, or play tag, or do something of this sort that my mom was not happy with. Mom did not like Uncle Chang, especially because Chang let me engage in rough-and-tumble types of plays that she frowned upon.

"Come on out and play with me like a man," said Chang. Ignoring Mom, I rushed out, and we started running out in the yard. I was chasing Uncle Chang with a toy pistol. Chang ran fast, and I tried to catch up with him when I stumbled on a rock and fell. Crack! I felt a stinging pain on my collarbone. My mom came to see what the commotion was, picked me up without a word, and took me to the doctor immediately.

At the university hospital, the doctors put my arm on a sling and reassured me and mom that it would be all right. "You know, when it heals, the broken bone becomes stronger at the place where it is broken because it gets thicker." My mother was not satisfied that more things were not being done than just a sling. She brought me to the osteopathic hospital, where the doctor prescribed "heat treatment." I had my shoulder under a 100-watt bulb in the hospital for about thirty minutes every day for about two weeks while mom stood watching. Her face was determined, and with each hospital visit, her dislike of Uncle Chang grew ever more.

Uncle Chang was my father's eldest brother's eldest son. He was the oldest and most legitimate brother, whose name was Sun. My Dad was the eighth and last son of a high government official and landowner and his concubine's first and only son. At that time, a *yangban* (noble person), like my grandfather, could have many concubines, but only the first wife and her children would enjoy legitimacy. My father, Suk, was the favorite of my grandfather's. Thus Uncle Chang was really my cousin, but he was so much older that I called him Uncle.

1920–30, Kangwon Province, Korea under Japanese Rule (37.9 N Parallel, 128 E Longitude)

Being less than legitimate had its advantages. For one, you didn't have to adhere to the prescribed custom of going to traditional Confucian schools like the legitimate firstborn son. Besides, the Japanese occupation that began when Suk was only four years of age put a damper on many of the old customs. When Japan annexed Korea in 1910 and dissolved its government, Suk's father retired to his family estate in the mountainous Kangwon Province, where he spent his leisure in the old noble tradition of writing poems, painting nature, and reading. Being his father's favorite, Suk persuaded his father that he should learn newer things by going to the capital city, Seoul, and enrolling in the Seoul High School, a school set up by the Japanese for the Korean elite, which eventually became the equivalent of Eaton in England. At the age of twelve, Suk went off to the high school, renting a room nearby.

When he was accepted by the new high school in Seoul, Suk's father called him to his private study, closed the door, and said, "You will be the first one in my family to go to a high school rather than a Confucian school. My blessings and best wishes go with you. Although I was a government official of the old order, I know that times have to change, and the old have to give in to the new. Some say I am a traitor because I have not opposed Japan's annexation of Korea. But Japan represents the new, and old Korea with its closed-door policy, its ingrained Confucianism, represented only what was wrong with Korea. Its caste system, its blind adherence to old customs and artificial legitimacy. You see, I really love your mother, and if I could, I would have obtained a divorce and married your mother as the one and only legitimate wife. But because of the old order, I could not divorce my first wife, whom I married when I was only five years old, an arranged marriage like all the others at that time. Go to Seoul and find your own destiny!"

He opened the door of his *tansu* and took out an exotic-looking traveling knife. He handed it to Suk, who accepted it with both hands. The knife had a shiny silver sheath and a green jade handle with silver bolsters at either end. The sheath had a small ring to which was attached a black leather strap, which could be used to hang it or attach it to a belt. It was surprisingly light, so that it could be worn inside the pants or a jacket.

"I bought this knife from an Arab merchant when I was traveling as a diplomat. You see, the knife blade is sharp and pointed like a sword, made of special steel. The handle is made of jade, with silver bolsters on both ends. And the sheath is pure silver. The Arab told me that this is a special knife that will protect me from all evil, and it has done so. Now it is yours. Stay safe, my beloved son!"

In Seoul, Suk felt free. Freer than he ever felt before in the house of his outranking "legitimate" brothers and relatives, where his mother lived in a small room in the back of the house. He was the concubine's son. No matter that his father loved him more than all the seven older half-brothers, no matter that he was the smartest of them all. No matter that even his half brothers loved him as the baby brother.

Seoul, unlike Kangwon Province, was a bustling city. The streets were crowded with horse-drawn carriages, rickshaws, occasional automobiles, and pedestrians, all sharing the same cramped roadways. Travel within the city was mainly by foot, or by packed coal-burning buses that spewed black soot. There was electricity in large buildings and even an electrically operated streetcar line, although most illumination in homes came from candles or kerosene lamps. There was a cacophony of sounds on the streets: wheels creaking, street vendors hawking, children shouting, and pedestrians seemingly arguing in various languages—Korean in various dialects, Japanese, and Chinese.

Suk learned Japanese quickly, the use of which became compulsory by then. The use of the new language seemed to give him an added sense of freedom from the old ways. He hungrily absorbed all the new information and knowledge that his teachers could offer. He learned about other nations, other lands, and science. About engines, chemicals, and painting. And music! For the first time, he saw a piano. Prior to that, the only musical instruments he had seen were the traditional Korean string and percussion instruments—*kayagum, komunko,* drums. But this huge black thing sitting on four legs, the piano, was really a marvel. Suk was entranced as his teacher played a melody on the piano. His teacher invited Suk to sit in front of the piano. Suk did as he was told and started to play with the keys. In a few minutes, he was playing the same melody that his teacher had played! The teacher was amazed and gave Suk private lessons, without charge. He did not encourage him to become a pianist, however, because being an artist or a musician was still not a prestigious thing in Korea, especially for a son of a yangban.

High school was a wonderful place for Suk to make friends. Being a naturally sociable and caring person, Suk made many friends. In spite of that, he experienced continuing hurt when a newfound friend would abruptly stop the relationship without giving any reason. Suk knew the reason—they were invariably "legitimate" firstborn sons who, upon finding out Suk's origins, decided to drop him as a friend. This occurred very seldom, but when it happened, it was as if an old wound were reopened and rubbed with salt.

Suk also discovered sports. Legend has it that when old Korean diplomats first saw a game of tennis in Europe, they thought it was quite amusing. When invited to play it, they were quite offended because they assumed, obviously, that only servants would play the game for the enjoyment of their masters. No yangban would demean himself with such physical activity! Suk had never been exposed to sports before coming to Seoul, but now he had learned tennis, table tennis, and even gymnastics! And they were exhilarating.

Suk always knew that he was liked by people. Now he learned that he was actually handsome. Of medium height and build, Suk had a very distinct, narrow, somewhat Caucasian-looking face with rather exotic and at times fierce-looking upwardly slanted eyes. Many girls found him to be practically irresistible. Yes, there were girls in high schools these days, although they went to all-girls high school. The students of the then-new high schools regarded themselves as avant-garde; they even sent letters to each other and in many ways were far more Westernized than the adults. So, Suk even received love letters from girls whom he hardly knew.

As he matured in adolescence, Suk's handsome face became even more interesting because he had a very severe case of acne. Eventually, his face developed a number of small pockmarks from the acne, which really did not detract from his handsomeness but gave it an added dimension of interest. He was nicknamed "Grapefruit" by his friends, which he did not mind at all.

October 8, 1925, Seoul (37.5 N Parallel, 127 E Longitude)
Suk's seventeenth birthday. He had a wonderful night out last night with his friends, partying into the early-morning hours. In those days, Koreans were considered grown up if they were over fifteen years of age, and the students of the elite new high schools behaved rather like college students of today. They drank freely and played freely. Today, however, was a special day, because Suk was planning to ask Ann Moon, the sixteen-year-old student from the Ewha Girls' School, to marry him. As he started dressing in the morning, his heart was filled with happiness. He recalled the walk with Ann three nights before and the eager face of Ann as he told her, "I read Pestalozzi today. He thinks that children will do just fine if they are allowed to grow up without hindrance from adults. They have the innate potential to become useful citizens of society!" Suk and Ann were walking hand in hand on the grounds of the Pagoda Park, often frequented by teenagers as well as adults.

"Yes, I agree," said Ann eagerly. "And as Rousseau says, all the problems in adulthood arise from the artificial restrictions set upon children by adults!"

Ann looked especially dashing in her newly pressed serge sailor's suit, which was the uniform of all high-school girls. Ann was a vivacious girl, about five foot three, with an oval face that tended to become somewhat comic with her rather pouting mouth. She was well-developed, and even under the uniform, Suk could picture her supple bosom that was heaving with excitement. Yes, I am in love, and Ann and I will build a home full of love and children who will grow up in freedom, who will fulfill their fullest innate potential! We will celebrate our engagement tonight in Ann's favorite sushi restaurant!

He awoke from his reverie as he heard the morning mail drop on the ground. In those days, mail as well as newspaper was dropped through an open slot in the door of the house and often landed on the ground with a thud. He walked out and picked up several envelopes addressed to him. Being a student, Suk usually received few letters, other than the occasional ones from his father that took more than two weeks to get from Kangwon Province to Seoul, usually by horse-driven mail carriage. He also received some love letters from unknown girls. One of the letters, in a thick envelope, had a black border—it was an old Korean custom to prepare the receiver for the news of death. Suk's dreams of happiness evaporated on this day, his birthday.

Suk met with Ann that night, as planned, on their favorite bench on the Pagoda Park. Suk was there first, his eyes full of tears. Ann, who was running happily toward Suk, sat down on the bench, startled, and looked at Suk. "Suk, my dear Grapefruit, what is bothering you on this glorious day, your birthday?" Suk could not stop sobbing for a while and then, finally, collecting himself, said, "Ann, I am sorry. I am truly sorry. I meant to propose to marry you today, on my birthday. Instead, I must say good-bye to you. This letter is the only thing I can give to you today." Suk left Ann, sitting on the bench, holding the unopened envelope, seeing but unseeing, as he ran away from the park, away into the darkness of the night.

In his little rented room, he drank himself to sleep, hoping never to wake up.

Dearest Ann,

Please forgive me. How I waited for today, and how I hate that today has ever come! I love you Ann, and I wanted to marry you, even if my father had forbidden me to do so (which he did not). But, Ann, I learned today that my father is dead! He died suddenly of a cerebral hemorrhage a week ago, and the mail being what it is, I just learned of it today. Not only that—upon my father's death, my eldest brother, Sun, has decreed that I must marry a lady of his choice, by the name of Min. You see, Min's father is the owner of a large parcel of land in Kangwon Province, and he offered a large sum of money as a dowry for his daughter. Sun found out, upon my father's death, that the family's finances were not what he thought they were and feels that he needs the money desperately. He persuaded my mother to write to me also, and she is pleading with me to agree to this marriage as Sun has threatened to put her out on the street if I do not consent to this marriage. I know how hard and desperate it must be for my mother to write this. I love my mother, and she is utterly in their hands. Ann, please forgive me. I have to marry this woman, who is five years older than me, whom my eldest brother has arranged for me to marry. I am leaving for Kangwon Province tomorrow. Please find happiness with another man, and try to forget me, though I shall never be able to forget you. I shall always live in the shadow of what might have been. Please forgive me.

Your undeserving
Suk

The wedding ceremony was beautiful, full of pomp and circumstance. Sun, Suk's eldest brother and now the head of the family, wanted to show the world that he was generous, and he treated the concubine's son just as though he were his own full-fledged brother. Min, Suk's arranged bride, was pretty and well-bred, and to Sun, her father's wealth and her dowry were, of course, of prime importance, now that he was planning to become an industrial tycoon in the Empire of the Rising Sun.

As he gazed upon the pretty, downcast face of his bride, Suk wondered. "Yes, I could love you, if only I could forget." Suk did forget, at least for a while, and Min gave birth to two children, Keh-Hoon (Hoon for short) and Keh-Kyung (Kyung for short), one year apart. Suk was only seventeen, a junior in high school, when he married Min. He was a man in a hurry, in school and at home. Two children and graduation came almost at once. He still lived in the small room in Seoul, now made smaller by his wife and two children. He mourned the sudden death of his father, whose funeral he could not attend, because he was three hundred miles away from home in the days before the telephone or even telegraph. Most vivid in his mind, of his father, were the words he had spoken to Suk as he left home for Seoul: "...Find your own destiny!"

The marriage was happy at first. Min was all support, cooperation, and submissiveness. She was also very fulfilling sexually. It did not matter initially that Min did not seem to be interested in anything but the family, gossip, and later, children. She was pretty enough, and she was definitely sexually gratifying. She did not understand Pestalozzi (I wonder where Ann is now), and she certainly had heard nothing of Rousseau. Having had no formal education at all, which was not uncommon for girls even from the richest families in Korea then, to her, painting meant house painting and all artists were lazy bums! And she wanted nothing more of Suk but to return to Kangwon Province and be a landowner ("Surely, your big brother would give you a sizable parcel of land if you asked, and serfs would work for you"). But Suk was only a high-school student, and he had in mind going to college and being a teacher of the young Koreans who needed knowledge and skills!

Soon, there were fights between Suk and Min and discontent that was soothed only by sexual fulfillment. It is a wonder that they had only two children. Though outwardly submissive, Min was a determined lady. She was a girl born of a proud old yangban family. The only child of a concubine, she was educated by a tutor in old social graces. Her parents were even more conservative than Suk's, and she led a very sheltered life. She saw her marriage to Suk as an opportunity to emancipate herself, but she soon found herself to be the symbol of the old order to Suk and a slave of her own two children whom she bore for Suk.

Suk was an obliging father, but whenever he could, he stayed away from the dingy little one-room home. He stayed in tearooms, in his friends' larger houses, and in the classrooms late at night when he would engage in a discussion with his teachers, oblivious of the passage of time.

Suk went to the teachers' college upon graduation from high school. He almost had no choice. Although Sun, Suk's eldest brother and now head of the family, sent him sufficient money to pay for his tuition and room and board for his family, Sun also made it clear that Suk was not welcome in the family home in Kangwon Province, that he had to find a livelihood in Seoul. Suk himself knew that he would never go back to Kangwon Province, as it represented to him the old order, the second-class citizenship. During this time, the only decent way a yangban Korean could make a living under the new Japanese order, other than by owning land, was in education. There was great fervor among Koreans then that, through education, they would recover their independence and dignity. Being a teacher was prestigious, and the Japanese encouraged Koreans to become educators because they also felt that resistance to Japanese rule and the new things it represented could be overcome by education on their terms. So Suk was, of course, accepted to the newly set up teachers' college.

1930–40, Seoul

In college, Suk continued to enjoy both academic success and popularity. In spite of his wife and two children, he had numerous outside romances, often misrepresenting himself as a bachelor. These romances were mostly fleeting ones, as he never seemed to be interested in one girl for any length of time.

Suk's two children were both rather morose. They grew up practically fatherless, under the strict tutelage of their conservative and limited mother. They cherished the rare times when Suk was home because, during those times, Suk was as always a loving and amusing father.

Suk graduated from college first in his class, a valedictorian. He was soon offered a teaching position with a new elementary school in the outskirts of Seoul. With this secure position in hand, Suk, Min, and their children moved to a somewhat larger three-room flat.

Suk's gifts as a teacher became apparent from the beginning. He cared for his pupils, and his pupils worshipped him. At a time when corporal punishment was accepted in public schools, Suk refused to discipline any child with a bamboo ruler, as was a common practice then. Once, a new boy in class was particularly unruly, and everyone was expecting Suk to punish the boy with the ruler that was given to all teachers specifically for that purpose. He did ask the boy to come up to the front of the class and took out the feared ruler in his right hand.

"Your disruptive behavior is making it impossible for me to teach the class," Suk said quietly.

"It is my fault that I am unable to impress upon you how important learning is for you as well as for the whole class."

Then, he held up his left palm and forcefully hit it with the ruler, one, two, three times. After a surprised gasp, the class was dead quiet except for the sound of the ruler hitting Suk's reddened palm. Whack! Whack! Whack!

Suk's palm started to bleed. The disruptive boy suddenly knelt in front of Suk, sobbing, "Please, my teacher. Stop. I will never disrupt the class again. Please stop. I will be your best student, I swear!"

In two years, in 1936, at the age of twenty-eight, Suk was elevated to the position of the principal of the school, the youngest principal in the young history of Korean public-school education. His already-busy schedule became even busier, meeting at night with other teachers, planning meetings, conducting the school chorus, teaching piano to gifted students, and continuing fleeting amorous adventures. Soon, among his students were both his children. Unlike the worshipful respect of other pupils, Hoon and Kyung felt mixed emotions toward their father and principal.

In 1936, the Berlin Olympics took place, presided over by Adolph Hitler, designed to be a showcase of "Aryan superiority." However, a black American athlete, Jesse Owens, startled the world and upset Hitler by winning four gold medals and breaking three world records. A storm was gathering in Europe as Hitler marched into Rhineland and the Spanish Civil War broke out. The fledgling Spanish Republic was under attack by Franco's forces sworn to restoring the old order, supported by the Catholic Church and actively aided militarily by the fascist regime of Mussolini and the Nazis. The military was consolidating their power in Japan after their successful invasion of Manchuria in 1931. In 1932, Japan set up the puppet state of Manchukuo and proclaimed Puyi, the last emperor of China, as the emperor of Manchukuo. In spite of the opposition of the United States, the Japanese "Empire of the Sun" was expanding rapidly throughout East Asia.

Although absent much of the time, Suk's home life seemed to stabilize a little once he became the principal. But there was practically no communication between Suk and Min by now other than purely perfunctory inanities.

Suk was in love, again. For the first time since he had said goodbye to Ann, he was feeling really alive again. The reason for this change in Suk was Yunhee, a small, smart, and passionate senior student at the teachers' college whom he met in a rehearsal for a performance of Handel's *Messiah* for Christmas. She was singing alto in the college chorus, in which Suk was often invited as a guest conductor. Being a respectable principal, Suk had to keep this affair, now in the second year, very quiet indeed. Especially since Yunhee graduated and became a teacher in Suk's school.

Suk would leave home at four in the morning, telling Min that he had to prepare for the early-morning physical exercise that he introduced to both pupils and teachers. At seven in the morning, pupils and teachers would gather in the school yard and exercise to Suk's commands: "Now, jumping exercise. One...two...three... four...Now turn head to the left. One...two...three...four...To the right. One...two...three...four." They would also exercise to the tune of waltzes and polkas that Suk played on the xylophone. Suk's preparations, however, included an initial detour—he went to the rooming house in which Yunhee lived. Yunhee, who would be anxiously waiting, looking out the window, would quietly open the door to her room. In Yunhee's room, darkened so as not to attract attention from other tenants of the dorm-like rooming house, they would make love, quietly, but with a passion known only to lovers for whom each second together is precious. Then, Suk would leave for school first, followed by Yunhee after a discreet interval.

In school, they would greet each other and talk to each other as though they were only casually acquainted coworkers.

Yunhee was known to her friends and coworkers as a quiet, serious, and no-nonsense kind of person. She was only one of two female teachers in the school, and one of the few Korean women to have gone to college. She was quite shy and reticent in high school and college, even though she went to girls' schools and some of her classmates were quite outgoing. Her teachers initially did not notice her because of her shyness but then noticed her later because of the excellence of her written work and her marks on the exams. In one of her classes, the students were given an honors assignment to look up a particularly obscure piece of poetry by an obscure English poet. Most of her classmates complained that the teacher really did not want to give any honors to anyone. Yunhee did not complain but wrote to the British consulate and obtained the necessary poem, which she delivered to her teacher with excellent annotations and critique. She received honors and also the nickname "Doer without Words."

4

LOVE, A HATEFUL STRANGER

1939, Seoul (37.5 N Parallel, 127 E Longitude)
Yunhee

Yunhee felt sore in her crotch. This repeated lovemaking was a bit exhausting, especially since she really did not enjoy it very much. Being a new woman, she tried her best to be responsive, to *enjoy* it, but all she felt was soreness in her crotch. To be honest, there were times when she felt rather excited when Suk fondled her breasts, and between her thighs, but when he actually went on top of her and inserted his organ into her vagina, all she felt was discomfort, and sometimes pain. She did her best to conceal the discomfort and pretended to be happy. She was, indeed, happy that Suk liked her, loved her, and she really did love him. Except for this physical thing. But men were men, and their animal needs had to be satisfied.

Yunhee loved Suk. From the first time she met him, when she was singing alto in Handel's *Messiah* and Suk was the guest conductor for the school chorus. Hall-eh-lu-yah. Suk was so handsome, so modern, so sophisticated, everything that Yunhee had yearned for. And now, he loved her!

For Yunhee, love was a rare feeling, which had to be nurtured and protected. Hate, on the other hand, was so familiar, so easy to remember. Hate for her stepmother who acted as though she were the legitimate ruler of her household! Hate for her father who rejected her mother and took on this hateful stepmother! Yes, hate for her own mother who died shortly after being cast aside by her husband and forced to return to her own parents' house. Legend has it that she had killed herself by drinking lye. Didn't she care for her daughter who was left in the clutches of the villains? Why had she not sent for her? Why had she not even said good-bye to her before she embarked on her journey of no return?

Yunhee's father was a landowner in the little island of Kangwha off the west coast of Korea. Kangwha was near enough the mainland to have mainland pretensions but isolated enough for the petit bourgeoisie to vie for hegemony, with attendant intrigue, backbiting, and worse. After the purported suicide of her mother that occurred when Yunhee was about twelve, she persuaded her father and her stepmother that she should go to a boarding school in Seoul. Her father, with mainland pretensions, was happy to send his daughter to a new high school in Seoul, and her stepmother was only too happy to send her away from her household.

Yunhee's introverted nature did not change when she came to Seoul. Her brightness was concealed in a cloak of brooding thoughtfulness, and her questioning eyes sparkled, distorted behind thick eyeglasses she started to wear for nearsightedness. She came across as a rather dull, bookish, intellectual sort of a person. Yunhee was desperately unhappy in Seoul, not that she felt any better in Kangwha. In fact, she was becoming obsessed with the image of her mother, her mouth dripping blood, dying from the ingestion of lye. She had bought a container of lye herself, without any particular idea what she wanted to do with it. Lye was often used in those days as a detergent, so buying it was not a particularly suspicious thing for a young woman. On the other hand, almost everybody knew that ingesting lye was an effective but particularly painful way to commit suicide. Yunhee finally planned that she would close her eyes and just drink the lye solution, as soon as her singing in the chorus was completed.

Then, she met Suk.

Suk would not probably remember the first time he met Yunhee, as he was surrounded by a number of aspiring females after the rehearsal. But the short girl behind the thick glasses whom he did not particularly notice decided that Suk was the man she had been waiting for. With the same kind of determination with which she would have drunken the lye, Yunhee permed her hair, bought new, more flattering glasses, and bought a whole new wardrobe with the money she had saved tutoring wealthier students, with the sole intention of attracting Suk. By carefully planned "chance" meetings and discussions on educational philosophy, music, and world affairs, she gradually won Suk's attention and love. Love was easy, carefree, and ephemeral for Suk. Love was planning, anticipation, and hard work for Yunhee, but it would be, for her, everlasting, eternal. Yunhee decided she deserved Suk, wanted him, and she obtained him.

1940, Seoul (37.5 N Parallel, 127 E Longitude)

Uniforms were everywhere. The Japanese military had successfully conquered much of China, and Manchuria (Manchukuo), though it nominally had its own emperor, was practically a colony of Japan. Unlike Manchukuo, Korea was to be, at least in name, an integral part of Japan itself. A campaign for the unity of Korea and Japan had been ongoing for some time. All Koreans now had Japanese names and would be treated just like Japanese born in Japan, especially if you went to Manchuokuo as a colonial. This was a new frontier for all Japanese.

Many things had changed in Korea by now. There were many "new roads"—paved roads for the newly introduced automobiles to travel to the provinces. There were more railroads for trains. There were schools everywhere, elementary schools, high schools, colleges, even graduate schools. War in Europe heated up—the Nazis were overrunning the Allied troops everywhere. A glorious year for the Berlin-Rome-Tokyo axis.

A sense of something in the offing was pervasive. Yunhee felt this zeitgeist more than anyone else, because she was a very sensitive person behind her shy, reticent exterior. "This must be a year for change. For the definite solution!"

When Suk came home that balmy August night, he noticed that something was very wrong. The house was in disarray, and he noticed a number of hastily packed cartons and luggage lined up before the door. Min seemed to be packing.

"What is the meaning of this, Min?" asked Suk breathlessly. Without looking at him, Min handed him an opened envelope. In it was a letter, written in childish block letters, that read,

> Do you know that your husband has a lover, who is a teacher in the school? Her name is Yunhee, and you can ask her landlord about where your husband is every morning at 4:00 a.m.

"I knew what was going on, Suk, for a long time. But now, everybody knows. I am a daughter of a yangban, Suk. I will not tolerate this shame of being cast aside by my husband, my legitimate husband. She is not even a concubine. This is common adultery, and I shall not stand it. My father has asked me and my children to come back home to the Kangwon Province. We are going. I have spoken with an attorney here in Seoul, who will sue you for damages and report you to the authorities for immoral conduct. I am sure that he will have you fired from your job as principal. I hope never to see you again." Her words came out like bullets, precise, explosive, and measured. Without another word, she ushered her children to the waiting carriage and sped away into the night.

> Opportunities in Manchukuo. Wanted: professionals, teachers, engineers. Those who speak Japanese highest preference. High salaries, high government positions. Apply with the Japanese colonial ministry.

"Yunhee, you are all I have now. I no longer have a wife, a son, or a daughter. I have only myself and my love. I shall resign from my job tomorrow, because I cannot continue in that job with this scandal. Yunhee, let's run away. Let's go to Manchukuo. We shall build a new life, in a new land, away from Korea. We will be like the American settlers in the West. We will build our own future together, with our own hands!"

In four weeks they were gone. With no forwarding address. With no good-byes. For a new world, up north, a vast wilderness called Manchuria.

5

A GLORIOUS DREAM

1940–45, Manchuria (Manchukuo, Japanese Puppet State and Colony: 44 N Parallel, 128 E Longitude)
Bo

An expanse of frozen ground, brownish black, and the indigo sky that is limitless in depth and in breadth…this is what comes to mind when I think of my birthplace, Manchuria. Perhaps there is a flag of some kind flapping in the wind somewhere up on a building. And I feel a cold wind that freshens my face and my whole being. Big, yes, very big…very cold…earthy…different…alien…home…

"What a wonderful baby, so fat, so cute…*Ding-hao.*"

My parents told me that people came to them and told them how very wonderful (ding-hao) I looked as a baby.

My father, who was now known as Daisin, was the deputy mayor of a small city called Daeduk, south of Harbin in Manchuria. Because of his administrative experience and his ability to speak Japanese fluently, he obtained this rather exalted position in the Japanese puppet state of Manchuria. The mayor, of course, was Japanese.

Suk and Yunhee believed that they were pioneers in this untamed land. They approached their new life with the spirit of exploration and adventure shared perhaps by the explorers of the

American West. As in the American West, the natives were badly treated in Manchuria. Wartime rationing was in effect, and depending upon your ethnic lineage, your rations differed. If you were a mainland Japanese, you were entitled to rice, sugar, meat, fish, and soybeans. If you were a "Japanese of Korean origin," you were entitled to a smaller portion of rice, sugar, fish, and soybeans. If you were a Chinese, you could obtain rice and soybeans. If you were a Manchurian native, all you were entitled to receive was soybeans.

Being a born diplomat and socialite, Suk did himself proud for his office. His superiors and subordinates alike loved him. Whether Japanese, Chinese, Korean, or Manchurian native, anyone who had dealings with him praised him as a true example of the kind of excellent government official that the "Greater East Asia Co-Prosperity Sphere of the Japanese Empire" must produce.

Suk was content, for the first time in his life, with himself, his family, and his work. He had a new name, a new position, and a new wife. Suk and Yunhee were married in a little Christian church in Daeduk shortly after their arrival. Since Manchukuo was supposedly an independent country, and Suk was the deputy mayor of the city, no questions were asked about his prior marriage outside of Manchukuo.

Suk had always been attracted to Christianity, a religion that represented something new and iconoclastic to a Korean yangban. In fact, he had attended some Christian churches during college and occasionally sang or conducted in the church choirs. He liked the Protestant churches better because he liked to listen to the hymns and sing along.

Converting to Christianity upon arrival in Manchuria was a stroke of genius on Suk's part. With his baptism, he got a new name, Daisin, which was a derivation of the biblical name Joseph that also meant, in Chinese characters, "Great Trust." He then formally registered his new name in the official government registry and shed the old name, Suk-jin, from which his nickname Suk was derived. No one who used to know Suk before he left Korea knew of Suk's new name or his new identity. Although Suk clearly wanted to have a clean break from the past, this level of secrecy was due, in part, to Yunhee's insistence, because she had secretly feared that Suk's first (and legitimate, as he never really obtained a divorce before leaving Korea) wife might come and reclaim him some day.

"Ma-ma, Da-da." Sixteen-month-old Bo was sitting in his playpen, babbling and pointing at Suk with his rattle.

"No, Da-da, then Ma-ma," said Suk laughingly to Bo and gently tickled him under his roly-poly chin. "Da-da will give you the whole world, my son. You will be unencumbered by the old ways, by Confucianism, by Korea itself. You are the son of two pioneers of the Land of the Rising Sun!"

Suk was filled with happiness with each landmark Bo achieved—sitting up, walking, smiling, saying "Ma-ma" and "Da-da" and then full sentences, real speech, all in Japanese.

Behind Bo's remarkable precocious achievements were hours of planning and effort on Yunhee's part. Yunhee did not work when they moved to Manchuria but, instead, concentrated on having a child. Secretly, she was concerned that she might be infertile, because during the more than one year of intimacy with Suk before their elopement, she had not used any contraception, even though she had repeatedly reassured Suk that she was (at that time, the only contraception available was the rhythm, vaginal sheath, douching, and premature withdrawal). She had indeed wanted to become pregnant even while their affair was kept secret, at Suk's insistence, to which she ostensibly acquiesced. In truth, she really had wanted to force the issue by becoming "accidentally" pregnant.

Now that Suk wanted to have a baby, she felt considerable fear and resentment at the implicit pressure. She carefully hid these feelings from Suk and went about the business of becoming pregnant in a methodical fashion. She made a temperature chart. She made love regularly, especially at times of higher fertility, literally seducing Suk several times a day with varying states of undress and provocative dress. Of course, Suk was very eager and cooperative.

Yunhee was pregnant within fifteen months. The joy that Suk and Yunhee shared was soon turned into energy for the deliberate preparation for the baby's arrival. Yunhee believed in giving a head start to the baby by educating him in utero. Oh, she was sure it would be a boy. It had to be. For her. And for Suk. And for himself, too, because it was, after all, a man's world!

The prenatal education consisted of a rigid schedule of yoga, classical music, reading aloud of classics, chanting of a Buddhist blessing, and singing of hymns. She never deviated from this educational endeavor up to the day of delivery.

Once born, Bo was in a truly enriched environment for learning. There were educational toys. There were books to look at when he was too young to read. And Yunhee read to him every day, beginning the second day of his life (on the first day, Yunhee had inadvertently fallen asleep before reading time). Yunhee also played with Bo: imaginary and pretend games, games for manual dexterity, games to develop coordination, and on and on.

Gifts, of nice little moon cakes, of sugar candies, of satin and silk. I remember them all—such an abundance of things, but also of love and goodwill, that surrounded me and our home then, in the distant past of my infancy and early childhood. Yes, I must have thrived in this exalted atmosphere. And I loved my *do-jang* and *oka-sang* ("dad" and "mom," in Japanese).

Yes, the flag flapping about in the wind, high on a pole atop the building, was that of imperial Japan, the Rising Sun with red spreading rays, rays spreading out like long fingers.

Night. Wind is howling. Everything is dark. I cannot stand this darkness; I am afraid. Where is everybody? Do-jang? Oka-sang? Smell of something burning—fire? The toad's house, the little box on the wall...circuit breaker...it is aflame, and the flame is spreading along the electrical lines. Help! I can't breathe. Suddenly, the darkness dissipates, and the room is brilliantly lit. I am rocking, as though on a boat. Mom! She is holding me, rocking me. "You had a nightmare, my precious. I am here. Everything is OK. Go back to sleep. Sleep, nehn-nehn-goroito...sleep."

Mysteries. I love to read mystery novels. I do not remember when I acquired the taste—maybe when I was in grade school, when I read Sherlock Holmes. No, I think I read Arsène Lupin before Sherlock Holmes. Mysteries have been my constant companion for as long as I can remember. I have read almost all classic armchair detective stories in print: Agatha Christie, Dorothy Sayers, John Dickson Carr...

Mysteries have given me comfort, escape from any and all stresses, major and minor. There is something profoundly comforting when you read of murders, many of them, and live the murders without doing the dirty work yourself and getting caught...All secrets will come out, and reason and logic will triumph at the end.

Dreamtime

Australian Aborigines speak of the "Dreamtime," a time in the ancient past when all things were created, when humans and animals and inanimate objects conversed with each other, when nature was in harmonious flux. When the Aborigines fall asleep, they often dream of the Dreamtime, and they paint their recollections of the events and images that reveal the essence of the timeless universe. Perhaps my infancy and early childhood in Manchuria represents a Dreamtime, a period seldom talked about by my parents, a period that seems to be filled with pride, shame, happiness, sadness, and dark secrets.

"Bo, when you came out, did you close the door or leave it open?" I did not know what to say to this cryptic question asked of me by my mom's friends, perhaps when I was about five or six.

"I don't know. But I usually close doors when I come in or out," I probably responded.

What they meant was whether I had closed the door for more babies to come out of my mother's womb. It was unusual for a married Korean woman not to have another child for six years after the first one. And, in fact, I know that my mom was trying. Then, I learned that there was a baby born to her some two years after I was born. And, somehow, it died. My parents were quite reluctant to talk about this dead baby. For some reason, I did not press them either. To this day, I do not know whether the baby was a stillbirth or died several days after birth or whether it was a boy or a girl.

6

THE THIRTY-EIGHTH PARALLEL

1947, Seoul, South Korea
Suk

The thirty-eighth parallel north dissects Korea almost evenly into two halves. It was this imaginary line that the United States and the Soviet Union decided in August 1945 to be the boundary that would separate the northern half of the Korean peninsula, to be occupied by the Soviet Union, from the southern part, to be occupied by the United States. Each degree of parallel is approximately seventy miles, or 111 kilometers. Thus, Seoul, the capital city of Korea, was about 0.5 degrees, or thirty-six miles, south of the thirty-eighth parallel. Pyongyang, the city that would become the capital of North Korea, was approximately on the thirty-ninth parallel, about seventy miles north of the thirty-eighth parallel.

In a matter of weeks after the last train from Manchuria was stopped forcibly at Sunjin, all the territory north of the thirty-eighth parallel was occupied by the Red Army and their Korean agents, Kim Il-Sung's People's Army. But before the Communists were in full control, millions of Koreans who lived in the North fled south of the thirty-eighth parallel.

The fortieth parallel that separates the United States from Canada is the longest unguarded border in the world. In contrast, the thirty-eighth parallel that separates North Korea and South Korea is one of the most impenetrable borders in human history even to this day. As soon as the Red Army secured control of North Korea, they declared Kim Il-Sung to be the president of the Democratic People's Republic of Korea. Telephone lines were cut off, as well as electric lines and railroad tracks. All communication and traffic between the two halves of Korea were closed.

For Suk, this state of affairs was not without advantages. Millions of North Korean refugees had arrived in South Korea without any kind of identification papers. Because of the closed border, there was no way of verifying any information such as birth and marriage registration. Suk wanted, above all, to hide from others the fact that he had been an official of the Japanese puppet government in Manchuria. Anti-Japanese feelings were running high, and Suk was fearful that his Manchukuo career would identify him as a pro-Japanese Korean. Such an identification could mean persecution, prejudicial treatment, or even arrest.

When all North Korean refugees were asked to register their names and birthplaces, Suk registered himself as Daisin and he and his family as refugees from a part of the Kangwon Province that was now a part of North Korea. He also registered Bo as having been born in that part of Kangwon Province, rather than in Manchukuo. There was no way the authorities could check the accuracy of any of this.

Thus began a new life for the Moons in the new country, Korea, a land of their ancestors that they had once abandoned.

In Seoul, Suk soon found out that many of his old friends from high school and college were in positions of influence in the provisional local government. Few remembered the circumstances of his disappearance more than ten years before, but many remembered the bright, sociable, and friendly Suk. Soon, he was again an elementary-school teacher in a suburban school district of Seoul. An old familiar job he had excelled in and outgrown more than a decade ago.

1947

Suk, Yunhee, and Bo lived in a small apartment in Seoul. Suk once again devoted himself to teaching and Yunhee to caring for and educating Bo. They tried to be oblivious of the political turmoil—power struggles, assassinations, rebellions—around them. Other than Suk's old school friends, no one knew of their whereabouts, or so they believed, until one day in 1947.

It was a clear September Saturday. As in many autumn days in Seoul, the sky was the color of the deepest of oceans, and the leaves were turning glorious gold, red, and crimson hues. There were only four hours of class on Saturdays. At about two o'clock in the afternoon, Suk was in the teachers' office, finishing up his preparations for the following week and preparing to go home. As usual, Suk was the last of the teachers to leave. As he was about to get up to leave, a coarse-looking young man in his twenties, dressed in an ill-fitting suit, hesitantly opened the door and came in.

"Excuse me, sir. Could you tell me where I could find Mr. Suk Moon?" said the young man.

"Er, yes. I am Suk Moon. What can I do for you?"

The young man seemed to be surprised and, for a moment, looked as though he wished to get out of the room. Then, he murmured, "Oh, I...You look younger than I thought. Are you sure you are Mr. Suk Moon?"

"Yes, I am sure, young man. And who are you?" responded Suk, good-humoredly.

The young man said, in a barely audible voice, "I am your son, Hoon, Father!"

Keh-Hoon. Suk's son from his marriage to Min, his first wife, who had left him in Seoul some eighteen years ago. Hoon, his son, and Kyung, his daughter, whom Min rushed away from Suk that day, to whom he had not said a word of good-bye. Whom he had not seen nor spoken with ever since. Whom he had almost successfully forgotten.

"Hoon? Are you sure?" Suk said, feeling stupid.

"Father, I have come for you. Mother is ill; she has been searching for you, waiting for you all these years. She is still your wife, and she is waiting for you. She lives, all of us live, in Kangwon Province, on her father's farm. She asked me to find you and ask you to come home."

"Hoon. How is your sister, Kyung?" asked Suk.

"She is well, Father. She is at home, helping Mother. She is now twenty years old, a beautiful girl. I have searched all over Seoul for you. Please come home. Mother needs you," pleaded Hoon.

Min's face appeared in Suk's mind's eye, pretty, smiling, suffering, and then angry. Memories of life with Min fleeted by—the marriage ceremony, the awkwardness of the arranged marriage, the gratifying lovemaking, Hoon's and Kyung's births, the cramped living quarters, the fights, the icy relationship during the last years of their marriage...I am sorry, my son...somehow, I do not remember you well...I know you were there, and I must have loved you, but somehow, I do not remember...

Suk said slowly, "Hoon, I am sorry, but I am not the man you were looking for. I am no longer Min's husband. I am the husband of another woman. I now have another family. I am glad you and Kyung have grown to be healthy and caring adults. I hope you understand that I cannot return to you."

The young man's expression became wooden. He said in a trembling voice, "No. I don't understand. You are my father. I wanted you back, I want you back. My mother hates that woman you live with, in sin. She hates you! I hate you! We all hate you!"

Hoon turned and ran out of the room, not quite able to hold back his tears and sobs.

Suk debated whether he should tell her but finally decided to tell her about the visit as briefly as possible, because he thought she should be prepared for a possible letter or visit to her. Yunhee became uncharacteristically hysterical when Suk told her about the incident that evening. Suk tried to reassure her,

"Do not talk to him or anyone you don't want to deal with. Just refer them to me." But Yunhee was not reassured by Suk. Her unending nightmares had just begun.

1991, New York (40.5 N Parallel, 74 W Longitude)
Bo

"Bravo! Brava!" Applause breaks out as the curtain falls on the last act of *La Traviata*. Ali, rising to his feet, exclaims, "Bravo, bravo! Brava, brava!"

Ali has been going to the opera since age three. Opera is a passion of mine acquired late in life, like skiing. In fact, I used to hate the opera, saying, "There is nothing more artificial and unrealistic. Even when you die, you sing with such a full voice that the theater shakes!" Little did I know how wonderful it can be, once you let go of yourself, your sense of being rooted in reality, and accept an alternate reality in which singing is the normal mode of communication. Little Ali enjoyed the opera from the beginning, when I took him to the Metropolitan Opera in New York for a trial run shortly after his third birthday. Dispelling my worries that he might embarrass me by crying or talking in the middle of the opera, he sat through it quite absorbed.

Ginny said that Ali would, even when he was in her womb, become peaceful and still when she listened to music. Ginny is quite musical herself, being an excellent pianist.

La Traviata and *La Bohème* are Ali's favorite operas. But Ali gets quite upset that the heroines die in both operas.

"Why didn't they get a doctor, Dad, and cure the disease?" asks Ali.

"Well, in those days, doctors couldn't do much for tuberculosis, which used to be called 'consumption' because the patient wasted away."

"Can doctors do something about tuberculosis now? Can you cure it?" asks Ali expectantly.

"Yes, now you can cure tuberculosis."

"I will become a doctor, Dad, when I grow up. And I will cure all these dying people!" declares Ali confidently.

Well, a doctor today. But maybe a fireman tomorrow. And, yes, a navigator and an ornithologist, too. Ali considers different occupations almost every day. Especially if the occupation sounds important. But I also know that Ali could be a good doctor—he has the gentle touch and a caring attitude. He really seems to feel for people who are in distress. But does he understand sacrifice? Like that of Violetta in giving up Alfredo?

My mom certainly understood sacrifice. She was the archetypal martyr. She sacrificed her whole life for the sake of her children and her husband. She woke up at four o'clock every morning, even before dawn, to make breakfast for her family. This was before the days of electric or gas stoves. She had to get the charcoal stove going by blowing into the kindling wood, then wash rice, put the pot on the fire, and wait so that she could turn the heat down by spreading the charcoal farther apart when the rice began to boil.

She worked like a slave, a maid. She would serve us food, she would wash and iron our clothes and leave them out fresh every morning, she would wait on us for the slightest need. When I wanted a glass of water, I didn't go and get it but called, "Ma, get me a glass of water!" My dad and I threw our clothes all over the house when we got home, and she would pick them up one by one and hang them in the closet. She would clean the house spotless every day. Yes, she was like a maid. And she would always praise my dad as the most wonderful person in the universe. Even when he treated her badly. Even when he came home every night drunk.

When he was not home by midnight, often she would walk outside of the house, waiting for him in the street. At times, when he did not come, she would walk even farther from the house and find my dad lying on the street, asleep, drunk. Then she would try to awaken him and bring him to the house, he leaning on her shoulder, practically being carried home. He would mumble, "It was such a nice party! My ex-pupils treated me to such a wonderful dinner!"

Sometimes, he would bring home some leftover food from such dinners. Beef ribs wrapped up in tissue paper, sometimes with teeth marks on them.

7

THE PATRICIDAL SOCIETY

1940–47, Kangwon Province, South Korea (37.9 N Parallel, 128 E Longitude)
Hoon

When Hoon told his mother about his encounter with Suk, she was a sick, crippled shell of a woman. At age fourteen when Suk left, Hoon had to be the man of the house, holding up a sickly mom and a frail twelve-year-old sister. Hoon remembered vividly that night when his mother suddenly packed her bags and dragged him and his sister out of their house, without even saying good-bye to his father. And the journey to Kangwon Province, to his mother's father's house, only to find that they were the objects of contempt. The concubine's daughter now cast away by her husband, and her two practically bastard children!

Though his mother, Min, was a daughter of one of the largest landowners in Kangwon Province, they were given a small shack of a house away from the main house, where they had to tend to a patch of land and some pigs and chickens, just like a sharecropper. This was the lot of a disgraced family, whose man of the house had eloped with a whore!

Hoon, who had been a bright student in Seoul, did not go to school in Kangwon Province. Min, unlike Suk, had no interest in education, and besides, Hoon felt too ashamed to go to school where the classmates would like to know where his father was. He, however, borrowed whatever books he could from the town library, which he visited at least twice a week. It took hours just waiting for the infrequent bus to town. In the library one day, a somewhat older young man called Kang struck a conversation with Hoon. Hungry for friendship, Hoon confided in Kang and told him about his father and how he hated him, as well as his mother's father, the landowner.

"Hoon, these evil people exist because of the evil system. We must overturn the capitalist system and build a society where everyone is equal, where there is no one born rich or poor, where all land belongs to everyone!"

"You are so knowledgeable, Kang. I never thought that there could be an alternative to the way things are, the way things have always been!"

"I am fortunate to have a teacher, Professor Lee, who taught me all these things," replied Kang.

Kang was a student at a university in Wonju, a city in Kangwon Province. He stayed in the college dormitory during the week but frequently came home on weekends and vacations.

"You mean you learn these things in school?" asked an incredulous Hoon.

"Well, not really—the Japanese fascists won't let the professors teach these things openly, but the progressive teachers do teach these truths to selected students in college. Professor Lee, who teaches at the university, is a very intelligent and progressive man. His wife is also a professor at the university, and they have just one teenage daughter, who is also knowledgeable about progressive ideas. She even attended our discussion groups. Too bad we had to stop meeting because the police have become more suspicious of 'dangerous left-wing subversive groups.'"

Kang gave him a list of books to read. The list included *Das Kapital* and the *Communist Manifesto* by Karl Marx and books and essays by Engels and Lenin. Hoon hungrily absorbed the revolutionary ideas, not only about how the old order must be shattered but also about how the whole human race must be remade to create an egalitarian, classless society, where each individual would serve the good of the whole, not of the self, and the society would provide to each according to his or her needs, not according to his or her ability, which in a capitalist system meant the ability to exploit the labors of the masses for selfish gain. Each individual's ability must serve the society! To create a classless society, the capitalist family structure, which is patriarchal, authoritarian, and antiegalitarian, must be destroyed, and this must be done decisively by killing your father!

This was the founding principle of the secret patricidal societies that sprang up in many parts of Korea, which Hoon joined with Kang's enthusiastic support. They did not know, and if they did, did not care, that these secret youth clubs were supported by agents of the KGB of the Soviet Union, which bordered both Manchuria and Korea.

Of course, Hoon could not kill his father then, as he and Yunhee had absconded to somewhere in Manchuria, and as a teenager during wartime, he risked being forcibly inducted into the Imperial Japanese Army if found unattached to a farm or other essential workplace.

But just wait, Hoon thought, till I grow up. You have betrayed your wife, your family, and your fatherland by collaborating with the Japanese imperialists. And you went to the Japanese puppet nation, Manchukuo, to be a colonialist for Japan! I will find you, Father, and I will show you what the people's justice means!

And now, he had found him, in Seoul.

And I know where you live, with Yunhee and your son, Bo. Just wait!

8

THE STICK OF THE PEOPLE

1948, Seoul, South Korea (37.5 N Parallel, 127 E Longitude)
Suk

In South Korea, after a United Nations–sponsored parliamentary election, the first election ever in Korea, Syngman Rhee was elected president of the Republic of Korea by the National Assembly. Rhee, who worked for Korean independence during the Japanese occupation, had been so severely tortured by the Japanese police that he developed a permanent twitch on his cheek. He had been in exile in Hawaii and had come back to Korea with American blessings, with the idea of forming a government widely accepted by Koreans. Rhee's method of obtaining and preserving power was ruthless—by the time of his election, all his rivals had been assassinated.

As Rhee consolidated his power, he set up a National Police as a tool of his exercise of power. Learning the tactics from the Japanese, the new National Police began to arrest political opponents of the regime under the suspicion of being Communists, tortured them to extract a confession, and, often, summarily executed them. Just like the Japanese. Some foreign journalists were not surprised at Rhee's dictatorial regime. After all, Korea never had a tradition of democracy. And Koreans never unlearned fearing the police.

"Thus, the Yi dynasty adopted Confucianism as state religion, as opposed to the Buddhism of the Koryu dynasty. Confucianism's basic tenets are filiality to ancestors and obedience to authority..." Suk was teaching Korean history to his class.

Suddenly, there seemed to be commotion outside, with loud shouts: "Make way!"

The students were looking out the window. "What is going on?" Suk also looked out.

In the school yard were several uniformed policemen, and Mr. Park, a coworker of Suk's who taught the third grade, was being led away by them in handcuffs. The police were pushing him with their sticks, shouting, "Hurry up, you Communist traitor!"

Suk felt a chill and goose bumps all over his body. The police in the school! And a teacher, in handcuffs, being abused by them! These were unimaginable things to Suk and to most Koreans. Because of the importance Koreans placed on education, schools had been immune to such incursions by state authority. Even the Japanese police did not show up in schools in uniform. When they arrested teachers, they took pains to do so in their homes.

Mr. Park was fired from work the next day. Suk had read in the newspapers a few months ago that one of his old high-school chums, Cho Il Whan, had become the police commissioner. He had paid him a congratulatory visit, with a box of candy as was the custom in Korea. Suk was socially facile and knew that he might need Cho's goodwill someday. Suk had paid Cho another visit after Park's arrest and told him that he felt quite certain Park was innocent and that many students and teachers in the school were worried about Park. If he were released, it would provide such a wonderful image of the new commissioner and of the police that he was now directing! The next day, Park was released.

When Suk saw him again, several weeks later, Park was a broken man. He had been tortured, he was limping, his eyes were bulging, his face was all black-and-blue. And Park said that more painful than the beatings were the electric shocks, to his penis and to his anus. He had "confessed" that he was a Communist and would have been hanged had it not been for Suk's help.

Park was eternally grateful to Suk. Having been arrested, however, Park could not find any work in the government and started working as a construction laborer.

A few months passed.

"Yunhee, Bo, where are you? I am home!" shouted Suk as he did not see either of them coming and greeting him as was their wont when they heard the door open. But there was no answer.

Suk found Yunhee shivering in the corner of their bedroom. Bo was holding her, trying to soothe her. "Mommy, it's OK. Dad is here now."

"What is the matter, Yunhee?" asked Suk. Without a word, Yunhee handed him an envelope that was lying on the floor. It was addressed to Suk, in a small, obviously feminine handwriting:

> *Dear Suk,*
>
> *I hope this letter finds you in good health. Hoon told me of his meeting with you and how cold and unfeeling you were. He had been talking about seeing you for many years, ever since we parted. He loves you and was very hurt when he saw you in Seoul. I must tell you that Hoon disappeared without a word a year ago, and I fear the worst. The police arrested me and Kyung and tortured us, saying that Hoon was a Communist and must have gone to North Korea. I've been limping and sick ever since. It's been a year, and still Kyung and I are crying every day. Kyung has now become a beautiful, quiet woman, a good traditional Korean woman, unlike those corrupt city women. We all need you and want you back.*
>
> *Suk, I know that we had problems in our marriage. Especially when you met that whore from Kangwha Island, the shameless whore who snatched you away from*

me and made you insane. That bitch of a whore that still lives with you!

But also think of the good times we had. The love and, yes, the wonderful love life we shared. And think of your devoted children, who pined for you once they learned that you were alive and in Seoul. And now, with Hoon gone, without a man in the house, you are needed here, and it is your duty to be with your family, in Kangwon Province, the land of your ancestors.

I am sorry about the way I left you when I found out about your affair—I was very upset and beside myself. But I never imagined that you would not send for me and your children—I was waiting for you every day to come to me and beg me to return home, to our home.

Please write to me immediately and tell me that you will be coming here. Your brother, Sun, has agreed to give you a parcel of land to cultivate if you come here. And he will let you manage a considerable portion of the family farm, as he is busy running his potato-processing factory.

And Suk, remember that if you do not come to me soon, I will curse you as I curse that whore! And I shall take revenge on her, and you, and your sinful offspring. Drop them immediately. Drop everything and come back to me.

With eternal love,

Min

Suk felt faint. Darkness closed in on him from all sides. He sat down. He knew that he had dreaded this moment ever since he had set foot in Korea again. He also knew that this moment would come, once he was back in Korea—that Min would contact him and shatter the new life he had made for himself, Yunhee, and now Bo. Because he had never obtained a divorce from Min, because he ran away to Manchuria without first putting matters in order, because he was too cowardly to face the scandal that the respected youngest principal was a lecher.

Confused images passed through his mind. Min's face, at first snarling and then laughing hysterically...then...her face as he remembered it when he made love to her...rapturous, voluptuous, crying out in joy...and then Yunhee's face, cold, rigid, suffering... she never seems to enjoy sex...yields to his desires, but it's obviously a chore for her...but Min really enjoyed sex...when he was making love, Min made him feel alive, a *man!*...unlike Yunhee, who made him feel like a heel, raping this reluctant woman who was sacrificing herself for his animal needs...such pain, such torture...faces, snarling...uniforms, handcuffs...policemen with their sticks! Fear, authority. Suddenly, an idea formed in his confused mind and took shape.

"Don't worry, Yunhee. Bo, Mom will be OK now that I am here. And nobody but nobody will threaten us again, and nobody will touch us—*never!*"

The very next day, he paid another visit to the police commissioner Cho's home. Suk told him that he would like to be a policeman. Cho was surprised but very eager to have Suk join the police, because he needed people who would be loyal to him in the force. Suk was not only a school chum but also from the same province as Cho. He also felt that Suk would be a good PR move, a teacher becoming a policeman. Gentle Suk could help change the bad image the Korean police had. The National Police of new Korea, and the sticks they carried, had to change from the image of beatings to the image of walking sticks to be leaned on.

After a month of training, Suk donned his sharp police uniform, with his lieutenant's brass insignia shining on his shoulders. Cho gave Suk a position as the department head for health and welfare in the police station in Kangneung, in the Kangwon Province. Suk had some reservations about going back to the Kangwon Province, even though Kangneung was by no means near the town of his ancestral home. But the likelihood that Min would not know his whereabouts if he moved away from Seoul was reassuring. Min would never imagine that Suk would move to Kangwon Province as a policeman! And even if she did, neither she nor anyone else could ever touch an officer, a lieutenant of the National Police Force!

Shiny brass bars on the shoulders. Sharp, well-pressed black uniform. Pants creases like knife blades. A round black cap with a shiny gold band and a shiny brass insignia in the front, that of an eagle atop a flower, the rose of sharon, the national flower of the new country, Republic of Korea.

I remember my dad in that uniform that late autumn day, when he graduated from his police academy. The sky was blue, the air was crisp, and so was my dad's uniform and his demeanor. He seemed so full of vigor and confidence. Oh, how proud I was! Little did I know how conflicted I would be about him, his uniform, what he was!

The flag of the Republic of Korea was flying in the wind on the flagpole. And spirits of the Moon family were also flying that day as they felt secure in Suk's new power and in the hopes of becoming invisible behind the powerful uniform, in Kangwon Province, the last place Min and her children would look for the fugitive.

9

IN THE LAND OF OUR ANCESTORS

1948–50, Kangwon Province, South Korea (37–39 N Parallel, 128–128.5 E Longitude)
Suk, Yunhee

Kangwon Province is a very large mountainous province in the central part of the Korean peninsula, dominated by the Taebaik Mountains and the coastal region east of the mountains that precipitously drops into the Sea of Japan. About one-third of the province is in North Korea. The Moon ancestral hometown, Hachon, was a town perched on the mountainside on the northwestern part of the province, just south of the thirty-eighth parallel. Kangneung was a small port city on the southeastern coast, one of the few port cities in Kangwon Province. It was a pretty town with a small pier, with tall mountains rising steeply just a few hundred feet off the docks and sheer cliffs falling into the sea to the north and to the south of the town.

Suk, a lieutenant of the Korean National Police, did himself proud in his new post. As a workaholic, Suk spent long hours working, often till dawn, and walked home to sleep for one or two hours before heading back to work. It was a good thing that the house was within walking distance, as there were only two automobiles in the police station—a truck and a jeep that was used by the police chief. Taking seriously his task of maintaining the health and welfare of the townspeople, whom he considered to be his ward, he inspected all the kitchens in the restaurants himself. Being a port city, albeit a small one, there were many restaurants and eateries, and they were filthy. Unlike his predecessor, he refused the bribes from the owners of the dirty restaurants. Instead, he ordered his subordinates to help clean their kitchens.

There were also houses of prostitution like at any other port. Although prostitution was nominally illegal, Suk realized that attempting to close them down would only drive them underground, that his duty to protect the health of the populace would be better served if he could ensure the health of the prostitutes. He asked for, and received, the help of the local physicians, who volunteered to examine the prostitutes regularly and treat any venereal disease they found. They also taught them better hygiene.

Suk bought with his own money pamphlets on disease prevention, on how to be rid of insects and vermin, and on nutritional values of foods and distributed them to his subordinates, restaurant employees, prostitutes, and anyone else he thought might be of influence. He went to schools and to workplaces and lectured on good hygiene. Many prostitutes, feeling cared for by the police rather than persecuted for the first time in their lives, quit their profession and obtained respectable employment, often going to night school to further their education. Many of them wrote thank-you letters to Suk. Suk would, of course, show them to his colleagues and subordinates, as well as to Yunhee and Bo. Yunhee would be annoyed that Suk was showing interest in prostitutes but would just bite her lips and say nothing. She would, however, suffer.

Yunhee was secretly jealous of the prostitutes who were receiving Suk's attention. Yunhee loathed prostitutes who sold their bodies for money. Yunhee loathed sex—the very idea of being touched by a man and having his dirty organ in her body was repugnant to her. But she was also jealous of the women who seemed to enjoy sex, who seemed to want it. She was jealous because Suk was always interested in women. And she knew that, probably, deep down, Suk knew that she hated sex, men, him. He would be so much happier with one of the prostitutes! She shuddered at the thought.

As far as Yunhee could remember, she had always been jealous. Jealous of her stepmother who enjoyed her father's love. Of her mother, who had left Yunhee with the evil stepmother and who had killed herself by drinking lye. She was in peace, dead, and Yunhee was suffering the pain of feeling unloved in the household where her father loved this evil woman. She was jealous of all her friends in school, because they seemed to enjoy each other and, yes, boys! They all had boyfriends. Yunhee did not have any. But then, when any boys approached Yunhee, she would never express any interest, and the boys would just go away, feeling rejected. Still, Yunhee was jealous of other girls, who could go out with boys, who could be kissed by boys, who could "have a good time" with boys. Then, she fell for Suk. Hard. She was determined to get Suk, at all costs, even her life. She gave herself willingly to Suk. She read about sex, was disgusted reading about it, but read it because she knew that Suk would want it. She prepared herself for it with the single-minded determination that she used to dig up that obscure poem, which earned her the nickname "Doer without Words." Finally, she was prepared.

That night, some six months after Yunhee met Suk, she invited him to her room. She knew that she was going to give herself to Suk. Instead of the usual light kiss outside the door, she asked Suk to come in and, once inside, held him tight and kissed him on the lips. Then, she groped for his hand, pulled his hand over her breasts, and slid it inside her blouse, letting him feel her bare breast and her hard nipple. Thank God, the nipple was erect. With the other hand, she then groped for Suk's other hand and slid it under her skirt, up her thighs, into her crotch. Yes, she was seducing Suk. She felt tense, excited, and determined. She was executing a very well-rehearsed act. Suk was clearly aroused; she could feel his hardened penis pressing against her. He then pulled up her skirt, pulled down her panties, pulled down his pants, and thrust his tumescent penis into Yunhee's well-lubricated vagina. She moaned, "Oh, Suk! Oh, Suk!" and thrust her pelvis back and forth with each moan. A very well-rehearsed act. A week ago, she had pierced her hymen with a sterilized razor blade. Her vulva was now well lubricated because she had put surgical lubricant on it earlier that evening. All to make it appear that she was aroused, that she was ready to receive Suk. An Oscar performance for Yunhee, especially because she did not feel any sexual arousal. She felt happy with Suk's penis in her vagina then, not because she was feeling sexual but because she finally had her man inside her.

Now in Kangneung, Yunhee was, as much as she was capable of being, happy overall. Bo entered the local public school, and she was going to school with him every day. It had never occurred to her that Bo might go to school by himself—the streets were so dangerous anyway. The school was within walking distance from home, and Yunhee walked with Bo, hand in hand, every morning to school. Bo, wearing his backpack that everybody wore to school these days, and Yunhee, holding a little lunch box for Bo.

She would stay in school, standing in the back of the classroom. Initially, quite a few mothers came to school with their children, but soon only Yunhee was coming to school with her child. In three months' time, it was Bo who asked his mother, "Mom, you are the only one who comes to school with a kid these days. Other kids sometimes call me a baby who needs his mom all the time. Perhaps I could go to school by myself sometimes?"

Reluctantly, Yunhee stopped going to school every day. But she would frequently drop by unannounced, and, at times, one could see her walking slowly by the school, attempting to get a glimpse of Bo in the classroom.

Yunhee adored Bo. He was smart, sociable, mature, and handsome. He was pure. He was an innocent boy. Unlike his father.

She saved everything Bo did—his doodles, his drawings, his colorings. Eventually, she made several wall hangings with them. One of them won a special prize at a school exhibition.

10

WAR!

June 27, 1950, Kangneung, South Korea (37.7–35.2 N Parallel, 128.6 E Longitude)
Bo

Hup! Two! Three! Four!

The amplifier droned on as I and all my classmates exercised at 8:00 a.m. in the school yard, as was the custom that was established with the help of my father, the head of the local Department of Health and Welfare of the National Police. Then, suddenly, the counting was interrupted by the voice of the principal.

"Students, I have been asked by the police to give you the following announcement. There is a national emergency. You are asked to go home as soon as possible and obey further instructions from the authorities."

We all hurried home. The Korean War had begun, two days earlier, on June 25, 1950. The North Koreans had crossed the thirty-eighth parallel, with massive ground and air forces, in an attempt to conquer the southern part of the peninsula within a matter of weeks. The South Korean government had kept the invasion rather quiet to the Korean people, while requesting emergency aid from the United Nations and the United States. The only radio station in South Korea then was a government-run station, which made no announcements about the invasion—just business as usual. There was no television in Korea then.

Five months earlier, in January 1950, Dean Acheson, then secretary of state of the United States, defined the "defense line of the United States in the Far East, a line bulwarked by firm troops commitment, running along the Aleutians to Japan and then…to the Ryukyus and from the Ryukyus to the Philippine Islands…" The Korean peninsula and Taiwan were notable exceptions.

June 29, 1950, 10:00 a.m.

Suk came home and told Yunhee to pack. He had heard, through police channels, that the North Koreans were invading the South across the thirty-eighth parallel. The United Nations had declared the North Koreans the aggressor and resolved to help the South Koreans, but the North Korean Army was advancing rapidly. The North Koreans had hundreds of tanks and airplanes. The South Korean Army had practically none! They had to leave Kangneung and head south, as the North Koreans were sure to advance to Kangneung in a matter of days. He, as a police officer, could not defend the town in peace unless he felt that his family was secure. Suk had brought with him his petty officer, Pai, whose family lived practically next door to the Moons. Pai and his wife were to accompany Yunhee and Bo. There would be a government truck waiting for them at the police station to drive them to Taejon, a city far enough south to be safe until the United Nations forces came to their rescue. Suk told Pai to go and help his wife pack and that Yunhee and Bo would join them shortly.

Dad was in the police uniform, not as neat and shiny as the first day. Dad told Mom in a hushed voice, "I will call you, or join you, as soon as I can. I have to stay with the police force, but you and Bo must be safe. Go south with the Pais. To Taejon. Go in the waiting truck, and we will be together soon." Dad took out a silver knife with jade handle from his desk drawer and handed it to Mom.

"Keep this for me, Yunhee. My father gave this to me, and now I give it to you to protect yourself and Bo."

Then he rushed out to return to the police station. He noticed that the street was becoming crowded with people—somehow the news of the invasion must have circulated quickly—heading south.

And Mom and I were left alone, to fend for ourselves! Yunhee packed quickly and joined the Pais next door. Pai and his wife had already packed. They were very happy to accompany and protect Yunhee and Bo to Taejon. So, Yunhee, holding Bo's hand on one hand, started out into the street, her other hand holding a small valise, together with her handbag. She walked with the Pais toward the police station and the awaiting truck.

"Please let me carry the valise for you; you are holding too many things already" said Pai as he took the valise in his hand. Once on the main street leading to the police station, they were swept away by waves of people, all with their families and with suitcases in their hands, all moving south, away from the invading North Koreans. It was chaotic.

In those days, the streets were narrow, and there were no sidewalks. There were very few automobiles on the road, and those few that were out could not advance. The street was filled with people, thousands of people, all pushing to get ahead. In that crowd, holding tightly to Bo's hand, Yunhee lost sight of the Pais. They simply disappeared into the crowds. With Yunhee's valise, containing some jewelry, clothes, and above all, the birthday pictures of Bo, from age one hundred days to his eighth birthday. Yunhee tried to call the Pais, but she could not see them, and they did not respond. She consoled herself that she would be reunited with them at the police station. But by the time they reached the police station, there was no one there. No truck. No policeman. Everyone in sight was walking south.

Bewildered, Yunhee joined the endless column of people, young and old, walking south, to avoid the onslaught of the advancing North Korean Communists.

I had never walked so much in my life. Walk, walk, walk, walk. Everybody was walking. I really couldn't complain. There was nary a car passing us; the road was filled with people, people with rucksacks, people with hand-pulled carts, people walking with children, people with suitcases, people.

"Mom, can we stop for a while and rest?"

"No, Bo. Let's at least walk till the next village."

Walk. Walk. Walk. Walk.

Arriving at the next town, Yunhee headed for the police station. She tried to call Suk on the police line but was told that Kangneung had been evacuated. All police that were in Kangneung had left for an unknown destination.

"This is the equivalent of a half a pound of beef," said Yunhee as she handed Bo a multivitamin tablet from a full bottle. Bo swallowed it hungrily and felt energy filling his body in seconds. Yes, a half a pound of beef in one tablet!

Yunhee never looked so strong, so determined, so full of energy. She knew that she was on her own. From that point on, she would never try to reach Suk until he found her. In fact, she had to conceal her identity as the wife of a police officer, because you never knew where the North Korean spies were. They would surely kill you if they knew that you were related to a South Korean police officer.

"If we ever get separated, tell people your husband is a carpenter. Never let others know that your husband is a policeman," Suk had told her.

A carpenter's wife and a carpenter's child. Walking south, not knowing where their final destination might be. Yunhee had very little money and very little jewelry in her handbag. They had had a substantial sum of money and a considerable amount of jewelry in the small valise that was now lost. Yunhee had only her small handbag in one hand and Bo's hand, firmly in her other hand. No, nothing would take that hand away from her.

Nightfall. Some continued walking. Many just stopped and rested for the night. Yunhee and Bo just rested on the side of the road. Bo could not continue to walk. Yunhee and Bo decided to rest awhile. They did not feel alone because there were scores of people right next to them, on the side of the road. Sleeping. The moon was bright. It seemed very natural that everyone should be sleeping on the roadside on this summer night.

Daybreak. They marched on. No breakfast. No morning toilet routine. They just woke up, got up, and started walking. They came across a small village. The whole village seemed asleep except for the small number of people on the road that early, just walking aimlessly south.

Yunhee and Bo were walking on the main street. They looked up and saw a sign that said, "Daiho Chinese Restaurant." Bo was famished. He asked, "Mom, a Chinese restaurant. Can we eat something for breakfast?"

Yunhee thought, "No. We cannot eat in a restaurant. We don't have the money." But she couldn't bring herself to say it to Bo, knowing how hungry he was, how tired he was. "Well, even if I have to spend my last penny, Bo will eat a decent meal."

She said, "Yes, Bo. Let's go in if it's open." It was open, and the smell of cooking inside the restaurant was simply mouthwatering. They sat down at the nearest table in a state of exhaustion. A middle-aged Chinese man came and said, "Are you refugees?"

"Yes. We come from Kangneung. We are the family of a carpenter, who couldn't get away with us just yet. Could we have something to eat for breakfast?" said Yunhee exhaustedly.

"Sure. In fact, I have prepared some food, a special nutritious food for the refugees, which I'll serve free of charge. I'm sure the boy would really enjoy it. It's a very nice chicken and dumpling soup."

"Why, thank you very much. We would really appreciate it," said Yunhee, surprised.

"Not at all. Koreans have been good to us Chinese, and this is only a small way of expressing my gratitude. Please feel free to ask for seconds."

The soup was delicious and filling. Even Yunhee had seconds. With the warmth of the soup within her belly, she felt a warmth in her heart, which was really a very rare feeling for Yunhee. Bo just continued to gulp, oblivious to her inner state. So many Koreans think the Chinese are just selfish people who care about nothing but money, thought Yunhee.

From the mountainous Kangwon Province, the only reasonable route south at that time was southwest, to the plains of Chungchong Province. Then, they could either head southeast to Kyungsang Province or southwest toward Chulla Province. Initially, Yunhee had hoped that she could just head for Taejon, in Chungchong Province, and wait for Suk to get in touch with her, as Suk had told her to do if ever they were to be separated from each other during the war. Days of marching, on foot, to reach Taejon. They lost count of days and nights they spent on the roadside, in abandoned sheds in villages, walking south.

Taejon. A midsize city. Yunhee and Bo could hear distant thunder, but the day was clear. They soon realized that the sound was artillery fire. The North Koreans must be near! They saw South Korean soldiers in trucks, headed toward the opposite direction that they were. The soldiers looked ill-equipped and seemed dejected while headed north, to fight the onrushing Communists.

Surely, we couldn't stay in Taejon if the North Koreans are so near, thought Yunhee. Besides, the streets were filled with people, resembling those of Kangneung as they were leaving it only a few days ago. Then they heard airplanes. Four airplanes flying in formation. The crowd cheered, "The UN planes. They have arrived to fight the invaders! To bomb the hell out of the North Korean Army!" Everyone strained to look at the silver airplanes flying in a neat formation in the blue sky.

Vroom! Bang! Vroom!

Tatatatatatatata!

The planes dived toward them as sirens wailed loudly out of nowhere, and they heard the explosions and the machine gun fire. The planes were bombing and strafing the crowds!

Tatatatatatatata!

The dreaded sound of machine-gun fire that was ingrained in Yunhee's and Bo's brains since that afternoon in North Korea, when they had nearly been mowed down by the "People's Army"!

They all fell on their stomachs. As they fell, they caught a glimpse of the insignia on the planes—red stars. North Korean warplanes.

The planes roared away. People got up, in a daze, and dusted themselves. Blood! A woman looked at her arm helplessly as the arm of her white dress turned bright red, soaking in blood. From her limp arm, blood was gushing out. She fell in a faint. People started walking, ignoring those who were still prone. Dead? Fainted? They did not have the presence of mind to care. They just walked. South.

Yunhee initially headed southwest, along the less mountainous route, toward Chunju, in Chulla Province. But as they were about halfway, they received the news that Chunju was already in North Korean hands. The North Korean Army was able to advance faster through the less mountainous parts and had overtaken them. They and others on the road took a sharp turn to the east and started their way toward Kyungsang Province, into the mountains toward Taegu.

They had been walking for hours without stopping. Bo's legs were hurting. Yunhee's shoes were now barely on her feet. Yunhee had made acquaintance with two other families that were walking south with them. One of the families consisted of a husband, a government clerk, his wife, both in their thirties, and a ten-year-old daughter. Another family consisted of a mother, in her early thirties, a son, age nine, and a daughter, age five. The mother said her husband was a soldier in the South Korean Army. Yunhee had told them that her husband was a carpenter. The three families, being similar in age and, in some ways, similar in situation found themselves walking together and being supportive to each other, including sharing food and stories.

They had again walked for miles and miles. It was getting dark. There were only a few people walking on the road, many having decided to camp on the roadside. The three families continued walking, until they came to a mountainside that seemed to have a small side road. The man who used to be a government clerk said, "Perhaps I'll try going up this road awhile. Maybe there is a house that can put us up for the night, from whom we might buy some food."

The rest waited on the road while he went up it. Soon, he came back beaming.

"Yes, there is a little thatched house up there. There is nobody there. It looks abandoned. But guess what! There is food there. Let's all go up there and live it up for the night!"

Indeed, the little house with the thatched roof, which was typical of a Korean peasant's house, was pretty well hidden from view until one was actually standing in front of it. Inside, it was rather clean, and the furniture looked expensive, unlike a typical peasant's house. And the house was well stocked with rice, dried meat and fish, and various pickled vegetables. The three families had a feast, and all fell asleep soundly on the floor of the living room.

In the morning, they again ate a hearty breakfast. Everyone was feeling rather content.

"What do you say," started the government clerk. "I am rather tired of walking. What if we just stayed in this house and pretended that we were farmers here? I don't think anyone will hardly notice this house. If the North Koreans overtake us, I doubt that they will bother poor peasants living in this country house. After all, the peasants are proletarians."

All the rest nodded their heads. Yes, it would be comfortable just to stay put in this nice little abandoned house.

Bo had a strange gut feeling about the little farmhouse that had given them shelter and food for the night. Wouldn't it be nice to stay put here till the war ended? No! He felt somehow trapped, suffocated, in that little house. In that house, on the slope of a rocky mountain, with a little stream on the side. It was a pretty enough house and outwardly peaceful. But Bo felt a violent aversion to the house. He said to Yunhee, "Mom, we have to get out of here. We must leave. I will not stay in this house. We *must* leave!"

Yunhee was tired. She agreed with the others that it probably made sense to stay put, pretending to be farmers, until the war was over. Who would bother little peasants living in this little house off the road? But she loved Bo, and she could not force Bo to stay when he was obviously feeling so strongly against it. She knew that Bo was very headstrong and that he would be practically impossible to live with if she forced him to stay there. So, she said good-bye to the others and started out on foot, again with Bo in one hand and, in the other, just the little handbag with the dwindling resources and a paper bag with a few rice balls that she had prepared in that house with the thatched roof.

They continued to walk southeast, over the great divide. Into Kyungsang Province. As they came down a winding mountain road into a valley at dusk, they found that the road led directly into a railroad station of a small village. And, miraculously, there was a train stopped on the platform! A black steam engine with at least ten cars, a train bound for Taegu and then Pusan. The southernmost port city of eastern Korea. The train was jam-packed and literally bursting at the seams. People were holding on to the train on the sides. And people were sitting on the roof of the train. Yunhee looked helplessly at the train. No room at all!

"Mom, my legs are so tired. Could we get on the train?" asked Bo, knowing that there was absolutely no room on the train. The train whistled. Southbound train. Lifeline. No room for Yunhee and Bo.

"Hey, climb on! Lift the kid up here. There is room for two up here. I'll give you a hand!" a man yelled to us from atop the roof of the train. He was holding out his hands, looking directly at Bo.

Yunhee lifted up Bo so that he could reach the man's outstretched hands.

The thought flashed through Yunhee's mind: "What if I lose Bo? What if the train leaves without me? But then at least Bo will be safe. Because if we kept on walking like this, we would probably both die of exhaustion."

Yunhee lifted up Bo, who caught the open window of the train with his hands and then the outstretched hands of the man on the roof of the train, who pulled him until he, too, was on the roof. And then Yunhee put the straps of her handbag around her neck and, using both hands, grabbed onto the man's outstretched hands and struggled up the window frame to the train's rooftop. Even before she could sit down on the crowded roof, the train started moving. Everyone had to duck as they approached a tunnel. Darkness. Smoke and soot all over. And the roaring sound of the engine. Bo held on to his mother tightly as the train rushed through the seemingly endless tunnel. Cough! Sneeze! It was a nightmare to ride the top of a train in a tunnel—the top of the tunnel was only a couple of feet away from your crouched back. With head on your knees, trying to breathe through a handkerchief. Endless tunnel. Eventually, the train emerged from the tunnel. Everyone was covered with soot. "Hey, we all look like Negroes," said the man who had pulled them both to safety and winked.

The train entered Taegu, which was a midsize city perched on the side of the mountain range. No one got off the train. No one could get on the train. But the train stopped. There were vendors on the platform, selling cheaply made sushi. Korean sushi, when properly made, is rice with morsels of fish, meat, fried egg, and vegetables, all wrapped prettily in seaweed. But the sushi they sold contained only rice and kimchi, the spicy Korean pickle. Spending practically her last penny, Yunhee bought a stick of sushi for Bo. Bo ravished the sushi. He did not even notice that Yunhee did not have anything to eat. From time to time ever since that train ride, Bo developed a sudden yearning for a cheaply made sushi, with nothing in it but rice and kimchi.

July 1950, Pusan (35.2 N Parallel, 129 E Longitude)
The last UN stand during the Korean War. South of the Nakdong River, inside the Pusan perimeter. Truly, the last patch of land in South Korea that remained unconquered by the North Korean Army. Finally, the train pulled into the Pusan station. Nowhere farther south to go, except into the sea, across which lay Japan. Pusan, the bustling port city, the population of which had swollen during the past several weeks to almost ten million, more than ten times the normal population. And the refugees were still pouring in.

Now, Yunhee had exhausted all her financial resources that were contained in her small handbag.

"Refugees, follow the sign to the Red Cross refugee camp!" read the sign on the platform. She followed the sign. They were eventually taken to a refugee camp that was set up in the outskirts of Pusan. It was a tent city, with hundreds and hundreds of tents, and unspeakably poor sanitary conditions. There was no running water and no sanitary toilet. There were holes in the ground, used as toilets, that were overflowing, and in the rain (summer is the rainy season in that part of the country), much of the excrement simply overflowed into the whole camp area. A walk in the campground was an adventure in filth. And the unbearable stink everywhere!

The food was also atrocious. A gruel consisting of mostly barley and unsterilized water, prepared by people with filthy hands. No condiments but a small dish of salt. No wonder dysentery broke out. Diarrhea. Bloody diarrhea.

Fortunately, because of the extreme caution Yunhee took concerning drinking water and food, Bo and Yunhee did not contract the disease.

11

A FATEFUL NIGHT

July 1950, Refugee Camp, Pusan, South Korea (35.2 N Parallel, 129 E Longitude)
Bo, Yunhee

The refugees spent their time reading the newspaper, listening to the radio, and watching the long line of army trucks go by in front of their camp. Freshly unloaded tanks, artillery, and troops! US troops, Filipino troops, Turkish soldiers. With their flags hoisted proudly, the troops rolled in from the docks of Pusan, in trucks, personnel carriers, and tanks, and they passed the refugee camp toward the defense perimeter. There were at least thirty or so refugees in one little tent. Forced togetherness. Some were gregarious and others reticent. Uncle Han was one of the gregarious types. He was not really an uncle, but almost any older man is called "Uncle" by children in Korea, so Bo naturally called him "Uncle Han." He was in his late thirties, a man who also used to be a carpenter. He was alone. He was separated from his family in Taejon—when he had come home from his shop the day the North Korean troops were pushing in, he found only rubble where his house used to be. The house had been bombed. A neighbor told him that he saw Han's wife leave the house with their seven-year-old son. Presumably heading south.

Han seemed to feel a kinship with Yunhee and Bo, perhaps because they reminded him of his own family. Han played Korean chess with Bo and saved some extra gruel for him and Yunhee and balls of barley rice, which was a rare and special treat in the camp.

Han was interested to know everything about Yunhee and Bo.

"Bo, did you see your dad use a bevel to cut wood?"

"Sure, Uncle Han. Lots of times," replied Bo, making up stories about his dad's carpentry shop.

"Did you know, Bo, that you can play a saw as a musical instrument? I used to be good at it," said Han. No. Bo had never seen a saw being played.

Han would often try to get Yunhee alone, while Bo and others were asleep, and talk about his own past. He would also sympathize with Yunhee about how hard it must be to be alone with a child in the refugee camp.

Night again.

Bo was sleeping soundly inside the sleeping bag that each refugee was given. The floor of the tent was littered with sleeping bags containing snoring people. There was a small naked light bulb hanging from the ceiling, attached to a power line that snaked its way out of the tent. Yunhee was not asleep. She had her eyes closed, but her face was outside of her sleeping bag. She was concentrating on what she should do. She felt she had to take Bo out of the filthy camp.

"Yunhee, I know you are not sleeping. Your eyes are closed too tight," a man's voice whispered. She opened her eyes and saw Han's grinning face.

"Yunhee, I have something to tell you. Could we take a little walk together?" said Han gently.

"OK. But we have to be back soon. I don't want Bo to feel abandoned if he should wake up" said Yunhee, getting up. Everyone slept fully dressed in the camp.

They walked in silence outside of the tent. They walked on the grassy knoll in the back of the tent site. It was a clear and moonless but starry night.

"Yes, Uncle Han. What is it you wish to tell me?" asked Yunhee.

"Yunhee, you know I like you and Bo very much. You remind me of my own family. And I have come to love you." He reached out and tried to hold Yunhee's hand.

Yunhee shook her hand free from Han and said, "Mr. Han, you know that I am married. And you are married. You should try to find your wife!"

"No, Yunhee. I love you now," said Han deliberately. He continued, "And, Yunhee, I know who you are. You are Suk's wife, now a lieutenant of the Korean Police. But I also know that you were in Manchuria and that Suk is a traitor who collaborated with the Japanese during the war. I know that you're hiding that fact. What would happen if the police found out that Suk is a traitor, and a bigamist at that?" whispered Han.

"But that's not true…how…how do you know all that?" stammered Yunhee.

"You see, I worked for the Korean underground in Manchuria. I know all about Suk and you. I am no more a carpenter than Suk is. I am a member of the Korean intelligence agency, and I am here to find Communist sympathizers in the camp. I could report Suk to the authorities—I am sure they can find him and put him in jail. I could also report to them about you and Bo and that I think you are also Communist sympathizers. But I won't do any of that, Yunhee, because I love you. I want you."

Han's breathing became heavier as he said these words. He stretched out his arms and forcibly embraced the trembling Yunhee and, kissing her, wrestled her down onto the grass.

Yunhee started to struggle and scream, but Han covered her mouth with his left hand tight. "If you scream, I'll have you and Bo arrested immediately. I do this because I love you, and I'll never hurt you. Oh, Yunhee, Yunhee. I will make you happy." His groping right hand pushed her skirt all the way up, as the left hand held her down. Now, his right hand found the top of her panties and yanked them down. The hand now found its way up again, onto Yunhee's thighs and her crotch. Now his rough fingers began to spread Yunhee's labia. Yunhee felt faint with revulsion. Struggling silently, she felt with her right hand for her hidden pocket under her skirt. She found the hard object, pulled it out by the jade handle, and swung her arm around and, with all her might, stuck the silver knife into the flesh of his heaving back.

Han slumped on top of Yunhee with a gasp as all air came out of his lungs. Yunhee struggled from under his weight, managed to stand up, and saw that the knife blade was completely buried in the small of his back. She straightened her clothes and looked around. No one in sight. Only the stars twinkling above. A peaceful night.

She turned and started running. Then she stopped. She turned back. She came back to Han, lying prone on the grass. The silver bolster of the jade handle of the knife shone faintly in the starlight. She grabbed the handle and pulled. It would not move. She pulled again, with all her might. Suddenly, the flesh gave in, and the knife came out, almost making her lose her balance. Blood gushed out from the wound, rapidly forming a little pool. Han was still, and no sound of breathing was to be heard. Yunhee put the knife back in its rigid sheath. On the way back, she stopped at the water well and cleaned the knife thoroughly. The silver knife that Suk's father had given him as he left for Seoul. "This will protect you from all evil."

The next day, the whole camp was in a state of excitement. Han's now-cold body was found on the grass by some early risers of the camp. He was obviously stabbed. The murder of a refugee right in the camp! There was talk that this was a political murder, that Han was stabbed in the back by an assassin while he was sneaking out of the camp. That Han was a government spy and that he had found some North Korean agents in the camp and they had killed him to prevent his reporting their identities to the authorities.

The police came and interrogated everyone about Han. Had anyone seen Han that fateful night? No one had. Many said to the police that they thought Han was a little suspicious, because, for a carpenter, he seemed to be well educated.

Yunhee told the police, yes, she liked Han. He was nice to Bo. No, she did not know what Han did that night. She had retired early in her sleeping bag as Bo was already sleeping. Yes, others had all seen Bo and Yunhee sleeping. No, no one saw when Han left the tent. His sleeping bag was at the other end of the tent from Yunhee's and Bo's, and nobody suspected the diminutive, four-foot-tall Yunhee of the murder. Eventually, the police arrested two people in an adjoining tent on the suspicion that they were North Korean agents who murdered Han. They were led away in handcuffs and never seen again.

With the murder presumably solved, life in the camp returned to normal. Normal drudgery and filth. Bo missed Uncle Han, his playmate. He hated the North Korean agents who killed his favorite uncle Han. At times from then on, he wondered how the saw sounded as a musical instrument. It was not until some six years later, in a school concert, that he would actually see and hear the saw being played as a musical instrument. By that time, Uncle Han was a faint memory for Bo.

Yunhee decided they could no longer stay in the camp. Without any money, without any resources, without any acquaintances in the city, she left the camp and took a room in a rooming house in the rather run-down downtown section of the city. This in itself was a great feat. The city was brimming with refugees. Finding a room was practically impossible even if one had oodles of money. But Yunhee managed to rent a room, without any down payment, in downtown, if in a run-down part. Perhaps Yunhee's determined and educated demeanor played a part. Perhaps the landlord took pity on Bo, who was clinging to Yunhee's arm as she asked for the room. The fact is she did get a room.

Now she had to make a living. One woman, all alone in the world, with her eight-year-old son.

12

A SHATTERED DREAM

1950, With Advancing Korean People's Army
(39–35.3 N Parallel, 127–28 E Longitude)

—from the Journal of Commissar Hoon Moon, Korean People's Army.

June 25, 1950

Our Great Leader, Comrade Kim Il-Sung, has given us orders to liberate all of South Korea! At the age of twenty-four, I am already a second lieutenant and a political commissar of the People's Army, leading my comrades across the thirty-eighth parallel, into the enemy territory! It is my job to round up the counterrevolutionaries in South Korea and to eliminate them. How long have I waited for this glorious day! Ever since I left my ancestral home in Kangwon Province to come north, to join the People's Army, I have dreamed of going back, to my mother and my poor sister, Kyung, as a man, a returning hero, to right the wrong, to mete out justice to my hateful father, Suk, and his whore, Yunhee! How I gritted my teeth for this day!

When World War II ended, I found out that my father, Suk, had returned to Seoul and become a teacher again. When I told her this, Mom asked me to go to Seoul and beg him to return to us, to her and Kyung in Kangwon Province. Against my better judgment, I went to see him in his office in Seoul. How coldly, heartlessly Suk refused! I remember vowing to kill him, and Yunhee, and yes, their son, Bo. I found out where they lived, too, but very soon they disappeared from Seoul. Later, I found out Suk became a policeman!

My father, now a South Korean policeman, the despicable capitalist dog! The same police force that arrested Kang, my friend and mentor, and tortured him to death, releasing his battered, dead body three days later. I was smart. I left for North Korea on the same night he was arrested because I knew they'd come after me, his closest friend.

Suk sold his soul, became a policeman to intimidate me and my family, *his* rightful family! Now, it will be my one ambition to find my father, and the whore and their bastard, Yunhee and Bo! I shall kill them both with my own hands. Their blood will purify my fatherland and calm my agitated soul!

June 27, 1950

Now, Seoul has been liberated! The capitalist dogs had blown up the bridge on Han River, south of Seoul, with four thousand people still on the bridge! That left most of the South Korean Army still on the north side of the river. We wiped them out!

How sweet it is to round up the traitors and execute them! All the government employees, soldiers, police, and their families. And landowners, bankers, and real-estate agents. Enemies of the people!

I looked for the faces of my father and his degenerate whore among the captured faces today. No, they were not there. But I shall find them!

Blood cleanses the land. Our fatherland.

Utopia requires pure people. A new breed of human beings, with only correct thoughts in their brains. Thoughts of the welfare of the society, the nation, the cause! No selfish thoughts, no greed, no thoughts of profit! Long live the Democratic People's Republic of Korea!

July 20, 1950
Our People's Army is crossing into Taejon, which had been guarded in strength by the American capitalists. Our partisans have already been in Taejon, fighting the capitalist dogs. Our glorious People's Air Force bombarded the cowardly crowds trying to escape from their own liberation!

General William Dean, the commander of the American capitalist forces, has been captured by the People's Army. How stupid the American imperialists are! Now he shall taste the hospitality of our Socialist state. Is there any question of our glorious victory? Our fatherland's total liberation is now a matter of days.

In each city we liberate, we round up the traitors, the counter-revolutionaries. I still look for the faces of my father, and the whore, and the bastard, Bo. No sign of them yet.

July 23, 1950
All the refugees that go south are traitors. Capitalists. Otherwise, why would they run and not welcome their liberators?

After so many days of running, some of them seem to be getting tired. Some of them find abandoned houses in little villages and pretend they are farmers! I have given orders to search every village and arrest anyone in the farmhouses who do not have rough hands. Capitalist dogs have soft hands. Not farmers' rough hands.

We found two such families in a little thatched-roof house, hidden in the mountainside off the main road from Taejon. A man and a woman in their late thirties and a ten-year-old daughter. And a woman in her early thirties, with a nine-year old son and a five-year old daughter. They pretended to be farmers living in the house, but my agents found fully packed city suitcases in the house. And their hands were soft as silk!

Even under torture, the man claimed he was a farmer. Until we tortured his wife in front of him and his daughter. We stripped them and tied them up. Then, we dunked their faces in a big pail of water, into which powdered hot pepper had been poured. First the wife and then the daughter. One should have seen how they gurgled helplessly in the pail. Then when they were almost drowning, after having inhaled at least several mouthfuls of the peppered water, we pushed their faces up. The agonized cries of the degenerates! But, finally, the man admitted that he had worked for the South Korean puppet government. We shot him, his wife, and their daughter on the spot.

The mother of the two children was so frightened that she confessed to everything. That her husband was a South Korean police officer, although she had told others that he was a soldier in the South Korean Army.

First, we shot her children in the head in front of her. Then, we tortured her. Not because we needed any information. We tortured her because she was the wife of a policeman. Like the whore, Yunhee. We strung her up naked and put her head in the pail of water containing hot pepper until she, in a gasp, breathed in the hot, filthy water. Then we suspended her from the ceiling by her ankles, upside down. She had big breasts, just like a capitalist whore! I crushed her nipples with a pair of pliers. She screamed deliciously. Then, I whipped her with a horse whip until her screams stopped and she was unconscious. Then I brought her back by pouring cold water on her face. She muttered, as she regained some consciousness, "Bo, you were so right."

"What? Who is Bo?" I asked her as she was fainting again. "Who is Bo?" I kicked her dangling face. Her eyes rolled. She was dead. Too late. Too late to find out if the Bo she mentioned was my hated half brother. How did she know Bo? Of course, the wife of a policeman. Maybe she knew him and Yunhee, the whore.

At least our fatherland has been rid of two families of traitors.

You just wait, Suk, Yunhee, and Bo, till I find you for your just deserts.

13

THE MATCH GIRL FROM KANGWHA

Bo

Night. It is snowing hard in the darkness, large white snowflakes pouring down from the blackened sky, only occasionally catching and reflecting starlight peering through the clouds. The little girl is selling matches to passers-by, but no one stops to buy a box of matches from the girl on this snowy night. The little match girl, half-frozen, huddled in the snow, strikes a match. In the spark, she sees her dead mother's face, smiling at her, beckoning her. The light goes out. She strikes another match. Another smiling face. Another match. Another match. It's as if each strike of the match brings forth a life that soars into the sky and fixes itself there, now a star, twinkling bright in the darkness. Soon, the last match goes out, and so does the life of the little match girl. Perhaps her life has joined those of the stars twinkling above the clouds...

A story I read as a boy that I remember as I think of the dark days of the war. And my mom. The match girl from Kangwha.

July 1950, Pusan, South Korea (35.2 N Parallel, 129 E Longitude)
Yes, she sold matches. In those days, the streets of Pusan were filled with vendors, selling pencils, flowers, candies...and plain beggars, panhandlers. My mom joined them, selling matches. She said,

"People always need matches. They need them for cooking, and they need them for cigarettes."

She pawned her wedding ring to raise the meager capital to buy two cases of matches from a wholesaler. Then she sold them on the streets to passersby. She held the matches in her raised right hand, saying aloud to passersby, "Matches, matches, buy matches for cigarettes, for cooking." Her other hand, of course, was tightly holding on to mine. Occasional passersby would take pity on this diminutive but dignified woman with a child and buy one or two boxes of her matches. Soon, she started ringing doorbells, selling matches door-to-door. She found that ringing doorbells paid off better. Once the housewife saw my mom, holding my hand, she usually invited us in. And, often, she would offer us food as she listened to my mom's story.

Yes, they took pity on us. My mom was successful, quite successful as a match girl. She used to tell the housewives in the middle-class neighborhoods how we were separated from her successful carpenter husband in the confusion of the war, and how wonderful I was in school, and how she meant to make sure that I continued my education through college. They listened, and they often bought all the matches she had. Yes, everybody needed matches. Also, in Korea, matches mean good fortune, fortune exploding like the strike of a match. So, when one moves into a new house, the customary present is a case of matches!

It is said that the Battle of Britain, during World War II, was England's finest hour. In spite of the daily bombardment by the Germans, they survived and finally won the air battle thanks to the courageous, tireless, determined pilots from England and from the Nazi-occupied lands—Poland, Norway, France, Holland. Churchill said, "Never have so many owed so much to so few."

July and August 1950, the darkest period of the Korean War, when the United Nations forces had finally retreated to the Pusan perimeter, with fears that the little patch of land left of South Korea would soon be engulfed by the North Korean troops, or that the United Nations would simply withdraw from Korea, chalking it up as a lost cause, was the finest hour for Yunhee. She became a successful proprietor of a small business as a match vendor. She made a reasonable living and was able to pay for the room that she rented, get back her wedding ring from the pawnshop, and even stash away some money. And she also gave Bo lessons. Lessons for school.

Bo, like many other refugee children, was missing school. During the walk south, he obviously could not attend any school. Once in Pusan, Yunhee inquired into enrolling him in school. She discovered that it was impossible to enroll him in a local school while they were living in the refugee camp, because one had to be a permanent resident of Pusan in order to enroll in the local school district. Now that Yunhee and Bo had a permanent address, albeit a rented room in Pusan, Bo could enroll in school the next semester, which began in September. To catch up, Yunhee began giving lessons to Bo. She bought all the textbooks, and she and Bo studied together in the early mornings, before they went out selling matches together. For the first time in her life, Yunhee felt whole. She felt confident that she could survive on her own, and she had Bo beside her. Bo was her constant companion. He was precocious, and he felt protective of his mother. They did everything together and felt they did not lack anything as long as they were together. And Bo was a better companion than Suk. Bo did not drink, he did not ask for sex, and he did not play around. He was devoted to his mom. He adored his mom. And he said, "All I need is you, Mom. I don't need anyone else, ever!"

Yunhee felt proud she was providing all the basic necessities, including education, to Bo all by herself. While she did not have her husband's position or power, she did after all make a living, a rather comfortable living, even though it was as a door-to-door salesperson. She had never imagined that she could survive selling matches, but she was doing it and even enjoying it!

No, she was not the helpless match girl of the fairy tale. She was the practical match salesperson, a businesswoman, from Kangwha, an island that endured all the storms and tides. Doer without Words.

September 15, 1950—December 1950, Korea (35–42 N Parallels, 128–31 E Longitudes)
General Douglas MacArthur's brilliantly conceived, boldly executed amphibious landing in Inchon, the port city and gateway to Seoul, turned the tides of the Korean War in a single blow. Within days, Seoul was liberated, and within weeks, the North Korean armies that had penetrated deep into South Korea were cut off and routed. The remnants were retreating back, north of the thirty-eighth parallel. By October, almost all of North Korea was in UN hands, and it seemed that the reunification of Korea and the end of the war was at hand. Then the Chinese Communists intervened, with their "human wave" campaign, where thousands and thousands of ill-equipped, ill-clad, chanting and screaming "volunteer" youths came down upon the American and South Korean forces, engulfing them with their sheer numbers. The UN forces retreated hastily, toward the south. Eventually, the UN forces regrouped and counterattacked. Seoul changed hands four times until March 1951, when it was firmly secured by the UN forces. The opposing forces were approximately where they began, around the thirty-eighth parallel.

In September, Bo was again a student, continuing his third grade in the local school in Pusan. Again, Yunhee walked to school with him and walked home from school, every day, for another two months, because, after all, Pusan, unlike Kangneung, was so crowded, with so many refugees, whom one could not trust at all. Bo caught up quickly, thanks to the studying at home with his mom.

Soon, Bo was the top student, who monopolized the teachers' attention and inspired the envy of his classmates. But he also made friends, many friends, and he was soon elected monitor of the class. Since Bo was enrolled in the local school, most of his friends were from established middle-class families in the city. Many of them had nice big houses. Bo was ashamed of his rented single room and was reluctant to let his friends know where he lived. When his friends said, "Bo, let's go play in your house," Bo would shake his head and answer, "No. Let's go to yours. I don't want to disturb my mom at home, who has many things to do that need concentration." The carpenter's wife with many things to do that need concentration.

As the winter approached, Yunhee decided to change her line of work, from selling matches to being a seamstress. In the course of her career as a match salesperson, she had met a number of rather wealthy women with whom she developed a friendship. She showed them the clothes she had made and offered to make or alter clothes for them. Yunhee was an excellent seamstress and an expert on the sewing machine. She was able to develop a steady clientele even while she was selling matches. She now purchased a used Singer sewing machine and went into the sewing business full-time. She did a good job, and her business again thrived. Now, she did not have to walk in the cold winter streets selling matches. But she did need to concentrate on her sewing!

14

SNOW, BLOOD, AND IDEALS

—from the Journal of Commissar Hoon Moon,
Korean People's Army. September 25, 1950.

The American imperialist forces have succeeded in their sneak attack on Inchon! In spite of the heroic fights of our comrades, Seoul has fallen again to the capitalists. Now the bulk of our army south of Seoul is cut off from the North. We have no supplies, no ammunition, no food. My comrades are starving. I will order them to become guerrilla fighters, glorious partisans, and fight on for our People's Republic till death!

But I must escape to the North. I have unfinished business. To see the resurrection of the People's Republic against the invading American imperialists. Like our leader, Comrade Kim Il-Sung, I will fight, if I have to, in Manchuria, until fatherland Korea is free again and justice is done!

September–December 1950, Jiri Mountains, South Korea (35.3 N Parallel, 127.7 E Longitude)
Hoon
The once-mighty Korean People's Army (KPA) was decimated by American and South Korean troops after its supply and escape

route was cut off by MacArthur's Inchon landing and encirclement of the KPA forces September 15–16, 1950.

Hoon Moon, second lieutenant and a political commissar of KPA, was the deputy commanding officer of the Jiri Mountain Second Commando group, which was hastily formed with the remnants of a platoon of twenty-five men. The platoon commander, a lieutenant, was shot dead almost at the outset by at least a couple of his subordinates as he tried to abandon the unit and head north, and Hoon, who was considered to be ideologically pure as the political commissar, was asked to assume command. There was no longer any military discipline, just a gang of armed men who were bent on preventing anyone from escaping. But they had nowhere to go—the escape route to the North was severed by the UN forces under MacArthur, and the regrouped South Korean paramilitary police force was mercilessly hunting down the remnants of the KPA from the South. Especially fierce was the cleanup operation Hoon's group faced, by the South Korean Police Task Force to Secure Jiri Mountains, or Jiri Mountain Security Force for short.

During the three months following the September Inchon landing, Hoon's platoon lost twenty-one men; twelve were killed in firefights with the Jiri Mountain Security Force, two were injured and "euthanized" with the bayonet to save bullets, two stepped on a mine and were blown up, two were shot trying to run away, and two just disappeared, perhaps successful escapes. The commando now consisted of five ragtag soldiers including Hoon. Hoon had planned to return to North Korea while ordering his subordinates to fight on as guerillas, but this was obviously impossible at this point. Yes, comrades, we must fight to the death!

December 24, 1950, Jiri Mountains, South Korea (35.3 N Parallel, 127.7 E Longitude)
Hoon
December is very cold in Korea, especially in the high altitudes. The mountainside was snow covered and beautiful, but for the most

part, it was devoid of trees, as many were cut down for fuel and others just died because they were denuded of bark. The starving farmers, whose crop had been confiscated by the invading KPA, stripped the trees of bark, boiled them, and ate them. At least it provided their stomachs some semblance of fullness, just for a while. The mountain was rocky, and there were many natural caves and crooks and frozen streams. The sun seemed pale and frail, though there were few clouds in the sky, and darkness descended quickly as the night approached.

Hoon's group found a little cave on the side of the rocky mountain and settled themselves in as darkness was descending. One of them, Private Park, was sick and was now curled up in the cave, his skin hot to the touch even in the freezing cold. Their food supplies were long gone; even the mountain rabbits and squirrels were nearly impossible to find in the snow. Even when they found an animal, they couldn't easily catch it, because they had discarded their rifles when they ran out of bullets. The only working firearms they had were one rifle that Kim carried, with only one bullet left, and Hoon's officer's pistol, which he kept in his holster at all times. Hoon also had a dagger, and the others kept their bayonets when they discarded the rifles, to be used for the few animals they were able to trap.

So, the five hungry men were huddled together in the freezing little cave, watchful of any movement, hoping for an animal to kill and fearful of footsteps as they knew the South Korean Police Force was advancing, climbing up the mountain to mop them up.

As night fell on this Christmas Eve, Hoon thought about the Christmases he had known, the midnight church service, the carols, the Nativity scene at the church, with the Virgin Mary and baby Jesus, and Joseph, and the animals in the humble barn. But above all, the Christmas dinner the family had, with his father, Suk, his mom, Min, and his little sister, Kyung, and the mouthwatering aroma of bulgogi, the strips of beef barbecued on the tabletop, the special dinner for special occasions. And the bowl full of steamed rice!

What he would give to relive this! And his father, saying a prayer as they sat down for the dinner, speaking in his clear, somewhat theatrical voice, asking for God's blessing for the family, especially for Hoon and Kyung! How loving he seemed! They even had a small Christmas tree at home, under which Hoon found presents from Santa Claus.

In spite of the frosty, cold mountain air that congealed his every exhaled breath, Hoon felt warm inside as he remembered his early childhood and how loved he felt, how secure he felt—until the fateful day when he was fourteen, when the world he knew was shattered, when his dad disappeared from his life!

I must escape this death trap of a mountain, thought Hoon, as he returned to reality and gazed at Park, who seemed to be delirious in his fever, muttering something incomprehensible.

Hoon finally said, "Comrades, we cannot just sit here waiting for death. Yum, you stay with Park. Lee and Kim, you come with me; we will steal into one of the police tents and get some food for us!"

There was no moonlight, but there was enough starlight. Clad in tattered People's Army khakis, the threesome carefully left the cave and furtively walked down the slope to where they had previously seen some activity—a little tent hidden among barren trees and a jeep unloading stuff.

Hoon told his two comrades to remain hidden behind the trees as he sneaked toward the tent. There must be supplies in the tent because I saw someone bringing stuff into it before. The tent was dark and seemed deserted. Hoon took out his dagger as he approached the tent and silently peeked inside. It was empty! And there on the little table was a little oil lamp whose light revealed several cans of meat and a plate with food—meat and dried fish. And even an opened bottle of sake, more than half-full! He quickly capped the bottle, put all the food he could find into the now almost empty backpack he always wore, and silently sneaked out of the tent with a big grin on his face.

"Comrades, we'll be OK for a while, and we can even celebrate Christmas!" Hoon knew that the materialist dialectics of Communism precluded religious celebrations, but Santa had just brought him wonderful presents!

Back in the cave, the starved comrades, Kim, Lee, and Yum, gulped the food down with sake. Even Park, in spite of his delirium, tried some sake. Hoon, however, did not touch the sake, though he ate some of the meat and dried fish. "I must keep my head clear tonight and store strength in my body, because I have much to do!"

On his luminous watch, Hoon saw that it was 23:50. All the comrades were snoring in their drunken sleep. Hoon was also pretending to sleep, but now he slowly sat up, pulled out his dagger, and quickly stabbed Yum, who was sleeping next to him, in the heart. Just a quick exhaling sound of blood quickly pouring out of Yum's chest. Lee was sleeping on his side—impossible to stab him in the chest without turning him over. Hoon grabbed Lee's hair with his left hand and quickly turned his sleeping head toward him and then slashed his throat with the dagger in one quick motion. The neck was almost severed, exposing the bone. Blood squirted out like two fountains from his neck, but only for a while. Kim started to stir and sit up, reaching for his rifle with one bullet left. Too late to stab him, Hoon pulled out his automatic pistol and quickly shot Kim in the chest and head. Park, looking at Hoon with delirious, unseeing eyes, mumbled, "Are you an angel or the devil?"

"I am both, and I am doing you a favor," said Hoon as he shattered Park's head with a bullet.

Hoon had to move out of the cave and be on his way north before dawn. The sound of gunfire might have attracted attention, and the police force might be after him. He knew which direction north was from the position of sunset in the west during Korean winter, and also he had a compass. Besides, the Jiri Mountain Range ran from southwest to north to the Taebaik Mountains, and he just had to follow the crest of the mountain range northward. Now there was a quarter moon in the sky.

As he made his way through the trees, a small shiny object half covered by snow caught his eye. He picked it up and saw that it was a silver Zippo lighter. This could come in handy, he thought and put it in his pocket as he continued his lone climb up the mountain, toward the north. It was a clear, cold night. Hoon looked up at the stars above, some bright, others faint. "I want to be like a bright star, guiding my people in the right direction. The North Star seems to have singled me out and is twinkling at me knowingly..." This thought seemed to have reduced the freezing sensation in his feet as he trekked up north on the frozen, snowy mountainside.

Hoon did not know how far north he had to travel. The last he heard about the war was that the People's Volunteer Army (PVA) of the People's Republic of China came to the rescue of the defeated KPA and that the tables were turning again. Maybe I don't have to walk all the way to the Yalu River to meet up with my comrades, Hoon thought.

Hoon could clearly remember the first week or so of the ordeal of his journey north, eating snow for water, hunting and eating small animals and anything else living, including bats in caves and hard-to-find insects, and stealing acorns stored underground by squirrels. At times, when he felt secluded and safe enough, he made a small fire, usually in a cave with dry leaves, using his Zippo lighter very sparingly. But as he made his painful way north, the snow was often frozen solid, and there were very few living things that could pass for food.

February, 1951

The next several weeks were a blur to Hoon; he did not know how he made his way finally to being rescued by the volunteer army of the People's Republic of China just south of the thirty-eighth parallel in February of 1950. He had nightmares of events he did not remember, such as being attacked by another KPA soldier in the slippery snow. Did I really stab him with my dagger as he was choking me? Did I really drink his blood?

It was only a nightmare and best not to remember. When Hoon was found unconscious, two of his toes had to be amputated because they were frozen solid. But for his uniform, he would have been left to freeze by the Chinese volunteers, who had now pushed back the Americans south of the thirty-eighth parallel.

15

AN OATH OF GREAT TRUST

December, 1950, Jiri Mountains, Korea (35.3 N Parallel, 127.7 E Longitude)
Suk

Suk, Lieutenant Daisin Moon of the National Police of the Republic of Korea, was with his police unit, which had become mobilized and attached to a military police unit. The function of the police unit was to guard and manage the prisoners of war, but during the initial phases of the Korean War, there were very few North Korean prisoners. Fortunately, however, that unit from Kangneung was kept together during the retreat to the Pusan perimeter. All the members of the unit had been cut off from their families as if they were in active military duty.

Soldiering was very alien to Suk. Even as a policeman, Suk had veered toward the educational aspects of the work rather than the law-enforcement side. As the head of the Health and Welfare Department, he had no occasion even to wear a gun. But now, he was issued a pistol and was directing armed men to protect supply trucks headed to the front.

Suk wondered about Yunhee and Bo. All he knew was that they must have headed toward the South when they could not reach the police station, where they were supposed to have gotten on a government truck. In fact, there was no truck waiting at the police station, because it had been commandeered by the army for military use. Suk had told Yunhee that, in the unlikely event they were separated during the war, she and Bo should go to Taejon, check into a hotel, and stay there until Suk sent for them. Well, Taejon was overrun by the Communists within a matter of days, and Suk hoped that Yunhee and Bo had not gone to Taejon, and if they had, that they had left it before the North Koreans occupied it.

With the Inchon landing, the tables were turned. The North Koreans were retreating in disarray, and a large portion of the Communist army was cut off from North Korea and was stranded deep in South Korea, without any hope of supplies or reinforcement. They headed toward the mountains and became guerrillas. The police force was given the task of mopping up these stranded guerrillas. Thus, Suk was made a commander in charge of the supplies for the Police Task Force to Secure the Jiri Mountains, also known as the Jiri Mountain Security Force. The task force's command post was located in the middle part of southeastern Korea, only about eighty miles northwest of Pusan as the crow flies. The Jiri Mountains, however, being a southwestern branch of the majestic Taebaik Mountain Chain, which forms the spine of the Korean peninsula, are tall, remote, and snow-covered at this time of the year. There were no roads except for a single highway constructed by the Japanese to traverse the range and narrow clearings made by the task force for jeeps and supply trucks.

The Communist guerillas, the remnants of the once-proud Korean People's Army (KPA), hid in caves, ate tree bark, hunted unlucky squirrels and deer with their bayonets, and raided villages at night, often killing everyone they could find.

Christmas Eve

Suk was in his tent, which was an outpost of the task force. He made frequent inspection visits to outposts where there were supply depots. Suk wanted to make sure that the supplies were not being diverted, which was rumored to happen frequently.

Whenever he made the inspection tours, he insisted on sleeping in a tent near the supply depot to see if anyone stole supplies during the night. Tonight, the unit commander, who had become quite friendly with Suk, drove his jeep to Suk's tent with a bottle of sake, some US Army canned meat, and dried codfish to celebrate Christmas Eve. "This is a small Christmas present, courtesy of the US Army," said the commander. They drank and reminisced about the old days, the peaceful days before war broke out. Since the outbreak of the war, Suk hardly had any opportunity to drink. Tonight, Christmas Eve, was an exception. After all, he was a Christian. Paradoxically, many Korean Protestant churches prohibited their members from drinking and smoking. But Suk was an enlightened, liberal Christian and did not feel bound by such silly rules. "I will go to the church in the village tomorrow and celebrate Christmas."

Being in a combat zone, they had to be careful about intoxication, and they stopped at less than half the bottle.

When the unit commander left, Suk thought of going to bed. Only 11:00 p.m. Somehow, he felt wide awake in spite of the sake. Perhaps I'll take a walk. There was a nice walkway within the compound that passed along a small stream that Suk had used a few times when visiting here. As he stepped into the walkway, a sentinel saluted him as he passed. "Please be careful, sir. There are guerillas in the area."

"Thank you, Soldier. I trust you will keep all of us safe!"

There was no moon but plenty of starlight, which gave the snow-capped mountains and darker valleys an otherworldly cast. Down in the village, he could see faint lights. He thought he heard "Silent Night" perhaps, the church organ playing in the distance. Suk felt nostalgic. He missed home, the hearth, and a normal life. Above all, he missed Yunhee and Bo. My flesh and blood, Bo! And Yunhee, who stood by me through thick and thin, through Manchuria and the perilous escape. Oh, where are you, my loved ones? Are you alive? Are you looking for me?

He lit a cigarette with his Zippo lighter. The lighter was a gift from his college friend when he entered the police force. A very reliable lighter that he prized. His lighting of the cigarette was almost automatic, but as he was about to put the lighter back in the pocket of his jacket, under the overcoat, a thought crossed his mind—I must find my family! Yunhee and Bo. Until I find them, I shall give up smoking! And I will give up my prized lighter, as a sacrifice, so that I may find them in good health! I swear to God that I will find my family. So, please help me, God! Suk crushed the lighted cigarette under his shoe and then, taking a long aim, threw the lighter into the woods. The lighter traced a long arc, the metal surface gleaming in the starlight. "I shall find my loved ones, Yunhee and Bo!"

Suk repeated these words like a mantra, over and over again, walking to his tent. In the tent, he found that the food and sake he had left on the table were gone. I guess my driver cleaned the table and is perhaps having a feast himself—well, it's Christmas Eve, Suk thought. He lay in his cot, picturing the faces of Yunhee and Bo and renewing his vow to find them over and over again until he finally fell asleep. Half-asleep, he thought he heard a burst of gunfire, but maybe it was fireworks? After all, it was Christmas.

Suk kept his word. He asked his subordinates to make discreet inquiries in refugee camps in Pusan and elsewhere. He himself telephoned local police stations in Pusan, Taejon, and other cities that had a sizable refugee population. He asked them if Yunhee had inquired about his whereabouts or if anyone had inquired about the whereabouts of the police contingent from Kangneung.

All these inquiries were to naught. No word of Yunhee or Bo. Yunhee was true to the scenario that she was a carpenter's wife. She never let anyone know that she was Suk's wife during this period, and she never made any inquiries of the police. She thought that Suk would be able to find her, somehow, if he wanted to.

One day, a colleague of Suk's who was making inquiries in a refugee camp in Pusan was told that a woman and a boy resembling his description had been in that camp for a while but had left. There the trail ended. No forwarding address. No way to know where they went. He reported this to Suk.

Suk tried to put himself in Yunhee's shoes, to think like her. Where would she be? If the woman and the boy were indeed Yunhee and Bo, they must be safe; they were in Pusan, and most likely they would still be in Pusan. But how to find them? Pusan was brimming with refugees. And, most likely, Yunhee would not be using her real name. She would be the wife of a carpenter. And Bo?

Bo! He is a schoolboy. Yunhee is an educator. Surely, she must be sending Bo to school! And since Bo does need his educational credentials, she must be using Bo's real name! Yes, I must look into schools in Pusan and find Bo in the third-grade class.

February 1951, Pusan

Bo

I still remember the day vividly. The day Dad came back into my life. February 15, 1951. I was in class—probably a geography class, since I seem to remember seeing a map in front of me, and I remember raising my hand to tell the teacher I knew the answer to the question. He called on me, and I gave the right answer. Then the bell rang. As I was about to get up and go out into the corridor for the break, I saw a uniformed man coming toward me. A rather familiar narrow face...and as he comes closer, I see his slanted eyes, his pockmarked, handsome face...Dad! Father!

We embrace. "Bo, is it really you?"

"Dad, is it really *you*?"

"Bo, where have you and your mom been? I have been looking all over for you!"

"Dad, Mom and I live in a little room downtown, not far from here," I reply, my eyes still bleary with tears. We hastily tell the teacher that we must go home right now, because I have found my dad.

Mom is home, in front of her sewing machine as usual. I rush into the room and yell, "*Mom!* Guess who's here!"

Mom looks up. Gets up slowly, as if in a daze. Rubs her eyes and looks again. "Suk!"

"Yunhee!"

A tearful reunion. Finally, Dad finds Mom. I find my dad. And the Moon family is reunited. In Pusan, in the little room that Yunhee made home.

Dad went back to the task force for only three more days. To resign from the force. He came back to the little room, now a free man, although without a job. We were happy, the three of us, in that little room. It was little, but it was home, a palace compared with the refugee camp. And above all, I was with both Mom and Dad. And Dad told me stories. Of the retreat from Kangneung, of the pistol that he was given, of how he learned to use the pistol but had never yet fired at any person. Dad was proud that he had never used a weapon against anyone.

He told us about the Christmas Eve. And how he swore to God that he would find us again! And about his quitting smoking, something he loved to do, until he found us again. And the Zippo lighter that he sacrificed so that he would find us! He lit his cigarette with a match, one of the leftovers from Mom's match-selling days, and puffed contentedly as he told us his stories.

Mom just listened quietly as she usually did, her hands busy sewing. "So, Yunhee, tell me your story. How did you survive?" Dad asked finally.

Mom told him. About the long, long journey south on foot. About the air raid in Taejon. About the little house on the mountainside, where we might have stayed had it not been for my insistence that we leave. "I wonder what became of the people who stayed there."

Mom and I told Dad about the ride on the roof of the train. And the refugee camp. And Mom's selling matches on the streets to make a living. Dad cried aloud, with tears streaming down his cheeks. He held us both tight and said he would never, ever leave us again.

For several weeks, when I was not in school, we just stayed in that little room and talked. At night, though, I began to feel afraid. I would hear my mom moaning, as if in pain, while Dad seemed to be on top of her, hurting her. Dad seemed to be breathing hard, and he seemed to pound on Mom. I was too scared to say anything; I would simply pretend to sleep. Then, somehow, Mom and Dad seemed to make up and disentangle themselves. They would then just fall asleep. I thought that, perhaps, Dad had become a little strange because of his being with the soldiers and maybe had nightmares that he acted out by hurting Mom.

I asked Mom one day, when Dad was out, if Dad had nightmares at night and if he hurt her during sleep sometimes. Mom smiled and said, "No, Bo. He does not have nightmares. But he sometimes becomes like an animal at night. All men do, when they are grown up. You will understand when you grow up. But, now, thank God you are still a child!"

I let it go at that. But I did not like the idea that I would become like an animal at night when I grew up.

16

DISLOCATIONS

February 28, 1951, Pusan, South Korea (35.2 N Parallel, 129 E Longitude)

Suk

Jiri Mountain Police Task Force Scandal!

Police Chief Arrested! Allegations of Misuse of Funds.

The headlines screamed that the Police Task Force to Secure the Jiri Mountains, the unit that Suk had been a member of only two weeks ago, had been involved in a major scandal. The top officials had diverted a major part of their supplies from the United States for private gain, while the men in trenches went hungry and had inadequate ammunition. All the top officials were arrested. Suk would certainly have been arrested had he not resigned two weeks before.

Suk was concerned that he might still be arrested. But he knew that he was one person who was innocent of the scandal. He, like anyone else, knew that there was something amiss. But, up to the point of Suk's responsibility, everything was according to Hoyle. Once materials left Suk's control, however, they were diverted for private gain.

Suk thanked God for another miracle. On top of the miracle of finding Yunhee and Bo, he was spared of this scandal, and the inevitable arrest and disgrace, all in the nick of time. All due to the promise he made to God, he believed, and his sacrifice of the Zippo lighter on that Christmas Eve.

March 1951, Pusan (35.2 N Parallel, 129 E Longitude)
Bo
Dad comes home, beaming, with a bag of sweet buns in his hand. He has been looking for work, but it was not easy to find any work in Pusan, which was filled with unemployed refugees. Every day, he has been coming home looking glum and tired. But, today, he is beaming!

"Guess whom I saw today. My friend, Cho Il Whan. You know, he used to be the police commissioner and gave me my first police job? For a while, he was retired from the police, but now he has become the police commissioner again, after the task-force scandal. And he gave me a job in the police force in Pusan! The coastal police, no less. Bo, Dad will be patrolling the seas in a police boat! And, Yunhee, no more work for you. Just take care of me and Bo!"

I am proud to see my dad in uniform again. The police have now become respectable because of the people's hatred of the Communists.

1990, Pusan
Bo
Pusan in Korean means busy and crowded. And that's how I remember the port city. The city where I grew up several years in a few months. And whose waters my Dad was now patrolling. Crowds of people, refugees, soldiers, both Korean and foreign, and street vendors everywhere. Selling chocolates, cigarettes, matches, condoms, everything under the sun.

And the smell of food. The smell of frying fish and the smell of sizzling meat. And sweat. And the salty smell of the sea.

And the noise of the streets, the port, the city! People talking loudly in a characteristic Pusan dialect. And others talking in all their various separate dialects, because Pusan was now the melting pot of all sorts of Koreans, refugees from all corners of the peninsula. And, yes, English spoken by the Americans, and other exotic tongues spoken by the UN forces. And the clang of the streetcars, rickshaws, bicycles, even ox-driven carts. And the honking of the car horns, jeeps, and trucks. Military and civilian.

Pusan, a city I loved and hated.

In 1990, Ali, Ginny, and I went to Seoul, Korea, for my medical school's twenty-fifth reunion. We had one day of free time during our busy schedule arranged by my classmates in Seoul. During that day, I insisted on taking a train trip to Pusan. I revisited the port city, forty years from the first time I had seen it.

Pusan had shrunk. While still a bustling city, it was a pale shadow of the city I remembered. The city that seemed so big to the little boy holding his mother's hand. A city of ten million people! With ten million sounds, smells…and lives! Ginny, Ali, and I hired a taxi and asked the driver to drive along the streets I used to know. But I did not recognize them. They were strange, relatively empty, and shabby. No street vendors. We ate rather sterilized Japanese-style sushi in a station-side restaurant. As I was reflecting in the train back to Seoul, I felt both disappointed and elated. The Pusan of my memory is no more, and so it is more precious now.

1951, Southern Korea (around 35–36th Parallel, 129–30 E Longitude)

Bo

The war was not over yet, but, then, it was no longer a real war. The front had stalemated again around the thirty-eighth parallel, with little costly fights over such mundane terrain as the Hamburger Hill. Most of the North Korean guerrillas had either surrendered or been killed. South Korea was in relative peace, especially in the southern provinces. But the country was in ruins, and people were desperately poor.

With the sense of life-and-death emergency dissipating, South Korea found itself full of pickpockets, pimps, prostitutes, swindlers, and outright thieves. The police were very much in demand. To protect against petty crimes as well as against the Communist threat.

I went to thirteen different grammar schools before I graduated—Kangneung, Pusan, and eleven more schools—because my dad was promoted from his job of patrolling the coastal waters of Pusan to the chief of small police stations, one after another. He was transferred eleven times during the two years till I graduated from grammar school.

With so many moves, I stopped trying to make friends. It was painful to make new friends and then say good-bye only in a few months. What's the use? I had been very outgoing and, perhaps, domineering before. Now I was shy, thoughtful, and introverted.

I dreamed. What I did not have in real life I fantasized about. I fantasized about all kinds of things: different parents, different lands, different cities. I was a grown-up hero, I was an orphan boy, I was a villain, I was a powerful general, I was a prisoner. I was a king, I was a slave, I was a knight, I was a damsel in distress. My fantasies seemed more real and enjoyable than the shadow of a life I led in school and at home.

17

OF STORKS AND OPEN DOORS

October, 1951, Kosung, South Korea (Just South of 35th Parallel, West of 128 E Longitude)
Bo

Kosung. A small poor southern port city. My twelfth, and penultimate, move during grammar school was to this remote old town. My dad was the new chief of police.

My new school was like any other, an old decrepit building filled with poorly clad kids. The kids were real countryish, rough, uncouth. As usual, I was shy and reserved and kept to myself.

I was now nine years old. One day, I was lying in bed, in my room, fantasizing as usual, when Mom knocked on the door.

"Bo, may I come in? I want to tell you something."

"Yes, Mom. What is it?"

She came in, closed the door behind her, and sat next to me.

"Bo, you are going to have a brother or a sister!" she said with a faint smile.

I was dumbfounded. "Did you close the door behind you or leave it open?" The old question came to my mind. Obviously, I must have left it open!

I do not really remember how I felt, then, other than surprised. Perhaps I was happy, because I was feeling desperately lonely, with no friends in school. Perhaps I was also a little apprehensive—I had always been Mom's only son, her most important person. Now, was I going to have a rival?

"Bo, remember that I love you the most. You are the only son for whom I sold matches on the streets!" She kissed me gently on my cheek.

"Mom, I love you, too. You are the only mom, the only girl, I shall ever love. More than anyone else in the world!" Somehow, I was sobbing and tasting the salt of my tears.

Soon, I noticed that my mom was changing. Her petite, slender figure was filling out, and her abdomen started ballooning.

"Mom, you look funny"

"Bo, it's because I am pregnant. The baby is now in my stomach," she said, pointing to her protruding abdomen.

"Mom, how are babies made?" I asked. Mom tried her best to maintain her composure and to explain that somehow, mysteriously, a baby was put in her stomach by my father. It didn't make any sense at all!

She finally said, "Bo, I can't explain this very well to you. You know, Dr. Lee is my doctor, who will deliver the baby. Perhaps she can explain it to you better than I." I give credit to my mother for knowing when to seek expert advice. She called Dr. Lee and asked her if I could pay her a visit and ask her some questions about the baby.

"Bo, Dr. Lee says to come anytime. She'll be happy to tell you all about it."

Dr. Lee, who lived only about two blocks away from our house, was a slender, tall, rather pretty woman in her thirties. There were few women doctors in Korea in the 1950s, especially in countryside like Kosung. In fact, at first I could not believe she was a real doctor. A nurse, maybe. But she was a real doctor, and a very kindly one at that. She showed me her office, and she let me listen to my heart and lungs through the stethoscope. Then, she said, "Bo, your Mom told me that you want to know how babies are made."

"Yes, Dr. Lee. I want to know how babies are made, and how one was put in Mom's stomach, and how it will come out!"

"You know, Bo, many people say that the stork brings the baby or that babies grow in cabbages. But you don't need a doctor to tell you that. I am going to tell you how babies are really made. Scientifically. If that's what you want."

"Yes, Doctor. That's what I want."

She brought down from her bookshelf a thick book full of pictures. She showed me the picture of a naked woman. She showed me where her vagina was. She showed me the picture of a naked man and pointed to the penis. She said, "When a man and a woman love each other and have sexual intercourse—which means that the man puts his penis into the woman's vagina and ejaculates a liquid that contains sperm, which comes out of the two testes—see this sperm seen through a microscope. Then the sperm travels upward into the womb, otherwise known as a uterus, and then into the uterine tubes here. Usually, a woman of childbearing age ovulates once a month—an egg comes out of one of the two ovaries and travels down the uterine tubes. If the sexual intercourse happens at the right time, one of the many sperm that traveled up the uterine tube meets the egg there and fertilizes the egg—that is, makes the egg now ready to grow. Then the fertilized egg travels down and implants itself in the womb. When the implantation occurs, this is called pregnancy. Then, the egg divides and divides, until it becomes a fetus, the beginnings of a baby...

"Bo, it is important to know that pregnancy is a serious matter and should occur only when the lovers want to have a baby. There are also ways of preventing it from happening, which I can explain to you when you are ready."

Her explanation was patient, thorough, factual, authentic, and at the same time, friendly. She encouraged me to ask questions to clarify anything I did not understand. She was an outstanding teacher. I became an expert in human reproduction from that day on. I understood! How wonderful it was to know, to understand, the mysteries of life, of love, of sex! I still remember the pretty, earnest, smiling, and eager face of Dr. Lee, the woman who taught me about love and about what true teaching was.

Now, I was eagerly following the development of the fetus in my mom's womb. I noted with excitement when it started to move about, to kick, and when it seemed to have settled itself in the lower part of the pelvis.

At times, I looked at my Mom's stomach and put some cotton balls on her full abdomen to make eyes, eyebrows, a nose, and a mouth to resemble a human face. Then, I called the stomach, laughingly, the "fatso baby"! Yes, I felt that I was a participant in the process of my mom's pregnancy.

My dad, by this time, was again staying late at work almost every night. He would come home late at night, often drunk. In retrospect, I think he felt increasingly frustrated at his work, which consisted mostly of what he hated, arresting and cracking down on the political opponents of the regime and keeping order by brute force. I also think that he became at least in part corrupt. Perhaps because he had to make some money in preparation for the baby. I know that, somehow, we had become rather affluent all of a sudden. Mom let me know that there was cash in an old handbag that she kept in the living room. I could help myself with almost as much cash as I needed to buy my books and candy. Perhaps Dad was also stressed by his wife's long-attempted but surprising pregnancy, some seven years after her last unfortunate pregnancy.

As my mom's pregnancy advanced, I found that I was becoming tense as well. The war was still going on around the thirty-eighth parallel; one hill would fall into the enemy one day, only to be recaptured by the UN forces two days later. The UN forces had clear air dominance, and every day we would see American jets streaking across the blue skies toward a target in the North.

As June 30, the expected date of delivery for Mom, approached, I found myself having to urinate frequently, almost as frequently as Mom. Also, somehow I found that my penis was itchy, and I had to keep on touching it, if not scratching it, almost at all times. I would put my hand in my pocket and feel my penis with my index finger, almost every fifteen minutes. Kids in class noticed that and called out behind my back, "Look at Bo. He's touching himself all the time!"

I did not know what they meant by "touching himself" then. Sure, I was touching myself all the time. My face, my hair, my arms, and so on. What was so funny or strange about it?

In bed, I found that I liked lying on my stomach and kind of pressing my penis on the mattress and rubbing it hard. I would feel a strange, tingly, tickly sensation in my penis, which was not altogether unpleasurable.

Rub, rub, rub. One night, the sensation got so intense, and then I found that my penis was swelling up. Then, with an intense pleasurable sensation, I felt as though my penis was exploding. I looked and saw that there was something liquid coming out of my swollen penis! Something thick and white oozing out of the swollen tip of my penis. The first thought was that there was something terribly wrong with my penis. The liquid looked like pus! I must have gotten some kind of an infection! I was frightened and ashamed. I should not have touched my penis so often with my hands. I should not have rubbed it against the mattress.

For days, I suffered alone. I could not ask Mom or Dad about it. My mom had an aversion to talking about body organs, especially the penis, the anus, and the vagina—dirty things. And my dad was not there, and even if he had been, I thought he might just think that it was funny.

Finally, I visited Dr. Lee, under the pretext of asking some more questions about babies.

"Dr. Lee, I wonder if I can ask you a private question. I am afraid I have a terrible infection in my penis," I said timidly.

"Yes, Bo. Why do you say that?" she asked seriously. I told her. About the discharge, about the swelling, about how I had rubbed it against the mattress, and about how I touched it with my finger.

She examined me. Then, she said, "I understand you are worried, Bo. Most boys get worried about that when they reach your age or a bit older. You see, what you had was an ejaculation. You are maturing, Bo, becoming a man. Remember what I told you about a man putting his penis into a woman's vagina when making love, having sexual intercourse? Your penis is becoming ready for that. When you become a man, your penis becomes swollen when it is stimulated, touched, or when you are aroused with love for a woman. Then, when it is continuously stimulated, as in the vagina of the woman, ejaculation occurs—and semen, the fluid that contains the sperm, comes out of your penis. That's what you saw, Bo, coming out of your penis."

"But it looked exactly like pus. Thick, disgusting pus," I said anxiously.

"Yes, semen often does look like pus. But it is quite clean and contains millions of sperm, the seeds that can become life."

"You mean I am not sick, Dr. Lee?" I asked.

"No, Bo. You are not sick. On the contrary, you are normal. And you may find yourself ejaculating while you are asleep, or while dreaming, as most growing boys and young men do. And at times, you may find yourself stimulating yourself, touching yourself. That's normal, too. Most boys do that.

"You must, however, be very careful that you do not have sexual intercourse, unless you are prepared to have a baby. If not, it's better not to do it, or if you have to make love but do not want to make a baby, then you must use protection, ways of preventing pregnancy. If you feel you must do that, come back to see me, and I will tell you how to protect yourself. But, for now, I think you should just relax and celebrate that you are now becoming a grown man!"

I felt proud that I was now really growing up, becoming a man. But in the back of my mind, I remembered what Mom had said to me shortly after Dad reentered our lives. "He sometimes becomes like an animal at nights. All men do, when they are grown up...Thank God, you are still a child!" But, Mom, I am growing up. I want to grow up...

June 30, 1952, Kosung (Just South of 35th Parallel, West of 128 E Longitude)

I remember that day very well. The day Claire was born. The day Mom and I gave birth to a new life in our family. Mom and I, because we were both there. I, a ten-year-old, precocious, brooding, introverted boy, full of fantasy, full of curiosity...I was there. I had asked Mom and Dr. Lee if I could be there when Mom gave birth. Mom hesitated in the beginning but said I could be there if Dr. Lee thought it was OK. Dr. Lee said it was OK as long as I was brave and helped her if she needed help, such as bringing her instruments and things.

Mom decided to have the baby at home, attended by Dr. Lee. It was common in Korea, then, to deliver babies at home rather than in hospitals or clinics. Dr. Lee came as Mom started having pains regularly with increasing intensity. She came with her black bag and put on a white coat. She put on rubber gloves and opened a green cloth packet that contained sterilized instruments.

Mom was lying on her back, grabbing her stomach, moaning periodically as the contraction came. Dr. Lee draped Mom's abdomen with a clean sheet and bent Mom's knees and put her thighs in an open position. She cleansed a wide area of Mom around her vagina and perineum. She took Mom's pulse and listened to her chest and her abdomen with her stethoscope. She felt her abdomen and the baby with her hands.

"Your contractions are good and strong, Mrs. Moon," said Dr. Lee. "I'll give you a little intravenous painkiller to ease the pain a bit, but try to push as you feel the contraction coming."

Mom seemed to feel better after the IV injection.

"Push! Push!" said Dr. Lee. I saw Mom's stomach tense and saw that her vagina was bulging! Something was coming out! Black something—hair! Now, the top of the head was visible. Dr. Lee put her gloved hand gently on top of the bulging head. Suddenly, the head was out, and then the shoulder and the whole body came out of the vaginal opening, followed by a gush of yellowish bloody fluid.

And also liquid feces, coming out of Mom's anus. And the smell! I was partly fascinated, partly disgusted. I had read that a human is born without dignity and dies without dignity. Being born between urine and feces and dying in urine and feces. Only during life's vigor does a human strive for an illusion of dignity.

"It's a girl, Mrs. Moon," said Dr. Lee, holding the baby after she had wiped the mucus from its mouth. The baby was crying—a healthy, loud cry: "I am!"

Mom smiled at the baby and at me. She was tired but happy. So was I. Very tired. Very happy. Also, rather nauseated.

Dad came home in about an hour, after Dr. Lee called him at his office and told him of the delivery.

Mom was lying with the baby. Dr. Lee had now gone. Everything was cleaned.

The baby, my sister, who was ten years younger than me, was named Claire, which, written in Chinese characters as *Kilah*, means Lucky Child.

1992, Guilford, Connecticut (41.3 N Parallel, 72.3 W Longitude)
Bo

I love to cook. I am an excellent cook. I cook French, Italian, Korean, and Japanese. I also like to experiment with cooking, making new concoctions of my own, as well as trying out the *New York Times* recipes. My *caneton flambé* rivals that of the *Tour d'Argent* of Paris, and my *entrecote au poivre flambé* is unrivaled. And my rack of lamb, with a special coating made of fresh garlic, parsley, and croutons rather than bread crumbs, is a true original. Maybe I'll open a restaurant someday. My few lucky friends know what I am talking about.

Cooking is a labor of love that transforms raw ingredients, each with separate tastes, some with no taste, some with rather foul taste or smell, into a unitary work of art.

As I say, "Cooking is the only creative endeavor, the fruits of which you can actually eat in a matter of minutes, or, at most, hours!"

My mom hated my being in the kitchen. I used to beg her to let me use her pots and pans to make food, but she would shoo me away. "Boys do not cook. Cooking is for girls!" I wished I were a girl so I could cook with Mom. But I think she hated being a girl.

Once, I saw her hand-washing something bloody. "What are you doing, Mom?"

She quickly hid what she was doing and said, "Nothing, Bo, nothing at all."

"But, Ma, I saw you washing something bloody!"

"It's nothing, Bo. Something dirty—female stuff. Don't be concerned about it." She was so upset about my asking about it. She should have known that I would have understood, that I had learned from Dr. Lee about menstruation as well. That it's normal for women to bleed from the vagina every month, that there is nothing dirty about it. But, to her, it was dirty. A curse.

I am glad that Ali often comes to the kitchen with me while I am cooking. He says, "Dad, can I help? I'll stir the mix!"

"Of course, Ali. Cooking is a lot of fun!"

18

IT ALL DEPENDS ON THE COMPETITION!

September 1952, Kosung, South Korea (Just South of 35th Parallel, West of 128 E Longitude)
Bo

Rodin's famous sculpture, *The Thinker*, sits at the entrance to hell. In Korea, then and now, two hellish entrance examinations stood at the gate of all opportunity. One for the combined middle and high school and then for college, which determined all job opportunities.

In fact, an examination is a very democratic process. Properly conducted, it is blind to your ancestry, origins, or place of origin; only the score, an impersonal number, determines whether you have passed or not, whether you are a success or a failure.

Korea had never been a showcase of egalitarianism, but Confucianism that permeated traditional Korean society had one virtue—its emphasis on learning. Thus, in spite of its emphasis on filiality, ancestry, and bloodlines, it also prescribed for the state an examination of the learnedness of the country's youths. A young man, regardless of ancestry, could study hard, pass the government examination for officialdom, and become a success overnight.

There are many dramatic Korean folktales that concern such examinations, such as the Choon-Hyang Jun (The Story of Spring Fragrance). In that story, a young man in a village falls in love with a *keisha* girl, whose nickname is Spring Fragrance. While the young man is away in Seoul taking the examination, the evil village head, a government official appointed by the king whose power was mayor, judge, and chief of police rolled into one, tries to force Spring Fragrance to become his concubine. Angered by her refusal, the village head arrests her. Even under torture, she refuses to become his concubine. He is about to execute her when her lover returns to the village as the king's special prosecutor, an office given to the youth who received the highest marks on the exam, to arrest corrupt or evil village heads and bring them to justice. Of course, justice is meted out, and the young man is reunited with Spring Fragrance, and they live happily ever after.

With the Japanese occupation, there were no more such officialdom exams. Entrance exams for middle schools and colleges replaced them. As the Japanese deliberately did not build enough schools of higher learning in Korea, however, the competition for a place in the schools became fierce. Not just a place in any school but in the best ones. This was the case not only in Korea but in Japan as well. The perceived quality and prestige of the grammar school to which one went determined the likelihood of the quality and prestige of the middle and high school, and that of the college, which determined what kind of job the person would eventually have. The situation did not change even after Korea's liberation from Japan.

Suk had gone to one of the most prestigious schools in Korea, the Seoul Middle and High Schools, the equivalent of Eaton in England. And then, he had gone to college, the Seoul Imperial Teacher's College, later to become the prestigious Seoul National University. It was thus taken for granted that Bo would first go to Seoul Middle and High School and then on to the Seoul National University. In spite of the thirty-to-one competition for the middle and high school. In spite of the fact that Bo was in a little backward town of Kosung, in a little backward school. In spite of the fact that Bo had now become a shy, dreamy, introverted child, who seemed to be spending most of his time reading novels and daydreaming rather than studying.

But Bo still maintained good grades in school. One of the best students, the teacher would say. Now Bo was in the final year of grade school, and the entrance examination to middle school was less than a year away. Now that Claire was born, Yunhee was busy taking care of her as well as the existing two family members. She, however, began to worry about Bo's upcoming entrance examination. When she said this to Suk, he would simply say, "Oh, don't worry about it. I am sure Bo will make it. He is smart, and that's what counts." He really did not seem to understand the enormity of the competition and how hard others were studying for the examination.

The entrance examination to the middle and high school was given nationally in February. Everybody had that one chance, one two-hour examination, to enter a middle school of his or her choice. The way it worked was as follows. You apply to the middle school of your choice and then take the national exam. The score of the national exam is, then, sent to you as well as to the school you applied. The school chooses the entering class solely on the basis of the score of the national entrance exam. For example, if Seoul Middle School had one hundred seats for the entering class, then the highest one hundred scores (students) among the applicants would be accepted. Period. One chance.

To be sure, there was another chance to go to a middle and high school, but not to a first-class one. If you failed to enter the school of your choice, there was a second go-around for a second-class school. Then, the second-class schools would use the same process and accept the highest scores to fill their entering classes. Of course, the prospects of entering a first-class college after graduating from a second-class middle and high school was practically nil. If you failed in your second go-around, you wound up in a trade school, or no school at all.

Most students in Bo's school in Kosung had no ambitions of going to any out-of-town schools. Most would go to no middle school at all and would become farmers and fishermen and their wives. A few would go to a local middle school, which was not competitive at all. Thus, there was very little incentive for most students in Bo's class to study for the national entrance exam. And it was easy for Bo to maintain his good class ranking in the absence of real competition.

Yunhee took a day trip to Pusan, Bo holding her hand and Claire on her back in the typical Korean fashion, to buy some baby things that were scarce in Kosung. In Pusan, Yunhee also wanted to see what was going on in some schools in preparation for the exam—whether there were any special preparations they were giving to their students.

The trip was an eye-opener for Yunhee, because she found that there were intense and systematic programs that the Pusan schools gave to their seniors in preparation for the national exam—early-morning and evening classes, mock exams, special individual coaching, and on and on. Nobody had even heard of these programs in Kosung. Yunhee returned in a state of agitation, abandoning all plans of shopping as originally intended.

"Suk, we must do something in a hurry! We must give Bo a chance to go to Seoul Middle School. The way things are going now, he won't have a chance. Not because he isn't smart but because he isn't prepared for the exam. Did you know that the national entrance examination is a new multiple-choice exam, unlike the essays and fill-in-the-blanks we used to give?" exclaimed Yunhee, out of breath, as soon as she returned home, calling Suk on the phone.

"Oh, don't worry about it, Yunhee. Everything will turn out OK," said Suk.

"We must worry about it, Suk. We must talk tonight."

Suk was home late again that night, as usual in a jovial mood, as usual reeking of alcohol. Yunhee was waiting for him, her head filled with cold fury. Bo heard his parents argue loudly that night, a rare experience. Then, he heard Yunhee say, "Suk, I have saved your life. Now, we must save Bo's life. He must go to Pusan to go to school; he must have his final months of grade school in Pusan, to be prepared for the national exam. If we don't go to Pusan within two months, I will take Bo and Claire to Pusan without you. I'll sell matches again if I have to. But Bo shall have his education in Pusan!"

They were in Pusan within six weeks. Suk had paid another visit to his friend, Cho, the police commissioner, and asked him for a job in Pusan, even if he would no longer be the police chief. He was appointed, once again, as head of the Health and Welfare Department of the police station in Yongdo, a district of Pusan, an island with a bridge to the port of Pusan.

October 1952, Pusan, South Korea (35.2 N Parallel, 129 E Longitude)

Bo

This move to Pusan was, then, the last and thirteenth move during Bo's grammar-school education. Although Suk made the move under duress, he found that he liked his new job much better than the old one. He no longer had to be concerned with harassing and arresting the political opponents of the regime or with keeping an eye on people suspected of being Communist sympathizers. He could now concentrate, again, on educating people about health and making sure that the restaurants and whorehouses were clean and sanitary. He drank less and was home more. He once again enjoyed being with his children, especially with the new baby girl, Claire.

I recall those months of grammar school with mixed feelings. They were some of the halcyon days of my life. Both Mom and Dad were home in the evenings, and they spent time with me and Claire. I was also enjoying Claire, the baby girl. It was a joy to see her shake her rattle and smile at me. I felt that, somehow, I had contributed an equal share with my parents in creating her.

School was something else. The bewilderment and confusion I felt when I first entered the fifth-year class in Yongdong Grammar School. To begin with, the class began at 7:00 a.m., full two hours earlier than in Kosung. And they were studying things of which I had not even heard in my school in Kosung! And all the students seemed to be studying every moment of the day. No, they would not go out to the playground. Even during recess, they would bury their noses in their books! A real culture shock.

And the mock exams! They had mock exams every week, every Friday. That first Friday I enrolled in my new school, I was exposed to my first mock national entrance examination. I had never seen an exam like that. Multiple choice! Often, there were two answers that were, I felt, equally good. But I had to choose one. I hesitated. I thought what arguments I might advance in favor of one choice rather than the other. I had not realized that there were more than three hundred questions in that exam booklet—that I had to skip to the next question if I was not sure, after making an almost random choice. No, I did not know how to take the multiple-choice exam at all. I agonized over the first several questions I was not sure of, all on the first page. I was unaware of the passage of time, immersed in thought, when the bell rang. The time was up. I was barely on the second page of the exam booklet.

I had failed an exam for the first time in my life! Even if it was a mock exam. I received the pitiful scaled score of eight out of a possible one hundred. Shame!

I thought about not letting Mom and Dad know about the exam. But Mom knew that there was a mock exam every week, and the first thing she asked about when I came home were the results of the exam!

I cried as I told her. I wished I could just wither away and die. But Mom hugged me and said, "No, Bo. It's not your fault. It's our fault, Mom's and Dad's. Remember, this was only a mock exam so that you will learn how to take the real exam!"

Next day, Mom bought a bunch of books on multiple-choice exams. In the evenings, both she and Dad helped me with my studies and made up multiple-choice questions for me. I realized then what wonderful teachers my mom and dad must have been! I had never actually seen them teach as teachers, although I knew that that was what they had been at one time. To me, up to that time, Dad was a policeman, and Mom was a housewife. The memories of Mom teaching me, reading to me, when I was a little kid came back to me, as well as of Dad telling me his wonderful bedtime stories in the dreamy, peaceful days before the war...Centuries ago.

Then there are memories of my dad playing the piano and singing and Mom singing along. I don't know where to place these memories, sweet memories that make my heart swell. Ever since he had joined the police force, my dad stopped playing the piano, stopped singing, and so did Mom. Music, which used to give joy to Mom and Dad...in fact, it was through the singing of Handel's *Messiah* that Dad met Mom for the first time in that little church...

I did finish the last page of the mock exam the following week. And my scaled score shot up to seventy-two. Not great, but a lot better than eight. I also became like my classmates, burying my nose in the schoolbooks during any spare time I had. I knew I had a lot of catching up to do in just a few months.

I had always been competitive, in order to get or maintain the number-one position in my class. I had also always known who my rivals were, and they also happened to be my best friends. In that school, however, for the first time in my life, I learned what real cutthroat competition was. One day, I found that my class notes that I had left on my desk were missing. I had taken careful class notes, and they were invaluable aids in studying. What had happened? I told the teacher of this, and he said to me, "Why, you left your notes on the desk? Never do that. Always take them with you. Some kids steal others' class notes for themselves, as well as to keep others from studying. It's called competition!"

From then on, I guarded my notes with my life. I also found out that the students were not at all helpful if you asked a question about a subject. They would either not answer you or, often, give you deliberately wrong answers! All to keep down rivals. Well, with a thirty-to-one ratio of competition to go to a good middle school, perhaps any rival you eliminated would enhance your chances. But what a way to educate children!

Weeks and months passed in a blur. Study, study, study! Exam, exam, exam. Multiple choice, multiple choice, multiple choice. The questions were coming out of my ears, and I was memorizing all sorts of trivia for the national entrance exam. How many ships did England have at the end of World War I? Name all the kings of the Yi dynasty. What was the name of Genghis Khan's second-in-command? How many miles is Saint Helena from Paris? And on and on.

There were so many things to learn, important or not, because other kids were learning them. Still a lot to catch up on. I was now one of the best students in the class, but not the best. And the time was up. The National Middle School Entrance Examination was tomorrow! And we had learned that the competition ratio for Seoul Middle School was not thirty to one as usual, but fifty to one this year.

April 1953, Pusan

It was a buoyant spring day. Beautiful blue skies with cotton-candy white clouds. All the graduating class in the school district of Yongdo who had applied to a middle school were gathered in the dingy auditorium of a local high school. The exam booklets were passed out. The next two hours would determine my entire future!

I felt the exam was what I had expected. Not too easy, not too difficult. It all depended on the competition. I would not know the results for another two weeks. And I would not know whether I was accepted by Seoul Middle School or not until April 30, at exactly 9:00 a.m., when the school would post the names of the entering class on the outside wall of the administrative offices. Names in the order of the exam score.

In two weeks, a letter from the exam office came. I had scored 482 out of a possible 600. These were raw, not scaled, scores. They used raw scores in ranking the applicants. Mine was a good score, an 80 percent correct rate, but it was not great, either. Again, it all depended on the competition.

April 30, 1953, 8:00 a.m., Pusan
Mom and Dad are with me, anxiously awaiting the posting of the names of those accepted to the entering class of Seoul Middle School. Mom had left Claire at home with a babysitter. The school yard is already bustling with the applicants and their parents, waiting for the posting to happen. Dad had been told, by one of his old pupils who was actually teaching at the Seoul Middle School, that I would probably get in easily with a score of 482. In the previous years, the so-called "cut line" had been about 460. After the posting, we would all go to an American restaurant that I liked and eat lunch to celebrate.

9:00 a.m.
Still no one comes out of the administration building. There is a "No Entry" sign in front of the door of the building.

9:05 a.m.
Still no one. No, wait, the door of the administration building opens. A man and a woman come out of the door, holding a long reel of paper. The man is holding a pail with a brush in it. He puts the reel of paper on the ground, facedown, and takes the brush from the pail and brushes it against the wall of the building. It's glue. Then, they both hold the rather long reel of paper and paste it on the wall. The names! The four hundred names of the entering class.

Everyone rushes toward the wall. It's impossible to get to the wall because of the people in front of us. We try to wriggle in. Already, some are shouting, "I made it! I made it!" Others slink away, some frankly breaking down in tears. Poor failures!

We finally inch our way in front of the crowd. Now we can see!

Heading the list is a Philmo Kim. Then, a Soonil Ahn…Where is my name? At first, I couldn't find it. There must be a mistake… let me try once again…Moon! But it was a Haesik Moon, not a Bo. There are other Moons. But no Bo Moon.

I had failed!

Everything seemed to turn gray and black. The wall, the playground, the sky…everything dark gray or black. Tears welled up and made even the gray difficult to see. A failure! At the age of eleven, I was already a failure. I would never be able to face my classmates, my old friends, my teachers, who always thought I would follow in my dad's footsteps and go to Seoul Middle School. I failed my mom, who had sold matches on the streets so that I could go to my dad's school, and my dad, whom I had secretly regarded contemptuously at times—I thought I was smarter and would make a better career for myself than that of a policeman—no, Dad, I am stupider than you are, much stupider, already a failure. I could never follow in your footsteps, even at a distance!

In the darkness that had descended on me at 9:05 a.m., on that day on which the sun shone for others but not me, I thought that the only thing left for me would be suicide. Yes, I would kill myself because that was the only thing that would put an end to the despair, the humiliation, the disappointment that I had caused to everyone I loved.

"Bo, it's not your fault! You simply did not have enough time to study. There is always another chance," a voice said as a familiar whiff of perfume filled my nostrils and I was engulfed in a soft, fragrant bosom. Mom! Oh, Mom!

I did not notice that Dad was not there with me until a few minutes later, when he came out of the administration office with the teacher in that school, Dad's old pupil. They came toward me, and

Dad said, "Bo, I know it's very disappointing that your name is not there. But Mr. Sung here tells me that there's still some hope. You see, Bo, the cut line for this year was four hundred eighty-three. You missed the cut line by one single point. Mr. Sung tells me that, almost invariably, every year there is at least one accepted applicant who cannot actually enroll, because of illness, because of the family moving away, or, even, because of death. If that happens, they accept the next highest score, and that is you! We simply have to wait for one more week, when the accepted applicants must declare their intention to enroll. If there is a single person who does not enroll, you are in!"

Fate had played a trick. Failing my first and most important examination by a single point! If I had known the right answer to just one more question! If I had been lucky on one single question the answer of which I was not sure! And the possibility that the failure might turn into a success by the failure of a single person who was ahead of me. If just one person would drop dead or be injured severely in a car accident! Or be murdered! I think I could have murdered to get in, to turn that failure into a success.

The days passed agonizingly slowly. I was mostly alone, buried in my mystery novels. Mom and Dad left me alone, understanding my need to be alone, to escape. I knew that they were as tense as I was, and as guilty, as disappointed, and as worried as I. They were feeling disappointed and guilty about themselves. They blamed themselves for my failure: "If we had only known about what the other schools were doing just one month earlier, if we had left Kosung just one month earlier, even one week earlier, Bo would have made it with flying colors!"

Four days after that fateful day, Dad received a phone call from Mr. Sung. I was in! Not one but three of the accepted applicants could not enroll in the school. I didn't know what happened to them, and I did not care. By some miracle, my failure had turned into a success. Barely, but a success, nonetheless. I was going to be a student in the same prestigious middle school that Dad went to. And, then, the same high school and college!

We celebrated that night by going to an expensive American restaurant. Dad ordered champagne and gave me a whole glass of it. Yes, by luck, by design, by fate, three of my rivals had to drop out, and I was clearly in! I thanked fate, whom I had cursed only four days before.

I finally enrolled in the Seoul Middle School. My sharp black uniform (yes, middle- and high-school students wore uniforms, then) resembled Dad's, with the shiny brass badge that said proudly, "Seoul Middle School."

When my first day in the Seoul Middle School came that summer, I found out that I needed not have worried at all. Since my acceptance to the school, the school had decided to increase its entering class size from four hundred to six hundred—and to admit the next hundred applicants in order of their exam scores, and then another hundred applicants on the basis of other criteria—in this case meaning monetary donations.

Too many children of the powerful Korean elite had failed the exam. High government officials, congressmen, generals, bankers. They had pressured the school and the Ministry of Education. Finally, the Ministry of Education had ruled that the policy of accepting students solely on the basis of the national exam scores applied only to the original class size, and if the school saw fit to increase its class size, with government approval, of course, then the school could make up the difference according to any criteria they chose! So, Seoul Middle School accepted a hundred students that year who did not come near qualifying on the basis of their intellect but who had rich or powerful parents. I had learned an important lesson in life—never give up hope. You never know what fate will bring. And never say never!

19

THE MAGIC OF CHEMISTRY

Brooklyn, New York, October 31, 1965 (40 N Parallel, 74 W Longitude)
Bo

I am an intern here at the Brooklyn College Hospital. Three months have already passed since I came to the United States. Three busy months of bewilderment and sleep deprivation. When I first arrived here as an intern, I was assigned to the obstetrics and gynecology service.

It is true that babies come only at night, or at least it seemed to me that was the case. Every night, at least three of the women on my ward delivered. And I had to scrub with the attending to deliver the babies. In those days, most babies were delivered in operating rooms. Often under general anesthesia. And the physicians were in full scrub. Three babies a night. Not a wink of sleep!

And the screams. The women always scream, "Ayeee-ayee-ayeeeee!" Most of the ward patients are Hispanic women. That's another thing! I thought that people spoke English in the United States. Not so in Brooklyn, New York. They speak Spanish. Or Yiddish. Or Italian. But no English. Not the ward patients, anyway.

The three months have passed like a bad dream. Like a dream from which you awaken and feel as though you had not slept a wink. I had, in fact, practically not slept a wink.

Well, the ob-gyn rotation is over, and now I am in pediatrics. A lot more civilized—at least, I sleep some nights. Although the kids are demanding and often difficult to examine. They cry, like the women, "Ayee-ayee-ayeeee!"

Well, I get this invitation to a "Halloween party" from the nursing-school students. I don't know what a Halloween party is. I ask Beverly, my internship classmate. She tells me, "You'll have fun, Bo. Halloween, the thirty-first of October, is the day that all the witches, hobgoblins, and ghosts are supposed to have a ball. People wear costumes, usually something scary like a skeleton or witch's mask, and have parties. Children also wear costumes and go trick-or-treating—that is, you give them candy or they may play a trick on you. It's a time when everybody, regardless of religion, has fun."

"Are you going, Beverly?"

"No, not to that party. Greg and I have a date, and we will go to the ob-gyn resident's Halloween party." Greg is an ob-gyn resident whom Beverly has been dating. I would be tempted to date Beverly if Greg were not around. And if I knew how to ask an American girl for a date. I am rather attracted to Beverly, with her dark hair, slender figure, and nice deep blue eyes. And she seems to like me.

"Well, I don't think I really want to be at a crowded party," I say. I really do not feel like going to a party; I am very tired. Besides, I really don't know much about what one does at parties, and I don't feel like being the novice in front of all the giggly nursing students.

"Come on, Bo, I think this would be your first party in the States! Why don't you go and meet some girls? This would be a good way of meeting some nice nursing students, you know. Go!" says Beverly.

"Oh, OK. Maybe I'll try it. By the way, what do you say if you like a girl?" I ask Beverly. After all, there is nothing to lose. Beverly seems to be rather serious with Greg, anyway.

"Well, that's a good question," answers Beverly. "It kind of depends, but, in your case, you might ask her to show you around the city. You are a newcomer!"

The party is at the nursing school's dormitory, which is a three-story building in front of the hospital proper. A bunch of students wearing various costumes greet me as I go into the hall where the party is being held. I am wearing my intern uniform—I decided that the uniform was the most scary costume one could think of, if one was intelligent.

"Hi, I am Ginny. Welcome to the spook's lair!" says a cute, very young-looking girl wearing the thickest pair of glasses I have ever seen. Ginny has light-brown hair and is not wearing a costume, either. She is wearing a soft white medium-cut woolen sweater and a cream-colored skirt.

"Hi, I am Bo. Short for *Bo*-geyman. How do you like my costume?" I ask.

"Your costume?" asks Ginny. Then, she says, "Oh, your costume! I think it's marvelous. Really scary! A green monster intern operates on the helpless nursing student!" Feigning a faint, she laughs. "Well, Bo. What do you think of *my* costume?" she then asks.

"Are you wearing one?" I ask. I really don't see anything out of the ordinary that she is wearing. Her face is oval and well contoured, with a hint of dimples on her cheeks. Her thick glasses magnify her hazel eyes, making them look enormous. But I doubt that the glasses are a costume; after all, how could she see at all through such thick lenses if she didn't need them?

Otherwise, just the sweater and the skirt, both white, both neat, both attractive, showing her young figure to advantage. I notice the supple white translucent skin on her face, throat, and into the V of the sweater. The gentle slopes at the V and the distinct mounds on her sweater indicate a pair of firm, full breasts. Her waist is narrow under her soft skirt, and her legs are long and shapely. A very attractive girl.

Ginny blushed as she said, "Well, Doctor, you are really giving me an exam! I am scary because I look so normal wearing a normal dress, but I am really a ghost!"

"I am scared stiff," I say, laughing. By this time, we are on one side of the hall, trying to hear each other. The room is crowded with all kinds of hobgoblins and spooks. Ginny and I seem to be the only people who are not wearing costumes specifically made for Halloween.

"So, you must be new around here," says Ginny.

"Yes, brand-new in this country. Are you from here?" I ask.

"Yes, I've lived in Brooklyn all my life," says Ginny.

"Then you must really know the city very well. Perhaps you can show me around the city sometime," I say with some hesitation. I am really becoming attracted to this girl. She seems bright, has a sense of humor like mine, and is also sexy. What if she says no? If she says yes, would it mean that she would be willing to date me? Would she have problems dating an Asian? Does she already have a boyfriend?

"Sure, Bo. Gladly. How about this weekend?" replies Ginny, vivaciously.

So, I date Ginny Mirabello, an eighteen-year-old nursing student at the Brooklyn College Hospital. A young, intelligent, attractive, sexy girl. And we fall in love. Love at first sight. Chemistry.

Summer 1953, Pusan, Korea (35.2 N Parallel, 129 E Longitude)
Bo

Now that I was a student at my dad's old middle school, Seoul, I felt a bit out of sorts. There were many things to learn, but I felt, in a way, shell-shocked to pick up my textbooks and study them for the class. I felt a bit guilty whenever I picked up mysteries.

I had to read something, because reading had become such a habit with me. I went to a bookstore and browsed. I deliberately avoided the mystery section. I first looked at some textbooks, bought some, and then looked at some science books. I came across a book on chemistry. This book was different from textbooks in that it gave a history of chemistry and moved on to some exciting experiments.

"Er, young man, you've been reading the book for a whole hour here. This is not a library, you know!"

Startled, I looked at my watch. He was right. I was so absorbed in reading that book. I bought the book and several other books on chemistry.

For the next several months, I was absorbed in chemistry. I read about the alchemists of the Middle Ages, about Alfred Nobel and his invention of dynamite, and about the Nobel Prize. I read about Madame Curie. And I began experiments.

I extorted my parents to buy me all sorts of chemicals, reagents, and equipment. Beakers, flasks, test tubes. Mom and Dad had very little understanding of modern chemistry. They were just glad that I had seemed to develop an interest in a school-related subject again. They let me go to the chemical wholesaler and buy whatever I felt I needed. After all, these things were not that expensive. Little did they know how dangerous they could be!

Most of the chemicals used in my experiments were, of course, poisonous. And many were abrasive, corrosive agents. And many could explode! I built a little laboratory in the walk-in closet of our apartment. If only they knew what danger lurked behind that door to that little closet!

Before long, as a freshman of the Seoul Middle School, I knew more chemistry than a college freshman. I thought of myself as an Alfred Nobel, or a Thomas Edison, or a Madame Curie.

Yes, I did pick up mystery novels again. But I alternated them with chemistry books. They were equally interesting, suspenseful, and magical.

20

PARADOXES

July 27, 1953.

Finally, the Korean War was over. A truce was signed by the United Nations forces and the North Koreans at Panmunjom.

November 1953, Pusan (35.2 N Parallel, 129 E Longitude)
Bo
The Seoul Middle and High Schools, which had been housed in military-style barracks in Pusan, announced that they would return to Seoul in January 1954.

Dad had had a standing application for a job in the Seoul Police, but there was never an opening appropriate for him. Finally, Dad decided to quit his job in Pusan. Then, he went to Seoul and stayed there until he found a job. And he did. Dad had finally found a job in Seoul, in his familiar capacity as head of the Health and Welfare Department of a police station in the suburbs of Seoul.

January 1953–1958, Seoul (37.5 N Parallel, 127 E Longitude)
So, we found ourselves again in Seoul, in a small rooming house. I was now back in the proper campus of Seoul High School in the northern part of Seoul.

I was introverted, shy, and unathletic. While others played stickball, I stayed in class and read. I also had a high-pitched voice, and they said my face looked like that of a girl.

My nickname these days was "Madame Curie." It was an apt nickname—a way of calling me a girl or a sissy, and at the same time recognizing my excellence in chemistry.

I was already an established scientist in their eyes. I knew almost everything there was to know in the science class with my knowledge of chemistry. I didn't just know chemistry—I understood it backward and forward, including its history, its physical underpinnings, and the basic principles governing the chemical reactions. I also knew the chemical formulas and the laws of interaction.

My less often used nickname was "Yankee." This simply meant that I spoke good English. I excelled in English. For some reason, I felt much at home learning English. And, later, German and French. Perhaps my experience with a foreign language at the age of three (after all, Korean was a foreign language I learned, after I had learned to speak Japanese fluently) helped me learn new languages easily.

I did poorly in math. Math was boring. You had to memorize the formulas for everything. And, then, the endless repetition of calculations. 87 + 26 + 136 – 34 + 7 x 4 = ? What is the circumference of a circle that has a radius of five centimeters? What is the volume of a cone that has a height of ten centimeters and a diameter of five centimeters? No, I did not like math. And I did not study. Consequently, my math grades were abominable. My teacher called me a "limping runner." I ran with Chemistry and English and limped with Math and Chinese character writing. A scientist with poor math, a linguist in English and reading Chinese characters, but an illiterate in writing Chinese characters! A contradiction, a paradox.

One day, a senior in the school pulled me aside and asked, "Bo, how would you like to join an English-speaking club? I know that you are excellent in English. There is a club of several good middle-school students that meets once a week. The purpose of the club is to practice speaking English. We even have an American adviser."

Initially, I hesitated. I liked the idea of actually conversing in English, especially with an authentic American, but I felt uncomfortable about the social club setting. But curiosity and the ambition of showing off my English won out. I joined Oak Club, an English-speaking club of middle- and high-school students, both male and female, that met in the Chosun Hotel, which had then also housed the American embassy. Yes, the membership consisted of both boys and girls, unlike my school, which had only boys. Most of the girls came from the girls' schools, mostly from the two prestigious girls' middle and high schools, Ewha and Seoul (the same name as mine, but not the same school). A Mr. Silverbell, who worked at the American embassy, was its adviser. Till then, I had never actually spoken English with an American. I found that I had no difficulty in making him understand what I was saying in English, but I had difficulty in understanding what he was saying. I needed to hear more spoken English. I decided to see American movies. I became an avid movie fan. On a Saturday afternoon, or a Sunday, I would tell my parents that I was going to do studying with some friends and then go to a movie theater that was playing an American movie. I would first read the Korean subtitles as I saw the movie, and then I would see the same movie again, this time concentrating on hearing the English dialogue, deliberately not paying attention to the subtitles. Often I would see the same movie again and again. By the time I saw the movie three times, I could practically recite back the English dialogue. Some of the movies I saw then were classics, such as *National Velvet,* with Elizabeth Taylor, *Citizen Kane,* with Orson Welles, and *Casablanca,* with Humphrey Bogart and Ingrid Bergman. These movies taught me spoken English.

I also fell in love. With Elizabeth Taylor! Who looked about my age in *National Velvet.* But, then, she was fully grown, beautiful, and sexy in movies like *Father of the Bride, Ivanhoe,* and *The Last Time I*

Saw Paris. I dreamed of her, and fantasized that I was Ivanhoe, the knight in shining armor, wooing her, rescuing her from the stake. I also made love to her in bed. Although I sometimes thought about some of the more attractive and mature girls I met at the club, or even on the streets, I really did not need a girl, or if I did, I was too shy to do anything about it. I had Liz Taylor whenever I wanted. At times, I thought of myself as Liz Taylor, beautiful and sexy. And I would be made love to by Ivanhoe. By this time, I was masturbating regularly. Without fear or guilt, thanks to the long talks I had with Dr. Lee some three years ago. The woman who taught me that there was nothing dirty or shameful about sex. Unlike my mom.

Soon, I became a star of the English-speaking Oak Club. In a year's time, I became the editor of the weekly bulletin of the club, which was written in English. I was shy and rather withdrawn in school, but at the club, I was outgoing and dynamic. I also learned I could work closely with a girl without feeling awkward or that I had to be overly masculine or sexual. Sue, who was a student of Seoul Girls' High School, became a close colleague of mine as she worked with me as an associate editor for the *Oak Bulletin*, writing brilliant opinion pieces concerning the youth culture. Sue was not attractive to me sexually, which was a blessing because I could work with her and be friends with her without any further expectations of the relationship.

21

OF CHANGING SEASONS

April 1956, An Apartment in Pyongyang, DPRK (39 N Parallel, 125.7 Longitude)
Kyok

You could almost smell the sweet fragrance of cherry blossoms all around Pyongyang, even in this small dingy apartment near the Kim Il-Sung University. Kyok awakens and finds herself still in Joonam's arms. How delicious it was to awake in the arms of your lover and breathe in the freshly scented air of Pyongyang, especially now that change was afoot and the true dream of a Socialist, classless society might come true! Khrushchev's reforms in the Soviet Union have been accepted and endorsed by the Great Leader, Kim Il-Sung, and now there would be more opening up to new ideas and ways of doing things, which, in her mind, was always the progressive way, the Marxist way. And she was in the arms of a diplomat liaison with the Soviet embassy, the epicenter of reform!

Kyok was so happy to be in DPRK, the Democratic People's Republic of Korea, where her parents brought her in 1947, as South Korea was about to become a capitalist colony of the United States. Born in Wonju, a city in Kangwon Province in South Korea, Kyok and her family would have been suspect and faced possible imprisonment because, in fact, they were ideological Communist intellectuals.

Kyok's father, Byung Lee, was a professor of economics and history at Wonju University and an ardent Marxist. He had written two books on Marxism that were published in Japanese during the Japanese occupation. When Japan became militaristic and fascist just before World War II, these books were suppressed. They obviously would not be acceptable to the fascist Syngman Rhee regime.

Byung Lee and his family were welcomed in Pyongyang when they arrived, and Byung was elected to the Central Committee of the Workers' Party and eventually to the politburo of the DPRK. He was an important member of the politburo group who were originally from South Korea. Unlike those politburo members already in North Korea, they commanded more respect as they had to go through the ordeal of living in fascist South Korea and escape in the dark of the night to reach North Korea.

Kyok, being the only daughter, was the apple of her father's eyes. Though she still remembered her painful days in South Korea when she felt ostracized because she was the daughter of a "Commie," she felt loved and respected in DPRK. In spite of the austere environs of North Korea, especially after the War of Fatherland Liberation, which was the official name of the Korean War in DPRK, Kyok had all her material needs met as the daughter of a politburo member, an exalted station in the Socialist state. As a girl, she especially enjoyed the respect she received when she would participate in intellectual discussions about philosophy, economics, and Marxism, because she remembered vividly how girls were dismissed in intellectual discussions in South Korea. As a teenager in Wonju, her hometown in South Korea, her enlightened parents let her participate in some intellectual discussions they had at home with selected university students, mostly about the theories of Marx and Engels. Kyok felt she understood the progressive ideas better than many students who were much older, but few would take her seriously. Except Kang, who seemed to treat her as an intellectual equal. I wonder what happened to him.

When she entered the Kim Il-Sung University, she became close friends with two classmates, a girl by the name of Myunghee Park and a man named Joonam Kim. They were in the same class as Kyok more than 80 percent of time, sharing their interest in Marxist dialectics, economics, advanced mathematics, and foreign languages. Kyok and Myunghee had much in common—both were daughters of politburo members, and both were born outside of DPRK, Myunghee in Manchuria and Kyok in South Korea. While Myunghee was of medium build and conventionally pretty, with long black hair, Kyok was taller and more curvaceous and had a rather longish, expressive face that was at once intense and beautiful. Both shared an independent streak. Joonam was a male version of Kyok, tall, full-bodied, born in the Soviet Union of Korean parents who had fled to Russia from the Japanese. Joonam spoke fluent Russian.

Kyok enjoyed intellectual arguments with Joonam, sometimes heated arguments in which Kyok became passionate, almost sexually aroused. Joonam seemed to become excited too, and they would argue through the wee hours of the morning in the dormitory cafeteria in Kim Il-Sung University. One night, in the midst of an intellectual argument, Joonam impulsively pulled Kyok and embraced her tightly. "Kyok, I know you are right—whatever you say, you will make me a believer with one kiss!"

Kyok kissed him, and they forgot where they were and who else was there. They hungrily sought each other, undressed each other, and made love passionately. Fortunately, they were in a deserted cafeteria, with no one around. They made love on the wooden floor, which did not seem that hard or cold in their own heat and flesh.

Now in this apartment Joonam rents to be near his new job as a DPRK liaison to the Soviet embassy, Kyok dreams of a future with Joonam, perhaps with a child or two. I'll be able to save a little now that I have a job teaching at the Special Technological High School for Girls. The school is a special school set up as a part of Kim Il-Sung University to train more women in technology. The students are carefully chosen among the many applicants from other schools on the basis of their intelligence, aptitude, and ideological purity. The graduates are to have preferential consideration for admission to the Kim Il-Sung University and a career in science, technology, and intelligence.

"Kyok, darling, I am glad to wake up with you in my arms!" says Joonam as he opens his eyes.

"Me, too, Joonam. And I hope to do this every morning once we are married." Kyok kisses Joonam on the mouth and climbs on top of him and feels his erect penis on her crotch.

They make love again, passionately and hungrily, as though they had not made love for months.

Yes, how sweet life is for the young in the morning.

August 1956, Joonam's Apartment, Pyongyang, DPRK (39 N Parallel, 125.7 E Longitude)

Kyok woke up in Joonam's arms again, feeling exhausted but happy. They had made love repeatedly till the wee hours of the morning, using various positions and techniques gleaned and loosely inferred from their readings. Reading Alfred Kinsey's books on male and female sexuality was an eye-opener for both of them. With the liberalizing trend since the death of Joseph Stalin, there were more books available for the intelligentsia, especially technical books in Russian. (Kinsey's books were considered technical even though they dealt with sex since they were couched in technical terms and few people in DPRK understood exactly what they meant.)

Kyok and Joonam explored each other's bodies and their functions like medical students, enjoying the touch and feel of each organ and each sensation, not just the sex organs but all of their bodies. But, of course, the exploration of sensuality was most gratifying with the sensation of the glans penis, the clitoris, the nipples (female and male), the labia, and so on. By exploration and experimentation, they became experts of each other's body as well as each other's mind.

Though Kim Il-Sung seemed to have embraced Khrushchev's reforms and declared that there should be more openness and less cult of personality, North Korea seemed to be behind the times in progressive ideas compared with other Socialist countries such as Hungary, Czechoslovakia, and Poland. But there was change in the air as Joonam remarked, "Darling, just wait. I think there will be some major changes in August in DPRK, based on my sources from the Soviet embassy."

"What changes, though? The Soviets are not going to make us change, and our leadership seems so ossified in their ways!"

"Yes, but I understand there are progressive people in the politburo who may bring about change, with the support of our Soviet brothers."

"I hope so. Oh, how much I hope so!"

November 1966, Kansas City (39 N Parallel, 94.5 W Longitude)
Bo

"Doctor Graves, I would like to go back to New York City beginning in January. I have written to the Manhattan University Hospital, which has offered me a residency position," I say with some trepidation to the chairman of the department. I am a first-year resident in psychiatry at the Kansas University Hospital. I miss Ginny, whom I left in Brooklyn some five months ago. Although I had wanted to move away from New York City and come to the Midwest where the air is fresher, and people look more like Americans, I am rapidly becoming homesick for the East Coast, which I have known only for one year. No, not homesick. Lovesick, really, for Ginny, whom I love with a passion that grows dearer with each day without her.

Kansas City. A nice city. Nice people, friendly people. Pretty, good-looking, buxom, prime-beef-fed females. Nurses. Social workers. Yes, I have gone to bed with a couple of them, luscious and wholesome. But I miss Ginny, with whom I had not yet even made love. Just chaste kisses and adolescent "heavy petting." But I love her, her youth (she is only nineteen), her pretty but humorous face, and—is it true?—her seriousness. Here is a woman to become, and I want to be a part of her becoming.

"My dear Bo, I certainly understand how you must feel," said Dr. Graves suavely. Dr. Graves is really a smooth operator, and when he talks, I think he could soothe even the wildest of psychotic bulls, his voice is so soothing and gentle.

"Could you tell me some more about why you would like to leave so soon after coming here? Is it because somehow our Midwestern culture is incompatible with yours?" asks Dr. Graves.

"No, not at all, Dr. Graves. The reason is more personal. You see, I am in love. I have a fiancée back east, and I would like to join her as soon as possible," I respond.

"I see. I understand very well how you feel. I am glad that you are in love, and I wish you the very best. However, I do feel that the Manhattan University Hospital does not quite do justice to your abilities, Bo. Although it is a university hospital, it is really not quite up to par as far as academic institutions go in New York. Also, it would be important for you to fulfill the contract you signed to serve a whole year as a resident here in Kansas City. These things are held rather as sacred commitments in the medical community. Tell you what—next week, the chairman of the Psychiatry Department of the Einstein University is coming here for grand rounds. If you want, I will introduce you to him personally and see if he can scare up a position for you for next July at the Einstein University Hospital in New York—as you know, it is one of the really top-notch academic institutions in the country. What do you say? And you might take a vacation and spend some time with your fiancée next month."

"I will have to think about it. It depends on my fianceé, too. I may have no control over it," I say, rather confused.

"Bo, you will realize that you have a lot more control over your life than you may think. Whatever your decision, I'll be happy to help in whatever way I can," says Dr. Graves, as suavely as ever.

Ginny agrees I can come in July. I meet with the chairman from Einstein, who apparently likes me and arranges a second-year residency position for me in his hospital. And I take a vacation for a whole month, to spend with Ginny, in a hotel in Brooklyn, New York.

December 1966, Brooklyn, New York (40 N Parallel, 74 W Longitude)
Her eyes are closed, her expression intent, vulnerable, moaning softly, with inviting, parted lips. As I kiss her lips, fondle her breasts, suck her nipple, she squeezes my penis with her hand and gently guides it into her moist vagina. I lose myself as I feel all of my being in my penis. The undulating movement of the pelvis brings forth the back-and-forth of the cradle. My eyes suck in her face—the curve of her cheek, the white throat, the eyes, closed but full of feeling, Ginny's face…no…a generic face…*woman*. Every woman who I have made love to—no, every woman who ever was, that ever will be. Woman, the primal cause of all being. And in the cradle is born heaven and earth, man and woman, yin and yang, all of being. The cradle is rocking faster now, violently. Danger! It might break and fly away! I feel a tightness around my penis, and I feel the quickening of her breaths and a certain tremor in her body as I explode within her. An exhausted peace. Peace of being out of nothingness. In the silence afterward, I hear the presence of time, the clock ticking, and realize that this is the last night of my vacation with my fiancée, Ginny. In this little hotel room in Brooklyn, New York, I desperately enjoy the joy of love with my lover, whom I shall not see for another six months. Although we made love every night for the last four weeks, still we both hunger for the desperate embrace, because we know that our time together is precious, that it has to be earned all over again in the next six months. Love is so dear when time is dear.

Counterintelligence Headquarters Bunker, Pyongyang, DPRK, August 1956
(39 N Parallel, 125.7 E Longitude)
"…so, we…plan to…attack Kim Il-Sung…new government…"

Several senior officers, including Kim Sangwoo, director of counterintelligence, and Hoon Moon were listening to the squeaky tape recording from the bug in the Soviet embassy.

"Traitors! Those Russian and South Korean faction of politburo members…How dare they plot to overthrow our Great Leader Kim Il-Sung!"

"Well, it's a good thing that Comrade Moon her was able to bug the Soviet embassy. Otherwise, they might even succeed!" declared Kim Sangwoo, who looked at his deputy and said, "Arrest all the sons of bitches, all their families and known associates, and then interrogate them—make sure they confess to everything and name everyone whom they know. I don't care if they are guilty or not—just knowing them is enough to be taken away to prison camps. Round up all their acquaintances and relatives, including uncles, aunts, cousins, nephews, nieces, and so on. They will all be sent to prison camps, where the sons of bitches and their immediate family will be executed, and others may be reeducated through hard labor. We must build many more prison camps—I know there will be thousands and thousands more traitors we must take into custody and reeducate or eliminate. *We cannot have this type of thing happen again!*"

Dormitory, Special Technological School, Pyongyang, September 1956
Kyok and three girls were sitting around a table in the Seminar Room. The Special Technological School was an experimental high school developed by the Kim Il-Sung University after Stalin's death to train the gifted and talented students to be the elite of the Socialist state. Though differing in ideology, the concept was similar to that of Eton in England or Seoul High School in South Korea. It had separate boys' and girls' dormitories, though the classes were

coeducational. The school boasted of classes and discussions at all hours including evenings, and thus all teachers and students were required to live in the dormitories except during vacation.

"So, what happens to surplus value in a capitalist society compared with a Socialist state?" asked Kyok.

"The surplus value, the amount of money that a product is actually sold minus the amount of money the workers were paid for, is pocketed by the capitalists in a capitalist system, which is an exploitation of the workers!" replied Lila Lee. Lila was an intense small-framed girl wearing horn-rim glasses, who seemed to be full of energy.

"Yes, that's absolutely right. So, what happens in a Socialist state?"

"In a Socialist state, there is no surplus value, as the workers own the means of production, and all income is shared by all the workers." replied Sunmi Song, the youngest of the students, who seemed to be highly intelligent as well as precocious.

"But it doesn't always work that way, does it?" asked Yoonja, who was Sunmi's elder sister by two years.

"Explain, Yoonja," said Kyok.

"Well, in DPRK, we have a Socialist state, and workers work very hard and produce a lot, but they do not get a fair share of the goods they produce. They go into sectors that the state decides are important—like the military and the political apparatus. Are they not like the capitalist corporations?"

Kyok was at a loss. She was an ardent Communist and believed in the ideals of a Marxist, classless society. But it was true that a new class was being created in DPRK, the military, the party...yes, she herself was an elite in the new class...

As she was debating what to say to Yoonja, who seemed to be seriously bewildered, there was a loud knock on the door.

When she opened the door, four uniformed armed men entered. One who seemed to be the leader faced Kyok and asked, "Are you the teacher, Kyok Lee?"

"Yes, and who are you and what are you doing in this women's dorm?"

Without a response, they stood Kyok up and handcuffed her behind her back. Then, the leader said, "And which one of you is Yoonja Song?" Yoonja stood up. The men handcuffed her behind her back.

"And Sunmi Song?"

Neither Sunmi nor Lila uttered a sound. The uniformed men looked at them, and the leader went in front of Sunmi. "You must be Sunmi; you resemble your sister."

Sunmi meekly nodded. They handcuffed her also. Facing Lila, the lead uniform said, "I do not know who you are, but rest assured that I'll see you soon." It was an ominous prophecy.

They led the three handcuffed prisoners into a waiting van and sped off into the night.

22

WORK WILL SET YOU FREE!

September 1956, Camp Lucky, DPRK (Somewhere around 40 N Parallel and 127 E Longitude)
Hoon

Special Counterintelligence Officer Kilin Oh stopped the Soviet-made GAZ-69 all-terrain utility vehicle in front of the nondescript wooden building that served as the processing center for this camp and jumped down from his driver's seat. Hoon Moon dismounted the vehicle from the passenger side. Kilin and Hoon then pulled out the three women who were seated in the backseat. Kilin motioned Hoon to join him on the driver side, and yanked the rear door of the vehicle open. The three women seated in the rear were blindfolded, handcuffed in the back, and tied to each other at the waist with a rope. They seemed startled, but sat motionless as if frozen. Without any warning, Kilin pulled the rope that tied them together outwards, causing them to yelp and stumble out of the vehicle as Hoon supported them from falling. They were barefoot, having been relieved of their purses and shoes at the State Security Detention Center before being put in the vehicle.

Kilin then retrieved his briefcase from the vehicle while Hoon took the prisoners' blindfolds off. Then, they guided the prisoners to the wooden building. Kilin and Hoon were in their khaki KPA uniforms, Kilin a captain and Hoon a first lieutenant. The black hawk insignia on their lapels indicated they were counterintelligence officers.

It was now dusk, and the five figures cast long shadows on the unpaved ground.

The camp was on the floor of a narrow valley with only one dirt road leading to it and was enclosed in several layers of barbed-wire fences. The wooden building was connected to another in the back, and they could see what looked like several army barracks interspersed on the grounds. There seemed to be construction going on in several areas in the back. To one side, there was a large clearing, perhaps an assembly ground. On one side of the clearing was a wooden platform with a pole and a structure that looked like a gallows. Since the founding of DPRK, a number of prison camps had been set up to "reeducate" some capitalists and other bourgeoisie who were not outright executed. Since the arrest of Pak Hon-yong, the foreign minister of DPRK, and his collaborators, who were shown to be American spies during interrogation by the DPRK counterintelligence forces, and then the discovery that the Russian faction of the politburo had actually planned a coup against Kim Il-Sung in August 1956, many more prison camps were being built in remote parts of DPRK for the traitors and their families. Hoon had read some of Pak's writings while he was still in Kangwon Province and had admired Pak's Communist essays. However, when he heard Pak talk as foreign minister in DPRK, he thought Pak was rather weak ideologically. I was right, Hoon thought. He turned out to be an American spy.

As Kilin and Hoon approached the building, the guard who was standing at attention saluted them and opened the door. They could see that there were at least ten guards in posts around the entrance with their machine guns ready. Kilin and Hoon returned their salute perfunctorily and pushed their prisoners forward into the door.

"Ah, Comrades, welcome to Reeducation Camp 0173, otherwise known as Camp Lucky! I see, Comrade Oh, that you have a new colleague," barked Colonel Il Kwak, the commandant of the prison camp. Kwak was a tall, thickset man with large and heavy features, somewhat giving the impression of a gorilla.

"Good to be back, Comrade. This is Comrade Hoon Moon, a very promising young operative who could use a little education in the ways of the world, which I'll do here. By the way, tell Comrade Moon why your camp is nicknamed 'Lucky,'" replied Kilin.

"Aha! It's because our camp is brand-new, built especially for the newly discovered traitors, the worst of the worst because they pretended to be our Workers' Party members—some even became politburo members. We have state-of-the-art equipment just for them here, imported from the Soviet Union, which is no longer using them since Khrushchev took over. Each lucky prisoner gets individualized, special treatment here."

"Very pleased to meet you, Comrade Kwak, and, indeed, Comrade Oh promised me I'll learn much about interrogation techniques and such here," Hoon said expectantly.

"I see that you brought us special presents—three females," Kwak said pleasantly. He walked over to the three prisoners, whose wrists were still cuffed in the back and who were tied to each other with a rope around their waists. He then gently touched the cheek of the prisoner closest to him, a young woman of about eighteen wearing a white blouse and navy-blue skirt. She had medium-length black hair and a rather plump, pretty face, which was white with fear.

"What is your name?" asked Kwak. She opened her mouth to answer but seemed to have trouble finding her voice because of fear. Kwak slapped her hard with his right hand, causing her almost to lose balance, which would have resulted in both her and the two other women falling as they were tied together. "Answer immediately when I ask a question!" thundered Kwak.

"Yoonja...Song, Yoonja," stammered the woman.

Kwak slapped her again, and this time she did not stumble, but blood seeped out of her bruised cheek.

"Never say anything to me without addressing me as Comrade Sir! Understood?"

"Yes, *sir*—I mean Comrade Sir!" stammered Yoonja, her face streaming with a mixture of tears and blood.

Kwak turned to the girl who was next to Yoonja. The girl was almost dressed identically like Yoonja, but her skirt was black rather than blue, and she had longer hair than Yoonja. She looked younger than Yoonja and as pretty.

"And what is your name?"

"Sunmi Song, Comrade Sir!" replied the girl quickly.

"So, you are a quick learner, eh? How old are you?"

"Sixteen, Comrade Sir!" answered Sunmi.

"So, are you Yoonja's sister?"

"Yes, Comrade Sir!"

Kwak touched Sunmi's cheek with his fingers and then slid his hand down her throat and toward the swell of her breast. Sunmi stood still, her breath quickening, but she did not move. Kwak withdrew his hand and then slapped Sunmi hard on the cheek. Sunmi gasped and almost fell, again almost causing others to fall as well. "What did I do…I mean Comrade Sir?"

"When I touch you, you must show appreciation…and you must learn how to do this as soon as possible, before I show you what happens to capitalist bitches who do not show appreciation!"

Now, turning to the third woman, Kwak asked, "What is your name?"

"Kyok Lee, Comrade Sir!" Kyok also wore a white blouse, but she wore ankle-length black pants rather than a skirt. Most women in DPRK at this time were attired similarly, with a blouse and dark-colored pants or medium-length skirt. Kyok seemed somewhat older than the others.

"So, are you also related to the others?"

"No, Comrade Sir, I am not related to them. I am their teacher."

Kwak touched her cheek with his hand and then slid his hand down her throat and to her left breast. Kyok started to make soft moaning sounds. Kwak gently withdrew his hand, smiled at her, and then—*crack!*

Kwak slapped her cheek so hard this time that she lost balance and fell to the floor on her side, causing the two other girls to fall as well in a heap. Part of Sunmi's buttocks was exposed as her skirt flung upward during the fall. Kwak kicked Sunmi's exposed buttocks and then kicked Yoonja's thigh, which was half-exposed, and then kicked Kyok hard in the butt over her pants. The three women squealed in pain, writhing on the floor.

Kwak picked up the document that accompanied the new prisoners.

"A teacher—a bourgeoisie intellectual, the worst enemy of our proletarian democracy. And you are also the daughter of a traitor, a South Korean faction politburo member! Sorry to tell you that your parents were executed yesterday right here. And these two girls are also the children of traitors who were executed yesterday. So, the girls and their teacher were in the school dormitory where they were arrested," spat Kwak.

"Comrade Hoon, now you've seen how some of the milder education is performed here," said Kilin to Hoon.

"Yes, I see. I think these bitches deserve much education."

Kwak said, "I'll take care of the older one, Kyok, here. I suggest you two take care of the two girls in the most fitting ways as usual."

Kwak summoned his minions and had them untie the women from each other and help them up from the floor. Kwak then lead Kyok away. The two Song girls were now the property of the two counterintelligence officers.

Special Interrogation Room Two, Basement, Camp Lucky

The large room had just one heavy metal door. The walls were concrete, but the ceiling and floor were hardwood. The room was illuminated by a single bare 60-watt bulb hanging from the ceiling. There were several large hooks hanging from the ceiling. There was a low sink with a large bowl and a water faucet.

In the middle of the room were two metal tables with what looked like stirrups, except they were on both ends of the table. They somewhat resembled doctors' examining tables or, more likely, autopsy tables because there was no cushion. They also resembled a gynecological examining table because there was a drop-down part on the bottom side, with metal stirrups protruding upward. There were metal cuffs attached to the stirrups with a metal chain. On the head side, the stirrups were leather loops with attached metal handcuffs.

There were also two metal chairs that looked like dental chairs with reclining backs and footrests, but metal cuffs dangled from both arms and each end of the footrest.

On one concrete wall, there seemed to be an electrical control box, with rows of switches, some buttons and others toggles. There were also dials and meters. On another wall were hooks bearing various tools and instruments of torture: ropes, handcuffs, ankle cuffs, leg-irons, vises, whips, chains, clamps, pliers, scissors, saws, knives, probes, and electric hot irons. In the middle of the room were two ominous nooses hanging from two hooks.

Kilin and Hoon led the terrified, shivering Song sisters into this room. Kilin had Yoonja standing in the middle of the room and, taking a pair of scissors from the hook on the wall, cut off her blouse and then her bra, revealing her bare breasts. Then he cut the skirt and the panties down the middle. She stood naked, shivering, with her wrists still cuffed in the back. Kilin told Hoon to do the same to Sunmi.

"Please spare me, Comrade," said Sunmi. "I am a virgin, and I'll give myself to you. Please let me live." Kilin put a finger on his mouth, indicating for Hoon to be quiet. Then Kilin came next to Hoon, in front of Sunmi, and slapped her already-bleeding cheek.

"You will learn to be quiet unless spoken to, you capitalist bitch! All you will do is obey, got that?"

Sunmi nodded. "Yes, Comrade Sir!"

Hoon cut off Sunmi's blouse and bra and her skirt and panties. Sunmi, though two years younger than Yoonja, had equally well-developed breasts though somewhat less pubic hair.

Kilin said, "Now the preliminaries. First, we have to teach these bitches that we can do anything we want to them and let them know what pain is, which is what they must experience to expiate for their capitalist sins."

Kilin ordered Yoonja to climb on the examination/autopsy table and then, spreading her naked thighs, clamped the ankle cuffs that were attached to what looked like raised stirrups at the foot of the table, removed her handcuffs from her back, and had her wrists separately cuffed to the handcuffs on either side of the head of the table. Thus, naked Yoonja was tied by wrists and ankles spread-eagle on the table. Then he dropped the bottom part of the steel table so that Yoonja's bottom was exposed as if in a gynecological examination. Kilin directed Hoon to do the same with Sunmi.

"Now, the serious business begins," intoned Kilin. He opened his briefcase and took out two sheets of paper and pens. He handed one to Hoon and said, "These are confessions, with spaces to fill in the names of their confederate traitors. I take one for this bitch, and you do one for your bitch."

He stood over Yoonja and spoke in a sharp but grave voice, "Yoonja, tell me about the counterrevolutionary capitalist cell you belong to in your school!"

Yoonja, shivering with fear, whispered, "I don't know what you are talking about."

Kilin cupped Yoonja's left breast with his hand and gently squeezed it and then suddenly placed her nipple between his thumb and index fingers and squeezed it hard. Yoonja cried out in pain.

"I know you belong to this capitalist cell. Who else belongs to it?"

Yoonja, still writhing in pain as he continued to squeeze her nipple, said, "I don't really know, Comrade. Please stop this pain. Pleeeease!" Yoonja was crying and screaming.

Kilin lifted his hand and said, "Well, if this is not enough for you, we have many other ways of persuasion." Kilin went to the wall where the torture instruments were hanging and brought some items to the table in each hand. He handed Hoon the items he had in his left hand.

He told Hoon, "Look, you and I each have here two metal nipple clamps, which will keep on squeezing the bitch's nipples, and here is a metal vaginal probe, which, like a penis, will penetrate the vagina and give the bitches a taste of heaven. For a male, you can use a penis clip, which serves the same function. You notice that the probe has two wires that can attach to the nipple clamps, and there is a dial on the plastic handle of the vaginal probe."

Kilin clicked in the plugs of the wires to the female sockets of the nipple clamps and showed Hoon the dial on the plump handle of the penis-shaped probe.

"When I turn this dial up, electric current from the powerful batteries in the handle flows to both clamps and the metal probe. Then the bitches will know what hell is like."

Kilin placed the nipple clamps on Yoonja's nipples, which made her scream out in pain. He then dipped the vaginal probe in a jar of jelly and forced it down into her vagina. Yoonja was screaming, crying out in pain, and sobbing at the same time. "Pl…ple*ase stop… pleeeease…*"

Hoon, following suit, placed the clamps on Sunmi's pink nipples. Sunmi, who was quiet, almost as if in a trance, cried out in pain. "*Ouch! Eee!* Please *help…*"

He dipped the vaginal probe in the jelly and penetrated her vagina with it. Drops of blood spilled out as it went into the tight vagina. "She is really a virgin!" thought Hoon. Sunmi was screaming and crying, and the probe was pushed out of the vagina. Kilin came over, picked up the probe, swiftly inserted it into Sunmi's vagina again, and held it there. "Now, take over, Hoon. Don't show any mercy to this capitalist bitch. Young as she is, she is the daughter of a capitalist traitor, an incorrigible enemy of our state!"

Kilin turned the dial on the handle of the vaginal probe halfway, and Yoonja became hysterical, crying and writhing in pain, trying to twist her torso and her pelvis, straining her wrists and ankles against the metal cuffs. Her screams were weakened by the intense pain in her nipples and her vagina, intense throbbing pain that took her breath away.

"Who are the members of the cell?" asked Kilin. "I'll turn this up more if you do not answer me immediately."

"No one…no cell…*aeeeehh*…Yes, there was a cell…please stop, and I'll tell you…anything…*pleeeeese* stop!"

Kilin turned down the dial. "So, who are they? I know there are at least five."

"Yes, five…Kim Il Won, Chun Dae Woo…Choi Byung…Lee Lila…I think that's all."

"I know there were at least five. Do I have to turn up the dial?"

"*No,* please…yes, there was also Park Yuni and Pang Soon."

"That's better. Anyone else?"

"No, Comrade Sir, I swear. No one else." As Kilin finished writing down the names in the confession, he turned to Hoon,

"OK, let's see what you can do, Hoon."

Before Hoon started turning up the dial, Sunmi cried, "Comrade, I'll tell you…yes, I was a member of the capitalist cell, and they included all the people my sister told you, and also, there was Yum Mira and Choi Kwon."

Hoon looked at Kilin, wondering what he should do. Kilin told him, "The bitch is lying. Turn up the dial and see what she says… which will be the truth!"

Hoon turned up the dial, and Sunmi screamed. Her scream was so loud that Hoon started turning down the dial when Kilin said, "No, keep it up. The bitch has to break and start telling the truth."

Sunmi screamed, "Pleeeeease stop! I'll tell you all!" Hoon turned down the dial, and Sunmi whimpered, "Yes, there was also Kim Okhi and Ra jin. That's all—I swear!"

Kilin said to Yoonja, "Now that you have told the truth, you'll sign this document. Then you will have a reward." He uncuffed her right wrist and had her sign the document he had prepared with the names just filled in and then cuffed her wrist again. He then told Hoon to have Sunmi sign her document.

Kilin unbuckled his pants, dropped them as well as his underwear on the floor, and approached Yoonja between her thighs. "You capitalist bitch, you will have the reward of your life by having me enter you and give you undeserved bliss." He took out the vaginal probe and set it aside on the side of the table, with the nipple clamps still on. He then thrust his erect penis into her vagina. Yoonja screamed again, which seemed to excite Kilin. As Yoonja struggled with her pelvis writhing in pain, Kilin thrust his penis back and forth in unison, and soon he ejaculated fiercely. "Take that, you capitalist bitch!"

Hoon tried to emulate Kilin, but as he took the vaginal probe out of Sunmi, he found he did not have a strong enough erection. He tried to enter Sunmi's vagina, but his penis was too flaccid. Soonmi moaned, "Please, Comrade, enter me! I want to live. Please save me."

Hoon silently shook his head and thought, "It's not your fault, Sunmi. I would save you if I could."

"What, you haven't rewarded this bitch?" said Kilin, who was watching Hoon fumble. He pushed Hoon aside and thrust his still-erect penis into Sunmi's vagina. Sunmi screamed and cried in pain as he kept on thrusting his penis until she seemed to pass out. "Young bitches don't appreciate it as much as the older ones."

After another ejaculation, Kilin put on his underwear and pants.

"Now we have the signed confessions of the capitalist traitor bitches. They are now to be executed according to our laws."

Kilin stood up the barely conscious girls, lowered the two nooses attached to the hook from the ceiling, and put them around their necks. "Please, Comrades, spare my life. I am only sixteen!" pleaded Sunmi.

Kilin slapped her on the face. "Remember to speak only when you are spoken to, you capitalist bitch!"

"You can kill me…maybe I deserve it…but please let my sister live. *Pleeease!*" cried Yoonja.

"You will die first then, and you deserve it!" said Kilin as he walked toward the electrical control box on the wall.

As the two naked girls, with the nooses around their necks, stood in the middle of the room, Hoon noticed that they were standing on two wooden squares that seemed to be trap doors. Kilin pushed one of the buttons on the wall, the trapdoor beneath Yoonja dropped down, and Yoonja fell into the dark chasm as the rope tightened from the hook. Then he pushed another button, and the trapdoor under Sunmi flung open, and she also disappeared into the darkness below, only the taut rope from the hook now visible. The execution of the two capitalist, counterrevolutionary daughters of a capitalist traitor had been carried out.

Special Interrogation Room Three

The room was somewhat smaller than room two, but otherwise it was almost identical, except there was only one each of what looked like the examination/autopsy table and the dental chair. There were still two nooses and trapdoors in this room.

Commandant Kwak withdrew his penis from the vagina of Kyok, who was tied spread-eagle like Yoonja and Sunmi on the examination/autopsy table. Kyok, however, was smiling.

"You are a good fuck, bitch, and for that, I'll spare your life. Even before the torture began, you confessed to all your crimes and named all the traitors in your school, among them your students Yoonja and Sunmi, as well as a number of your colleagues. Of course, you know what happened to Yoonja and Sunmi and what will happen to the others."

"Yes, Comrade Sir! I am a good soldier of our proletarian cause!"

"Remember, Kyok, you must work for me, meaning that you have to satisfy me at every turn, if you want to live. Work will set you free—nothing but work!"

Commandant Kwak, in spite of his crude behavior, was an intellectual, a student of history, and knew the Nazi concentration-camp slogan, "Arbeit macht frei" (Work will set you free). A lie, because no amount of work would set the doomed free. Only death did.

Commandant's Office, Later after Supper with the Commandant

Kilin gave Commandant Kwak a thick envelope from his briefcase, and Kwak gave Kilin a large metal box from his safe. Kilin unlocked the box with the key Kwak gave him and opened the lid of the box. The box was full of sparkling jewelry, gold, silver, diamond, sapphire, and many other small precious articles. Kwak opened the envelope and counted the currency—American dollars!

"So, it was a fruitful week of harvesting" said Kilin.

"You know, the capitalists you bring here do have a lot of jewelry on them—they have the notion that they might bribe us to buy freedom. Ha-ha."

"Ha-ha," said Kilin. "Hoon, don't you agree that the capitalists are stupid?"

"Yes, Comrade. I do," Hoon responded mechanically. Hoon knew that the jewelry would be sold overseas by a special branch of the DPRK intelligence assigned to the diplomatic corps, and the American dollars would be distributed among the party hierarchy and Kwak and then some of the officers directly involved, including a few dollars to Kilin and a smaller amount to Hoon himself.

Kilin and Hoon drove off Camp Lucky in the early hours of the morning. The weather was still warm during the day, but there was a chill in the air in the early September morning.

During the four-hour drive back to Pyongyang, Hoon could not get over his experience of the last several hours, of torturing the young girl, Sunmi, and being unable to fuck her when she wanted him to. She reminded him of Kyung, his younger sister, whose whereabouts he did not know. Sunmi looked so vulnerable, so terrified, and so desirable. Why was I not able to penetrate her and maybe save her life? No, I couldn't have; she was already condemned, by the system, by her birth, even before she was brought here. But still, could I have done something? She begged me to spare her life. Could I have set her free, even if I had to kill Kilin? No, she was a capitalist bitch, and her pleas were to save her own life. No wonder I did not want to have sex with her: she was a lowly capitalist running-dog bitch. Nevertheless, Hoon resolved that he would never do this "courier and prisoner management" duty again. He would have no problem in passing it on to someone else, because this job was one of the most sought-after duties of the counterintelligence section. And no wonder, considering all the fringe benefits.

23

A HOME FOR EVERY PATRIOT

1955, Seoul, Korea (37.5 N Parallel, 127 E Longitude)
Yunhee, Suk

Yunhee's one dream in life was having a home of her own, ever since her home in Kangwha Island turned overnight into a stranger's house when her mother left. She lived in the dormitory of her high school, and in dormlike apartments during college and while she taught. In Manchuria, she and Suk lived in a house provided for them by the government.

Back in Korea, they lived in rented rooms or rented houses. They could not afford to buy a house, not only for the lack of funds but also because Suk was transferred so often. When he was not transferred, he had to move for other reasons, like the move to Pusan for Bo's sake and the move to Seoul so that Bo could continue to go to Seoul Middle School. But this time, Yunhee was determined to realize her dream of owning a house.

"Suk, now is the time to buy a house. We are not moving away from Seoul. Ever! Bo must finish his education, and now we have Claire to think about."

"But how are we going to get the money to buy a house?" asked Suk. "I am an honest policeman. I do not take bribes. You know as I do that my salary is barely enough to live on and pay Bo's tuition.

And you know what happens to dishonest cops, like those in the Jiri Task Force- Prison!"

Suk was in the habit of reminding Yunhee of his old colleagues of the Police Task Force who had gone to jail each time he felt Yunhee was complaining about financial things.

"We have to find a way, Suk. I have saved a little money, perhaps about half of what is needed for a down payment. We have to find a way!"

"Yunhee, I am impressed that you were able to save at all from the little I bring home/ But it costs so much to buy a house. I'll see what I can do. But I am not at all optimistic" said Suk. He was not surprised that Yunhee was able to save money—she would rather save than even eat. He was also grateful that she did not offer to sell matches!

Both Suk and Yunhee looked at available houses in Seoul. But the prices were astronomical. Even with Yunhee's savings, Suk's salary was woefully inadequate for the monthly mortgage payments, even if they had been able to find a sufficient sum for the down payment.

"Guess whom I ran across today, Yunhee!" said Suk as he came in. Yunhee greeted him with a gloomy face, as usual these days.

"You mean with whom you drank!" said Yunhee icily.

"Sure, we had a drink to talk about old times. Chang—remember the son of my elder brother, Sun?"

"You mean that ruffian, who broke Bo's collarbone?"

"Come on, Yunhee, he did not break Bo's bone. He was playing with him, and Bo fell accidentally. Anyway, he is now in the real-estate business. And you will like this, Yunhee. He is building new homes here in Seoul, in the Chongyang District. These homes are built with a special grant from the government specifically for patriots and their families! They will be sold at about half the market price, only for qualified patriots. And he thinks that we can qualify because I have been in the police force, fighting the Communists and crime, for more than five years!"

For once, Yunhee did not mind Chang. Anything to have a home of her own!

"Chang also told me that his father, Sun, died during the war of heart disease and, in a matter of months, all my other brothers died, one after another, of heart disease or stroke. And that my mother had died of tuberculosis just before the war broke out. Sun's factory was destroyed during the war. Chang sold what was left of the estate and divided it up among the surviving children. Then, he moved to Seoul and has been in the real estate development business ever since. I am sorry that I didn't have a chance to see my mother before she passed away. And Sun, too."

"I'm sorry, too, Suk. But you didn't know, and there was no way then that you could have seen them." She also wondered what had become of her father, whom she had not seen ever since she left Kangwha more than a quarter of a century ago. He must have been dead a long time.

Suk did not tell Yunhee that he also heard about what happened to Min, his first wife, and her family. Shortly after the end of World War II, Hoon, Suk, and Min's firstborn son had left Kangwon Province and gone to North Korea, presumably because he was a Communist. The South Korean Police arrested Min and Kyung after that on the suspicion that they also sympathized with the Communists. They survived the torture and were eventually released. Min, however, developed a severe and painful limp in her left leg because of a broken bone that did not heal properly. She died shortly afterward. Kyung had left Kangwon Province after her mother's death and disappeared without a trace in the fog of war.

Suk said to Yunhee, "You might visit Chang at his office one of these days. He asked about you. And he could tell you more about the new development!"

She did pay a visit to Chang, who gave her detailed instructions concerning applying for the housing, about the mortgage, everything she needed to know to make her dream come true.

So, in about six months' time, Yunhee, Suk, Bo, and Claire moved into their new house in the Chongyang District. Across the railroad tracks.

The one-story house was built with clay bricks and stucco. The house had a foyer leading to the living room with a dining area and kitchen and a hallway to the bedrooms. The first door opened to a combination bedroom and study that Bo used, and past that there was a door to the master bedroom, another door to the bathroom, and then a door to the small bedroom for Claire. At the far end of the hallway, opposite Claire's room, was a small den that Suk used as a study/hobby room full of birdcages and potted plants. There were various leafy and blooming plants and cages and cages of canaries, parakeets, finches, and so on. The room was called the "bird room." Though the external walls of the house were made of clay bricks and thus thick, the internal walls were plasterboard and rather thin, and the doors were made of flimsy plywood. Any sound made in any room could be heard from any other room.

The house had a small backyard, with a covered hole of an entrance with a ladder leading down to a small basement-like dirt room, which could be used as an air-raid shelter, as well as for storage of kimchi. This type of underground air-raid shelter, though just a hole in the ground, was required by the government for every new building in Seoul.

Yunhee's dream was finally realized. And Suk boasted, "We live in a house built specifically for patriots!"

24

PERRY MASON VERSUS SIGMUND FREUD

1956–57, Seoul (37.5 N Parallel, 127 E Longitude)
Bo

As I listened to Dad's stories of his own past, I envied him, his many interesting experiences as a young man, his handsomeness and popularity during his school days. Especially among girls. Dad had received love letters from girls. I had never received any love letters from girls.

When I think of my dad, I think of something warm, smelly, and juicy. This is in contradistinction to my mom, who was always clean, aseptic, and, yes, mineral. But a mineral that bled, because another part of my memory of her has to do with the blood-soaked sanitary napkin and her discomfort with it.

My dad liked animals. All kinds. Mom did not, and would not tolerate one in the house, mainly because of the unsanitary conditions they produced, such as the excrements and the smell. Nevertheless, Dad had birds. Many birds, including canaries, parakeets, and other birds whose names I do not remember. In fact, he had a whole roomful of birds at one time. And plants. He grew various potted plants, including those that moved when touched, and very elaborate miniature Japanese pines, which were so artistically curved and twisted. He had to apply judicious pressure and ligations to the branches to achieve this artistic effect.

He really seemed to enjoy all living things and made them thrive. He did not mind the extra work he had to do, including feeding the birds and cleaning their cages.

I am in some ways more like my mom than dad. I do mind very much the stink of animals, including birds, and I hate to take care of them. In fact, I do not like plants indoors, either. I do like to see trees and flowers outdoors, but not in the house. As I used to say, they compete with humans for oxygen! And living space.

Yes, I prefer nonliving things. Such as fancy rocks, electronic equipment, and sculpture. They are clean, they never soil, they do not compete against you for oxygen. Above all, they do not need to be taken care of by you. And they never die or reject you or leave you...

Even though I was still in love with Elizabeth Taylor, I felt by now that I needed a flesh-and-blood person whom I could touch. My daydreams now invariably included an as-yet-unnamed girl, perhaps someone in one of the girls' high schools, to talk to, to hold hands with, to kiss, and, eventually, to make love to. The dreams also included the possibility of marriage and building a home together. The thoughts were still vague and unformed, but I felt that my desires were real and becoming stronger every day.

My face was changing. Like my father, I also developed a rather severe case of acne. It was not quite as severe as Dad's, but I was still quite self-conscious about the multiple pimples on my face, which made me even shier among girls.

The only place where I did not feel shy was in the English-speaking club. There, I was confident and assertive, in spite of the girls, because of my excellence in English, which was commonly accepted by all members. The second year of high school was the last year high-school students could participate in extracurricular activities, such as the English-speaking club, with a clear conscience. Because in the third year, another examination was coming up—the national entrance examination to college!

The Korean school system was modeled after the American one. The grammar school lasted six years, followed by three years of middle school and then three years of high school. Middle-school seniors who were in good standing were usually accepted to the same high school. Then, there was college that was available for about half of the high-school graduates. Grammar school was compulsory. Attendance at any of the higher school levels wasn't mandated by law, but it was essential for any success—to get a decent job.

While the entrance examination for the middle and high school was very important, and determined one's fate at an early date, the entrance exam for college was the *real thing*. Almost everything before was a lead-up to this big event that actually decided the future of the student. Furthermore, the competition was the fiercest. There were only two universities that were considered to be the best in Korea at that time—Seoul National University and Hyundai University. Seoul National was the more prestigious and was the alma mater of Suk. Hyundai was a missionary school, built by Protestant missionaries from the United States. In almost every department and school, Seoul National University excelled over Hyundai University except one—the medical school. Being the oldest medical school in Korea, Hyundai University's medical school, the Providence College of Medicine, was at least equal to, if not more prestigious than, the Medical School of Seoul National University.

Of course, every member of the graduating class at Seoul High School aspired to enter the Seoul National University. If everyone from Seoul were accepted, they would account for approximately 50 percent of the entering class at that university. Of course, not everyone got in. About 20 percent of the entering class of Seoul National each year were graduates of Seoul High School.

Once again, early-morning classes and mock exams. The mock exams were given every week, and the students' names were posted in order of score on the wall of the corridor! One knew exactly where one stood in relation to each other this way. Up to the junior year of high school, class rank was a confidential matter. No more. Anything to motivate the students to study, to compete!

I was particularly worried because of my status as a "limping runner." The college entrance exam tested all subjects, the subjects in which I ran, such as English and chemistry, and those in which I limped, namely math. Overall, consequently, I would be just average, not good enough for the fierce competition to enter the prestigious Seoul National University. And this time, I couldn't blame my parents for keeping me in a backward city. I was already in Seoul High School.

I just had to do better in math! I had to get over my disinterest, my contempt for the memorization and routine of math. How would I accomplish this? I did not know. My parents were of no help. Finally, I turned to my books again. First, I bought several books on how to study math. One book, *Math for Those Who Hate Math*, said that those who hate mathematics, by and large, are good at memorizing, not reasoning, and, therefore, should try to attempt to use their memory in math—by memorizing not just the formulas but also the answers to most questions that are likely to be asked in entrance examinations—thousands of them! I put the book down disgustedly.

Another book was more encouraging. It said that most people who had little interest in math, and consequently were poor in it, were, in fact, approaching it from the wrong direction. Mathematics could be interesting and challenging, if one did not think of the numbers but rather the question behind the numbers. The essential questions that math asked, the book said, were really philosophical questions—how things were related to each other and how one could deduce an answer logically by having clues to the answer—just as in a detective story! Now, this was something I could relate to!

The book had one such question for each day of the year for one year—365 questions. Questions, and a guide to approach these questions, answers, and corollary questions. By following this book,

I would solve 365 basic questions and their corollaries. I had a little more than 365 days before the entrance exam.

I studied every night. After dinner, from eight thirty to one o'clock in the morning. Every night. Like everybody else. The thought of the possibility that I might fail the exam was, however, absolutely horrifying! It would bring back in a flash the morning of April 30, 1953. When the world was suddenly bleached of colors and turned gray and black. And the despair, the humiliation! I could not, I would not, have that experience again!

"Mom, I have trouble going to sleep after studying at night. Do you think I could ask the doctor for a sleeping pill?"

My parents were gratified to see me study so hard, all on my own. My mother obtained a prescription for me from the doctor for some sleeping pills. For ten capsules of Seconal.

I made copies of the prescription. Then, I went to ten different drug stores, and bought altogether one hundred capsules of Seconal, a hundred milligrams each. I knew that would do the job—of successful suicide. I had vowed that I would commit suicide if I failed to enter Seoul National University. Absolutely, and without hesitation. I put all the capsules together in a plain bottle and hid it in the bottom drawer of my desk in my bedroom/study.

I had thought of suicide when I thought I failed the exam for the middle school. Then, however, I had been absolutely unprepared. I did not know how to kill myself. Now I thought about jumping off a bridge, the bridge on the Han River, south of Seoul, where some four thousand people perished during the war when it was prematurely blown up by South Korean soldiers. It would have been effective, and I believed I would do it if the situation warranted. But it was not aesthetically pleasing and not my style at all. And jumping in front of a truck or a train was even messier! So was stabbing myself or shooting myself. Actually, I knew that there was a pistol in the house somewhere, and I could have found it if I wanted to. But, somehow, I felt that that was not how I would kill myself. No, sleeping forever, and dreaming forever, was far more attractive, even romantic.

Mine was a pact with a deity. I shall pass the exam, or I shall kill myself. If I pass, you shall have me here on earth, where I shall remain a part of your design if there is one. If I don't, you will lose me on earth, or you will have me, or my "soul," if that is your wish.

During the war, I was a rather devout Christian. Being with my mother, to whom it never occurred to go to church, I sometimes missed being in one. I prayed that we would be reunited with Dad and that the war would end. At times, I felt that I had some sort of a direct line with God and could influence him, because he really liked me, and loved me, just like Jesus Christ. By the time I was a high-school student, however, I had become an ardent atheist, thanks to the fire-and-brimstone preachers I read about and occasionally heard on the radio and the devout, almost fanatic Christian classmates I had. To them, Christianity was perfection and righteousness itself—no room for questioning, no room for discussion. Anyone who disagreed with them was advocating the cause of Satan and must be condemned to hell. End of discussion!

The God that Dad had preached was full of love, forgiveness, and understanding. But their God was the God of dogma, vengeance, and intolerance.

I read the Bible several times. Both the Old and the New Testaments. I read philosophy books. I read books on other religions, Buddhist, Islamic, Confucian, Zoroastrian, Hindu, and others. I came to realize that all gods of organized religion were instruments of the perpetuation of irrational authority, that they grew fat on the ignorance of the populace. I also realized that the gods reflected the best hopes and the worst fears of the people who believed in them. Indeed, man made God in his own image!

Among gods, I felt much more attracted and sympathetic to the Greek gods. They were so human! I felt they represented human aspirations and human frailties far better than the monotheistic gods. Much more worthy of being gods. But I was also, in part, praying to an all-powerful God and, at the same time, making a bargain with the devil. Like Faust.

I was also attracted to Karl Marx's atheistic dialectical materialism. Religion was the opium of the masses! Marx's economic theories made much sense, though Communism was anathema to Syngman Rhee's fascist regime. Had I been born earlier so that I was about my age now when World War II ended, perhaps I would have become a Communist, and maybe gone to North Korea. But here I was, in South Korea, and I did not want to be persecuted as a Communist, which I really was not. While I was attracted to dialectical materialism, I did not believe in the totalitarian aspects of Communism—I believed that freedom and the free exercise of one's abilities in creating wealth would best serve the society as whole. But perhaps Communism was evolving! Following Stalin's death, Nikita Khrushchev was bringing significant liberalization to the Soviet regime and the satellite states. I was hopeful that, with the liberalizing trend, North and South Korea might eventually be united to form a more just and democratic nation.

I was in the upper half of the class of six hundred when the exams began. I excelled, as expected, in English and science, did very well in most of the humanities, and did only so-so in math. Yes, I had gotten over the terrible problems with math with the daily workbook problem-solving exercises, but I still did not enjoy memorizing formulas that one just had to do. I did enjoy the more theoretical aspects of advanced math, including the probability theories, combinations and permutations, and the calculus I was now learning in school. As months passed, and I continued in my "study mode," my scores made drastic improvements, and my standing shot up to twenty-five out of six hundred. There I stayed, with only minor fluctuations such as climbing up to twenty and then dropping to twenty-eight.

Everyone including me felt that, as long as I maintained my class standing, I would have no difficulty in passing the entrance exam for Seoul National University. After all, about two hundred students from Seoul entered Seoul National University every year. I had to decide, however, what my major would be in college. To apply to Korean universities, one had to apply to specific departments—for example, history, physics, English literature, Korean literature, political science, premedicine, or law. To enter a Korean medical school, one usually applied to the premedical curriculum, although one could apply to it after college as in the United States. The premedical curriculum was usually two years, the successful completion of which was followed by promotion to the medical school. The law school was not a graduate school, and one could apply directly to it.

The choice was between law and medicine. Although I had dreamed of becoming a scientist, especially a chemist like Alfred Nobel in my younger days, I decided by now that I really wanted to deal with people rather than spend all my time in a laboratory. I felt more comfortable with people with my success in Oak Club, and also, with maturity, I became more interested in people. In addition to mysteries, I had read novels and plays voraciously, such as Shakespeare, Dostoyevsky, Hemingway, and Sartre. I also read all of Erle Stanley Gardner and identified myself with Perry Mason. Mason's courtroom dramas came alive to me, and I felt I could bring to the gray authoritarian Korean courtroom a taste of judicial brilliance and much-needed reforms. Law, then. Besides, I really did not like the sight of blood, which one would have to see much of if one was going to be a doctor.

On the other hand, I had become entranced with psychology and psychoanalysis and read voraciously about these subjects during high school. Freud, Jung, Adler, Meyer, Pavlov, and so on. I was especially enamored with Freud and psychoanalysis. Reading about psychoanalysis was like reading a mystery novel—the tracking down of an idea or a symptom to the very genesis in early childhood, completely repressed from memory! Following clues gleaned in dreams and in everyday slips of the tongue! And undoing the repression of the sexual instinct! Somehow, to me it made sense that the root of all problems was traceable to repressed sexual drives. And such repression was quite strong in Korea, perhaps even more so than in nineteenth-century Vienna. No, I had to become a psychiatrist.

I really had to make up my mind now. The application deadline was only one week away! Then, Cousin Soonkil appeared out of nowhere! Soonkil Moon, MD, diplomate, American Board of Surgery, diplomate, American Board of Thoracic Surgery! Soonkil, who was the second son of my dad's eldest brother, Sun.

Soonkil had been in the United States ever since his father died during the Korean War. Soonkil had finished Providence Medical College of Hyundai University just before the Korean War and had gone to the United States, sponsored by a missionary, to study surgery. He had trained mostly in Christian universities in the South, finished his residency in surgery and thoracic surgery, and come back to Korea triumphantly as, perhaps, the most qualified thoracic surgeon in Korea. And Soonkil came to see my dad, after more than fifteen years.

I was impressed with Soonkil. He was tall and spoke with a deep, strong voice that projected authority. He was also kind and gentle. For a cousin, Soonkil was a bit too old, I thought. After all, he was in his forties, compared with my seventeen. But what an impressive man! And he was going to be teaching at his alma mater, the Providence College of Medicine!

Dad told Soonkil about my indecision between law and medicine. Soonkil invited me to take a walk with him to talk about medicine. It was a long and enlightening walk. I asked about the training involved in becoming a doctor and then a psychiatrist. I told him about my qualms concerning blood and asked whether it would keep me from becoming a physician. "Not unless you want to be a surgeon," said Soonkil. He explained that, during medical school, one had very little exposure to blood, other than perhaps drawing blood into a syringe. He also explained how, in a way, medicine itself, not just psychiatry, was like detective work—one had to make a diagnosis on the basis of clues and then confirm the diagnosis with laboratory tests, like trapping a criminal. He also told me about the busy schedule and the amount of hard work needed in becoming a doctor. But then it was gratifying because you could really help people, and even save lives!

For a surgeon, Soonkil showed considerable understanding of and support for psychiatry. He thought psychiatry was an intellectually challenging and gratifying specialty. He also told me that I definitely had to study in the United States if I wanted to be a top-notch psychiatrist. There was not even a psychoanalytic institute in Korea. And he suggested that I apply to Hyundai University, rather than Seoul National, because there one learned everything in English—they used English textbooks and even had American professors.

Sigmund Freud had won out finally, thanks to a surgeon. I made the astounding announcement that I would apply to the Hyundai University Premedical Course, not the Seoul National University.

Having decided to enter Hyundai University if accepted, I felt a sudden relief from my anxieties. Even before the decision, I had felt much more at ease about the entrance exam to college. Knowing that I had a very good chance of entering any college I wanted certainly played a role. But I no longer felt that my life depended on my success at the entrance exam. Even if I failed, I no longer resolved myself to commit suicide by taking the whole bottle of Seconal, which still stayed in my desk drawer, half-forgotten. If I failed, I would wait another year and try again, while trying something else, such as writing. I might even try working for a year, perhaps in a library, or, if necessary, as a waiter.

Working as a student, especially while preparing for an entrance examination, was quite unusual in Korea. Especially for the students who went to Seoul High School, as most of them came from privileged, wealthy families. Students were supposed to study and enjoy life, not work. While my family was by no means rich, Dad did make a reasonably decent living, and I had never had to work. I, however, felt that working was a valuable means of learning about life and would have welcomed such an opportunity. Besides, I knew that my parents were making considerable sacrifices in order to buy all my needs and, now, Claire's too. Claire was now in grammar school, and soon she would be ready for college as well!

25

OF CHERRY BLOSSOMS AND MAGNOLIAS

April 1957, Pyongyang, DPRK (39 N Parallel, 125.7 E Longitude)
Hoon

The cherry blossoms in the Moranbong Park were glorious this year, especially along the promenade of the Taedong River. On this Sunday, there were a number of couples walking along the bank holding hands. Many men were in their military uniforms and Mao suits, and women were in various monochrome uniforms or in dark knee-length skirts and white blouses. The brilliant colors of the blossoms seemed to make up for the lack of color in the young people's attire. And the tender smiles and occasional laughter reflected the joy of young love everywhere.

Hoon and Myunghee were one of the couples walking along the riverbank. Hoon was in a smart military uniform, and Myunghee was wearing a pink cotton blouse and a navy-blue skirt. The color of her blouse harmonized with the pink and red of the cherry blossoms, enlivening Hoon's heart.

Myunghee was now twenty-three, a graduate of the prestigious Kim Il-Sung University in Pyongyang. The daughter of a Communist guerilla who fought with Kim Il-Sung in Manchuria, she was now working as a secretary in the Section of Cultural Affairs of the Korean Workers' Party, the only political party in the Democratic Republic of Korea. Myunghee was of medium height and medium build, with a very pretty oval face and medium-length black hair. She also had a very cute smile, but she was no frail damsel. Having grown up with the guerillas in the harsh environs of Manchuria, she was tough as a nail as well as highly idealistic.

"I can hardly wait till we are married!" Hoon murmured as he squeezed Myunghee's hand.

"Me, neither," whispered Myunghee. Privacy was scarce for young people in North Korea, especially in cities like Pyongyang where there were prying eyes everywhere. In the countryside, young people could easily escape into the mountains and fields for privacy. In spite of the egalitarian principles of Marxism, the brand of Communism in North Korea being practiced was a hybrid of Confucianism and Communism and was rigidly puritanical when it came to sexual matters. Public displays of sexual affection, including embracing and kissing, were considered to be decadent, and the only thing young lovers could do was hold hands.

Four years had passed since the Korean War ended in a truce in 1953, but Pyongyang still bore the scars of the massive air raids by the UN forces, and there was a great housing shortage. Though there was massive construction going on, it would take years for newlyweds to find an apartment in Pyongyang. But because of their positions in the Communist Party hierarchy and because of Myunghee's father, a ranking member of the politburo, Hoon and Myunghee were promised an apartment for October of this year, when they would be married.

January 1957
Political Committee Quarters, Korean Workers' Party
Counterintelligence Headquarters, Pyongyang

"Hoon, I think you have a good chance of being chosen for the Covert Operations Section, but there is a problem," said Commissar Kim, his boss.

"What is the problem?" asked Hoon, with a crestfallen look.

"The Special Intelligence Unit doing your background check found out that your birth name is Keh-Hoon Moon and you changed it to Hoon when you arrived in North Korea in 1948. That's OK—you wanted to start a new life—but they are concerned you may still have some relatives in South Korea and that you do not have any personal attachments in DPRK."

Hoon felt a lump in his throat, and his heart began to pound. Relatives in South Korea!

Being a counterintelligence officer of KPA, he knew that having ties with South Korea had become dangerous! It had not always been this way. When Hoon came to North Korea in 1948, many forward-thinking, idealistic South Korean Communists came to Pyongyang, as well as Koreans and their descendants who had escaped to China and Russia during the Japanese occupation of Korea.

Pyongyang had been a lively, thriving city then, with so many diverse Communist intellectuals—so diverse that many spoke in different languages, mostly Mandarin and Russian, at home, but still argued and debated in Korean, their mother tongue. After the Korean War ("War of Fatherland Liberation" in DPRK), those intellectuals and technocrats who had come from China and the Soviet Union were suspected of being disloyal. Then, in August 1956, there was a coup attempt by the Chinese and Russian factions in the politburo. Only the uneducated former guerilla fighters from Manchuria who fought with the Great Leader, Kim Il-Sung, turned out to be truly loyal to DPRK. In fact, Hoon was one of the officers who played a major role in uncovering and foiling the coup attempt.

"But I am the one who, with other comrades, played a major role in discovering and putting down the traitors last year! I came here in 1948, crossing the thirty-eighth parallel in the dark of the night, voluntarily, to join the KPA, even before the DPRK was founded! And I lost two toes, walking north in the freezing snow, to join my comrades in DPRK during the war. Don't these prove that I have strong attachments and loyalty to DPRK?"

"Hoon, no one is questioning your loyalty to DPRK. What they would like, though, is a personal attachment...you know, family in DPRK whom you love, to whom they know you will return, even when you may be outside of our Socialist paradise, even if you are on assignment in Japan or South Korea."

"I see..." replied Hoon, suppressing the thought. "You mean as a hostage if I do not return?"

"Hoon, the intelligence report says that you have no known living family and you have never had any known liaison with the opposite sex—that you dedicated yourself only to work and ideology. Is this true?"

"Yes, Commissar. That is true. It never occurred to me to do anything other than dedicate myself to our great Socialist cause."

Hoon thought, for a moment, of the fleeting attraction he felt to a girl in his class when he was just thirteen, but he did not even have an opportunity to strike up a conversation with her before the catastrophe of his life, his father's elopement and his exile to Kangwon Province, his mother's birthplace. It was such a long time ago—is it possible my life has been so constricted because of this trauma? To Hoon, the near sexual encounter with the sixteen-year-old female prisoner in Camp Lucky did not count as anything resembling "liaison with the opposite sex," as the commissar put it. Of course, the commissar knows about these activities—almost everyone in his unit did the same thing.

"Hoon, I would like to introduce you to a beautiful, ideologically pure, and intelligent girl I happen to know because of her father, who is a friend of mine and is a member of the politburo.

"He is a great comrade and friend of our Great Leader, having been a guerilla fighter with him in Manchuria. I happen to know that he is looking for a promising man for his daughter."

The lump in Hoon's throat melted away, but his heart still kept on pounding. What a break! Practically having a marriage proposal to the daughter of a politburo member who was a guerilla fighter with Kim Il-Sung! This would certainly put Hoon in the loyal camp of ex–guerilla fighters and erase any concerns about his South Korean origins! He realized once again what a great mentor Kim had become, just like a father he no longer had. With the warmth he felt in his heart for Kim, he also tasted bitter bile in his mouth as he thought of Suk, his biological father who had rejected him.

Arranged marriages were the norm in Korea before the Japanese occupation, as was Suk's first marriage to Min. However, during the Japanese era, more and more young people adopted the new ways of dating, falling in love, and marrying for love. In North Korea, however, the unique blend of Communism and Confucianism that was the ideology of the new regime dictated a return to the old ways of doing things, including arranged marriages, especially for the ruling elite. Thus, through this marriage, I might even be invited into the elite of North Korean society, thought Hoon. Maybe I should broaden my life a little. As he contemplated the idea of introducing a woman into his life, he felt a mixture of fear, excitement, and anticipation. He was no stranger to these emotions in his career as a soldier, but the excitement was quite different this time, a strange sensation, perhaps the stirrings of sexual arousal?

"I am greatly honored, Commissar. I would be happy to meet her."

Hoon and Myunghee met that very Sunday.

October 15, 1957

The wedding was a festive affair by North Korean standards. Unlike in South Korea, North Korean weddings take place twice, in the bride's and then in the groom's house. However, as Hoon had no relatives in Pyongyang, his boss, Kim, and his wife stood in for his parents and invited them to his house after the wedding ceremony in Myunghee's parents' house.

Myunghee's father, Comrade Park Sangjoo, had a rather large traditional-style Korean house that had survived the UN bombing during the war. There was a large enclosed garden with flowering trees, evergreens, and a koi pond, as well as a small stone bridge. To get inside the house itself, one had to take off one's shoes and climb onto a wooden floor, which led to the living quarters, including the living room and bedrooms.

The rooms had *ondol* floors, cement covered with thick, smooth, coated paper glued onto it. These floors are heated from beneath when it is cold. There were stacks of small pillow-like cushions against the wall, which one took as one entered the room and sat on. North Korean weddings are usually performed by an elder of the community or an official of the government or the party. For Hoon and Myunghee, Comrade Lee Moo-il, the director of Covert Operations, offered to preside over the ceremony, which was gratefully accepted by all concerned, including Hoon's boss and mentor, Park.

The ceremony itself was a brief affair. Myunghee, the bride, was attired in traditional Korean wedding dress consisting of a short red silk jacket and a long, flowing, high-waisted red silk skirt. The jacket had long ribbons that were tied in the front. She also wore a dainty white tiara. Hoon wore a traditional Korean court dress for males—a white silk jacket, loose white silk pants, and a blue silk overcoat. She looked beautiful and radiant, and he looked proud and confident. They made a happy, handsome couple.

There was a long low black lacquer table with mother-of-pearl designs on one side of the room, on which were two porcelain ducks facing each other and an arrangement of magnolias. The ducks represent fidelity, as they mate for life, and the magnolias are the national flower of DPRK. These highly scented yellow magnolias that brightened up the room must have been specially grown in a greenhouse, as the season had passed in frigid Pyongyang in October. There were also two ceramic sake cups and a small bottle of sake on the table.

The bride and groom were seated on the cushions on one side of the long table, and on the opposite side sat Myunghee's parents and Park and his wife, surrogate parents for Hoon.

The master of ceremonies, Director Lee, sat at one end of the table on the side of the bride and groom. On the other side of the table, behind the bride's and groom's parents, sat the guests in several rows of cushions.

Lee stood up and said, facing both the bride and groom, who also stood up, "Now the wedding ceremony for Comrade Moon Hoon and Comrade Park Myunghee will begin."

"Comrade Moon, do you take Comrade Park Myunghee as your spouse and swear to serve together, throughout your life, the Democratic People's Republic of Korea and our Great Leader, Comrade Kim Il-Sung?"

"Yes, I do," said Hoon firmly.

"Comrade Park, do you take Comrade Moon as your spouse and swear to serve together, throughout your life, the Democratic People's Republic of Korea and our Great Leader, Comrade Kim Il-Sung?"

"Yes, Comrade," responded Myunghee in a clear voice.

"I now declare that Comrade Moon and Comrade Park are man and wife. Please bow to each other."

Both Hoon and Myunghee knelt and bowed to each other in the traditional Korean style, touching the floor with their heads. As they sat up, there was a stir in the garden and a muted commotion followed by footsteps. Everyone stood up to see what was happening.

A tall man walked in through the open door. The room was hushed, and then someone said, "Our Great Leader!" and bowed in front of the tall standing man. Everyone else fell to their knees and bowed. Kim Il-Sung!

Walking toward Park, Myunghee's father, and Hoon and Myunghee, the Great Leader said, "I can stay just for a moment, but how could I miss the wedding of my good friend's daughter?"

"Why, it's such an honor that you came to my humble house!" stammered Park.

"It's my pleasure, Comrade Park."

Turning to Hoon and Myunghee, Kim said, "I know that you have done great work for DPRK, Comrade Moon. Myunghee, you have made a truly wise choice. I wish much happiness and long lives to both of you!"

"We are honored beyond belief, our Great Leader!" said Myunghee.

Hoon just kept on nodding, tongue-tied. "Yes, honored, Great Leader!"

"Here is a small gift for your happiness. Now don't let me hold up your party." Kim gave a small gift-wrapped box to Myunghee and then swiftly strode out of the room and the house and entered the black sedan parked just outside the house. There were rows of identical sedans and armed guards everywhere. They immediately sped east to Kumsusan Palace, the official residence of Kim Il-Sung.

Hoon and Myunghee re-collected themselves and poured a cup of sake each and then gave it to each other to drink. Then they passed the cup around, pouring sake, to Lee and to their relatives and other guests. Then they repaired to the enclosed garden, where a feast of *bulgogi*, *kalbi* (barbecued beef ribs), and the required noodle soup was waiting. Noodles are traditionally served in a Korean wedding because of the long length of the noodle, signifying long marriage and long life.

Myunghee's father was a rotund man who maintained the military discipline he must have acquired during his guerilla days. Behind the jovial exterior, one could feel the cold, calculating mind. His wife, who was a guerilla herself, was a handsome middle-aged woman who seemed quite comfortable with everyone. Hoon liked her because she seemed so competent and in control, compared with his own mother who was so dependent and frail. There had been no communication between them ever since he left South Korea. He made discreet inquiries and found out that his mother had taken ill and died about a year after he left for North Korea. Then, his sister Kyung left Kangwon Province and disappeared without a trace during the war. They would have been so happy if they could have been here today, thought Hoon wistfully.

The ceremony at Kang's house was a simple one, where the bride and groom again bowed to each other, and to Kang and his mother, who gave them a large chest filled with gifts. Traditionally, the bride went to the house of the groom to live with him and her in-laws, but this was modern Communist DPRK, and they both wanted to be on their own after marriage. And they were lucky enough, or by dint of her birth and his accomplishments, to get an apartment of their own in a new high-rise in a prestigious neighborhood near the Kim Il-Sung University.

The wedding night was a deliriously happy blur for Hoon, who had never had sexual intercourse with a woman before. It was Myunghee who seemed to be more knowledgeable and taught her husband how to make love, passionately and compassionately. Hoon, in happy exhaustion, felt truly grateful to fate.

Later that night, Hoon and Myunghee opened the box Kim Il-Sung had given them. In the gift box were two identical gold-chain necklaces with gold pendants shaped like ducks. On the back were identical inscriptions: "Loyalty, Love, Happiness. 10.15.1957. Kim Il-Sung."

Hoon's son, Chulgi, was born the following year. Now Hoon was a father, and he vowed to himself that he would always be present as a father, unlike Suk, who disappeared when he needed him the most.

Fortune had smiled on Hoon since his marriage to Myunghee. Hoon found that he was capable of intimacy with a woman; in fact, he wondered how he had survived without the warmth, excitement, and pleasure of sex and the feeling of contentment in simply lying with another human being without having to be on guard, as he had been accustomed to. Myunghee was all of what he had hoped she would be: a passionate lover, a trusting partner, and a fiery ideological Communist. And the visit at their wedding by Kim Il-Sung, who gradually assumed the position of the sun god of North Korea, was a decisive event in Hoon's fortune.

He was soon promoted to the rank of colonel of the KPA and, more importantly, was inducted into the elite Covert Operations

Group of the DPRK. Hoon became a specialist in lone-wolf operations—assassinations, sabotage, and abduction performed single-handedly. This suited Hoon's meticulous, brooding personality. Hoon did not enjoy working with others, especially when danger was involved, because he did not want to be responsible for the others, who were usually not as smart or careful. A little-known fact except by the really in the know was that he was responsible for the blowing up of a South Korean airliner in Bangkok and the abduction of a South Korean actress who was filming in Kenya. He had not yet, however, fulfilled his dream of infiltrating into South Korea and taking revenge on his father, Suk, and Yunhee. Not yet, but just wait!

Hoon kept his operations secret even from Myunghee, and especially Chulgi. As far as they were concerned, Dad worked for the Political Committee of the Workers' Party and had to be away for days or weeks sometimes for field-education tours and strategy planning and other full-time activities. This was not only a requirement of Covert Operations—it meant, Hoon hoped, peace of mind for his family.

Of course, Myunghee knew that Hoon was more than what he said he was and vaguely knew that he was responsible for the discovery of the plot to overthrow Kim Il-Sung, for which he was rewarded handsomely. She wondered about what happened to so many people she used to know, who disappeared suddenly never to be seen again. She wondered about her close friend in college, Kyok, who she knew was the daughter of a South Korean faction politburo member who was purged. Could I do something for her? But she knew any attempt would be in vain and that the egalitarian society she had dreamed about, in which women have an equal voice as men, was crumbling in the new order of *juche*, an ideology created by Kim Il-Sung that supposedly fused Communism with a traditionally Korean Confucian patriarchal authoritarianism. She decided to be silent for the sake of her son, Chulgi. She mourned the image of herself of the olden days, when she was accepted as an equal pal of the male comrades, with a clear voice that was heard by all.

26

THE COST OF SURVIVAL

September 1956. Camp Lucky, DPRK (Somewhere around 40 N Parallel and 127 E Longitude)
Kyok

For the first two weeks, Kwak seemed to have forgotten about Kyok. Kyok felt thankful that she was able to get out of interrogation room three in the basement alive—she knew that she could very well have been executed just like her two students, who seemed to have just disappeared that night. She had practically seduced Kwak as she was about to be tortured while tied up spread-eagle on the examination/autopsy table. After being savagely raped by him, she was led to one of the female inmate quarters—a cinder-block building with dirt floor that housed about one hundred inmates. It had hard wooden bunk beds with no mattresses or sheets. On one end of the large room was one sink and one latrine, a hole in the ground. There were two small windows with iron bars. There was one bare light bulb hanging from the high ceiling, which could be controlled only by the guards from outside. There was only one thick wooden door, which was bolted from the outside every night. Kyok later found out that the camp was surrounded by an inner 3300-volt electric fence and an outer barbed-wire fence, with traps and hidden nails between the two fences. One touch of the electric fence, and the would-be escapee would be burned to a crisp.

Kyok was naked and shivering in the autumnal night when the two male guards took her from the basement to the female quarters. Here, she was given all-purpose prison garments—a gray striped blouse, a gray striped knee-length skirt, and a pair of ill-fitting sneakers. They were not new and not well washed. She reluctantly put them on, still shivering.

"In October, you will be issued a top and a pair of slacks. You will be punished if you don't take good care of your clothes," snarled one of the guards as he threw the clothes on the dirt floor. "Your work day begins at five in the morning when the door opens from the outside. You get up and hurry to the Assembly Grounds. Any laggards will be severely punished!" barked the other guard as he cracked his whip on the closed door. Everyone was looking at Kyok, standing there naked and shivering. Fear was palpable.

Kyok woke up at 4:50 a.m. to the loud siren. Immediately, all the inmates were herded to the large clearing, which was called the Assembly Grounds. It was a gloomy dawn. In the dim light, she could see that there was a wooden platform with a flagpole on one side and a tall gallows and a pole on the other. The whipping pole, the name of which Kyok learned later, was about eight feet tall, with metal hooks at different heights. The platform was a terrifying sight.

The inmates stood at attention facing the platform. There were some three hundred inmates so far, but more were arriving every day. There were about a hundred women and about thirty children, who were separated from the men and stood on the left side. They were all dressed in the prison garb, men in gray cotton striped shirts and gray cotton striped pants, women in gray cotton striped blouses and gray striped cotton knee-length skirts. They waited about forty-five minutes at attention. There were guards with machine guns surrounding the inmates.

Suddenly, the loudspeaker blared the DPRK national anthem, and everyone saluted the flag. As the anthem ended, the guards were seen rushing to two inmates, a man toward the rear of the assembly and a woman on one side, and they cuffed their wrists behind their backs and led them to the platform. Other guards led a group of three men and two women, who were similarly cuffed in the back by the wrists, to the platform. Then, Commandant Kwak walked up the platform and addressed the inmates.

"We are greeting another day in this Camp Lucky because of the benevolence of our Great Leader, Comrade Kim Il-Sung! It is he who gives us this day, and our food and shelter, and who protects us from the American capitalist imperialists and their puppet South Korean running-dog soldiers. And we must repay our Great Leader with our undivided loyalty and sacred work.

"Today, as usual, I am ashamed to say, there are inmates who have not repented their old ways and have been disloyal or otherwise counterrevolutionary. They will be executed. And there are those who have been lax. They will be punished. We are a camp of reeducation. We will reeducate you by whatever means necessary. Those who would not be reeducated successfully shall be eliminated so that our society can be safe!"

Kwak looked at the five men and women who were on the platform. Kwak then looked at the notebook he was holding and said, "Prisoner three-oh-one-one, prisoner three-seven-oh-four, and prisoner three-eight-three-six, you are guilty of disloyalty to DPRK and our Great Leader, Comrade Kim Il-Sung, and will be hanged."

Two guards brought two handcuffed men and one woman from the group of five up the steps to the gallows and placed the nooses around their necks. Then one of the guards pushed a lever, and the plank on which the condemned prisoners stood dropped down, and the three bodies swung. The woman's skirt blew in a sudden gust of wind, exposing her pale, freshly dead thighs.

Kwak continued, "This is what happens to you if you betray your loyalty to our Great Leader, Comrade Kim Il-Sung! Now, prisoner two-three-six-one and prisoner three-seven-one-four, you have been lax in your work. Two-three-six-one, you did not carry your load of rocks from the quarry within the allotted time, and three-seven-one-four, you broke a hoe, property of the people, while working at the farm. Each of you will be flogged twenty lashes. Two-three-six-one first!"

Two guards led the trembling man, who looked like he was in his thirties, to the whipping pole and, opening the handcuffs in the back, cuffed his wrists in the front and hooked the handcuffs to one of the hooks on the pole so that his wrists were secured arm length above his head. Then they cut the man's prison shirt in the back to expose his bare back. Then, each guard took a whip that was stored in a case near the pole and started whipping the prisoner's back hard, counting each stroke in turn..."One, *two,* three, *four...*" The man tried to be silent in the beginning, but soon, he was screaming with pain, until he seemed to pass out by the count of fifteen. Blood was oozing out of the welts in his back.

When it was finished, the man seemed quite unconscious, and the guards poured a bucket of cold water on him to revive him, and then they dragged him away.

Now, the woman's turn. She seemed to be in her twenties, a petite woman who was pale and trembling with fear. She was placed on the whipping pole like the man before her, with her prison garments cut to expose her bare back. She was whimpering, "Please, forgive me...Please don't flog me...I am weak...I'll die...*Please!*" The guards began the whipping, with the same intensity as for the man.

"One."

"*Aaahhhggg!*" the woman screamed. "*Please...pleeeeese...help... stop!*"

"*Two,* three, *four...*"

With each stroke, the woman's scream seemed to become higher pitched, until it was no longer audible. By the stroke of ten, she seemed unconscious. They poured a bucket of cold water on her, and she began to stir.

"Eleven, *twelve,* thirteen..." The whipping resumed, and now she just emitted weak moaning sounds with each stroke, until she became utterly quiet again by the stroke of eighteen. They poured cold water again on her head. This time, however, she did not stir. One of the guards unhooked her handcuffs and laid her on the platform. He checked her pulse and shook his head. "She is dead." The guards unceremoniously dragged her body away.

Then the guards brought the man and a woman whom they had handcuffed as the assembly was beginning to the platform.

Kwak said into the microphone, "Now, these two inmates were seen not being attentive and not singing our anthem loudly enough during this morning's assembly. Vigilant attention and passionate love of the symbols of our state, like the anthem, are prerequisites for loyalty to our Great Leader, Kim Il-Sung. This is a first task in reeducation. Ten lashes each for them, so that they can correct their errors."

With ten lashes each, the man and the woman survived, though half-dead and bloodied. Four people, two men and two women, died during the morning assembly, which lasted about two hours. Two hours of horror for the inmates.

Then the backbreaking, hard work began. Men were marched to the quarry, where they dug up rocks by hand and carried them to a pile to be transported later by trucks. Kyok, with other female inmates, was marched to the fields to dig the ground with a primitive hoe and pull weeds out with her bare hands. The guards carried whips that looked like riding crops and used them liberally on anyone whom they deemed slow, or just for the fun of whipping women and hearing them scream in pain, because it was unclear why there were so many whippings and screams everywhere. Kyok was trying to be as efficient as she always was, rapidly pulling out the weeds with her bare hands when—*crack!*—she fell to the ground as the whip landed on her bare legs. Then, two more blows on her thighs and back. The fiery, stinging pain!

"Get up and work harder, or else you will be flogged at the whipping pole in the morning!" barked the guard with the whip. The whipping pole! Kyok clenched her teeth, pulled herself up, and started digging.

October 1956, Camp Lucky, DPRK
Kyok
It's been a month since Kyok arrived at Camp Lucky, a month of sheer hell. Kyok remembered the first night she arrived, blindfolded and handcuffed in the back, with a rope binding her to the two other prisoners, her students Yoonja and Sunmi. Poor Yoonja and Sunmi, who were executed the same night. And she herself would have died had she not seduced the commandant, Kwak, on the torture table. Kwak had brutally raped her but spared her life.

She worried about what happened to her fiancé, Joonam. Of course, she had not heard any news about anyone: Joonam, her parents, her students with whom she had been arrested. There were rumors that there was a massive purge of traitors in DPRK after a coup attempt by the Russian, Chinese, and South Korean faction members of the politburo against Kim Il-Sung in August and that there were mass executions of immediate family members of all the traitors. Joonam, being the son of a Russian-trained politburo member, must have been arrested and probably executed! The love of my life, with whom I was so happy only a month ago, gone with all the hopes and dreams of our young lives! But I will cherish our memories together, and all our dreams and hopes, foolish as they may have been—how comforting they are as memories!

And her own parents—probably murdered, too. Her father, being a South Korean–born member of the politburo, must have been active in the reform movement, and now he was branded as a traitor. Dad, oh, how I wish I had also died the first night I was brought here. Being your daughter, I am sure I was to be murdered that night. I actively sought to live, and the only cowardly way was to seduce the brute of a commandant! How I wish I let him kill me, by insulting him, resisting him. But I wanted to live to see a better egalitarian society, and I know that what is going on now is an aberration, a corruption of Socialism. Unless I live, I cannot help turn this tide of despotism, even in my small way! Yes, I must live at all costs, for now, until I can make some difference, for all that you stood for, Dad, and for all that Joonam and I stood for, stand for, for a spring of true egalitarian Socialism!

After two weeks of backbreaking work, and witnessing every morning the hangings and floggings, Kyok gave up any hope that she would escape the fate of all inmates—death by flogging or hanging—as she was sure she would collapse one of these days and be brought up to the platform in handcuffs. She also learned that there were other secret means of torture and punishment in the camp about which the inmates only whispered. They included

- Water torture: The prisoner has to stand on his or her toes in a tank filled with water to the nose for twenty-four hours.
- Hanging torture: The prisoner is stripped and hung upside down from the ceiling to be violently beaten.
- Box-room torture: The prisoner is detained in a very small solitary cell, where one can hardly sit, and not stand or lie at all, for three days or a week.
- Kneeling torture: The prisoner has to kneel down with a wooden bar inserted near his or her knee hollows to stop blood circulation. After a week the prisoner cannot walk, and many die some months later.
- Pigeon torture: The prisoner is tied to the wall with both hands at a height of about two feet and must crouch for many hours.

There were beatings every day if the inmates did not bow quickly or deeply enough before the guards and if they did not work hard enough or obey quickly enough. Inmates were also often used as martial-arts targets by the guards. The guards raped women routinely and in public. Kyok was advised by the female inmates that she should submit quickly if a guard tried to rape her, or else the guard might simply kill her with whatever was nearby, a hoe, a hammer, or as a last resort, his machine gun. She was also told that many inmates were taken away several times for "major construction projects." None of these prisoners ever returned to the camp, and it was rumored that they were secretly killed after finishing the construction work to maintain the secrecy of these projects.

Kyok also learned that there was human experimentation carried out in the camp. Inexperienced medical officers of the Korean People's Army (KPA) practiced their surgery techniques on prisoners. She heard numerous accounts of unnecessary operations and surgical experimentations killing or permanently crippling inmates. Getting sick in the camp was tantamount to offering your body for experimentation!

Nights were no better than days in the prison camp. The back-breaking work ended at 8:00 p.m., when the inmates were herded to a common dining area where they were given a cup of cornmeal that passed for supper, and then there was an hour's class instruction on Communist ideology, which was unlike any Kyok had studied previously. The class was mostly about the great deeds of the Great Leader, Kim Il-Sung, and his ideology of juche, which was a blend of nationalism, chauvinism, xenophobia, and authoritarian Confucianism, far from the egalitarian Communist ideals that Kyok cherished. Juche was imposed as a guiding principle to justify the top-down Confucian order of DPRK and its brand of Communism, which was, if anything, the opposite of the egalitarian Marxism-Leninism Kyok had studied and taught. This was followed by two-hour "self-criticism" sessions in small groups of seven or eight, during which each person had to confess in public to various shortcomings and infractions they had committed. These included having "impure thoughts," such as coveting material possessions, wishing they were not in the camp, not thanking Great Leader Kim Il-Sung when eating, and so on. No one confessed to really serious crimes, such as thoughts of escape or rebellion—they knew that anyone who did so would be immediately led away for torture and secret execution.

Almost worse than the constant beatings and fear of torture and execution was the acute and nagging hunger. Each inmate was given exactly 180 grams (6.3 ounces) of cornmeal twice a day, without any meat or vegetables. The only animal protein was secretly caught frogs, rats, or snakes, which they ate raw out of sight of the guards. Especially for the female inmates, this was hard to come by. Kyok, being of a larger and more athletic build than most Korean females, felt the hunger more acutely. She even caught a frog, killed it, tore the flesh of the limbs, and gulped it down her throat. She gagged several times but forced it down. I need the protein!

She wondered what happened to her college friend, Myunghee. As the daughter of a politburo member belonging to the guerilla faction who fought the Japanese with Kim Il-Sung, she is probably doing fine. Could she help me? But there is no way I can communicate with her from this prison, and besides, she probably does not want her friendship with a "traitor's daughter" known to others.

Kyok thought about suicide—the simplest way might be to run to the electrified fence surrounding the camp, but the idea of frying to death was abhorrent to her. The simpler way might be to say something counterrevolutionary in the earshot of a guard—but Kyok was an ardent, idealistic Communist, and she did not want to die being branded a capitalist counterrevolutionary...Could I just stop eating and drinking? Kyok wondered. Then, during the third week, things changed drastically.

Kwak entered her life again. One night, before the ideology class, she was escorted by a guard to Kwak's private quarters, a separate house connected to the main building. The house had a bedroom, an office, and a basement equipped with various torture instruments. The basement was for his own private sexual pleasure and lacked the elaborate examination/autopsy tables, hanging facilities, and trapdoors to the subbasement that the real interrogation rooms had. Instead, there was a rather comfortable double-size bed. But the basement was equipped with enough whips, lashes, ropes, handcuffs, ankle cuffs, vises, electric prods, and so on for his purposes.

With wrists handcuffed in the back, Kyok was led to the basement, where Kwak awaited. Kwak dismissed the guard and turned to Kyok. "So, I am hoping you are enjoying the hospitality of Camp Lucky! I brought you here to further your reeducation by first reorienting your brain!"

"Yes, Comrade, sir! I will cooperate fully."

Crack! Kwak slapped Kyok hard. She fell to the floor on the right side. He kicked her exposed thigh.

"Comrade, sir, what did I do wrong?"

Without any reply, Kwak walked to the wall where various instruments of torture were hanging by hooks. He pulled out a horse whip and walked back to Kyok still lying on her right side, trembling. Kwak raised the whip and cracked it hard on Kyok's buttocks and thigh, twice.

"Aaaeeeee! Pllleeease, Comrade, sir, what did I do?"

"You did not do a thing, bitch! It is who you *are* that needs fixing. You need to experience pain to cleanse your mind, which is full of impure thoughts. You have to be rid of your willful mind!"

Kyok did not know what to say or do. So, I am just to be punished to experience pain? I feel so helpless! *Crack, crack, crack!* The unbearable stinging pain, and the burning pain afterward. Kyok heard herself scream…tried to stop it but couldn't and then, with further whippings, just moaning sounds escaped her mouth.

"OK, I hope you are experiencing enough pain to start to cleanse your mind! I am the one who saved you from death, and now I have to save you from yourself. I am going to take your handcuffs off now, and I want you to take your clothes off and crawl. Got that?"

"*Yes,* Comrade, sir!" Kyok answered, sobbing. Anything to stop this whipping.

Kyok forced herself to stand up in spite of the pains all over and undressed herself completely. She could see the welts on her body and blood oozing out from the welts on parts of her body that had been exposed and were hit directly by the whip.

"Now, crawl on all fours!" ordered Kwak as he cracked the whip on her bare thighs.

Kyok fell on her knees and then started crawling on all fours. *Crack!* The whip fell on her bare bottom. "Faster, bitch! Faster!" Kyok crawled faster and faster.

"Now bark like a dog, the bitch you are!"

"Arf! Arf!" barked Kyok. I am losing all dignity, thought Kyok. I need to survive, though, and anything to stop the pain…*Crack! "Please, I am barking and crawling as fast as I can! Arf, arf!" Crack!*

"You forgot to say, Comrade, sir!" Crack!

Kyok couldn't keep up anymore; she was exhausted and hoped she would pass out, but she didn't and was still feeling pain. She crawled toward Kwak and then prostrated herself with her head down. "Comrade, sir! Please kill me. I am afraid I can't bear the pain any longer, and I am too exhausted to be able to serve you as I would like. Please kill me!"

Kyok felt her wrists picked up and then the familiar handcuffs closing on them. Now he is going to hang me, Kyok welcomed the thought. Then I'd be free. But, suddenly, she found herself turned around into a supine position. Then she saw Kwak standing in front of her, naked, with an enormous erection. He looks like a bull, thought Kyok.

"OK, now for your reward. Open your legs!" Kwak dropped down on top of Kyok and entered her violently, almost crushing her. Kyok's bruised, welted skin was afire, but so was her vagina, and she felt a degree of contentment amid shame, humiliation, anger, disgust, and guilty pleasure.

The nightly torture continued for several weeks. Pain for pain's sake, for "reeducation." Each night, Kyok would be stripped and suspended in the air by either her wrists or upside down by her ankles and whipped or tortured with electrical current. She was often ordered to crawl on all fours while being whipped with the riding crop until she became almost unconscious with pain and exhaustion. Then Kwak would rape her, from behind while she was crawling on all fours, or while suspended in air, or in a supine position with her wrists cuffed in the back. He would also have her suck his cock kneeling, with her hands cuffed in the back. When she did this, she had to swallow every drop of his semen or else!

Gradually, Kyok found herself being treated somewhat differently. For one thing, Kwak would often give her food, as a "reward" for good sexual performance. The food was presumably left for him on a tray by his attendants for his own consumption. Real food, with meat and vegetables, which she hungrily gulped down.

She was reassigned to a sewing crew that worked in a sweatshop, sewing on buttons on various uniforms or sewing various garment parts together. While arduous and tiring, this work was a piece of cake compared with the fieldwork she endured before. And there were not the frequent beatings during work, as it was impractical to whip one inmate without disrupting all six or seven women working side by side in close proximity. She was moved to a different cell in a different building, where "more reeducable" prisoners were housed. Her room was a single room on one corner, with a measure of privacy. Her cell had a portable electric heater, and her bed, which was double the size of the normal bunk beds in the camp, had a decent mattress. Here, the food in the communal dining room was a bit more generous, if not qualitatively better. She was even given a small cupboard that Kwak stocked with dry snacks. And even books! Books by Marx, and the usual propaganda, but also subversive books, like *Gone with the Wind* by Margaret Mitchell and *Lady Chatterley's Lover* by D. H. Lawrence! The latter two books were published in South Korea, and simple possession of such books in DPRK was reason enough for arrest and possible execution. She was supposed to critique them as a part of her reeducation, but Kyok knew that Kwak really wanted to provide her with some intellectual stimulation. Kyok was especially grateful that her arduous nightly classes and self-criticism sessions were now replaced by "individualized reeducation" in Kwak's basement.

I feel like a whore, thought Kyok. Being paid for sadomasochistic sex! But though I don't enjoy the pain part, I do really enjoy the sex part. My having read Kinsey with Joonam (the love of my life, where are you?) and our sexual experiments have helped me in tolerating Kwak and even making sex enjoyable for him. Memories of happier times with Joonam would enter her mind from time to time, but she suppressed them immediately because she knew she would burst out in tears or do something rash to ensure her being put to death. I wonder if Kwak is really brutal because he can't be otherwise. Could I teach him to be otherwise? Could Kwak be a closet intellectual, a sensitive, empathic person behind his gruff exterior? Kyok wondered.

Kwak

Kwak tested Kyok's limits by torturing her, but always taking care not to disfigure her because it would defeat the purpose by reducing the desirability of her body. No matter how much pain was inflicted on her, she seemed to appreciate the sex act that followed, no matter how it was done. This both excited and puzzled Kwak.

Deep down, Kwak had some serious conflicts over his sexuality. Kwak's father was a teacher in a Confucian school in Pyongyang during the Japanese occupation and instilled strict Confucian values in his three children, Kwak being the youngest. When Kwak was in the first year of college in Pyongyang, he befriended a particularly handsome man in his class. Having an intellectual bent in common, they talked about various works of literature as well as progressive ideas like Marxism. Kwak was aghast when, one day, his friend was summarily dismissed from the college because he was found to be a homosexual! And Kwak had such a yearning to be with him at all times! No, I am not a homosexual, thought Kwak. What if my father found out that I was a close friend of a homosexual? I have to prove that I am a normal virile heterosexual man!

Kwak deliberately and methodically found a college student, Yang, in a women teacher's college in Pyongyang. Yang was the daughter of a professor in the same college and was a very liberated, progressive girl, who was willing to experiment with sex when Kwak suggested they go to a hotel one night. They had wonderful foreplay, but as Kwak was about to penetrate Yang, he found his penis to become flaccid. "Sorry, Yang, I never did this before."

"It's OK, Kwak. Maybe it's my fault. But you say you never made love to a woman before? Maybe you like men!"

This remark made Kwak boil—a fuse snapped, and he saw red in front of his eyes.

"I am not a queer, you *bitch!*" Kwak screamed and then slapped Yang hard and started punching her naked body, her chest, breasts, abdomen. As she recoiled and turned her back, he kicked her butt. But then, he felt his penis become erect, enormously erect. He turned Yang around, moaning with pain, and thrust his penis into her vagina and let it explode.

"So, there, bitch!" said Kwak triumphantly and left the hotel room, with Yang in a state of almost comatose, utter exhaustion.

So, I had to run away from Pyongyang before they could arrest me. I ran and ran to the border, and to Manchuria. Of course, I was wanted by the Japanese police, who also controlled Manchuria. The only place I could find refuge would be with the guerillas! By joining the guerillas, I met Comrade Kim Il-Sung and was able to rise in the ranks because of my hard work, and now I am the king of this prison!

The guerilla years gave Kwak a measure of camaraderie and respite from sexual conflict. There was much physical contact and horseplay with men, which Kwak enjoyed, and a dearth of women, which gave Kwak the excuse not to have to prove his heterosexuality. On the occasions when they had captive women, Kwak found that he could have satisfactory sex by first tying them up and inflicting physical pain and seeing them suffer. None of them seemed to enjoy it, though. Maybe it can be enjoyable for some special people like Kyok? In many ways, in spite of being a woman, Kyok is like me, thought Kwak, an intelligent and survival-oriented person.

Eventually, Kwak wondered what it would be like to be fucked while tied up.

"Kyok, I tried to break your will by torturing you and tying you up each time we had sex. I know that your will is broken by now, but you really seem to enjoy sex. Right?"

"Yes, Comrade, sir! I no longer have a will of my own—your will is my will, and it will always be. And I always desire you, no matter what you do to me!"

"Hmm, you know what? This time I'll have you cuff me and blindfold me, and you will suck my cock. If you do it right, I may go easier on you."

Kwak enjoyed it very much. Feeling helpless for a change, while this slave made love to him, knowing, of course, that he was not really helpless, that he could kill her if she did not behave. She did behave perfectly, though. It was clear, from the beginning, that she was enjoying the kinky sex as much as he did, which made him feel more potent and powerful. Soon, the torture was gone, and Kwak usually took turns in tying her up and being tied up. When the sex was particularly enjoyable, Kwak would tell Kyok, "Now you deserve a wish—you can ask me for anything within reason, and I'll try to get it for you. What is your first wish?"

"Thank you, Comrade, sir. It's always my desire and pleasure to please you. My first wish is to do just that—can I make love to you without either of us being tied up?" It was delicious, and Kwak, for the first time in his life, had sex without any element of domination or submission. Kwak and Kyok still alternated among various sexual modes and positions, including tying and being tied up, because they provided spice and intrigue to sex. Kyok seemed especially to enjoy tit bondage—having her nipples clamped or tied with a thin rope and pulled from above. Kwak felt aroused when doing this, partially regretting that his tits were not big enough to experience it.

Kwak felt grateful that he was still single so that he did not have to find excuses for his wife and that he saved Kyok's life that day a year ago—Kyok turned out to be such a wonderful sex mate for him, who proved to him that he was really a potent heterosexual man and let him discover aspects of sex he had never imagined before. How did a schoolteacher learn these techniques?

July 1957, Camp Lucky
Kyok
Kyok found herself getting used to Camp Lucky and considered herself to be lucky to be a special prisoner of Commandant Kwak. Though she still had to endure the torture and beatings as a prelude to sex, they were now more foreplay than serious punishments, and she often inflicted some pain on Kwak as well. Like most female prisoners, Kyok had ceased having her periods when she came to Camp Lucky, but as her living conditions improved with her special status, her periods returned.

She was thus dumbfounded when she failed to have her period this month. Am I pregnant? After all, I've had sex with Kwak almost every night for the last eight months or so, without any protection! But how could I be pregnant under these conditions? As weeks passed, she felt her breasts becoming fuller, and when she missed her second period, she knew that she must be pregnant. She knew that women became pregnant in the camp, often as a result of rape by the guards, but sometimes with fellow prisoners. Some pregnant women were allowed to give birth and stay with their children in separate quarters. Their children were treated as prisoners, with no hope of escape from their destiny as lifelong prisoners. Others seemed to disappear without a trace. What determined their fate seemed to be a mystery. What would happen to me if I told Kwak I was pregnant? Would he acknowledge he was the father of the baby? Would he simply kill me and the baby before my pregnancy shows? Would he let me have an abortion?

Kyok did not know what to do. She had hoped—it seemed such a long time ago—that she would have two children with Joonam, but now, having a child was the furthest thing from her mind in her survival mode at Camp Lucky. What choices do I have now?

27

A SILENT NIGHT

Christmas Eve, 1958, Seoul, South Korea (37.5 N Parallel, 127 E Longitude)
Bo

It was a cold, windy, wintry night. Cold wind from Siberia was blowing, chilling pedestrians to the bones. The sky was gray, and there had been some flurries during the day, but, once again, a white Christmas was not going to materialize.

The decade of the fifties was coming to an end. A decade of war, poverty, misery, and political turmoil in Korea and a decade of postwar prosperity and complacency for the United States, until the Sputnik, in 1957. The launch of the first manmade satellite into earth orbit by the Soviet Union shattered the status quo understanding that the United States had absolute military and scientific supremacy in the world. There was change afoot.

I accepted an invitation to attend an all-night Christmas party at Sue's house. Neither I nor Sue had attended Oak Club for almost a year, studying for the national college entrance exams, which were now behind us, for better or for worse. It was a relief to know that I would probably get in Hyundai Premed with the score I got—I'll be informed of the acceptance or rejection in January.

All-night parties were common on Christmas Eve in Korea. Although most young Koreans were not Christians, most celebrated

Christmas Eve by holding all-night parties with friends or, if one had a serious girlfriend or boyfriend, by having a special date. A date on Christmas Eve was a serious affair, however, as it was the only night of the year when sex, for the first time, was expected and accepted between unmarried couples.

Contrary to the name, "all-night parties" really did not last all night. Everybody more or less fell asleep anywhere, on the floor, on a sofa, by about two in the morning, fully clothed. Young people slept at the party rather than going home because there was still a midnight curfew in Korea. After midnight, one was at risk of being arrested at gunpoint if one was caught on the streets. And there were no cabs, buses, or streetcars running past eleven at night, or past ten in the suburbs, where my home was located. The ostensible reason for the curfew was to prevent North Korean agents from infiltrating and spying, but the real reason was for Syngman Rhee's regime to exercise its authoritarianism and intimidate people. And my dad, as a police officer, was part of the establishment enforcing this curfew.

Korean high-school students were rather naive then. Even though the parties were for both boys and girls, there was very little sexual activity. There was, at times, some dancing, but not many Korean students knew how to dance. It was not taught in schools, and with so many exams and so on, not many really had the opportunity to learn. It was the 1950s still, when people still danced to waltzes, cha-cha-chas, and big-band jazz. Rock and roll was just being introduced to Korea, though it was already popular in America, with Elvis Presley releasing "Jailhouse Rock" in 1957.

When I arrived at Sue's house that evening, Sue warmly greeted me, "Welcome, Bo. It's really been a long time," and shook my hand. Koreans did not embrace or kiss in public then.

"Nice to see you, Sue. You look more mature since I saw you last!" said I. This was not an insult but rather a compliment, as being "more mature" meant one was more feminine or sensuous. She led me to the living room, which was adjacent to the dining room and a larger music room. There were already several boys and girls drinking soda and chatting in the room.

I greeted the others, whom I knew from the club. Three boys from the Seoul High School and one from another high school. There were three girls besides Sue, one from Seoul Girls' High (like Sue) and two from the Ewha High School. That made four girls including Sue and five boys including me. Well, perhaps I am the odd man out, I thought. I knew that Sue was dating one of the boys from Seoul High School, whose English nickname was Joe. Joe, unlike Sue, was a tall, thin man, who was surprisingly handsome, considering how unattractive Sue was (at least to me). Joe was also an athlete who played basketball. He was applying to the law school at Seoul National.

"Well, we are expecting only one more person!" Sue said. That very moment, the doorbell rang. Sue opened the door to admit a bundle of fur.

"Welcome, Sungja. Nice to see you. You look all bundled up, like a roll of cotton candy," greeted Sue. Cotton candy was what she resembled—the overcoat she was wearing was all fluffy, with fur lining the bottom in such a way that it looked like an upside-down piece of cotton candy.

"Brrr! It's cold!" said the cotton candy.

"Sungja, meet my friends. This is Joe, this is Duksoo..." Sue introduced all of us to the cotton candy, who unwrapped herself from the fluff and emerged as a very petite but fully developed attractive girl, approximately my age. Underneath the fluffy coat, she was wearing a low-cut black dress. Her black hair was of medium length that formed a sort of a circular half frame around her roundish face with a full mouth. She had full lips that seemed to form a pout as she spoke, in a cute, comic sort of way. I felt an instant attraction to this new arrival. She seemed like a feminine version of Santa Claus that appeared on Christmas Eve with a mysterious bag of promises.

We had a wonderful sit-down dinner in the dining area of the living room. A Christmas turkey and roast pork that had been cooked by Sue and one of her friends. As Koreans did not customarily celebrate Thanksgiving, turkey was still an exotic rarity and most fitting for Christmas. We also had delicious chocolate cake from the German bakery. And champagne. Unlike in Suk's time, high-school students usually did not drink, and the drinking age was twenty-one. But on special occasions such as parties, high-school students did drink beer or sparkling wine.

After dinner, we moved to the large music room and played some parlor games. There was a state-of-the-art stereo system, and Sue and Joe danced the cha-cha, and a few others joined in. I did not know how to dance and found myself watching the couples dance. On the other side of the room, on the sofa, was Sungja, also sitting alone.

"My name is Bo, in case you didn't catch it before," I said as I walked over to her. "It seems we are the only klutzy people who don't know how to dance."

"And my name is Sungja, in case you didn't catch it before," repeated Sungja, with her full lips forming a humorous smile that looked a bit like a pout. "And I know all about you, Bo. Sue told me. That she knew you from Oak Club and that you speak English like an American. She invited me to come to the club, but my English is understood only by Donald Duck!"

"Oops, Sungja. It seems all my secrets are out. Well, I am at a terrible disadvantage. I don't know anything about you!"

"Bo, with that music blaring we can't really talk. You know, there's a very nice atrium in the center of the house. Would you like to walk with me there for a while and get away from the noise? Sue's parents are in the States, and we have the house to ourselves," said Sungja.

I felt an inner excitement as I stood up. The lights were dimmed in the music room, the stereo was blaring, and everyone was now absorbed in dancing a tango, holding each other quite tight. No one paid any attention when Sungja and I slipped out of the room.

As we walked out into the corridor, I held Sungja's hand. She did not pull away.

Sue's parents' house was one of the most beautiful houses in Seoul. It was on a slope of the Pukak Mountain on the northern side of Seoul, almost completely hidden from view by trees and shrubs. The entrance to the house was unassuming, but once inside, one realized how spacious the house was. It was shaped somewhat like a horseshoe, the front door leading to one side that was occupied by the large music room, which was built to Sue's mother's exacting specifications. Sue's mother was a concert pianist, who often gave performances at the house. On the same side, there was also a smaller living room with a dining area, a bathroom, and a kitchen. The horseshoe partly enclosed, with a glass wall, a well-tended garden with flower beds, shrubs, and a water fountain. The garden connected by a glass door to an indoor atrium in the middle of the horseshoe with a glass ceiling and ventilation, in which were exotic rubber trees, flowers, and parakeets. There was also a fishpond, with many brilliant colored carps. There were tree-stump chairs and wooden benches here and there both in the atrium as well as in the garden.

Then, on the other side of the horseshoe were the more private sleeping quarters, which housed the master bedroom, a number of smaller bedrooms, bathrooms, and also a kitchenette. The music-room side of the horseshoe was thus rather isolated from the bedroom side by the atrium and the garden.

Sue's father was a textile magnate. Being an only child, she was the apple of her parents' eye. She was always able to hold parties for her friends in her house, and she and her friends had the run of the house, especially when her parents were traveling. Her parents traveled frequently, often separately as her mother had to give piano concerts all over the world and her father had to travel to his various factories in Korea as well as to his company's outlets abroad. In fact, her parents had several houses, one in Seoul, one in a resort area in Cheju Island, and a small condominium in New York. Sungja told me that Sue's parents were in New York at the moment.

We talked as we walked into the atrium. It was like being outside, except it was warmer and more beautiful. The lights were off in the atrium; the only illumination was from the skylight above, the pale light dancing in the water fountain outside in the garden, and from the pale light that shone inside the fishpond, illuminating the colorful fish as they swam.

We talked about many things. About Sungja. That she was a student at Ewha Girls' High School. She was a close friend of Sue's, although she went to a different high school. In fact, her mother, who was also a musician, a violinist, was the closest friend of Sue's mother. Sue and Sungja had played together as children, often sleeping in each other's houses. Sungja intended to become an artist, a sculptor. She also played a flute. We talked about my plans to be a doctor, a psychiatrist, to help people with emotional turmoil, to free people of their sexual repressions. We found we liked each other's company and were excited about each other's plans. In the dim light of the atrium, amid the sound of the little water fountain mixed with the sound of the stereo from the music room, I began to become more and more aware of Sungja's bodily presence, the warmth her body emanated, and I knew she felt the same about my body. We were now walking, holding each other's waist.

"Sungja, I can't believe that I have just met you. It seems like I have known you for a long time," I said, as I put pressure on my arm around her narrow waist.

"Me, too, Bo. It seems I've known you for a long time. In fact, I've heard of you for so long." She also squeezed her arm around my waist.

We turned to each other and faced each other. As our eyes met, they engulfed each other, and we felt an intense spark of lightning between our bodies. We reached out simultaneously and embraced each other. Her full lips parted, and my lips met them in a hungry gasp as I held her tight. Sungja kissed me back passionately. It was a long, hungry, breathtaking kiss. As we were kissing, we eased ourselves onto a bench nearby and, still kissing, groped around each other's clothes. I found the zipper on the back of Sungja's dress and slowly unzipped it. Still kissing, Sungja whispered, "No. Bo. Not here. Let's get into one of the bedrooms!"

"Do you know how to find one?"

"Yes, this way."

Sungja led me into the side of the horseshoe opposite the music room, where the music was still blaring and the outline of the dancers could be clearly seen from the atrium.

"This is the room where I usually stay when I am at Sue's house," said Sungja as she opened the door to one of the rooms. She turned on the light. It was a small neat bedroom with one full-size bed and a night table. Hanging on the wall opposite the bed was a reproduction of Van Gogh's painting *The Starry Night*.

"Let's turn off the light. It's more romantic." I switched off the light. The shade on the window was open, and a pale half-moon shone. I kissed Sungja again and, this time, still standing, unzipped her dress. Sungja also reached out and unbuckled my belt. I slid her dress off her to the floor and then kissed her smooth neck and shoulders as I unhooked her bra. Then I gradually moved my hands gently, rubbing her back, and then following the bra line as I pulled the bra, around her back, over her upper arms, on her smooth throat and collarbone, and down. Still under the loosened bra, my fingers caressed her firm, full breasts, and her tumescent nipples. The bra finally fell, and I cupped both of her breasts with my hands as I gently eased her down on the bed.

I kissed her erect nipples and sucked on one and then the other, first gently, then hard. Sungja drew in her breath in a gasp and then moaned softly. "Yes, Bo. Yes." I had fantasized about lovemaking before, had thought of every move I would make with a girl, but much of it came spontaneously at the sight and feel of Sungja's naked breasts, her hard nipples, and the warmth and the fragrance of her body, as though I had made love to many women before. I licked both of her firm, supple breasts and around the now-reddened nipples, and then I poured kisses on her soft belly. I then gently pulled down her panties and kissed her soft mound, the inner thighs, and her vulva. She uttered a gasp as I covered her clitoris with my mouth and gently sucked on it. It tasted a bit salty in my mouth, but a delicious, tingling, tactile sensation accompanied it on my tongue. Sungja's breathing accelerated, and her pelvis began a slow undulating motion as her moans, stifled lest others might hear, became more urgent.

"Bo, please, Bo. Please come on! Get inside me!" I pulled down my underpants and kissed her nipple, sucked on it hard, as I went on top of her. I kissed her mouth, put my tongue inside her mouth, and felt her tongue entangle mine. Sungja put her hand on my erect penis and, squeezing, guided it into her vagina. As my penis entered her well-lubricated vagina, I felt a tightness around my penis, a feeling of belonging, and a surge of joy—this was the very first time that I had ever entered a woman! But the joy was mixed with the sudden realization that I was apprehensive. To be sure, I was a little apprehensive before, about whether Sungja would accept me, whether she would let me undress her, how far she would go. But now that I was actually inside her, I realized that I was not taking any precautions. What about Sungja? Should I ask? I felt in a bind. What if she becomes pregnant? Why didn't I think of buying a condom and wearing one? Because I didn't think I would be making love to a girl tonight, at a party!

I finally stopped kissing, and, still on top of her, with my penis still inside her, I whispered in her ear, "Sungja, I love you, but I am not wearing any condom. Are you taking any precautions?"

Eyes still closed, with labored breathing, she whispered, "No. Please, Bo. Let's not worry. I love you. That's all that counts. Come! Please! Please, Bo!" She held me tight around my back, and her pelvic movements accelerated. But my penis did not respond. It was losing its erection. I did not quite understand—I did not mean, necessarily, to become flaccid. But I lost my erection, and my penis, now flaccid, slid out of her vagina.

"What's the matter, Bo?" asked Sungja in alarm.

"Nothing, Sungja. It's just that I must be more tired than I thought." I replied guiltily. "But let me continue and stimulate you, Sungja." I hastily kissed Sungja again, on her mouth and on her breasts, and, covering her abdomen with kisses, I moved my mouth down to her moist vagina and put my tongue into it. And I sucked her clitoris. Many repeated movements of the tongue, in and out of her vagina. She started moaning again softly, and soon I felt a little convulsion in her vagina on my tongue as she gave a gasping sound.

"Oh, Bo! It was wonderful!" said Sungja.

"It was wonderful for me, too," said I. I wished I meant it.

"I'm sorry you got so tired, Bo. But I really loved having you in me," said Sungja meaningfully. "I'd love to have you come in again."

It never seemed to occur to Sungja that she might have also stimulated me. On the other hand, I was in such a complex mood then that it might not have done any good. I was elated and disappointed and angry. Elated because a woman wanted me and let me make love to her. An attractive, sexy woman. Disappointed that my erection disappeared as I became distracted—when I became anxious about taking precautions. I still remembered Dr. Lee's remark some seven years ago—"Do not put your penis into the vagina of a woman unless you take precautions, unless you really want to have a baby with the woman." Well, I am really not ready to have a baby with Sungja, although I am desperately attracted to her. I was angry with myself for not having the foresight to be prepared for the eventuality that I would have sex with a woman, even though it might be in a most unlikely place, at a most unlikely time. Perhaps I should have been a Boy Scout: "Always be prepared!"

When we sneaked back into the music room, the others were still absorbed in dancing. To be sure, they were really holding each other tight and swaying to music, with the lights dimmed. In fact, some of the couples were actually kissing. French kisses!

Sungja and I stretched out on the sofa and soon fell fast asleep. It was two o'clock in the morning. Santa Claus had come and gone.

28

IN GOD I DISTRUST

January 1959, Seoul (37.5 N Parallel, 127 E Longitude)
Bo

The new year brought the news that I was accepted to the Premedical Department of Hyundai University! Not a big surprise but a big relief. The matter was settled! I was happy, but I was curiously unhappy. Was it because of Sungja? I had felt extremely attracted to her that night when I had made love to or, more precisely, almost made love to her youthful but fully mature and willing body! I blamed myself for not being prepared, not being in a position to give and take fully what we had both wanted so much. In the light of the half-moon, in that little bedroom away from the blaring music of the party, I had a perfect opportunity to consummate my first love with a beautiful and eager partner. And I had botched it. Because I was unprepared.

The cold morning light to which I had awakened on Christmas Day returned reality to me with full force. Here I was, lying on a sofa next to Sungja, still looking disheveled in her low-cut black dress. Somehow, in the sunlight, she looked paler and unhealthy, as compared with last night, when she looked so supple and full of energy. Yes, she had exuded a certain sexual energy last night that called to me like a siren in Homer's *Odyssey*. But now, she was lying in carefree abandon, still sleeping soundly, with a little saliva drooling out of one corner of her mouth. She looked lovely, nonetheless, and I kept on staring at her partially exposed breast, the curve of which was moving up and down gently with each breath. "Ah, I would enjoy this sight every morning, perhaps, if I were married to Sungja!"

The fact is, I felt seriously conflicted about Sungja. I loved her, or at least I felt I was in love with her, with her willing, yielding body, her humorous pouting mouth, and what I knew of her as a person, a budding sculptress. Art would complement my career as a physician. As a psychiatrist, I would appreciate art and, perhaps, provide her with psychological insights that might contribute to a more profound level of artistic creation. But her willingness to have sexual intercourse with me without any precautions bothered me deep down. What if she became pregnant? What if my body had not had the wisdom to make my penis flaccid at that moment, preventing my having an ejaculation? I had not known about it then, but as I learned physiology later, I became more and more profoundly impressed by what Walter Cannon called "the wisdom of the body"—the unconscious physiological reactions that protect us from potentially fatal danger.

Sungja had wanted me to come, to ejaculate in her, to do what seemed right and natural for the moment, without consideration for the consequences. I desperately wanted to do exactly that, but I was also worried, upset, and, yes, angry, too. The last thing I wanted to be was be irresponsible! Dr. Lee's warning came back vividly in my mind that very moment I might have let go: "Do not put your penis into a woman's vagina unless you take precautions, unless you really want to have a baby with the woman." I was going to become a doctor, just like Dr. Lee, just as learned, as skillful, as rational, as courageous, and as caring. Yes, Dr. Lee was a remarkable woman, living and practicing in a small backward, conservative town like Kosung that did not readily accept a woman professional. She had the courage to teach a nine-year-old boy everything about sex, factually, scientifically, using charts and models. She later taught me how to use a condom, when to use it, and why it was necessary to do so. If some of the town's conservative old guard had known about what she had taught me, and shown me, they might have tried to lynch her for "corrupting" the morals of a youth. Never realizing how important it was for youths to learn about the facts of life, to become prepared! But I had failed her in not being prepared tonight, and therefore failed myself.

At about ten in the morning, Christmas Day, everyone was finally awake. Sue made a pot of coffee and took out some pastries. All of us were so tired that we barely ate before we bid "good morning-night" to each other and went home. I did squeeze Sungja's hand as I shook hands with her.

"I'll call you."

"So will I."

We had exchanged our phone numbers the night before during a game. In fact, everyone had the phone numbers of everyone else.

But I never called. And she never called, either. In a way, I was waiting for her to call. It's possible that she was waiting for me to call, too. The fact is, I suppose, that my conflict over her continued—perhaps I could not really forget or forgive what I considered to be her rashness, or her willingness, to put both herself and me in jeopardy by having sex without precautions. Still, I am sure that if she had called, I would have been only too happy and eager to see her again, to take her into my arms again, and to kiss her full, pouting mouth, her smooth throat, her firm, full breasts, and her tumescent red nipples. Yes, this time I would make love to her properly, fully, and completely, with full protection. But she did not call, and I did not call.

Weeks passed, and my thoughts of Sungja took on a different dimension. I now masturbated thinking of Sungja (a step down into reality from Liz Taylor), visualizing her naked, in various poses and situations, with various parts of her anatomy, some from memory, some from imagination, becoming vivid focal points of my erotic fantasies. She lived very vividly in my fantasies.

In reality, however, the thoughts of her as a real person, flesh and blood, diminished with each passing week. I no longer thought about calling her. I doubt that I would even have agreed to date her if she had called me by that point. She had now become a vivid living person in my fantasy land. Her existence in real life was an unnecessary duplication.

March 2, 1959, Seoul
My first day as a college student began with a ceremony in the amphitheater of Hyundai University. As a college student, I was now considered to be a full-fledged adult, even though I was still only seventeen going on eighteen. I could now drink or smoke, if I wanted to. I could even go to a brothel!

Hyundai University, being a school run by American missionaries, always included a prayer in the beginning of any ceremony. So, the university chaplain droned on, "In God we trust the destiny of our country, and of our youths…their future, their success…"

I felt conflicted about going to a Christian university, although I decided on doing it for the benefit of being prepared for postgraduate education in America. I was still an atheist, although by now I had become more tolerant or, perhaps, more mellow, an atheist bordering on being an agnostic. Nevertheless, it irked me to hear grown people praying for some supernatural salvation rather than attempting to shape their own destiny with their own efforts!

Only three graduates of the Seoul High School were in the entering class of seventy premedical students at Hyundai University. This was in contrast to the much larger entering class of Seoul National University, at least 30 percent of whom were from my high school. In addition to me, there was Philmo Kim, a really brainy guy whom I remember as the first name on the list posted on the wall on that dark April day some six years ago, when I failed to find my name on the same list—the list of the entering class of Seoul

Middle School. And then there was Chulsoo Paik, a handsome guy whom I didn't know very well during high school. He tended to hang out with the wealthier, happy-go-lucky playboy types during high school. Then, Kwangsoo Park, a rather bright but lightweight sort of fellow who had rather prominent ears and whose nickname, consequently, was "Rabbit."

From the beginning, almost by necessity, we stuck together. We shared a sense of paranoia of the elite. We felt somehow that we were different from the others who came from lesser schools and that, unless we stuck together, we might somehow be persecuted. Philmo was very short but perhaps the most mature of us all. He also tended to be a wise, mediating influence. Rabbit was usually full of jokes and introduced a certain lightheartedness to the ensemble. Chulsoo was the entrepreneur, supplier, and black marketeer of the gang, always providing us with cigarettes, liquor, candies, and other consumables. His father owned a big department store in Seoul, and Chulsoo was happy to keep his friends happy with material things.

The rest of the class consisted of a mixed bag. The majority were quite decent students from reasonably first-class schools. Then, there were some students from high schools in the provinces, such as Pusan. Some of them were quite bright but lacked the sophistication of Seoul natives.

Then there were some students whom I can only describe as ruffians. From unknown, rough-sounding high schools. There were some women students, too. Seven, to be sure. Just 10 percent of the entering class. Two from Seoul Girls' High School, two from Ewha, and one each from three separate girls' high schools. By and large, the women students were rather shy and tended to blend with the crowd. There were, however, two coeds who caught my eye from the beginning, a rather heavy girl by the name of Soonil Kang, from Seoul Girls, who was obviously very bright and very self-assured and tended to assume the role of the spokesperson for the women students, and Kaehee Chung, whose English nickname was Katie, from Ewha Girls' School, who was slender but buxom, vivacious, sharp-tongued, and quite competitive.

It was obvious from the beginning that the university was influenced strongly by Americans. There were several American professors, and quite a few American missionaries were on the board of trustees. The university received millions of dollars from the United Methodist Mission. In fact, as my cousin Soonkil said, most of the textbooks we used were in English.

The university was on the fringe of the city of Seoul, in a wooded area on the slopes of a mountain that formed the western edge of town. Most of the buildings on campus were neo-Gothic in style, and provided a truly collegiate atmosphere. The Premedical Department was housed in a neo-Gothic building of the main campus. The medical school proper was at the south end of Seoul, attached to the Providence Hospital.

The premedical curriculum was a concentrated form of liberal-arts education plus science, all to be completed in two years. In the United States, with some exceptions like Brown and Dartmouth Universities, which have two-year premed programs, one usually has to finish four years of regular college, making sure that one takes the required prerequisite courses for admission to medical school, such as biology, comparative anatomy, and chemistry, to be eligible to apply to a medical school. In Korea, however, all the premedical education was cramped into two years, presumably to save time. I enjoyed the premedical curriculum, especially the liberal-arts courses that included philosophy, history of civilization, English, and Korean literature. Being a missionary school, there was also a course on religion, which I did and did not enjoy.

The religion course was run in a seminar format and consisted mostly of discussions of articles written by religious philosophers, such as Buber and Kierkegaard. There were also discussions of passages from the Bible and how one might interpret them. In these discussions, I made it clear from the outset that I was not a Christian and that I considered religion to be superstition and, at best, a crutch that the weak feel they need. I felt that religion was the single biggest obstacle to human progress throughout history. My position naturally generated much heated discussion, especially with devoutly religious students who had come to Hyundai because it was a religious school.

The professor, Dr. Min, was an enlightened but religious man, who was a fan of Kierkegaard. While he did not push religion in an authoritarian sort of way, he seemed to be pained when I was at my fiercest in pointing out the contradictions in the Bible and the crimes of organized religion throughout history. I also discovered that I enjoyed these heated discussions; they were somewhat like a wrestling match. After such a discussion, I felt rather exhausted but also invigorated. It was fun!

Philmo, forever the arbiter, would point out that Confucianism was a religion, too, but that it contributed to Korea's authoritarianism and stagnation while Christianity brought in new ideas of equality and progress. On the other hand, Philmo continued, Confucianism did contribute to Koreans' valuing of education and social order. Hard to argue with that!

I discovered, also, that I really got to like those with whom I had had a heated discussion—for example, Bob Lee. Bob's Korean name was Roh-bu, which sounds like his baptized name, Robert. He was a devout Christian, but he also liked to discuss religion in a rational manner, rather than just emphasizing faith as some others did, who I felt were too dumb to be able to make an intelligent argument. Bob argued for the need for a superordinate order and that a deity was necessary to symbolize such an order. While our discussions were heated at times, and at times we seemed to be at complete loggerheads with each other, I found myself also being at least partially influenced by his point of view. But I held strongly that human beings were better off trusting their own abilities in shaping the future, rather than relying on, or trusting, a bearded old man somewhere up in the sky who would influence all matters capriciously.

Bob had gone to a second-round high school—that is, he had failed his entrance exam to the Seoul Middle School and had gone to his first choice among the second-round high schools. Thus, he had the experience of having failed an entrance exam at a young age, which was an experience I had almost shared with him and with which I empathized. Bob was the most honestly sincere person I had ever met. I had met many hypocritically sincere people, mostly "devout" Christians, whose sincerity, I felt, was shallower than their skins but worn like a badge. Not so with Bob. He did not even come across, at times, as being particularly sincere or pious. But deep down, I knew that he really cared about people and about human suffering. Bob was now accepted as a full-fledged member of our elite little clique of Seoul boys.

29

THE WHITE DEER DAYS

Spring 1959–Winter 1960, Seoul (37.5 N Parallel, 127 E Longitude)
Bo

"White Deer" was the name of the tearoom that my friends and I frequented. The "four musketeers," as we were called by others. Philmo, Bob, Rabbit, and myself. The premedical students from Hyundai University. We were always together, discussing, arguing, studying, chatting, always talking. We were together at school, and we were together outside of school.

On many evenings and weekends, we spent hours in that little tearoom in Myungdong, the entertainment district of Seoul. Tearooms, abundant in most cities, were the meeting places for young people. Tearooms provided coffee, tea, and other nonalcoholic beverages. You could stay there for hours and listen to excellent stereo music. As long as you drank at least one cup of coffee or tea every two hours or so, they did not mind how long you stayed.

Many young people had made tearooms their second homes, practically living there, reading, writing, and meeting friends. Each youngster had his or her favorite tearoom. Ours was the White Deer. We liked the tearoom because it was rather spacious and there were nice nooks formed by potted plants and fish tanks.

There was a particularly secluded nook in a corner that was our favorite. We spent hours and hours there, discussing philosophy, religion, politics, and metaphysics, sprinkled with gossip and small talk. Eventually, we were rather well-known to the waitresses at the tearoom. We could even use the tearoom as a message center. One has to remember that this was long before the days of cell phones and the Internet. There were only wired telephones found at home and in offices, and they afforded little privacy. Telephone answering machines had not been invented yet. Since the owner of the tearoom knew us, we could phone her and ask her to take messages for the other members of the gang that would certainly be there later. In this fashion, we were able to leave messages for each other. Rabbit often used the message system for his private affairs. For example, his girlfriend might leave a message with the owner concerning their next date. Because of my interest in mysteries, we had developed a code language for messages as well. For example, I might leave a message to Philmo saying, "The egg is unfertilized," which might mean that I was not going to be able to make it—that is, waiting would be futile.

Among the four musketeers, Philmo and I had a special relationship. I had always admired Philmo from the first day of Seoul Middle School. He was the first in rank among the entering class, and he remained the top student throughout high school. It was commonly accepted that Philmo was a genius, and his surprising decision to enter Hyundai University gave credence to the notion that Hyundai was as prestigious as Seoul National.

In high school, Philmo and I had not been close. Although we knew each other (both of us were rather prominent students, Philmo as the all-around genius and I as the uneven genius in English and chemistry), we had little occasion to speak to each other. In fact, I did not have any close friends in high school, except for close working relationships in Oak Club. When my high-school days were coming to a close, I had wished that I had made some close friends. During the final months of high school, I deliberately decided to develop a friendship with Yulak Ahn, a student who was applying to the premedical course at Seoul National. I had admired Yulak for a reason a bit different from why I admired Philmo.

In addition to being bright, and being especially good in English and a frequent competitor of mine in that regard, Yulak was particularly well versed in fine arts. He was able to discuss works of art with authority and seemed to have a real appreciation for the nuances of modern art. Art was something to which I had not been exposed to any extent. My parents simply did not seem to know anything about, much less appreciate, art. I had been almost completely oblivious to the existence of fine art until, one day, the high-school class went to an exhibition of modern art at the National Museum. Yulak happened to be walking with me, and I asked him if he liked what we saw. He explained to me why he liked one painting more than another and showed me how one might interpret the artist's intentions by the way he had painted the canvas. I was enchanted. I began to see that the paintings had messages, and I realized that I wanted to know more about fine art. Around that time, I saw the movie *Moulin Rouge.* A great sentimental movie about the French artist Toulouse-Lautrec, who was a midget. My interest in art grew.

After the event at the National Museum, I realized that I had been very deficient in culture in general, not just fine art and painting. Especially in music. Up to that point, the only music that I had been interested in was jazz and the newly introduced rock and roll from the American Eighth Army radio. My parents did listen to the government radio station that had mostly popular music, but they did not seem to show any enthusiasm for music. They never took me to concerts or operas. I still wonder why. My parents were well-educated people who used to love music. In fact, they had met each other while singing Handel's *Messiah* together. What had made them lose that common interest, that spice of life?

I was determined to catch up in this area of deficiency. After all, I had now overcome my deficiencies in math and was, in fact, rather good at advanced math.

I decided to make friends with Yulak and adopt him as a sort of a mentor in cultural education. That he was going to be a doctor like me gave me an excuse to approach him and to make conversation with him. I told him that I wanted to be a friend of his, that I wanted to maintain contact with him even after graduation, as our careers would be related, and that I wanted to see what the premedical students at Seoul National were learning and compare it with what I was learning. Yulak was very pleased with my approach to him, and he welcomed me into his circle of friends. A cultured bunch of people!

Yulak was the youngest of four children. His father was a professor of French at Ewha Women's University. Yulak's eldest brother was a certified genius, a nuclear engineer, studying in the United States. I visited Yulak at his house a number of times during high school and after graduation. We talked about art, literature, and philosophy, as well as about what we were learning in our respective premedical schools. Whenever I visited his house, I was impressed by two things—the number of books and artistic artifacts that his father had around the house and also how everyone was subdued when his father was at home. He demanded absolute peace and quietude around the house—Yulak's father seemed to carry an authority that I was quite unaccustomed to in my own home. My dad was always down-to-earth and unassuming—he was like a friend rather than an authoritarian ruler.

Eventually, I invited Yulak to join the four musketeers at White Deer. It made so much sense for all of us to get together, talk philosophy like we liked to do, and enjoy our college life together. Yulak also made unique contributions to our discussion through his cultural perspectives and by injecting into it his expertise in fine art and literature.

Ah, these halcyon, White Deer days! They were some of the happiest, most fulfilling days and nights of my life. I felt at ease with my friends, and I truly enjoyed their company and the intellectual and artistic stimulation that I obtained from them.

30

LUCKY AGAIN

September 1957. Basement in Commandant's House, Camp Lucky, DPRK (Somewhere around 40 N Parallel and 127 E Longitude)
Kyok, Kwak

Kwak is standing naked, with his hands handcuffed behind him. His eyes are blindfolded. Kyok, who is also naked, is kneeling before him and sucking his erect penis vigorously. With a loud groan, Kwak ejaculates a copious amount of semen, which Kyok swallows eagerly. "That was good, Kyok!"

Kyok opens the handcuffs with a key, and Kwak removes his blindfold. Kwak holds Kyok in his arms, almost crushing her. "Do you know that you are the best sex performer in the world? As a reward, I'll give you another wish!"

Of course, at first Kyok was just a prisoner whose sole purpose was to satisfy Kwak's every whim, which tended to be mostly raping her in various poses, usually hog-tied. In the beginning, Kwak tried to make Kyok into a helpless slave by abusing her mercilessly. He would have her suspended naked, with her raised arms tied up, and whip her with a horse whip until she begged him to kill her—he would then untie her and have her crawl on all fours while he whipped her until she lay prostrate in front of him. Then he would fuck her from the rear or turn her around and enter her from the front. Almost unconscious, Kyok would still make appreciative noises when he touched her or entered her—was she really enjoying her torment?

"Comrade, sir, do you realize today is the anniversary of our first meeting last year?"

"No, I didn't realize that, but you are right; it was last September that you came here, brought by Captain Kilin and Lieutenant Hoon. "

"Yes, Comrade, sir. And I was so scared to be in that interrogation room. But that's where we had our first lovemaking. As my wish, could we revisit the room? And maybe reenact the lovemaking? Perhaps this time you could torture me a little, like what happened to my poor students."

Kwak felt excitement building in his body—yes, the special interrogation room, where they had sex the first time after he threatened to torture her to get her to confess to being a member of a capitalist cell and to extract names of people who had to be eliminated. He was surprised that Kyok told him exactly the names even before the torture began, including those of her students Yoonja and Sunmi, and seemed so aroused sexually that he proceeded to rape her immediately, if this could be called rape—she seemed so eager and willing. And she seemed to enjoy the rough sex, the rape, at his hands. Almost like a wedding night! And now, she is even begging to be tortured! Well, I'll show her.

Special Interrogation Room Three, Basement, Camp Lucky
Kyok is lying spread-eagle, with eyes closed, on the steel examining/autopsy table with both wrists and ankles cuffed to the four posts. She is moaning softly as Kwak places on the metal nipple clamps with wires. Kwak then pushes the metal vaginal probe with the thick plastic handle with a dial into her lubricated vagina. Kyok lets out a small scream as the cold metal enters her. Kwak clicks the male plugs of the wires from the probe handle into the female sockets of the nipple clamps.

Kyok is now breathing rapidly, with her face flushed. "Are you sure you want this?" Kwak asks, feeling rather confused. The bitch should be petrified, not excited.

"Yes, Comrade, sir. I want to experience what Yoonja and Sunmi experienced, which you spared me out of your kindness."

"OK, then. Here it goes..." Kwak starts turning up the dial on the handle of the probe halfway.

"Aaaaghhhh! Aaayyyeee! Please stop, pleeeese! I'll do anything, anything, aaaaagh!" Kyok screams as she almost convulses, with her pelvis and body twisting against the metal restraints.

Kwak immediately turns down the dial and turns it off. "See how this will make anybody tell all they know?"

"Yes, Comrade, sir! And I know how lucky I am to serve you. Please fuck me like the first time."

Kwak drops his pants and enters her, fully aroused by her pleading, flushed body. He ejaculates almost immediately.

"Thank you, Comrade, sir. And now, I'll do oral sex the way you like, with you cuffed and blindfolded." Kwak is able to ejaculate two or three times during an encounter, and he particularly enjoys having oral sex this way.

"But before I do that, could you show me how Yoonja and Sunmi died? Were they executed in this type of room?"

"Yes, but a double room, interrogation room two. But here, you see these two nooses?" Kwak pulls one of the nooses hanging from the ceiling and puts it around Kyok's neck.

"You stand here on this trapdoor, and I go there and push that button, and then the trapdoor drops and you are no more. They will remove the body later and bury it without any mark. That's the way they died, and you would have, too, if I hadn't spared you." Kwak removes the noose and puts it around his own neck.

"OK, now you can cuff me and blindfold me and suck my cock."

Kyok puts the handcuffs on Kwak's wrists behind his back and puts a blindfold around his eyes.

"I know what you are thinking—you are debating whether you should press the button while I am tied up like this. But you see, there is no way you can escape because this building is heavily guarded, and the camp has an electrified fence. Once you are caught, you will be tortured a thousand times more painfully than what you experienced just a moment ago, and then you will be executed in the most painful way possible, such as being burned alive. We have all these facilities here. With me alive, you are enjoying special status here, well worth your services to me."

"Comrade, sir, I am truly grateful to you, and I truly enjoy making love to you." Kyok kneels before Kwak, puts his penis in her mouth, and sucks first gently and then vigorously as it gains tumescence. Making soft moaning sounds, Kyok expertly brings Kwak to orgasm.

Kwak says breathlessly, "That was good, Kyok. Now I'll give you another wish."

"Thank you, Comrade, sir. It was my pleasure. Here is my wish—that you would think of me lovingly as you die—I'll think of you lovingly as I die, too. You see, I love you, but I cannot let you or me live, knowing what you and your prison have done to my students, Yoonja and Sunmi, and to my parents and are doing every day to hundreds and thousands of innocent people here and in other prisons.

"And I cannot, in good conscience, bring another life to this earth. Yes, dear Kwak, let me call you this, because I am pregnant, and you and I would have had a child, but he or she will never be."

Without waiting, she runs toward the wall with the trapdoor switch and pushes the button. The door drops down with a thud, and Kwak disappears into the darkness, with the rope straightening taut.

Kyok then puts the other noose around her neck and jumps into the same hole into which Kwak disappeared. In her mind are the vivid images of the prison life, the hard toil in the quarries for men, in the fields and sweatshops for women, daily public hangings for the smallest infractions, the public floggings of innocent men, women, and children at the whipping pole, and the starvation and disease, all of which she had witnessed but escaped under Kwak's protection and for which she felt as responsible. As she is dropping down with the noose on her neck, she has fleeting images of the days before her arrest, the smiling faces of her students, her colleagues, her parents, her loving parents, her fiancé, Joonam, the passionate love they used to make, herself once so idealistic and full of hope, and Kwak, her love and hate rolled into one, and that of a baby, forever unknowable. We exit life together through the same door...

31

BO ERECTUS

October 1959, Seoul, South Korea (37.5 N Parallel, 127 E Longitude)
Bo

The White Deer Tearoom was in a section of Myungdong that bordered on the red-light district. Although prostitution was still nominally illegal, there was a large red-light district in Seoul as in any other large city. After leaving the tearoom around eight or nine in the evening to head home, Bo sometimes took a walk through the streets of the red-light district out of curiosity.

The district had two distinct parts. The lower part of the district had its streets lined with streetwalkers in various states of undress. The girls would directly negotiate a price with their customers and lead them to one of several run-down hotels nearby. The upper part, nearer the famous Myungdong Cathedral, a Norman Gothic edifice, consisted of a number of relatively middle-class houses. There, the girls would wait inside the houses, and an older woman or man would stand in front of the house, telling passersby of the availability of "nice, clean girls inside."

Bo felt a certain thrill as he took walks through both parts of the red-light district. He was at times tempted to talk with one of the attractive-looking girls on the street and follow her, or to explore what "nice, clean girl" was inside one of the houses. But he did not have the courage—he was too afraid of the possibility of contacting a venereal disease through such contact.

Bo was content at school, he was enjoying his liberal-arts education very much, and he felt very happy with his circle of friends. Except for the lack of a girlfriend.

Since the Christmas Eve of the previous year, Bo had not made any attempts to make any girlfriends. His fantasized ongoing relationship with Sungja, who by now bore no resemblance to the flesh-and-blood Sungja, was sufficient to maintain his sexual appetite at a masturbatory nirvana. But with the air turning crisp, and the leaves changing colors into the symphony of autumn, Bo began to feel the need for another kind of companionship, one based on flesh and blood, one that complemented the purely intellectual companionship of his White Deer friends. Above all, he felt a need for physical intimacy. As his masturbatory fantasies became more and more vivid, he somehow felt the need to translate the fantasy into reality, to have sexual intimacy with a real person. One autumnal evening as he passed through the red-light district, Bo decided that he would make use of their services.

Utilizing the services of a prostitute was not an uncommon thing for college students, then or now. Many of Bo's classmates talked about the red-light district and about some of the girls they had known. Some talked about how they learned to make love better by learning the techniques from a prostitute. Although this was before the days of AIDS, Bo felt quite uncomfortable about the thought of having sex with a prostitute mainly because of the danger of venereal disease. But, now, he was determined to have sex with one to prove his manhood and to release himself inside an accepting woman (no matter that money rather than love caused that acceptance), fully and without fear of irresponsibility. Yes, he would use a condom, to protect himself as well as, possibly, the girl. But he would complete the sex act!

Bo had bought a box of condoms long before tonight. Even though there were many vendors of condoms and candies on the streets of Myungdong, Bo bought the box of condoms, "Silvertex," in a reputable pharmacy. Even the act of buying a box of condoms took some courage. But he bought it with aplomb. And he had two condoms in his pocket, in their airtight tinfoil.

10:30 p.m., Saturday night.

He had been at the White Deer Tearoom, talking with his friends. He did not give any hint of what he was about to do after they broke up their meeting. He had told his parents that he was going to an all-night party and not to expect him till next morning. He first walked through the lower side of the red-light district, slowly, paying some attention to the girls on the street.

"How about spending some time with me, young man?" said a rather plump girl, who had garish makeup on her face. She wore a skirt that was too short to conceal her plump, fat thighs. Like a naked pig, thought Bo.

"Come and play with me, handsome," said another. She was slender, tall, and had shapely legs. But when she approached Bo, he felt a sudden revulsion as he saw her eyes, eyes that seemed hollow and without life, like those of a vampire. Bo shuddered and walked on. I am becoming too picky, he thought. Perhaps I shouldn't pay any attention to how she looks; after all, all I want is sex with a woman, to prove that I can do it in real life!

He walked to the upper part of the section and followed one of the male pimps who advertised "nice, clean girls inside."

Bo was led into a small dim cubicle inside the middle-class-looking house. The inside of the house had been remodeled to accommodate a number of small cubicles, each with a small mattress and a bedside table. On the mattress sat a girl about Bo's age, wearing nothing but a black slip. She looked young, bored, and tired. Bo felt embarrassed as he walked into the cubicle.

"Hello there," said the girl. Her face was round, and her make-up was smudged. She gestured to Bo to sit next to her, in a careless, abandoned manner. Bo sat down. He did not know what to say or what to do.

He stammered, "Hi, I am Hoyoung, a graduate student. I am doing some research on the sexual habits of Korean young men. I thought, perhaps, you could help."

The girl looked at Bo tiredly and said, "OK. Ask me questions." It was obvious to anyone but Bo that she knew Bo was lying but that she thought it best to humor him.

"Er, tell me about yourself. How you came into this business," said Bo.

"Young man, that's none of your business. Either you ask me objective questions or you do what you are supposed to do and get fucked!" she said icily.

Bo found himself becoming angry and aroused at the same time.

"OK, if that's how you feel about it," spat Bo, as he put his arms around her bare back.

He tried to hold her and kiss her on her lips, but she pushed him away, saying, "No. You don't kiss me. That's not part of the deal."

Bo was taken aback but then remembered what he had heard from a braggart of a classmate, who had said that the whores would let you fuck them but wouldn't let you kiss them. I have to learn not to take this personally, thought Bo.

"OK, then take your things off!" said Bo. She complied by pulling her slip over her head. For a young girl, her breasts were pendulant, She had a rather full stomach, and her pubic hair was curly. Overall, a rather sexy but vulgar sight, thought Bo.

"Well, big boy, I am ready! How about you?" said the girl, in a false, coquettish voice. She gestured to Bo's pants. Bo hastily took off his jacket, his shirt, his pants, and then his underpants. Then, he suddenly remembered that he had a pair of condoms in his jacket pocket. He fished around it until he found the tinfoil, took the condom out, and then showed it to the girl. "Gee, you are prepared, Boy Scout!" said the naked girl.

Bo took a condom out and tried to put in on his penis. But his penis was only half-erect. It would be futile to put it on a less than fully erect penis. Bo felt embarrassed and then angry. He suddenly grabbed the girl and kissed her on her breast and then her nipple and sucked it harshly, savagely. She made a yelping sound, tried to push him away, but Bo became more savage in sucking her nipple. He practically covered her mouth with his hand. She stopped struggling and just lay still. Bo felt his penis harden, put on the condom, and tried to insert his penis into her vagina. But the vagina was not lubricated. It was dry. The penis felt resistance, and as Bo moved his penis up and down to attempt penetration, he found himself suddenly ejaculating, on the girl's vulva but outside of the vagina. The condom was filling up with semen. Bo felt exhausted. He just pulled off the condom, threw it into the garbage, wiped his penis with tissue, and put on his underpants.

The girl just rolled back on the mattress and was fast asleep. Bo lay next to her, feeling confused, sore, realizing that he had been extremely tense. Soon, he was fast asleep, his hand lying on her naked belly.

At the crack of dawn, Bo awoke at the sound of the crowing of a distant cock. The girl was sound asleep next to him. He looked at her young, peaceful, over-made-up face, her breasts, her abdomen, a little too fat, and her smooth thighs and legs. How many men have fucked you? And you seem to know men very well. But have you loved any? Bo thought not and felt a wave of sadness sweep through him. And I have not really loved any woman yet. I have had sex, or near sex, with two women, but I have not really loved any yet. And I have not yet had complete sex. Yes, perhaps I should wait. Until love and sex should meet. Inevitably, they must! Bo quietly put on his clothes and left. He had already paid the pimp for the services the previous night, before he even set his feet in that cubicle.

1973, New Haven, Connecticut (41 N Parallel, 73 W Longitude)
Psychoanalytic couch.
Bo

"Ja, Das ist good," said Dr. Lowmann. "Continue..."

"Well, I could not dissociate my physiology from my brain I suppose...hmmm, it's funny...the first two times I came near having real sex with a woman, I had suddenly lost my erection, or I ejaculated prematurely...my physiology failing...or was it actually succeeding...?"

"Ja, you really vanted to have sex?"

"I am not sure...with Sungja, I really did, but I was fearful that I would impregnate her...and I was mad that she didn't think of it... that's how some people really get tied down!"

"But you say you thought of the woman doctor..."

"Yes, Dr. Lee. She had impressed upon me the importance of being prepared and being responsible...do you think, perhaps, she was so emphatic because she herself had an experience? Could it explain why she was in Kosung, a backward town?"

"Please, elaborate..." murmured Dr. Lowmann.

"I mean, maybe she'd become pregnant by a man at the wrong time. Maybe she moved to Kosung with him...and then, maybe it didn't work out...I don't know...but I didn't want to fail Dr. Lee... she gave me knowledge and wisdom and perhaps even taught my brain to think for me, even when I was not thinking...Cannon's wisdom of the body..."

"And Dr. Lee must be the goddess Athena!"

"Funny you should say that! Athena is my favorite deity. She was not born of a woman but was born out of Zeus's head...hmmm... do I have a conflict about sex, Dr. Lowmann? I prefer aseptic birth, nonanimal procreation..."

"And I recall you witnessed the live birth of your sister," added Dr. Lowmann.

"True. I have seldom...no, that's not true...I remember, yet I don't... but it was yucky to see Claire coming out between urine and feces"

"Ja, and blood!" thundered Dr. Lowmann.

"Yes, blood. Do you think that has something to do with my initial hesitation about medical school for fear of blood? Yes, I wanted to be like Dr. Lee, but then I didn't want to deal with blood, unlike Dr. Lee. And I like nonliving things, sculptures, pyramids, rocks, works of art, but not the animals, pets, and so on that my Dad liked. In that sense, I'm more like my mom!"

"But she gave birth to your sister…"

"Yes, maybe I wish she hadn't. Instead, she could have sculpted a nice statue of a girl…ha-ha, my Pygmalion complex again, *ja, Docktor?*"

"Maybe you wished you could have given birth yourself?"

"Yes, maybe I wanted to go through it myself. Or maybe give birth to a sculpture, or a novel!"

Sunday, February 28, 1960, Seoul, South Korea (37.5 N Parallel, 127 E Longitude)
Bo

The national elections were coming up in three weeks. The election in Korea then was really two elections—one for president and the other for vice president, so that they could come from opposing parties. Mr. Cho Pyong-Ok, the opposition Democratic Party's candidate for president, had died of stomach cancer one month before the election, while receiving treatment in Hawaii. While this news put a damper on the enthusiasm of the populace that the authoritarian regime of Syngman Rhee and his Liberal Party would finally be turned out of office, there was every indication that the vice presidential candidate of the opposition party, Chang Myun, would be elected by a landslide and would eventually inherit the presidency from Rhee, who was becoming senile at age eighty-five. But the ruling Liberal Party's vice-presidential candidate, Lee Ki

Bung, was obviously attempting to rig the elections so that he would be elected. There was tension in the air.

A major event occurred in Dad's career at this point. Dad found himself increasingly pressured to do more and more political dirty work for the ruling party. He was asked to pressure restaurants to eavesdrop on parties attended by the opposition party members. He was asked to harass businesses that gave contributions to the opposition party. He was ordered to prepare duplicate ballot boxes and stuff one of them with precast ballots in favor of the Rhee regime and to switch them at the end of the election day, when the ballot boxes would be in police custody being transported to the central ballot-counting office. And he was ordered to stand by, armed, in preparation for the anticipated riots after the March presidential election. Dad shared all this information with me two weeks before and said, "I have done many things that weigh on my conscience. I have done many things that I thought I would never do. But everything I did I did for my family. And I've never actually hurt anyone, no matter what I did. Even when I was fighting the guerrillas during the war, I never really shot at any human being. Yes, I have taken bribes, and I've bent the law to benefit the ruling party. But now they are ordering me to kill, both symbolically and literally. They are ordering me to kill whatever feeble hope for democracy remains in this country by blatantly switching ballot boxes, and they are ordering me to shoot at demonstrators, who will probably be young men and women, like my own children.

"I have thought about this for a while, ever since the secret orders came down about a month ago. I decided that I have to draw the line somewhere, if I am to maintain any self-respect at all. I shall resign from the police, with two weeks' notice, unless, Bo, you feel strongly that I should do otherwise."

I was extremely happy to hear of Dad's decision to resign from the police. Ever since I became a teenager, I had felt ashamed of my father's job, not so much because of what he actually did but because of the stigma attached to being a policeman, the handmaiden and enforcer of the corrupt dictatorial regime. In fact, I told few of my friends about what my father did. When asked, I would simply say, "My dad's in business." While I was happy about his decision, especially at this politically tense time, I was also a bit worried about money. If he quit his job, how would I be able to pay my tuition? Unlike the Seoul National University, which had only a nominal tuition, Hyundai was a private university whose tuition was considerable. Although I was now tutoring a high-school student twice a week, the money I earned would surely be insufficient for Hyundai's tuition.

I said, "You know, Dad, that I'll be very happy when you are no longer a policeman. You know how I feel about the police and what they have been doing politically. I know, Dad, that you've not been involved in them, I mean the brutal suppression of political opponents, and now the election fraud, at least not willingly. But I've always felt upset that others can't tell the difference between you and the thugs who wear the same uniform. Yes, Dad, you have my full support. And if we need to, I'll take a leave of absence from college and work full-time to make a living for all of us!"

"I appreciate very much what you say, Bo. I don't think that will be necessary, not yet, anyway. I've spoken with one of my ex-pupils, Sungwoo Kang, who is in the advertising business. He invited me to join his business, which is really very small. He leases space on the rooftops of a couple of buildings and rents advertising billboards to companies. I think I'll be able to eke out a living and pay for your tuition, at least for the time being. And I hope that the business will expand. We are talking about getting a Diners' Club franchise, for example."

I felt a heavy burden being lifted from my shoulders and realized how ashamed I had felt deep down about my father's occupation. Now I could honestly tell my friends that my dad was a businessman!

The national elections were held on March 15, 1960. According to official records, Syngman Rhee had won the election with more than 88.7 percent of the votes, and Lee Ki Bung defeated Chang Myun, 8,225,000 to 1,850,000, and was declared the vice president elect. It was reported that most of the ballot boxes had been stuffed before the election and that most ballot boxes from Seoul and other opposition strongholds were switched before the ballots were counted. No one in Korea believed that the elections were fair, that the results represented the will of the people. There were sporadic demonstrations everywhere after election day.

32

KISS ME, KATE

April 1960, Seoul, Korea (37.5 N Parallel, 127 E Longitude)
Bo

Comparative-anatomy lab. They had dissected frogs, guinea pigs, and now rabbits.

The class had a number of dissecting tables, usually with five or six students surrounding it. Only two or three students had the opportunity to do real dissection of the animals.

The women students, by and large, shied away from it and tended to wait for the men to do the dissection, passively watching what was being done. Not so with Katie! She was one of my group of five students at table six in the lab. She was perhaps the most enthusiastic about the dissection. She would be the first person to anesthetize the animal with ether, the first to make the incision with her scalpel, and the first person to dissect out the organs. She didn't seem to mind the blood or the sight of the internal organs like other girls. In fact, as she dissected, she seemed to become excited, with her face flushed, her ample bosom heaving, and her eyes agleam. I thought that she felt sexually aroused as she dissected! Watching her, I felt myself becoming aroused as well.

Katie was slender, rather tall, with long legs and with a bosom that resembled Marilyn Monroe's. She wore low-cut sweaters, or blouses half-unbuttoned, showing her cleavage and the beginnings of the slopes of her breasts to maximum advantage. She also wore miniskirts. Her dress was, according to then Korean standards, quite outrageously revealing. It was clear that most of the other women students envied her and disliked her. Many men students seemed to dislike her as well and would whisper, "Slut" or, "Whore," barely out of reach of her earshot.

Her sexiness was paired, however, with a sharp tongue and a competitiveness that was fierce. I rather liked talking with her from the beginning. I often found myself debating with her in our philosophy and psychology classes. We would often disagree on a minor point, although we found ourselves agreeing on the whole. But we enjoyed picking at the weaknesses of each other's arguments. This was a very unusual behavior for a Korean woman, as they tended to avoid intellectual discussion with men, much less arguing with one. And, for that matter, not many men dared arguing with Katie. She had the intelligence to talk circles around most men in our class. She also had the ability to put down a man with just one wilting glance. If that was not sufficient in itself, she would say something like, "If you had real balls, you wouldn't say something as cowardly as that!" The male offender would just slink away. However, I found myself not at all intimidated by her as others seemed to be, and, in fact, the heat of our debate often made me feel closer to her.

At times, I used to joke with her, and she joked right back, with her characteristic throaty laugh. As I told my friends, she reminded me of a rose, beautiful, alluring, but also with thorns capable of protecting itself!

She and Soonil, the heavy spokesperson of the women students, made a good match. They were about equally bright, had strong characters, and were rivals. Soonil had her constituency of women, and Katie had herself, her sex appeal, and some men, including me. When the class was asked to elect a liaison with the medical school proper, which was at that time at another end of Seoul, Katie ran for the position as did Soonil. Katie won by one vote—probably mine (and yes, other men—I am sure all the other women voted for

Soonil). Yes, I often found myself on her side, with or without her near me. I felt she had spunk, and also she was attractive, although I had not done anything about it, yet.

April 16, 1960, Seoul

It was a particularly bleak Saturday afternoon that third week of April. It was raining on and off, the sky was gray, and the last of the cherry blossoms were being blown by the raw wind into the gutter swollen with rain. Along with democracy in Korea—into the gutter. President Syngman Rhee had won the rigged presidential election "in a landslide" for the fourth term last month, and the mood of the country was as gloomy as the weather. It was just too gloomy for me to take the long bus ride to White Deer, and, apparently, all my friends felt the same way. I found, when I called the White Deer, that all of the White Deer musketeers had called and left message that they wouldn't come. I felt lonely at home and was immersing myself in a particularly bloody mystery novel when the phone rang.

"Hello, this is Bo."

"Hello, Bo. This is Katie Chung. How are you?"

"Hi, Katie. I'm in the middle of my *Weltenschmerz*"—a pun on *Weltschmerz* (worldpain) and *Mittelschmerz*, a medical term for mid-cycle pain due to ovulation—"but how about you?"

"Me, too, Bo. As well as the Mittelschmerz! Anyway, I feel like having some good company and seeing a good movie. It's so depressing nowadays, with the rigged election and all. How about joining me at the New World Cinema, which is playing the revival of the musical *Kiss Me, Kate*?"

"Glad to, Katie. I'm finally glad to have a date with you. I've been thinking of it for some time but didn't have the nerve to ask," I said on the phone.

"Me, too, Bo. I had to have a drink of scotch before I mustered enough courage to call you. The movie starts at four o'clock. Let's meet in front of the theater at ten of."

"Sure, Katie. I'll be there. And perhaps afterward we can have supper together and talk. Let's make it into a real date!" I said.

Katie was waiting for me inside the theater, just before the ticket booth. She was holding her raincoat in her arm. She was dressed in a low-cut, soft, fluffy, creamy sweater and a very short plaid skirt that accentuated her shapely, long thighs and legs. She wore a pair of leather boots with white inside fur lining. Overall, she looked squeezably soft and voluptuous.

The theater was nearly empty. We sat in a row all by ourselves. I don't remember much about the movie, because I was concentrating more on Katie during it. I was quite self-conscious with her, and conscious of parts of her body. Her face, her eyes, her mouth, her throat, her neck, her shoulders, her chest, her breasts, her abdomen, her waist, her hips, her thighs, her legs, her feet. My eyes were darting back and forth between the screen and my left side, where Katie was sitting. I hoped she couldn't see my eyes moving. I was acutely conscious of her breathing and her breasts moving up and down under her fluffy sweater. I finally put my hand on hers, on her lap. Her hand was a bit cold and clammy, but it opened and held mine, our fingers intertwining. I felt a thrill through my whole body as our fingers intertwined. I suddenly realized that our hands, made into an intertwined ball, were resting on the inner side of her bare thigh! Her skirt was so short that her midthigh was exposed when she sat. The skin of her thigh was cool and soft, and she didn't seem to mind the tips of my fingers, intertwined with hers, feeling the softness, rubbing it gently, and moving up under her miniskirt. I flushed and felt excited, with a strong hard-on. I hoped others could not notice me, but, in a way, I did hope that Katie noticed me. She must have, because a little later, she transferred my hand that was holding her right hand into her left, still under her skirt, and let her right hand slide onto my thigh and onto my crotch! Her hand then swooped down, felt my erect penis, gave it a little squeeze, and then withdrew it quickly and held my left hand again, now with both hands, once again on her thigh. Soon, the movie ended. I still don't remember much about the movie.

"Katie, it was a wonderful idea to come see the movie. I really enjoyed it very much, and my April blues are almost gone!" I did not specify what *it* was that I enjoyed. "Let me treat you, Katie, to a Western dinner, for coming up with such a wonderful suggestion!"

"Me, too. Yes, it was a wonderful idea, if I may say so myself. Thank you, but no, thank you—that is, if you don't mind, we can go to my place, and I'll fix you a nice curried chicken and rice. In fact, it's already made waiting for us. You see, my mom's away today on business, and I have the house completely to myself. If you are wondering, I am an only child, my dad is deceased, and I live with my mom."

"Gladly, Katie. Absolutely and gratefully!" I replied. Katie's house was near the theater, in a middle-class neighborhood. Her house was a rather modern three-bedroom house with a comfortable living room. In the living room was a mantelpiece with a number of photographs, several of Katie at various ages and several of an older woman, in and out of a military-looking uniform.

"That's my mom, whose name is Ann Moon," said Katie. "She used to be the commander of the Girl Scouts of Korea"

"Wow, I am impressed," I said, giving her mom's picture a military salute.

I also noticed, half-hidden behind a picture of Katie, a black-and-white photo of a young couple, all dressed up as in a wedding photo. "Is this your parents' wedding picture?"

"Yes, this is about the only one that survived the war. Both my parents were teachers when they met."

"That's great. Few women worked in those days I think, let alone taught."

"My mom believes in educating girls. She was the first in her family to go to high school, and then college, and to work outside of home. Mom also believed that girls should be active outdoors and became active in the Girl Scouts when it was first introduced to Korea. Dad agreed with her, too. Both taught at Ewha Women's University. My dad died of cancer about five years ago—one of the reasons I want to be a doctor."

It must have been exciting to be young in those days, I thought. Being in the vanguard of a modernizing country, albeit as a colony of the Japanese Empire.

Katie served dinner in the dining area of the living room, with candlelight. The curried chicken with rice was deliciously spicy, complemented by a fruity white wine.

Katie and I talked about the courses in school, our teachers, philosophy, friends, and especially politics. Katie was passionate about democracy, women's rights, and above all, individual freedom. She was also passionate about more women becoming doctors and how medical schools should actively recruit women. "That's one of the reasons I ran for the liaison position with the medical school—I am representing the whole premed and liberal-arts school when I meet with the medical-school student leaders and faculty! You know, Bo, I envy you and the four musketeers! You seem to have so much fun together. You should hear what we women talk about when we get together!"

"Well, we do have fun. I do wonder what women do talk about when they are together by themselves!"

"Mostly nonsense! Small talk. Gossip. I get sick of them," said Katie. "That's why I like to talk with men. It's more fun, and there is more substance to what we talk about. Even if men don't often take us seriously!"

"I do take you seriously," I said. By now, we were finishing coffee, sitting on the sofa.

"I know you do, and that's why I like you!" said Katie, holding my hand. I held her hand, kissed the back of it and then her arm. She giggled, "Bo, Prince Charming!"

I put my arms around her head and gently pulled her face against mine and kissed her lips gently. She closed her eyes, parted her lips, and kissed me back, first gently and then passionately. My tongue found hers inside, and our tongues intertwined. I slid my hands behind her back, pulled her sweater upward, and felt her bare back upward, under her sweater, until I found the back of her bra. She continued to kiss me while I unhooked her bra and felt her bare breast with the palm of my hand, and her hard, erect nipple. I squeezed her nipple gently with my fingers and slid my hand down, outside of her sweater and over her miniskirt, to feel the inside of her thighs and upward to her crotch. I rubbed the inside of her thighs and her crotch with my fingers, first gently, then harder, feeling more and more excited as her breathing became more and more labored and her face became flushed. Then, suddenly, she opened her eyes, pushing my hand away, "Bo, please, slow down a bit before we reach a point of no return...We must do some things before."

"Yes, Katie, I know. You are lovely, Katie!"

Thank heavens I am now prepared, I thought as I disentangled myself slowly and fished in my pants pocket for my wallet. I now carried two condoms in my wallet at all times. Katie collected herself and disappeared behind the bathroom door.

In a few minutes, Katie came back into the living room, wearing a semitransparent black negligee. "I am yours, Bo, if you want me now!"

Katie came to me as I stood naked, feeling a little embarrassed but fully aroused. She knelt down and kissed my penis, sucked on it gently, and took the condom that I had out and put it on my erect penis, as she kissed the length of my penis. I gently pulled her up, took her to the sofa, and gently lay her on it, legs spread apart. I pushed her negligee up, all the way over her head and off, and covered her naked body with kisses. Her mouth, her nipples, her abdomen, her navel, her vulva, her clitoris, her inner thighs, all over. I then sucked her clitoris, and her vagina, and her nipples, and her mouth. She was breathing hard, with barely audible moans, with her eyes closed, but eyes moving rapidly back and forth under the lids, and her face looked so intense, so excited, so exciting...I could wait no longer: I thrust my penis into her vagina, which was warm, well lubricated, welcoming…my penis was inside, feeling the depth of her, feeling the tightness of her, the warmth of her, and her pelvic movements—no, my movements—no, ours together, and then, I felt a tightness around my penis, a squeezing sensation that made me explode inside her…joy…relief…peace…happy peace…and the exhilaration of success…I have finally made love to a woman, a beautiful, willing, and loving woman…love…peace…

I stayed inside her for some minutes after orgasm. She also held on to me on top of her. "It was lovely," we said simultaneously and laughed, as we disentangled ourselves finally. "Good sex is a good thing, as Freud would say, according to Bo," said Katie laughingly. "Well, after all, we are premedical students!"

We promised to meet again next Saturday for another movie and…

I felt elated that night. Katie had entered my life, and my life was changed forever. I had real sex for the first time with a remarkable woman, someone who, I hoped, could be my life's companion.

33

APRIL IS THE CRUELEST MONTH

April is the cruelest month, breeding
Lilacs out of the dead land, mixing
Memory and desire, stirring
Dull roots with spring rain.

—from The Waste Land, *"I. Burial of the Dead," by T. S. Eliot (1888–1965)*

Monday, April 11, 1960, South Korea (Thirty-Third to Thirty-Eighth Parallel)

In Masan, a small port city on the southeast of Korea, the bloated body of a young student who was active in calling for fair elections was discovered floating in the harbor, obviously a victim of police torture. The students demonstrated en masse and were fired on by the police. A number of deaths ensued. The minister of interior, who was in charge of the national police, declared that the police were given live ammunition so that they could use it against the demonstrators. He declared that the demonstrators were disloyal Communist sympathizers and, consequently, would be punished severely.

Tuesday, April 19, 1960, 10:00 a.m., Seoul (37.5 N Parallel, 127 E Longitude)
Bo

Bo, Philmo, Chulsoo, Bob, and Rabbit were sitting on the grass at the university, smoking and chatting. They had a free hour between classes. It was a beautiful spring day, and the campus was lit up with fiery red and pink azalea blossoms everywhere. The rain and wintry wind of last weekend was replaced by brilliant sunlight and warm, fragrant air. Bo was feeling particularly content, relishing in the memory of his night with Katie and anticipating the coming weekend with excitement.

"You know, we must really do something about the rigged election! We cannot tolerate Rhee killing off the last hope of democracy." Bo said with feeling. He felt especially good saying this, now that his father was no longer a policeman.

"Yeah, we should try to mobilize the country, somehow. Demonstrating, by itself, I think is not going to work. Somehow, we have to persuade the United States and the military not to support Rhee's regime," said Philmo, the strategist.

"I don't quite agree," said Chulsoo. "The opposition party is going to be Socialistic and not encourage business. For business to prosper, there has to be law and order and political stability. Although authoritarian, Rhee does provide order and is trusted by our allies abroad."

"But that was while Rhee was claiming to be a champion of democracy and when we had elections that were at least not as blatantly rigged as the last one!" retorted Bo.

"I think Rhee has gone one step too far. By doing so, he has betrayed all the people who believed that, deep down, he believed in democracy, that he would ensure democracy when he died. The way it is now, Lee Ki Bung will inherit the presidency and become even more dictatorial," said Bob. Rabbit did not really participate in discussions but just nodded at what each said. He probably doesn't care, thought Bo. As long as he has fun, Rabbit doesn't really care about anything else, especially serious stuff like politics.

"An emergency student-body meeting at the amphitheater!" the loudspeaker suddenly blared. The campus had a loudspeaker system that was installed primarily for emergencies, such as possible air raids from North Korea. The message was repeated several times.

"Now what?" said Bo.

"Perhaps we will demonstrate, too!" said Philmo. They got up and walked down to the amphitheater, which was on the other side of the newly built auditorium.

The amphitheater was large enough to accommodate some eight thousand people, about the size of the student body. It was filling up rapidly. On the stage was the president of the student body, with a megaphone. Several senior students were busily making placards by writing on long sheets of white cloth:

"March Election Was Rigged. We Demand a New, Fair Election!'

"Down With Dictatorship!"

"We Demand Syngman Rhee's Resignation!"

By eleven, the amphitheater was completely filled. The president of the student body, Sungwhan Kim, spoke through the megaphone, "Fellow students, we are here to decide whether we will participate in a massive demonstration of all college students today. As you know, the March election was rigged in a most blatant way to ensure the succession of the presidency to another dictator! Last night, the presidents of the student bodies of all the major universities in town met secretly and decided to organize a massive student demonstration today, to commence at twelve noon. Each university's students, each of you, will decide whether you will participate in the demonstration or not. Before you decide, please understand the following:

"We anticipate that today's demonstration will be massive, with all universities in Seoul participating. And it may spread to other cities. We will demand that the results of the rigged election be nullified, that a new election be held within a month to elect a new president and a vice president. We will demand that Syngman Rhee step down from his presidency immediately in favor of a caretaker government that will oversee the new election.

"Through our demonstrations, the world will note what is happening in Korea. World opinion will support our demand for democracy in Korea, for a fair and honest election. The United Nations forces, from many countries around the world, shed their blood during the Korean War, for what purpose?...to ensure democracy, to ensure that the hope of freedom will not be snuffed out by naked aggression on this Korean peninsula. With their help, we have repelled aggression from the North, but their blood, the blood of our fathers, mothers, brothers, and sisters, would have been in vain if we cannot protect our freedom, our democracy, from our own rulers!

"There is much danger in participating in our demonstrations today. The police are given live ammunition, and the minister of interior has publicly declared that the police will shoot to kill any demonstrators. Rhee may declare martial law. The authorities may close down our universities, arrest us, and torture us. Please take heed—there is danger—and remember that whether you participate or not is up to you as an individual.

"My friends and I who have organized this demonstration are prepared to sacrifice our careers, and our lives, so that freedom will be preserved for our people. If not in our generation, then in the next generation. Even if we fail, God and history will heed that the youths of Korea protested the death of freedom and democracy, that they did not let it happen without a fight."

"Now, I would like to ask our liaison with the medical school, premed Ms. Chung, to take the megaphone!" Katie! Katie was speaking into the megaphone!

"Please know that all the medical students and premedical students are behind us! With all our medical skills, knowledge, and honor, we support the cause of democracy. We will do whatever is needed to provide any emergency care, should the need arise.

However, to be effective, our demonstration must be peaceful. We must show to the Korean people, and to the world, that we are not the agents of North Korean Communists, that we are not trying to create turmoil to benefit the Communists. Our fight must be peaceful, and our means must be democratic. We will not trample on the freedoms of others to make ourselves free.

"Even if they attack us, shoot at us, we will just march, singing and chanting our demands. We will not throw any stones; we will not even push any policemen. Our demonstration will begin at noon and end at five. This is to give all of us plenty of time to go home before the curfew. We do not want to give the regime the excuse to arrest any of our demonstrators for curfew violation. If you agree with our goals and our means, and if you want to be a part of this demonstration, please follow us and march to the Presidential Palace!"

Katie! The liaison with the medical school, organizing this march! Bo found himself deeply moved. His eyes were filled with tears, and he felt a surge of determination sweeping through his body. He noticed that others were also wiping their eyes with handkerchiefs. Ever since the rigged election on March 15, the students felt as if a prized possession had been ripped away from them by a band of gangsters—freedom and democracy, an ideal that they all shared. In spite of the reality of the authoritarian regime, the youths had clung to the notion that, eventually, Rhee's regime would give way to a more enlightened, more democratic regime. But the election, blatantly and publicly rigged, made a mockery of the term *election* and ensured the perpetuation of authoritarian rule by an even more authoritarian dictator, Lee Ki Bung. We cannot let freedom die without a protest! They all felt this imperative. Protest! Let the world know!

Bo felt personal pride and thrill about Katie being a leader of this movement and could hardly wait till the coming weekend when he would show her how proud and thrilled he was!

The foursome nodded to each other, their eyes still filled with tears. "Yes, let's go! Let's join the demonstration." Even Chulsoo joined in. And Rabbit. They all marched together, in a long column of five or six students across, holding each other's hands so as not to break their ranks, toward the Presidential Palace. Bo was proud to see Katie in the front of the line, with Kim and other organizers of the march.

As the column from Hyundai reached a main intersection of town, they were joined by the students from Koryu University, coming from the other direction, from the other side of town. And as they marched together, they were joined by students from the Seoul National University, who came from another side of town. Then they were joined by the students from the Ewha Women's University, all women, all determined. Then, by the students from the Sungkyoonkwan University, the traditional Confucian university. Then by the students of the Catholic University. Then the Yonsei University. Then the Hanyang University. And on and on.

There were endless columns of students, tens of thousands of them. The cream of Korean youths, men and women, boys and girls, all shouting for democracy, for freedom, with their voices becoming hoarse, still shouting, "Give us freedom or give us death," "We demand new elections," and, "We demand Syngman Rhee's resignation!"

By midafternoon, the streets were lined with people. People who came out of their places of work. Women who were shopping. Old men and women who came out of their houses and apartments to see what was going on. They all cheered! They cheered the demonstrating students. They brought pails of water for the students to drink. They brought bags of candy, fruits, and donuts for the students. And they joined in.

Soon, all the streets of Seoul were filled with demonstrators, thousands and thousands of students and hundreds of thousands of ordinary people, who cheered and then joined the demonstration. Everything else stopped in Seoul. The news of the massive demonstration filled all the places of work, all the elementary and high schools. Everyone stopped what he or she was doing and joined the demonstration. They all converged toward the Taepyong-ro, the "Road of Great Peace," the main road to the Presidential Palace.

The Presidential Palace was well prepared for the demonstration. There were divisions of specially trained riot police guarding the palace. They had set up several barricades, at least some twenty blocks away from the palace. They had stationed machine guns, tanks, and thousands of police to protect the barricades. But they had not been quite prepared for the number of people converging on the palace. They decided to take no chances. They fired their guns and machine guns point-blank at the demonstrators. Scores of demonstrators fell to the ground, some dead instantaneously, others bleeding. The riot police spread out in a V, partially surrounding the demonstrators, and systematically shot at them. Some students started throwing stones at the police. "No, no stones. No violence!" others shouted to the students.

Bo and his friends heard the gunfire at some distance. They were still marching toward the Presidential Palace, as the column from Hyundai University was still several blocks away from the police barricades. Bo saw a number of stretcher-bearing medical students wearing white coats, running. On the stretcher were students who were obviously injured and bleeding. They were taking them, weaving through the throngs of people, to the nearest hospital. There were ambulances parked far in the rear of the demonstrators. No cars could pass through the crowds of people, demonstrators, their supporters, and onlookers. The column stopped their march as more gunfire was heard. They heard the medical students shout to them, "The police are shooting machine guns at us. Stop, and do not proceed. It's a massacre!"

Still, the students persisted. Even though the sound of gunfire was coming closer, they chanted their demands and sang patriotic songs. The Korean national anthem. Military songs. "Children of Democracy" based on the melody of "Let Freedom Ring."

The sound of gunfire was coming very near. Bo could see disruption in the front of the crowd and saw an armored truck in the distance shooting directly at the front of the column. People were falling. Then, Bo saw Kim, the president of the student body, shout through his megaphone, "Students of Hyundai! Please take cover! And disperse! We must not let our lives be taken so easily! We must live for our continuing struggle!"

Bo could hardly hear anything because he was running toward the front where Katie was marching with Kim. Katie! He saw her holding on to Kim as he seemed to have been hit by a bullet. "Hurry! Stretcher!" Katie was screaming as Bo tried to run toward her and Kim, but he was pushed back as the students were running toward the rear, away from the police. Two medical students in white coats with a stretcher finally reached Kim, but as Kim was put on the stretcher, the white coat of the medical student lifting up Kim began to turn red as he collapsed.

Katie! Now she took the place of the medical student, lifting up the stretcher and carrying it toward the rear, as Bo tried to reach her. As she came near, Bo saw that her blouse was blood soaked. "Bo, please bring this stretcher to the ambulance in the rear, and remember I love you!"

Bo, together with the other medical student holding the stretcher, who seemed uninjured, managed to put both Kim and Katie on the same stretcher and slowly made his way to the ambulance. Bo tried to ride in the ambulance, but it was too full with the injured with stretchers almost piled on top of each other. Katie!

When Bo arrived at the emergency room of Providence Hospital, where the ambulance must have gone, it was full of people, both injured students and families and friends looking for their loved ones.

"I am a medical student here, and I am here to help," Bo lied to get into the ER. He found Kim in one section of patients with non-life-threatening injuries. "Kim, where is Katie?"

"Katie is gone…she saved my life—as they were shooting directly at me while I was on the stretcher, she shielded me and took the bullet to her chest, and she still kept on going with the stretcher till you took over…" Kim's words reached Bo as strange sounds, just sounds devoid of meaning…then his world seemed to lose all color and all reality…

Katie, gone, so much to give, so much already given. Collapse of a dream, so sweet while it lasted, in the midst of gloom and waste.

It was impossible to even get a glimpse of Katie's body as all the dead were quickly moved away into the morgue to make room for the influx of freshly arriving casualties to the ER. And the morgue was strictly off-limits to anyone, including and especially the police.

Bo walked all the way home, weaving through the crowds, walking for three hours to get home. As he was walking like an automaton, the merciful dense fog in his brain that buffered his pain cleared somewhat, and the pain was mixed with fury and regret. If only I had reached Katie before she took the stretcher, I would have carried the stretcher, and Katie would be alive! If only I had taken the bullet instead of Katie…It was long after nightfall when he finally came into the door of his house. His parents and Claire were waiting for him anxiously.

"Thank God you are OK!" said Yunhee.

"Welcome home, Son. We were all so worried about you!"

"Did you participate in the demonstrations, big brother?" asked little Claire.

"Of course not. Bo wouldn't do something as silly as that!" said Yunhee reproachfully.

"Yes, Claire. I did participate in the demonstrations! We had to do something to protest the rigged election! We can't just watch freedom being robbed from us! They shot at us and murdered many of us, including some of my really good friends. I am sad, and

I am furious!" Bo said, his voice tremulous, exhausted, deliberate. If they only knew how much! Oh, Katie!

Yunhee just made faces but did not answer. Suk said, "Well, I am glad you are home safely. I heard that many students were shot and quite a few died. I was really worried stiff!"

"Dad, I am truly glad that you are not a policeman today. I am truly, truly grateful to you for having the foresight to quit the police just days before today!" said Bo with eyes filled with tears.

"I am, too, my son!" said Suk. His eyes were also filled with tears.

Wednesday, April 20, Seoul

Syngman Rhee declared martial law throughout the country and closed down all the universities and all other schools. Tanks rolled out on the streets of Seoul. Strict censorship was imposed on all newspapers and radio stations.

With the imposition of martial law, order seemed to return to the streets of Seoul initially. But tension mounted among the populace as hundreds of students were rumored to have been killed by police gunfire and by police torture after being arrested following the demonstrations.

In spite of the surveillance and martial law, people whispered on street corners, in their workplaces, and in their homes, about the need to make their support of the students' cause known, the need to respond to the students' call for democracy, for the end of the autocratic regime.

They spoke of a new demonstration, this time of ordinary people, defying the orders of the martial-law command. Bo tried to call Katie's home, but there was no answer. Obviously, her family was in mourning and did not want to be disturbed. Had they only known of our budding relationship, her mom would have called me, Bo thought. Bo wanted to go to Katie's house, but all public transportation was suspended for the week.

Bo spent April 23, the Saturday he would have had a date with Katie, alone in his room. Katie! The first bloom of my life so cruelly snuffed away—will this be the fate of all the hopes of the young, for freedom, democracy, and love?

Monday, April 25
With daybreak, thousands upon thousands of people, ordinary people, converged, on their feet, on the Road of Great Peace. People who knew they had to protest, to let the world know that they would not tolerate freedom and democracy being robbed from them so blatantly. People who wanted to let the world know that they stood with the students and that they would not let the bloodshed of their children be in vain. Hundreds of thousands, millions, of people, unorganized people, converged on the road, in spite of the tanks, chanting, "Freedom," "New elections," and, "Syngman Rhee, resign!"

They stuck flowers into the turrets of the tanks. They confronted the soldiers peacefully, still chanting. Soldiers had replaced the riot police during the last several days. Rhee thought that, with this massive show of force, the demonstrations would simply die away. But it was a miscalculation. Among other things, he did not quite understand that the soldiers, who were conscripts, really sympathized with the demonstrators. They were the sons of ordinary people, people who might be demonstrating that very moment in Seoul, or in Pusan, or in Masan. The demonstrations had now spread across the country. People everywhere in South Korea were demonstrating for new elections, for the resignation of Syngman Rhee.

Unlike the police, the soldiers did not fire on the demonstrators. They let the demonstrators climb up on their tanks. They let them put their placards across the tanks:

"New Elections!"

"We Want Democracy!"

"Rhee, Resign!"

Tuesday, April 26
Another day of demonstrations. The demonstrators of the previous day had not left the Road of Great Peace. They stayed overnight, still chanting for freedom and for the resignation of Rhee. With daylight, hundreds of thousands more people joined the demonstrators.

General Yo-Chan Song, the chief of staff of the army and commander of the martial law, declared, "The army will not fire on the demonstrators. The army shares the people's demands for a democratic Korea." The United States ambassador declared that the Korean people's demands for democracy should be heeded and that there were clearly irregularities in the March elections. The embassy also denied reports that Lee Ki Bung, the vice president elect of the ruling party, was hiding in it. Lee Ki Bung had disappeared from sight during the demonstrations, and it had been widely rumored that he was hiding in the American embassy.

That afternoon, Syngman Rhee, president of the Republic of Korea, declared that he was resigning from his office. In a dramatic gesture, he left the Presidential Palace on foot to a hastily put-together house that very afternoon, after transferring power to a caretaker government headed by Chung Hur, a respected scholar, as acting prime minister. The students had won! The people had won! The April student revolution was triumphant!

Bo did not participate in the final demonstrations that resulted in the fall of Syngman Rhee. He thought about sneaking out of the house to participate, but that meant having to go by foot into the center of town, which would take three hours, as no public transportation was operating after the first day of demonstrations. And he did not have the heart to leave his parents, who were begging him not to go out of the house. They had no way of knowing what was really happening downtown, whether there were more demonstrations, more shootings. The government-controlled radio had announced the martial law, but no other news was forthcoming until the dramatic announcement of the resignation of Syngman

Rhee. Bo was monitoring the radio of the American Eighth Army stationed in Korea, broadcast in English. It was through that station that he learned of the subsequent demonstrations by the people, of the refusal of the Korean military to shoot at the demonstrators, of the declaration by the US ambassador, and then, finally, the resignation of Syngman Rhee.

Friday, April 29, Seoul
Former president Syngman Rhee fled Seoul for Honolulu with his wife, Francesca. Lee Ki Bung and his whole family committed suicide by shooting themselves.

The streets of Seoul returned to normal, after two days of jubilant celebration at the departure of Syngman Rhee's regime. The new caretaker government was now in place. The martial law was lifted. The midnight curfew was lifted. All censorship was abolished. All schools reopened. People were intoxicated with their newly found freedom and the sense of empowerment. Syngman Rhee, who seemed to be so entrenched, so powerful, so immovable, was in fact removed by the people. There was some scattered violence against some police stations, but otherwise, the aftermath of the revolution was remarkably peaceful.

People cheered soldiers on the streets. They also cheered Americans. The Korean people knew that the support of the military, and of the United States government, was crucial in the downfall of Rhee's regime. People felt a special kinship to the young boys in the military, their own sons, who refused to fire against their own families. They felt grateful to the Americans, who helped save their country twice, first from aggression by North Korea and now from the tyranny of Syngman Rhee.

Soon, they returned to their day-to-day lives, with their hearts filled with hope for a brighter democratic future, for themselves and for their children, who proved themselves to be so deserving of it.

Bo was happy about the outcome of the demonstrations, but the loss of Katie filled his heart with sorrow. Bo felt his sadness was worsened because nobody had yet known about his relationship with Katie, and thus of his loss.

Bo returned to his class that morning. He was a little late, as was usual for him, as he had to take an hour's bus ride from home to get to the campus. The first class, an English-literature lecture, seemed to have been canceled. He noticed that his friends, Philmo, Bob, and Rabbit, were sitting together in their usual seats, talking to each other with solemn faces.

"Hi, gang! Nice to see you guys again! Hope you went home OK on the nineteenth!" said Bo as he took a seat next to them.

"I am so sad about Katie. She was such a wonderful, beautiful, energetic person. And I know you really felt close to her," said Philmo.

"Yes, I do feel devastated. She had so much going for her, and she was the liaison between us and the medical school…which she will now never attend…"

"How about Chulsoo? Is he here yet?" Bo asked.

His friends looked at each other. Finally, Philmo said, "Bo, we just found out that Chulsoo also died! He was shot and killed on the nineteenth."

"How is it possible? He was never close to the front of the line; I remember his running to the rear as I was trying to get to the front, where Katie was."

Bo realized that Chulsoo must have been killed after they separated. Since Chulsoo's house was in the downtown area, he must have been exposed to danger longer, unlike Bo, whose house was almost outside of the city. Chulsoo, who actually supported Syngman Rhee as a stabilizing force. Bo had been surprised that Chulsoo even decided to participate in the demonstration. But he did, and he died.

Chulsoo, the entrepreneur. A handsome playboy, who grew up in wealth and privilege, who enjoyed life, and who had a bright future ahead of him. Dead at age eighteen. Killed, demonstrating against the excesses of a regime that he had once believed in! And Katie, who was a beautiful, articulate, and committed woman, an organizer of the demonstration, and who helped save another life!

April. The cruelest month.

34

THE HOUSE WITH THE DARWINIAN GARDEN

October 1976, Guilford, Connecticut (41.3 N Parallel, 72.3 W Longitude)
Bo

The indian summer finally gave way to autumn. A northeastern autumn with a symphony of brilliant colors of foliage. The house by the apple orchard that Ginny and I shared was on a hill, through whose picture windows one could easily enjoy the seasons in the comfort of the indoors. A house fashioned after Frank Lloyd Wright, it blended well with the trees surrounding it. And it had a Darwinian garden. Survival of the fittest!

Neither Ginny nor I knew gardening. Growing up in Brooklyn, Ginny barely saw potted plants. I, unlike my father, did not really enjoy gardening or taking care of any living things, plant or animal. Besides, I liked the idea of a Darwinian garden—let nature take care of itself, and I shall just enjoy the fruits, whatever they might be. The house was on about one acre of land, and being a new house, there was no landscaping. There was no lawn, just bare ground. We did not have the money then to have it landscaped professionally. The only thing I did to the garden was to plant a number of twigs of pine trees that I got free from the local hardware store on Arbor Day. Some twenty twigs. And then I did scatter some seeds of wildflowers.

There was one exception to the principle of the Darwinian garden. I set aside a patch of ground just in front of the house, just before the driveway, for a rose garden. I had that patch of land tilled, and I planted some thirty rosebushes. Hybrid tea roses, as well as floribundas. I do love roses! Their beauty, their fragrance.

Nature had been kind to us in Guilford. Both of our gardens flourished, the rose garden as well as the Darwinian garden. Every spring, flowers of every description, every shape, and every color would spring up and bloom, a chaotic but orderly procession of wildflowers, shrubs, leaves, and fruits. And my roses, stately, delicate roses, would also bloom in the full glory of their colors, red, yellow, white, pink, even blue. And I would bend down and smell their fragrance and enjoy their beauty. Then, I would cut a few of the prettiest roses, bring them in, and put them in a vase. I did not mind working in the rose garden. It was the one place outside of the house in which I felt really at home, tending the lovely thorny roses.

With the autumnal crispness in the air, most of the roses stopped blooming, except for one stately rose. A pink grandiflora, called Queen Elizabeth. Grandiflora, because it had the attributes of the wilder climbing roses, floribundas, in being especially thorny and resistant to disease and harmful insects like the japanese beetles, but also had flowers that were truly exquisitely grand. Tall, slender, noble. With a delicate, sweet fragrance. The single flower on the tree was now in a state of perfection, the inner petals not quite open, the outer ones open to reveal the inner bud, which looks very much like a young girl's breast, creamy pink, delicate, firm…

I smell the fragrance, inhaling deeply. Then, solemnly, I cut the flower at the stem, a long stem, and bring it inside. I put the single rose in the vase on the piano. Somehow, I feel moved to tears. Perhaps it is the sadness of the autumn, prelude to the cold winter…

"Come on into the kitchen, Bo. Your coffee is getting cold," I hear Ginny calling.

35

SALT AND TEARS OF THE EARTH

How countlessly they congregate
O'er our tumultuous snow,
Which flows in shapes as tall as trees
When wintry winds do blow! -

As if with keenness for our fate,
Our faltering few steps on
To white rest, and a place of rest
Invisible at dawn -

And yet with neither love nor hate,
Those stars like some snow-white
Minerva's snow-white marble eyes
Without the gift of sight.

—"Stars," by Robert Frost

October 1960, Seoul (37.5 N Parallel, 127 E Longitude)
Bo

To Bo, the autumn of 1960 was a gray void. His world had collapsed as if sunken into a black hole. His dreams of a vibrant future with Katie were shattered in a single instant.

So alive, full of life, only six months ago! Now dead, buried, gone. Bo again experienced the draining of all color from his universe—everything turned into shades of gray, shadows of what used to be reality.

Bo went through the motions of going to school, participating in discussions, even going to the White Deer Tearoom. Bo took long walks at night, into the countryside near his home. At times past midnight, past the midnight curfew of Syngman Rhee's regime. He gazed upon the stars above and wondered where Katie was. Perhaps she had become one of the stars above, twinkling at Bo, whispering to Bo! As in the story of the little match girl! Bo talked to the stars, to Katie among the stars. He still had the Seconal, hidden away in the bottom drawer of his desk, which he had not even thought about since the time when he had procured it some three years ago, in preparation for the results of the college entrance examination. But the stars twinkled, and Katie's star seemed to whisper to Bo, "No, I want you to live, for both of us, and be happy, for both of us!"

Ah, Minerva's soft white marble eyes, without the gift of sight! The sight of Bo's suffering.

As weeks passed, Bo eventually identified a star, a faint but distinct star near Polaris, as Katie. Because he had not noticed it before, it might just be Katie, who had assumed that place; perhaps she was visible only to Bo and twinkling her messages only for him. Her twinkling whispers were always encouraging and always forgiving. Eventually, Bo felt comfort in talking with her at night and, guided by the starlight, found the courage and the strength to go on and immerse himself in work. And in friendship with the White Deer musketeers.

Yulak said, "You know, our White Deer days are coming to an end with our entrance to medical school proper. We simply will not have enough time to come to the tearoom as we do now."

They all agreed sadly. It would be truly disorienting not to have the White Deer to go to almost every day and every weekend. Yulak continued, "You know, I was thinking, why don't we form a formal club, an inter–medical school students' social and academic club? I understand that there are such clubs in America. I spoke with some of my friends at Seoul National, and they were very much in favor of the idea, too."

"I think it's a great idea. We could have regular games and parties together," chimed in Rabbit.

"Yes, and we could have symposiums on medicine, invite some top-notch people from each medical school, and that way we would be exposed to the faculty of other schools!" said Bob.

Bo and Philmo agreed, too. So, the following week, the White Deer musketeers met with a few more premed students from Seoul National, as well as some premed students from Ewha Women's University, one of whom was a girlfriend of Rabbit's.

The Medical Students' Society, MSS for short, was born. The preamble of the society, written largely by Bob, was strewn with religious metaphors: "Through our friendship and pursuit of the truth, we dedicate ourselves to becoming the salt of the earth in bringing humankind health and comfort…"

MSS was to be Bo's main outlet for social life for the next several years. He dedicated himself to study, which was clearly necessary in the medical school. Up to that time, studying was largely to pass examinations. But, upon entrance to medical school, Bo felt that, now, he had to study for the sake of knowing, because as a doctor, he had to know. To be a good doctor, he must know—he must understand! Passing an examination was now secondary. He had to study to digest the information, to know it backward and forward, because he had to *apply* it to real people, whose lives would be in his hands!

36

THE ICE CASTLE

Ice sculpture. Ice castles. Resplendent, glistening turrets and spires, castles that gleam in the cold sunlight. The artist has spent hours, days, and weeks perfecting the castle that shines so brightly in the brilliant sunlight!

Miniature rooms, miniature cannons that will never be fired. And miniature people populating the ice castle, all of ice, all of which will melt.

The splendor of the moment, the glory of being. Transformations of water, eternally amorphous. The magical union of two atoms of primordial hydrogen with one atom of oxygen.

Hydrogen. The lightest atom. The stuff of the universe, the oldest inhabitant. Star stuff. Energy stuff. Have you memories of the big bang, the creation of the universe? Have you any structure that changes with experience, with memory? Or is memory the whole of you, unchanging, memory that is, was, and ever will be?

June 19, 1960, Seoul (37.5 N Parallel, 127 E Longitude)
Bo
President Eisenhower's visit to Korea was one of the most memorable events in the history of the two countries' relationship. Literally millions of people lined the streets of Seoul, cheering and welcoming him. With the memory of the crucial American support for the

April revolution fresh in their minds, the United States, symbolized by the benign, smiling face of President Eisenhower, was perfection itself!

Bo was among the crowds cheering Eisenhower. He felt proud to be a part of the welcoming crowd. He was proud to be a Korean, to have participated in the student demonstrations that changed the history of democracy in that country.

Fall 1960, Seoul

By September, Chang Myun, who had been the vice-presidential candidate of the opposition Democratic Party, became the prime minister of the newly democratic Republic of Korea. The government system was changed from a president-centered one to a cabinet-centered one, along the lines of the parliamentary system of Great Britain. Having been burned by too strong a president in Syngman Rhee, the populace wanted what they perceived to be a more democratic, less centralized political system.

People felt intoxicated with freedom. Freedom to express. Freedom to criticize the government. And people used the newly found freedom. The number of newspapers and periodicals increased from six hundred to fifteen hundred. There were street demonstrations almost every day, for whatever cause, from labor disputes to calling for the resignation of university presidents.

Some of the populace worried about what they perceived to be chaos and anarchy. They worried about Communist infiltration of some student organizations. There was talk about strengthening the police to deal with the daily demonstrations. Others were worried about the Japanese influence again. Chang Myun's government, unlike Rhee's, favored an open-door policy and had gingerly started to reopen commercial and cultural exchange with Japan. But overall, the country was peaceful, and the slow pace of democracy rolled on nevertheless.

November 1960
John F. Kennedy was elected president of the United States. His programs of the New Frontier were enthusiastically supported by the Koreans. "Ask not what your country can do for you—ask what you can do for your country!"

Spring 1961, Seoul
All the White Deer musketeers were now in medical school. The White Deer days were now over. The Medical Students' Society met once a week.

Bo set aside the hours of 9:00 p.m. to 12:00 midnight, every night, for study. He found the "real" medical-school subjects hard but also gratifying to learn. Anatomy. Physiology. Biochemistry. Histology. Basic sciences for the first year. Foundations of clinical medicine. Subjects a doctor must master. To be a good doctor, a competent doctor. There were only two kinds of doctors to Bo—competent doctors and quacks. Bo had to become a competent doctor. Like Dr. Lee, like his cousin, the famous thoracic surgeon, who was a professor at the medical school.

May 16, 1961
Bo woke up to the radio as usual. His radio had been tuned to the independent commercial station that had the best news in the morning. But, instead of the usual news, it was playing martial music. He turned the dial to the American Eighth Army broadcast.

"Early this morning, a group of Korean Army officers appear to have staged a coup. The military junta, headed by Colonel Park Chung Hee, has dissolved the Cabinet and the National Assembly. They have taken President Yun into custody, and he has signed a proclamation supporting the coup. Unconfirmed reports indicate that Prime Minister Chang has been arrested by the military junta, as well as most members of his cabinet. Stay tuned for further developments throughout the day."

On the other radio, in his parents' room, the Korean government broadcasting station had a high-pitched male voice making announcements: "President Yun Bo Sun has decreed that the government has been transferred to the Military Revolutionary Council. The Military Revolutionary Council that took power early this morning has declared the following:

"One, the Military Revolutionary Council has taken control of the government in order to save our country from further anarchy and chaos that would have led the country to Communist takeover. The first principle of the new government will be anti-Communism.

"Two, we pledge continuing close ties with the United States of America.

"Three, all corruptions and social evils will be eradicated from the society.

"Four, a fresh moral system will be created for our society, based on traditional values of law and order and of respect. Students shall return to their proper duties of study and leave the area of politics.

"Five, we shall strive for a self-supporting economy, not relying on ties with other countries, especially Japan.

"Six, upon completion of aforementioned duties, the military will turn over the control of government to clean, conscientious civilians, and we will return to our proper duties.

"Martial law is in effect throughout the country!

"All political activities are prohibited for the duration.

'All universities and secondary schools will be closed until further notice.

"All press will be censored!

"Any assembly of more than two persons is prohibited!

"No demonstrations of any kind will be allowed!

"The curfew of midnight to four in the morning will be reinstated to curtail North Korean Communist infiltration.

"Any violators will be arrested without warrant and tried by the military tribunal under martial law!"

Barely a year-old democracy in Korea, dead, trampled by the boots of the soldiers. The leaders of the military coup were not the sons of the people who had brought democracy to Korea last April. They were a clique of army officers who had been trained by the Japanese during the occupation days, in the discipline and values of the Japanese Imperial Army! Their leader, Park Chung Hee, a diminutive man with a solemn, melancholy face, had planned a military takeover even before the April revolution. His dream was an authoritarian regime, with himself as the leader, that ran the country like a well-disciplined military.

It was remarkable how quickly and effectively the military took control. The democratic forces, including students, were stunned and demoralized. They recognized that they were powerless against a well-armed force of half a million young men, who were trained to the hilt in anticipation of a North Korean attack at any moment. They also feared that if they confronted the military, the North Koreans might indeed take advantage of the split between the South Korean population and the military and march in. The behavior of the United States concerning the coup was also bizarre. Although the ambassador expressed concern, the language was extremely mild, and there was rumor that the coup was actually engineered by the American CIA, because they feared Communist infiltration of the Korean society!

Eventually, schools reopened. But there were military guards posted at the gate of every university, even the medical school, and there were strange men attending classes and generally mixing with the students—obviously agents of the newly set-up Korean Central Intelligence Agency.

Fear permeated the campuses. Some students, including Kim, the former president of the student body of Hyundai University, whom Katie had saved in the stretcher she carried, just disappeared and never returned. There were rumors that they had been arrested, tortured, and executed. Other rumors had it that the arrested students were forcibly inducted into the military and sent to remote areas of the country. Some said that many of these students died in the military, often by the "accidental" firing of a gun.

The brilliant colors of spring lost their hue. May 1961 ushered in a gray regimented, fear-laden society where the idea of escape provided the only hope for youths like Bo.

37

THE TROPHY

Spring 1962, Seoul (37.5 N Parallel, 127 E Longitude)
Bo

The second year of medical school. There was a sense that things had settled down among Bo and his friends. They had all survived the first year of medical school, with all its new and intense subjects like anatomy, histology, and biochemistry and its new and serious schedule of classes that began at eight in the morning and often lasted till late at night in the laboratory. They now began to feel confident that, somehow, they would make it through medical school.

Their club, the MSS, provided for most of them the only opportunity for social gathering during the hectic first year, except for those who had steady girlfriends, like Rabbit. Bo knew that Yulak, undaunted by the trial by fire of the first year of medical school, had one or two romances going. But, otherwise, their getting together with other medical students from other schools and discussing what they were learning and listening to lectures by professors from other schools, which included subjects such as medical ethics and economics, proved to be adequate out-of-school socialization.

Another important source of entertainment was television. Commercial television had come to Korea late. The first TV broadcast occurred during the explosion of communication media following the April revolution. Within two years, TV had spread like wildfire, and by now, even under the censorship of the military government, it thrived as an entertainment medium.

There was a new TV show that was particularly popular among college students called *Scholastic Competition.* The show was a spin-off of the American TV show *It's Academic.* A team of four students representing a university would compete with another team in answering questions that covered the broad spectrum of liberal arts and sciences. The winning team would then face another challenging team the following week. And so it went until one team beat ten challengers in a row, when it would be crowned the champion of the season. Then, at the end of the year, the three seasonal champion teams would compete again to be declared the "grand champion of the year." The winning team of the year was awarded a trophy, which it would bring to its university. In 1961, Seoul National University had won the championship of the year.

Bo and his friends were chatting about the TV program one day during an informal meeting of the MSS. All the original four musketeers were there except for Bob, who had to attend a church function that evening.

"You know, the Sungkyoonkwan team seems to be very good in Korean and Chinese history, but they don't know a thing about science," Yulak said.

"On the other hand, this Koryu team knows all about science but knows very little of Western civilization," said Philmo.

"Yeah, they are not at all well-rounded, like us, for example," chimed in Rabbit.

"Perhaps it would make sense for us to enter as a team!" said Bo.

"An excellent idea. I'm sure that we can beat all other teams," said Rabbit.

"True, but we have a problem. You know, the competition is between universities. We represent more than one university. I don't think they will allow an MSS team!" Philmo said. Thoughtful as ever.

They were so accustomed to seeing themselves as a unit of friendship that they had forgotten that they came from different and rival universities. They eventually decided that they would form separate teams representing two separate universities. This would also be the first ever competition between the two rival medical schools of Hyundai and Seoul National Universities.

The Hyundai team consisted of Bo, as the captain, and Philmo, Rabbit, and Taewon, who was an extremely bright and intellectual person who was especially good at remembering small details, such as the year in which Gutenberg invented the printing machine. The role of the captain was to press the buzzer as soon as his team decided they had the answer. The Seoul National University's team had Yulak as the captain and three other exceptionally capable students who were members of the MSS.

The Seoul National University (SNU) team was first to go, to compete against Koryu University, which had now won eight games. But they were no match for the bright students from MSS, headed by Yulak. The SNU team won and kept on winning, until they became the seasonal champions.

Then, the Hyundai team came in and beat the Sungkyoonkwan team, the Catholic University, Hanyang University, and so on and also became the seasonal champions, as had been anticipated from the outset. They had not, however, thought far enough. They had not actually realized up to that point, although they should have, that eventually the MSS friends would be competing against each other.

The other seasonal champion was Yonsei University. The "World Series" of *Scholastic Competition* had the three teams competing against each other.

The first competition was between SNU and Yonsei. SNU won handily. Then, Hyundai won over Yonsei. Thus, the final and decisive competition for the grand championship was between SNU and Hyundai.

Excitement was running high on all college campuses. The final showdown between the rival universities, Seoul National and Hyundai!

And it was their cream of the crop, the medical schools! Most students and even nonstudents took sides, and there was even betting as to the outcome. Although SNU was more prestigious in general and was expected to win in most games against Hyundai, this was the Providence Medical College they were competing against!

The evening was a seesaw. First, Hyundai would score. Then, SNU would catch up. Then, Hyundai. Then, SNU.

"Who were the members of the second Roman triumvirate?"

Taewon nudged Bo. Bo pressed the buzzer. "Yes, Hyundai!"

Taewon answered, "Octavian, Mark Antony, and Lepidus!"

"Correct! Hyundai eighteen, Seoul National eighteen."

"Cosima Wagner, Richard Wagner's wife, was the daughter of which famous composer?"

Yulak pressed the buzzer. "Yes, Seoul National!"

"Franz Liszt!"

"Correct! Seoul National nineteen, Hyundai eighteen."

"Now, please listen carefully. Please identify the following music, the composer, the name, and the movement."

The live music questions were the most demanding, and very few of them were correctly answered by any team. And the time was running out. Only about two minutes more to go. And SNU was leading by one point. "Would my school forgive me if we lost the grand championship to Seoul National, our archrival?" wondered Bo. He looked across the table at the SNU team and Yulak, in the center, his finger on the buzzer.

The music started with an ominous note. The auditorium's packed live audience was still. Tension filled the room. A march. A dark, mocking march! Flash! The answer! Bo pressed the buzzer quickly.

"Yes, Hyundai!"

"It's Berlioz's Symphony Fantastique, fourth movement, the 'March to the Scaffold'!"

"Correct, Hyundai. Now, the score is even, nineteen to nineteen."

Applause broke out in the audience.

Now we are even! A tie! Perhaps the game could end in a tie? wondered Bo. How would Yulak feel if he lost the contest for his school, Seoul National? But what if I lose it for Hyundai, the school that has treated me well, that made me blossom, made me the top student? Oh, why do we have to compete against each other? Why must one of us win and the other lose?

"The next and final question, the tiebreaker. Who was the Spanish painter who painted the famous mural depicting the horrors of war, *Guernica*?"

Bo's finger was about to press the button. This was too easy a question. Of course, the answer was Pablo Picasso. Even a high-school student would know that. And, of course, Yulak. Bo looked at Yulak, whose finger was on the button. Hurry, he will beat me! But Bo's finger did not press the button. It lay flaccid on the button. Let this be a tie! I know you know the answer, Yulak, but you have not pressed the button. And you know I know the answer, but I haven't pressed the button. Bo and Yulak looked at each other, and a flash of understanding swept through them. The buzzer sounded.

"Time is up! The answer was Pablo Picasso! The final score is Hyundai nineteen, Seoul National nineteen. A tie! We declare that, for the first time in our history, we have two grand champions! Seoul National University and Hyundai University are both the grand champions of this year!"

Everyone in the audience was on their feet, cheering. Bo and Yulak got up from their chairs, walked toward each other, and embraced each other.

November 1962
Pyongyang, DPRK (39 N Parallel, 125.7 E Longitude)
Central Intelligence Committee Headquarters, North Korean Workers' Party

Hoon glanced at the pile of newspaper clippings on his desk with disgust as he came into his cramped office. Being a covert field operative, he hated doing paperwork in the office, but one of his duties was going through news coming from outside DPRK.

In DPRK, the only source of news was the government-controlled Korean Central News Agency, which fed government-approved news to several print papers, such as the *Workers' Daily*. Of course, Hoon knew all the news before it was printed.

The female clerks did most of the preliminary work by going through the many South Korean, Chinese, Japanese, and English newspapers and clipping items that were of potential interest to the higher-ups. This included mainly news of travels of dignitaries or major political and cultural events, which might be targets of espionage, assassination, abduction, or sabotage.

As Hoon was flipping through the clippings, he noticed the photo of two groups of young people seated behind two desks, with the caption, "Hyundai and SNU Tie for Quiz Championship!"

One of the faces in the Hyundai team caught Hoon's eye as it looked vaguely familiar. What is his name? Hmm, Taewon Cho, Kwangsoo Park, Philmo Kim, and Bo Moon (Captain). Bo Moon!

Could he be hated Suk and Yunhee's son, my half brother?

38

SAVING LIVES

September 1962, Seoul (37.5 N Parallel, 127 E Longitude)
Bo

An outbreak of cholera was sweeping the southern part of the country. Cholera is a rapidly spreading, potentially fatal infectious disease caused by a bacterium called *Vibrio comma.* Its symptoms are severe abdominal cramps and severe watery diarrhea that leads to dehydration and death. It is primarily spread through contamination of food and water by human waste. The disease can be prevented by proper sanitation and immunization. It can be effectively treated by forcing fluids, intravenously if necessary, and antibiotics.

Bo and his friends were discussing an upcoming talent show of the MSS that was going to be held in the municipal auditorium when the loudspeaker blared, commanding everyone's attention: "All medical students, please come to the auditorium. A special announcement by President Park Chung Hee to medical students and the general public will be telecast!"

"What the hell does the Tin Man want again?" asked Rabbit. The "Tin Man" was a nickname given to General Park Chung Hee, the head of the military junta, after the Tin Man of the Wizard of Oz, but really meaning a tin-pot dictator. He continued, "Maybe he wants to draft all of us into the army to fight the cholera with bullets and artillery. Come out, you goddamned Communist *Vibrio comma*! Take that, bam, bam, bam."

Rabbit was not too far off. Park had declared a state of emergency for the cholera epidemic and was, in fact, mobilizing all medical students to form a "Public Health Corps" to be sent to the southern provinces where the epidemic was raging. The medical students would provide vaccinations and teach the inhabitants sanitation and hygiene techniques, such as drinking only boiled water, making sure that the septic tanks were far enough away from the water wells, and so on.

Park wanted to show the populace how effective his military regime was. He would commandeer the medical students and stem the tide of the epidemic in one blow!

While most students resented the high-handed tactics of the Park regime, they decided to cooperate with the mobilization because the cholera epidemic needed to be stopped. Besides, Park was going to pay the mobilized students doctors' salaries for the period of the mobilization!

Each medical school was given a geographic area to cover. Hyundai was assigned to the southwestern part of Kyungsang Province, not far away from Kosung, the city where Claire was born. A field team of about eight medical students was assigned to each hamlet. Of course, the four musketeers formed a team, which included, in addition to them, four others from the same class.

September 1962, Songjin, South Korea (35.2 N Parallel, 128.7 E Longitude)

Their team was assigned to a seaside fishing village called Songjin, near the city of Chinhae. It was a picturesque town perched on a hill that dropped into the sea in a foam of tiny islands. That part of the Korean coastline is famous for the small islands that change numbers depending upon the tide. At full tide, there may be only a handful of islands visible, but at low tide, one could count literally thousands of little islands, rock formations, and other protrusions out of the sea. The town had two elementary schools, one middle school, one high school, one movie theater, two inns, one post office, and a small medical clinic, run by one doctor and one nurse. And one high-school student was also subbing as a student nurse.

The task of the team was to form links with the medical clinic, the police, and the schools in setting up an emergency cholera clinic at the elementary school, inspecting the wells in the town, and giving vaccinations to everyone, beginning with the elementary-school children. The single doctor in town was an elderly man, who was very happy to have the help of eight medical students from Seoul. He made both the nurse and the student nurse available to assist the students. He would also be available in case someone needed serious medical care. Fortunately, there had been no actual cases of cholera in Songjin.

Bo was busy giving vaccinations to first graders in the elementary school. He and Philmo were assigned to one of the elementary schools, together with the student nurse, Mirah Noh. The regular nurse was assigned to the other elementary school with Rabbit and Bob. All vaccinations were to be done in the two elementary schools. Today and tomorrow, the grammar-school students. The next day, the middle-school students. The following day, the high-school students and the general public. The other four medical students were testing all the wells in town, as well as examining the distance and relationships between the wells and septic tanks. Songjin relied on well water; there were no reservoirs or rivers to worry about.

4:30 p.m.
Only about twenty children were still waiting in line to be inoculated. "At this rate, we should finish by five," said Bo as he looked at his wristwatch.

"It would be nice to finish!" said Philmo. The phone rang. Mirah, who was preparing the children's bare arms with an alcohol sponge for the injection, went to the phone and picked it up.

"It's the other elementary school. They are asking if we could lend them a hand. Somehow, they still have more than a hundred children to be inoculated, and they wondered if someone here could come and form another line for them."

Philmo volunteered to go. It was important that the vaccinations be finished before dark so that the children could go home safely. Most of them walked home from school.

5:15 p.m.
The last of the children waiting in line was inoculated. Bo smiled at the student nurse as he said, "Well, that's that for today. You worked really hard, all day long, practically without a break except for lunch!"

"Oh, I enjoy working, especially with kids!" Mirah replied. Mirah was eighteen years old, a high-school senior, who was studying to be a nurse. She was enrolled in a special nursing course at the high school, the completion of which would qualify her as a practical nurse. She had told Bo, at lunch, that she was hoping to work as a nurse for a couple of years for the local physician, until she saved enough money to go to college in Pusan.

Mirah was a slender, petite girl who looked younger than eighteen. She had a bright, ready smile and a youthful freshness about her that made people around her feel more alive, thought Bo. Bo welcomed this feeling that she gave him, of being alive, because Bo felt he had not really felt that feeling for a long time, ever since he entered medical school, or even before…yes, ever since that fateful April of 1960, when Katie was plucked away from his life. Ever since then, although he worked with women, even closely, through MSS and other functions, Bo had not had any interest in dating them or even simply seeking sexual companionship with them. He did not even masturbate much. Somehow, Bo had felt rather asexual; his focus was on the study of medicine, which was interesting, fulfilling, and demanding.

But in this little town away from home, Bo felt a certain stirring within him as he looked at Mirah's bright, smiling, pretty face, as she said, breathlessly, "And I enjoy working with you. You are so skillful with your injections, and I love the way you talk to the children, teaching them about sanitation. You talk to them like adults, and they listen to you so seriously. You know, they'll go home and teach their parents to boil water before drinking and how to make sure that the cholera germs don't get into food!"

"Well, you were very good with the kids, too, I noticed," said Bo. "You have the knack of soothing them, the ones that are afraid of the needle, and you make them laugh and smile by the stories you tell them!"

As they were cleaning up the area to close up for the day, an elderly man came into the makeshift clinic, supported by a woman. He was dressed in the traditional Korean garb of white linen and looked obviously sick. The woman said, "Doctor, please help us. This man is my husband, and I'm afraid he is sick. He's had severe diarrhea and also vomited several times. We live near here, and we don't have a phone. I thought I'd bring him here. Can you help us?"

The man was barely standing and barely conscious. Without the wife propping him under the shoulder, he would simply have fallen. Bo quickly helped his wife lay him down on a cot on the corner of the clinic and quickly took his blood pressure. Eighty over forty-five millimeters of mercury. Very low. He took the man's pulse. One hundred twenty per minute. Very high.

With Mirah helping, Bo did a quick physical examination. The elderly man's skin was sallow and lacked elasticity. His eyes were sunken, as were his cheeks. His mouth seemed dry. He could hear very loud and rapid bowel sounds with the stethoscope, indicating increased peristalsis. With the history of diarrhea and vomiting and the degree of dehydration, cholera was, indeed, the most likely diagnosis. Should I call the doctor? Bo wondered. But what could he do, other than send the patient to the hospital in Chinhae? I think he is too weak and too dehydrated to be managed at home. Most importantly, he needs to have fluids!

Bo put an intravenous line into the man's arm and hooked it to a physiologic saline solution. Then, he asked Mirah to call the doctor in town. First, she tried the clinic. There was no answer. Then home. Again, no answer. He must be with one of the medical student groups, maybe inspecting a well. There was no way to get in touch with him. Once the IV was running well, Bo got to the phone and called the hospital in Chinhae. He spoke with the Emergency Cholera Team of the hospital.

Yes, they would send an ambulance. Yes, it should be there within two hours. In the meantime, they said, "Make sure that you have an IV saline going. The patient will be dehydrated and also likely have electrolyte depletion, too. Then, wait. We will be there. In two hours."

Bo told the man's wife, "I called the hospital in Chinhae, and they'll send an ambulance. It should be here within two hours. I think your husband has the cholera, which can best be treated in the hospital. With vigorous treatment, I expect that he'll recover. But it's important that he receives the treatment as soon as possible in the hospital, where they can make sure that he receives everything he needs. Right now, I am giving him fluids that he lost through diarrhea and vomiting. We'll check his blood pressure, pulse, and other vital signs frequently while we are waiting."

"Thank you, Doctor. Thank you very much. Will he be all right? He looks so pale and weak!" said the woman.

"Once he gets enough fluids back, I think he will feel stronger. Just in case his diarrhea starts again, we will get this bedpan ready on the cot."

"Yes, Doctor, yes! I am so glad that you are here!"

Bo was secretly afraid that the man might die before the ambulance arrived. His wife seems so trustful of me, thought Bo. How could I face her if he died?

An hour passed. Bo and Mirah were taking his vital signs every thirty minutes. And waiting for the ambulance. The vital signs were still precarious. The patient was hanging on to life by a thread. The wife was sitting rigidly by the side of the cot, holding on to her husband's hand. What thoughts are going through her mind? Bo wondered. What thoughts would go through your mind as your lover lies dying before you and there is nothing you can do? Tears welled up in Bo's eyes as he thought. Yes, I could have been you! I could, should, have been holding Katie's hand as she lay dying...

But I can do something for your husband. At least keep him alive, even if only by a thread!

He took his blood pressure again. One hundred over seventy. Pulse one hundred. An improvement. Perhaps the IV fluid is helping!

Suddenly, the man stirred and opened his eyes. He blinked, opened his eyes again, and then focused on his wife. "Is that you, my wife? Where am I?"

"Oh, darling! I am so glad you are awake! You are here, at the emergency clinic set up at the school! This doctor here, Dr. Moon, has been taking care of you every minute since I brought you here!"

He was awake! And his color was better. He said, "Thank you, Doctor. I suppose I got sick—shouldn't have eaten those raw clams!"

It was well past nine o'clock when the ambulance finally arrived. An intern jumped out of the ambulance, shook hands with Bo, listened to Bo's report, and examined the patient. He said, "Thank goodness you gave him the IV. I think he will be OK, once we put him in the hospital and treat him vigorously. If you hadn't put in the IV line immediately and rehydrated him, I doubt very much that the ambulance and I would have done any good. OK, we'll put him on the stretcher—easy now—and put him in the ambulance—that's right." Then facing the wife, he said, "OK, ma'am, you can stay with him in the ambulance. We'll be going to Chinhae Hospital. Thank you very much, Dr. Moon," he said as he faced Bo. Bo was proud to be called a doctor by a real doctor.

"Dr. Moon, you should be proud of yourself. You saved this man's life. Go and get a good night's sleep so that you can be there tomorrow for others who may also need your help in a hurry!"

With those words, the intern jumped up onto the ambulance, which roared forward, leaving only the sound of its wailing siren behind.

"Well, that's that," said Bo as he looked at Mirah. He had not realized up to that point that Mirah's hand was holding on to his arm.

"Goodness, Mirah. You must be tired and starved!" said Bo. He added, "Listen, let me buy you dinner. I missed my dinner with my colleagues anyway. Let's go to a nice restaurant."

"Good heavens, I didn't realize how late it was! My parents must be worried to death about me! Let me call them and let them know that there's an emergency with a patient," exclaimed Mirah.

She went to the phone and called her parents. She came back and said to Bo, "Well, they understand that as a nurse I must have emergencies from time to time. Sure, let's have dinner. Unfortunately, there aren't many choices for dinner at this time of night here in Songjin. Only one place, a Chinese restaurant, is open. And we can walk there!"

Bo walked to the restaurant, one arm around Mirah's waist. Like many Chinese restaurants in Korea, it had private rooms rather than tables. They ordered sweet-and-sour pork and "eight treasures," a seafood dish that contains a delicious combination of shrimp, sea scallops, sea cucumbers, and abalone. Over the delicious meal and green tea, they talked about themselves, their dreams, and their lives. Mirah said, "Gee, Bo, you lead such an exciting life already! How would your life be when you're married and have kids, too? It would be so hectic, so exciting!"

"Well, Mirah, I don't think I have to worry about that. I doubt I'll ever be married or have a family. I have too many other things to do, like practicing medicine, probably teaching, and also research."

"But you can do all these and also have personal happiness! I'm sure, Bo, that you can do both. Perhaps there's another reason why you don't think about personal happiness, about marriage and a family?" asked Mirah earnestly, with a puzzled expression.

"Yes, Mirah, perhaps you are right," said Bo. "Yes, at one time in my life, so long ago, I dreamed about all these things. I thought I could be happy as a man, with a woman I loved. But that was such a long time ago. And I know that it won't happen, not in this life, not with me."

"Bo, can you tell me about it? I so very much want to know," said Mirah.

"No, Mirah, I really can't tell you. Other than to tell you that I loved a girl once, by the name of Katie, a long time ago, and that she died. And I can never love again!"

"Bo, how sad! Was it an accident? "

"No, it was not an accident. She was a student leader of the April revolution, and she was shot while carrying an injured student to the ambulance."

"I am so sorry…she sacrificed her life for all of us, to save an injured student, to save democracy, to save our country! If she loved you, she would want you to be happy again!"

"But how can I be happy, without the source of my happiness?" Bo said bitterly.

"I understand, Bo. And I also understand that if she could hear you now, she'd cry and say, 'But, Bo, I'd be so happy if I saw you try, try to find another source of happiness, because my happiness now depends on your happiness—you're the only one of us who is alive—you can do this for me.'"

After dinner, they walked in silence, toward Mirah's house. Bo was in a pensive mood. Mirah, unlike her usual bubbly self, was quiet during the walk. As they approached Mirah's house, she said, "Bo, let's say good night here. I've been thinking about you. I understand how you feel, and I respect you for that. But please think—as you saved our patient's life tonight, you will save many others, as a doctor. But, as a human being, you could also give happiness to at least one woman, someone who could share your life as Katie would have and who could give you the kind of happiness Katie would have given you. Why don't you give yourself, and another human being, that chance?" Mirah put her hand on Bo's face, around his neck, and brought his face down onto hers. She whispered, "Bo, I'd love to be that woman. But I am not. But kiss me tonight! I think I deserve it. But tomorrow, I'm again Mirah, just the student nurse!" She pulled Bo's face down so that her lips met his. He kissed her tenderly at first and then passionately.

...Yes, Mirah. I am truly indebted to you. I feel in my kiss the presence of Katie and of love. Even though Katie is dead, my love is not, and my ability to love lives on. Yes, love lives, as I feel myself stirred again, feeling aroused again. Thank you for reawakening love, my dearest Mirah!...

Mirah released Bo from her embrace. She kissed Bo again on his cheek, lightly, and then, with a vibrant smile that matched in brightness the full moon above them, she ran into her house.

Bo heard the animated bark of a dog in the distance as he walked back to the inn where he and his friends were staying. Somehow, Bo felt as though he were walking on air. A transfigured night! A night in which he found that love still existed and life still existed, on this crazy big little flat round planet with an outsize moon circling around it!

39

REGRETS OF DYING YOUNG

October 1962, Songjin, South Korea (35.2 N Parallel, 128.7 E Longitude)

Bo had successfully treated the only case of cholera in Songjin. His patient was released from the hospital the following week, full of smiles, and with undying gratitude to the young doctor, the student doctor from Hyundai called Bo Moon. He and his wife brought Bo and his friends a whole satchel full of dried persimmons that they had made themselves from their farm.

Bo and Mirah worked hard inoculating every single one of the inhabitants of Songjin and making sure that every single well in town was tested and properly sterilized when called for. They often had lunch together and took walks, but their relationship remained that of friends. At one point, Bo asked her for a date, but she said, "No, Bo. I really love you, but I think our love should remain that of friends. Soon, Bo, I think you'll be able to love someone as you did Katie, but not quite yet. And I don't want to be hurt, and I don't want to hurt you. You've had enough hurt and suffering already, and I'm not ready for it yet!" Then she smiled radiantly and took Bo's hand and squeezed it gently. Bo understood that she was right, and he was grateful. How wonderful to see her smile, her bright, radiant smile, thought Bo. How infectious it is to be with you, and how lucky is the man who will be with you all his life!

By the middle of October, the cholera epidemic had petered out, and the national mobilization ended. The epidemic may have run its course. Or the end of the outbreak may have owed itself to the decisive and effective measures of the military government that mobilized the medical students across the nation to fight the national emergency!

Bo acknowledged that at times of real emergency, extraordinary measures, including dictatorial ones, may have a place, but his distaste for the military regime and their high-handed ways continued. He was happy to be back at home, in Seoul, attending his now-familiar, even mundane classes again.

November 1962, Seoul (37.5 N Parallel, 127 E Longitude)

"Please come back in two days for the next treatment," Bo said to the emaciated, bald woman as he led her to the therapy room, feeling his own neck with his right hand. A rotation to therapeutic radiology. Treatment for cancer.

Perhaps I should set up an appointment for myself, thought Bo. Here? No, maybe my family doctor near the Pagoda Park. But does he know anything about cancer? Maybe I should see the chairman of the oncology department here at Hyundai. No, then everyone may find out, my friends, even my family. Perhaps I should just ignore it, as I've done for the past month or even longer. When was the first time I felt this lump in my lymph node on my neck? A month? Two months? More? This firm nodule feels just like cancer, like the one I felt on the patient I just saw. And I feel another enlargement of the lymph node in my armpit, too. So, if it's cancer, it's probably too late. It's a malignant lymphoma, leukemia, or metastatic cancer, cancer spread from somewhere else. No use in treating a metastatic cancer. It will just prolong life, and the agony, to myself and to others. Maybe there is no need to see anyone. Either it's malignant or it's benign. If it's malignant, then it's too late, and I'll just die. If it's benign, then there's no need to do anything about it. Either way, there's no need to do anything about it. Or is there? You call yourself a scientist? A would-be physician? Who's too scared, too chicken to find out? As Katie would have said, "If you had any real balls, you wouldn't act so much like a coward!"...Maybe I should face whatever I have...Yes, I'll see someone...Whom?...the family doctor or the chairman? Well, the family doctor at least would keep a secret.

Finally, Bo made an appointment to see his family doctor, Dr. Woo.

"Hello, Bo. How is the medical school treating you? And what brings you here today?" asked Dr. Woo, shaking Bo's hand.

"Well, Dr. Woo, I think I have the flu or something. My lymph nodes are enlarged a bit," Bo said apprehensively.

"Hmm, well, tell me about it. When did you notice the enlarged lymph nodes?"

Bo wanted to minimize his concerns, hoping that Dr. Woo would say there was nothing to worry about, that it all was in Bo's imagination. But Dr. Woo appeared very serious as he took a careful history and did a thorough physical examination. Bo's armpits were dripping with sweat as Dr. Woo examined him. Then, Dr. Woo ordered a number of laboratory tests, including a complete blood analysis, urine test, and a chest x-ray. Then, he said, "Well, Bo. My guess is that it's nothing very serious. We will know for sure when all the lab tests are back. My feeling is that you have infectious mononucleosis, otherwise known as the 'kissing disease,' presumably because the virus is transmitted by kissing, but we know that you can get it without kissing. This is a common disease among medical students, for some reason. Anyway, I have ordered a specific diagnostic test for that, and the results should be back within a few days."

Although Bo had wanted Dr. Woo to say that what he had was not a serious disease, Bo did not somehow feel reassured or optimistic. In fact, even when the results of the test came back positive—indicating that Bo did, indeed, have infectious mononucleosis—Bo did not quite believe it. "Yeah, I probably do have infectious mono, but I may also have leukemia or malignant lymphoma. Yes, the blood test was negative for leukemia, but sometimes leukemia does not show up in peripheral blood for a while, and lymphoma cannot really be diagnosed without a biopsy…and Dr. Woo did not do a biopsy!" Infectious mononucleosis is usually a benign viral infection for which there is no specific treatment. Usually, with the passage of time, almost all symptoms, which can include mild fever, fatigue, and enlarged lymph nodes, tend to disappear gradually, although, at times, they can last for several weeks to months. Bo kept on feeling the enlarged lymph node on his neck from time to time, which gave no indication of shrinking. Eventually, Bo convinced himself that he had Hodgkin's disease, a slow-growing but malignant disease. The lump in the neck served as a reminder to Bo that he was dying of Hodgkin's disease, which idea made him feel stoic and philosophical about everyday concerns.

To be convinced of impending death at the age of twenty-one, to die young, to be nipped in the bud before the full bloom of life, just like Katie—these thoughts brought Bo sadness that was at once bittersweet and romantic. And made him feel detached, above everyday concerns and worries. What does it matter? I won't be alive next year or the year after that. I shall probably not live to graduate from medical school. If, by some miracle, I did, I certainly wouldn't be alive ten years from now, at age thirty-one, or at the latest, by age forty, I would surely be dead!

December 1962
Saturday afternoon.
Bo was in his room at home, reading a mystery novel. Something he had not done much lately. But he felt so pent up that he needed a good murder. But the murder did not take place even though Bo was already about fifty pages into the book, and he felt bored.

The sky had been gray, the streets had been gray, and people's expressions had been gray. Bo wished it would snow so that all the grayness might be covered, at least for a while, with the sparkle and purity of snow. They had not had any snow at all that year, but it had looked like snow for the last several weeks. The holidays will be here soon, thought Bo, but there was no reason to celebrate, and no one to celebrate them with! Except maybe Claire. Of late, Claire had become rather a young lady, at the age of eleven. She made a point of talking with Bo whenever she had the opportunity, and she seemed to want Bo to do more things with her. Maybe she is already becoming an adolescent, thought Bo. Funny I have not really paid much attention to Claire for a long while—in fact, years—because of my busy schedule, first with the White Deer friends, then with medical studies and MSS, and now with my preoccupation with my own disease and anticipated death. Poor Claire!

The phone rang. Bo thought of not picking it up; he really did not feel like talking to anyone. But since he was alone in the house, he felt he needed to take a message if it was for someone else. He reluctantly picked up the phone.

"Hello, may I speak to Mr. Bo Moon, please?" said a woman's voice.

"Speaking."

"I am sorry to disturb you, but this is Okhee Kim, the psychiatric nurse at the Providence Hospital Emergency Room."

"Yes, hullo. How are you?" Bo had met Ms. Kim, the psychiatric nurse, during his summer clinical elective in emergency psychiatry. She was a very efficient and considerate nurse, who, Bo felt, often helped the patients much more than the psychiatrists. She tried to soothe the disturbed patients and understand them as human beings far more than some of the psychiatric residents.

"Fine, thanks, Bo. Listen, I have a patient here, named Taewon Cho, who is a classmate of yours—you know, one of the TV-show tetrad. He doesn't know me because he didn't have his summer elective here. He's been calling your name, and he's been just awfully agitated and impossible to handle. I thought I'd call you before I called the psych resident, because, in his current state, the psych resident will probably commit him to the hospital in a straitjacket.

I think you might be able to help him calm down so that we don't have to commit him."

"OK, I'll be there as soon as I can." Bo quickly changed into his street clothes, called a cab, and arrived at the emergency room within an hour.

"I am Bo Moon, a medical student here. I understand that my classmate, Taewon Cho, is here at the ER," Bo told the receptionist.

"Yes, Dr. Moon, we've been expecting you. Please come this way." The receptionist personally led Bo to the psychiatric area in the back of the emergency room. The psychiatric suite consisted of an outer reception area, an examining and interview room, and a seclusion room. Ms. Kim shook hands with Bo and led him to Taewon. Bo was surprised to see Taewon standing in the middle of the examining room, looking quite abnormal. His hair was disheveled, his eyes had a peculiar, wild glint, and he was extremely agitated, pacing back and forth, muttering to himself. He seemed to be oblivious of Bo.

"The ball has dropped! The great apocalypse…do not stare at me so…*no, no, no!…*"

Bo gathered those words, although much of what Taewon was muttering was unintelligible. Bo tried to approach Taewon, but the nurse said, "Perhaps you should talk to him at some distance, I understand that acutely ill patients may be a bit too frightened if someone approaches them too close. And if at all possible, would you persuade him to let us give him an injection of a tranquilizer, chlorpromazine? I called the resident on call and told him about the patient, and he said it would be OK to give the injection before he came down. It would help him calm down and sort out his thoughts."

"Thank you. I will try my best."

Bo spoke to Taewon, some fifteen paces away.

"Hi, Taewon, it's me, Bo. I hear you asked for me."

Taewon looked around. At first, it seemed as though Taewon did not see Bo, and then he walked around Bo, and then came nearer to Bo, looking at him intently,

"Yes, I see you, Bo. But I have trouble seeing you—there's so much going on. All these people and images. Frightening! Yes, the ball…it's dropping again!" Taewon put both his hands on his ears, as if to ward off an explosive sound. "Bo, I know that they will get me…help!"

"Taewon, I am your friend. I'll do anything to help. Tell me what's happened."

"No, you don't understand—you won't understand. But then, maybe only you other than the bastards, because you are smart, because you are number one…no, not really, not because of that or that or that or that…but because maybe you understand…you are a psychiatrist, or you will be…No! Another ball dropping!" Taewon again quickly put his palms on his ears and closed his eyes tightly.

"Taewon, are you hearing a loud noise?" asked Bo.

Taewon looked at Bo and said, "The end of the earth as we know it…the big ball…the big bang…Bo, I'm afraid and tired…of what's happening, of Sungja…of Mom, Dad…everyone…"

Sungja! Could he mean the Sungja that Bo knew, whom he met and almost loved on that Christmas Eve? But Sungja is not an uncommon name. Bo asked, "Sungja? Who is Sungja?"

"Sungja, Sungja, Sungja," said Taewon in a singsong voice.

"Of course, you know Sungja, Bo. Sungja Oh, who knows you. Who said such nice things about you. She said she used to be your girlfriend…ya, ya, ya, Sungja, Sungja! No, another ball!"

Taewon closed his ears with his hands again, visibly shrinking. Bo was curious about Sungja and how Taewon knew her, but it was obvious to Bo that Taewon was suffering terribly. Whatever the descending ball meant, it was frightening him unbearably. Now Taewon was sitting on the stool before the examining table, quite near Bo, with his head between his hands that were propped up on the table. Bo approached Taewon and gently put his hand on his arm.

"Taewon, listen, why don't you let me help you get the injection the nurse has been trying to give you. You'll feel much better once you have some tranquilizer in you. You are very hyperalert, and your nerves are extremely sensitive. Probably you didn't sleep much at all. Listen, remember the time of the cholera epidemic? And how we gave vaccination injections to so many people? Now, it's your turn to get a shot. OK?"

Taewon did not protest. He let Bo roll up his sleeve and motion the nurse to come and give him the injection into the deltoid muscle in his arm. Bo helped the nurse take Taewon's vital signs, and stayed with him when the psychiatric resident finally arrived. Bo did not know the psychiatric resident and felt glad he did not. Bo was not at all impressed by the resident, whose examination of Taewon, Bo felt, was too cursory and lacked empathy. Taewon was rather sedated now and told the resident that he came to the ER because he knew that he was going crazy, that he was hearing and seeing things that couldn't be true, such as a big ball, a wrecking ball, coming toward him and then crashing into anything near him, buildings, windows, cars, and so on. The resident promptly admitted him, under the diagnosis of "schizophrenia, acute." No, Bo could not accompany him upstairs, but he could come back tomorrow to visit. During the visiting hours.

Well, at least Taewon was not committed against his will. In fact, he did come on his own, didn't he? But Bo felt certain that if the resident had seen Taewon the way Bo had initially found him, before the injection of chlorpromazine, Taewon would have been committed to the hospital. Well, he would come back tomorrow and talk with Taewon on the ward.

As he left the hospital, Bo found himself in a complex mood. On the one hand, he felt alive because he had helped and was helping Taewon. He was at once gratified and puzzled that Taewon had asked for him. I am already seen as a psychiatrist? It was gratifying to talk with Taewon, as he became calmer in Bo's presence. But it was terrifying to see Taewon suffer! He seemed to have such vivid hallucinations! What could have gone into Taewon's illness? He is such a normal kind of person, someone who knows all the details of history and everything else. A bright and careful person. The last person one would expect to go crazy!

But crazy he was! With his hallucinations and what seemed to be paranoid thinking...people being against him and doing things to him...most frightening. Bo thought of his own experiences of reality seeming to dissolve into nothingness...the first time was when he thought he failed the entrance exam to middle school, and then he had experienced it again only two years ago when Katie died...yes, I could have been Taewon...reality is as tenuous to me as it may be for Taewon, but I am still "normal," and he is now on the psychiatric ward as a patient. Bo felt a determination forming within his mind to try to understand and help Taewon, yet he also understood that he could help only as a friend—he was not Taewon's doctor, and he could not and should not be that. A friend. Not the doctor.

Sunday Morning
Bo went to the hospital at 10:00 a.m. Visiting hour. For some bizarre reason, the psychiatric inpatient service in a general hospital, almost anywhere in the world, is usually found in the worst possible location, either the top floor, where so many depressed patients are tempted to jump out of the window, or in the basement, the most dingy and depressing unit, where not even sunlight comes in. The Providence Hospital was no exception. The psychiatric ward was on the top floor, 7 East.

The nursing staff on 7 East knew Bo and let him in without any hassle. In fact, they were pleased to see him and called him Dr. Moon. This implied that he could come anytime, not just during visiting hours. He was one of them. He asked the head nurse about Taewon and was pleased to hear that he was doing much better, his hallucinations seemed to have stopped, and he was much more coherent. His parents were visiting with him now. Bo chatted with the nurses, waiting for the parents to leave, as he did not wish to intrude during their visit.

In about twenty minutes, Bo saw Taewon walking in the corridor with his parents. Taewon saw Bo and said, "Hello, Bo. I am so glad to see you." And turning to his parents, he added, "You know Bo Moon, my friend. He saved my life! Yesterday, he came to the emergency room and calmed me down enough to be admitted to the hospital. I heard from the nurses that I was so wild then that if Bo had not calmed me down, I would have been committed to the hospital. Commitment to the hospital for insanity stays on your medical record, and I would never have been able to go back to medical school again!"

Taewon's parents, whom Bo had met at one of the MSS shows, thanked Bo immensely. They were so happy that Taewon had a friend like Bo, someone who was so smart, so dedicated, so caring! Bo felt a bit embarrassed listening to them but also felt gratified that his friend's parents were so grateful to him.

After his parents departed, Taewon sat alone with Bo in the interview room on the ward. Taewon was visibly better; the wild glint and mutterings were gone. He still seemed agitated, and, at times, he seemed suspicious and hypervigilant. Nevertheless, Bo felt that Taewon was much more like his usual self now.

"Bo, I meant what I said to my parents. I really appreciate your being there yesterday. It really calmed me down!"

"I am glad I could help, Taewon. And I am glad to see you looking so much better. Are you feeling better, too?"

"Yes, I am. I am a bit groggy, probably because of the chlorpromazine. But it certainly helps! I wouldn't have believed it if I hadn't experienced it myself. You see, I was hallucinating like crazy…I mean, I was crazy, probably still am. But at least I now know that I am. Well, I knew it yesterday, too, or otherwise I wouldn't have come here in the first place, but, at the same time, I really thought I was being pursued by a bunch of gangsters, and the wrecking ball! It just kept coming toward me, to smash me into mush!" Taewon said as he shook his head. "I still have that image of the wrecking ball, and sometimes I see it coming, but it's not as vivid as it was yesterday, not as threatening."

Bo asked, "How did it all begin?"

"I don't really know how it began. I have been under considerable stress lately. Among other things, I broke up with my girlfriend about a month ago, shortly after we came back from the cholera mobilization. My girlfriend, whom you know—I understand she used to be your girlfriend—Sungja Oh and I broke up. Then, I was convinced that I had leukemia, with swollen lymph glands. Then, suddenly, I knew the answer to everything…the wrecking ball, swinging back and forth. That was the answer.

"To be honest with you, Bo, I took some Dexedrine, just to give myself a little lift. You know there are bunches of packets of Dexedrine lying around in the clinic pharmacy that the drug companies are providing free to doctors and patients who want to lose weight? I just took a bunch of them, saying something about my patients who are obese. Then, I took them regularly, for at least three or four weeks now."

Bo had been concerned about these packets of Dexedrine lying around the clinic pharmacy. Dexedrine, in those days, was not a controlled substance and was readily available in pharmacies for weight loss and also as a stimulant. It was often prescribed as a "picker upper" with cold medicine as well. But Bo felt concerned because he knew that the stimulation of the central nervous system by Dexedrine was known to cause paranoid tendencies in many people, according to published articles. Furthermore, there was often depression following Dexedrine stimulation. It seemed that Taewon's symptoms were easily explainable by the Dexedrine abuse.

"Did you tell your doctor about the Dexedrine?"

"No, I haven't seen him yet. Today is Sunday, remember?" said Taewon.

"Well, be sure to tell him when you see him. I think you had an amphetamine-induced psychosis, which is now under control. You certainly had paranoid thoughts, had hallucinations, both visual and auditory…" said Bo.

"I hope that it was a simple drug-induced psychosis, but I am not sure, Bo. You see, my grandmother had a nervous breakdown and had to be committed to a psychiatric hospital. She died there, I understand. I was less than ten years old then."

"By the way, Taewon, Sungja was not really my girlfriend. I did know her, a little, for a brief time. I didn't know that she was your girlfriend," Bo said.

"Yes, we were in love, or so I thought. We were going out for about two years. I met her shortly after coming to the medical school and fell in love. She told me that she used to be your girlfriend in high school. Anyway, she said you were such a perfect gentleman that she found it difficult to break up with you. It seems she didn't find me to be as perfect a gentleman as you, because, obviously, she did not find it as difficult to break up with me as with you."

"Taewon, we did not break up. We never got to that point. We just had a fling one night, that's all," said Bo.

"Well, it was much more than a fling between us, Bo. We really loved each other, and we had great sex, too. Then, she meets this sculptor, and—bingo!—she sleeps with him and doesn't care about old Taewon anymore! You know, she's in the Fine Arts Department at Seoul National. Her new lover is a lecturer in her department."

"I am sorry to hear that, Taewon. I had no idea that you were going through all this. I know how painful it is to lose someone you love, no matter what the cause!"

"I know you understand. We all knew about you and Katie and how much pain you must have suffered. Well, Sungja's not dead, but she is dead to me!"

"Does that have something to do with the wrecking ball?" Bo asked.

"I don't know, Bo. Maybe it does symbolize something: my wish to smash everything to smithereens! Sungja herself, maybe myself—yes, the ball comes at me, directly! If I don't duck, it will smash my head like a ripe persimmon, and blood and brain will be splattered all over the floor!"

"You say you were convinced you were dying of leukemia?" asked Bo.

"Yes, it's funny. As I was feeling rejected and that life was not worth living without Sungja, I became preoccupied with the idea that I had leukemia. My glands were a bit swollen. Then, I decided that I had leukemia, and, you know, Bo, I did not want to die—I was afraid of dying. But I didn't see any doctor, because I did not want to find out that I was going to die. I took the Dexedrine mainly to stop worrying about dying. And it did help me with that. I stopped worrying about dying of leukemia but got afraid that people, gangsters, the Korean Mafia, were going to kill me—yes, with the wrecking ball. You see, the Mafia was hired by this guy, Sungja's new lover, who sees me as a threat and tries to kill me! I know that the idea is far-fetched, but when you see this giant black wrecking ball coming right at you, and then, as you duck, you hear it crashing into the brick wall behind you with a tremendous *crash*, then you know that it's all true…that they are going to get you. Thank God that's stopped! Now I feel more like a rational human being."

"Listen, Taewon, be sure to tell your doctor about what you told me. I have the hunch that you will be completely OK very soon and come back to class!"

During his long bus ride home, Bo wondered about Sungja. What would have happened if that Christmas Eve had turned out differently? If I had made love to her completely? What if I had dated her after that night? Would we have become lovers, as Sungja seemed to have told Taewon? Would I have been rejected by her as Taewon was now? Would I also have become psychotic, with or without amphetamines? After all, I am perhaps at a higher risk of becoming psychotic in view of my experiences of reality dissolution before, thought Bo. Fate deals such strange, twisted cards.

Taewon was discharged from the hospital within two weeks and was back in class within the month. He would be able to catch up and graduate with the class. Taewon was very grateful to Bo for helping him. Bo did not feel he deserved any credit for Taewon's recovery. After all, what he had was, in all likelihood, just a drug-induced psychosis. The prognosis was good. The class as a whole was gratified that Taewon was back to being his old self again. It could not afford to lose another student under tragic circumstances.

Bo found that he did not think about his own "fatal" illness at all ever since that phone call on that Saturday afternoon from the emergency-room nurse. The idea that he had fatal Hodgkin's disease seemed so remote now, yet it seemed so real, so urgent then, thought Bo. How is it that a close exposure to someone else's real illness makes your preoccupation with your own supposed illness so trivial? Perhaps we should draft all hypochondriacs into national health service, thought Bo.

1974, New Haven, Connecticut (41 N Parallel, 73 W Longitude)
Psychoanalytic Couch

"So, you see, Dr. Lowmann, somehow I was cured of my Hodgkin's disease by Taewon's psychosis. As they say, 'mind over matter'...but really, I think that the reality of seeing Taewon really sick emotionally kicked me back into reality...it's one thing to fantasize about being sick and dying, but it's another thing to see it happen to someone...I mean actually see the symptoms of psychosis, see how that the person had changed so drastically...Taewon was such an obsessive-compulsive, detailed, careful sort of guy, and the way he acted in the emergency room was so strange...so different...in a way you would never expect him to be capable of changing so much..."

"Ja, perhaps, you were afraid of that happening to you, too?" said Dr. Lowmann.

"Do you mean changing or becoming psychotic?"

Dr. Lowmann does not answer. Although Dr. Lowmann doesn't exactly fit the stereotype of the psychoanalyst who just says "hmm-hmm," it is still maddening when he does not answer your question, which he does from time to time. He just sits there. But, then, this time, anyway, my question is rather silly. I continue, "Maybe both. The idea of dying itself is not that scary; in a way, it is a consolation when you are in pain. I also had some romantic notions about death, you know, of being free, being one with nature, being with Katie, and being the tragic hero... but what happens before you die is something else, the pain, the suffering, and, yes, in Taewon's case, the loss of your identity or pattern of behavior...after all, what defines you other than how you feel, how you think, how you act, and how you perceive reality?...but all that was changed with Taewon...and that possibility was frightening to me, too. And that Taewon and I had something in common...we both knew Sungja...although she was definitely his girlfriend, and I don't quite understand what she was to me, we almost had sex...maybe some would say that we did have sex...insertion without ejaculation!...and she told Taewon that she was my girlfriend..."

"Ja, what do you think of that?" says Dr. Lowmann.

"I am at a loss. Maybe she thought she was intimate with me, although we never followed through with it...I wonder if she really loved me...but, then, why didn't she call? True, I did say I would call, but I never did...but she had my number, too! Were we waiting for each other to call? Did I miss an opportunity to develop a truly gratifying relationship? But, then, maybe I was afraid of it, afraid of what might happen if we really got together. Maybe I was not ready, then, to be fully in love. Seeing what happened that Christmas Eve, the next time we were together, if we had gotten together, we would have had real sex and maybe real commitment...She was lovely, but maybe I was afraid of too deep an involvement with her...but I did get very involved with an image of her, in fantasy...I had a torrid affair with a fantasized Sungja, with daily masturbation...it was almost as real as reality itself..."

"And safe, too." murmurs Dr. Lowmann.

"Yes, safe. No real bodily contact. I wonder if she had a similar period when she fantasized that I was her boyfriend. Maybe that's why she told Taewon what she did! Maybe we thought alike and acted alike! Maybe she should have been my girlfriend. Then, maybe I would have had the psychotic episode, not Taewon…what a frightening thought. As you know, my relationship with reality is not the Rock of Gibraltar, either. I sometimes wonder…"

"You mean, what it might be like if you became psychotic?" murmurs Dr. Lowmann. Dr. Lowmann pronounces the term *psychotic* as *see-ko-tyk*.

"No, er, yes, I mean…what if, indeed, I crossed the threshold and lost it? Ha-ha, I could blame you, of course! You know, 'psychoanalysis may be hazardous to your health—it can make you crazy?"

"You mean if you face your real self that may make you psychotic?"

"But what is my real self? Isn't it really whatever I am, at any given moment? Is there really a reality? Ja, Herr Docktor Lowmann, Ich know that I am intellectualizing, but what is life without intellectualization? And you know and I know that all of us, both Taewon and myself, and probably the rest of the class, were suffering from an endemic disease of the medical school, known as the 'medical student's illness'! In medical school, almost all students experience, at one time or another, the feeling that they have a dreaded disease."

"You mean medicine causes illness?"

Sometimes, psychoanalysts can be impossible.

40

SECRET MISSIONS

November 4, 1963, Pyongyang, DPRK (39 N Parallel, 125.7 E Longitude)
Central Intelligence Committee Headquarters, North Korean Workers' Party
Hoon

They were listening to Kim Il-Sung, prime minister and chairman of the Central Committee of the Workers' Party of the Democratic Republic of Korea (DPRK), on the remote PA system broadcast from his office in Kumsusan Palace. "Comrades, the corrupt government of South Vietnam has been replaced by the puppet generals of the South Vietnamese Army, in a coup engineered by American imperialist CIA. American imperialists are likely to increase their aggression against the heroic freedom fighters in South Vietnam, but I know that our comrades will prevail, under the heroic leadership of Comrade Ho Chi Minh!" Martial music followed the announcement from the loudspeaker above the blackboard on the wall. The loudspeaker also served as a local PA system connected to a microphone. Kim Il-Sung's speech had also been broadcast on the government-provided radio found in every household in DPRK. All these radios had been prewired in the factory to receive only one channel, the government propaganda station.

Actually, in this very secret place, there were three sets of radios and even a TV set. The first TV broadcast in DPRK occurred in March 1963, some seven years after TV was introduced to South Korea, and like the radios, all TV sets in DPRK were pretuned to the only government channel. Unlike the radios and TVs outside of this building, the three radios and TV here could be tuned to any station, including the many South Korean stations and even shortwave stations around the world. One of the radios and the TV were in the conference room, another radio was in the office of the chairman of the committee, and the other was on the desk of the chief of covert operations.

Today, all the officers of the committee were gathered in the conference room to hear Kim Il-Sung. There were twelve men in the conference room, all senior officers of the elite intelligence corps of the Democratic Republic of Korea (DPRK). At the head of the table was the director, Kim Sangwoo, a man in his fifties attired in a Mao suit. Next to him sat Lee Moo-il, also a man in his fifties, identically attired in a Mao suit, who was the director of covert operations. Two seats down sat Moon Hoon, a young man of thirty-six, who attained the level of senior covert operations officer. He was the youngest man in the group and a hands-on operative. Hoon, unlike the others, was dressed in a plain blue worker's cotton suit, but one could tell his rank by how well pressed it was. He had distinguished himself in several lone covert operations, including the infiltration into South Korea earlier in September to blow up a munitions factory near Seoul to disrupt the presidential elections scheduled for October, the first election after the military coup by General Park Chung Hee. Hoon received a medal from Kim Il-Sung himself for his bravery, though the South Korean presidential election was won, albeit narrowly, by General Park Chung Hee.

Although the act of blowing up the factory itself was lone-wolf, considerable resources had been deployed to bring Hoon to South Korea. The land border between North and South Korea was practically impenetrable because of miles of minefields and machine-gun posts on both sides of the border. The only road between the two Koreas was through Panmunjom, the notorious abandoned town in which the 1953 Korean Armistice Agreement was signed. It was heavily guarded on both sides.

The only way agents of either Korea could infiltrate into the other half was through the sea. Korea, being a peninsula jutting off Manchuria into the Sea of Japan on the east and the Yellow Sea on the west, has a very complicated coastline, which cannot be practically patrolled at all times. Thus, a North Korean submarine had sailed underwater to Kangwha Island and deposited Hoon on a desolate coast.

Armed with fake identify papers and plastic explosives that he had brought from the submarine, stuck in an innocent-looking garment carrier, Hoon had checked into a busy, cheap hotel near the main train station in Seoul, after traveling by ferry and train from Kangwha Island. Hoon marveled at how South Koreans could travel freely from town to town in ferries and trains without once having to show an ID. In North Korea, it was very different—you had to first obtain a travel permit to travel outside of your town of residence, and there were checkpoints at every town and almost every intersection on the road and train station, where you had to show not only your ID but also your travel permit. If you were caught traveling without a permit, let alone an ID, you faced arrest, torture, and imprisonment, internment in a concentration camp, or even public execution.

In the hotel, Hoon plotted out his exact plans of blowing up the munitions factory in Yongsan District, a southern suburb of Seoul. Unlike in North Korea where private property was banned, there were private taxicabs in Seoul, but it would be too conspicuous to take a cab to a place you will blow up. Besides, there were not many of them, especially in the night and early morning. There were no rental cars in Seoul yet. The only public transportation available was the bus, as the subway, while planned, was not constructed yet.

The bus would serve the purpose, as it was usually crowded, and nobody would pay attention to him. He would take the bus to Yongsan and then walk to the factory and wait for nightfall. But before he blew up the factory, he had to do one other thing—find out where his archenemy lived. Suk.

My father, who abandoned his own flesh and blood, not just me but his daughter, Kyung, too. And his devoted wife, my mother, Min, whom I left behind when I came north to join the Red Army. I often imagine her dying in my arms of *han*, the psychosomatic disease caused by the bitter hatred and regret that grew like cancer in her heart. I had begged him to come home that day, but he spurned me, because he was bewitched by Yunhee, the witch! Since that day, my single purpose in life was to take revenge on Suk and Yunhee. I must find out where they live!

Suk's name was not listed in the phone book, and Hoon was at a loss as to how to find him among the three million residents of Seoul (if he lived in Seoul, that is) or among the thirty million South Koreans. Hoon's eyes suddenly lit up—but wait! Suk and Yunhee had a son called Bo. Didn't I read in a South Korean newspaper, about a year ago, that a student named Bo had been on a South Korean TV quiz show representing his university, which won the trophy? Yes, representing Hyundai University! I remember I was in the headquarters building reading the paper, and I was going to find out more about Bo, especially where he lived. But then I was urgently summoned by my director and ordered to interrupt everything and carry out a particularly daring and risky operation in Thailand.

He picked up the phone.

"Hyundai University, student affairs."

"Hello, I am calling from the Munwha TV station. We need to send some material concerning the quiz show to Bo Moon, who represented your university. Can you give me his mailing address?"

"Sure, it is 2413 Hwi-jo Dong, Seoul."

"Thank you very much. I am sure he will be delighted." So simple!

Hoon found the address on the Seoul map—very much on the east side. He found that there was a bus line that went near the address, but the bus stopped operating at 10:00 p.m. If only I had a car, thought Hoon. Of course, in DPRK, I always had a government car at my disposal. But a bus will have to do. He marked the address with an X and then folded the map and put it in his secret, inside trouser pocket.

2120 hours
Hoon arrives by bus a block from the factory entrance. He knew the layout of the factory by heart from the intelligence reports gathered in Pyongyang. It's dark, and there are a few passersby. Hoon, wearing dark workman's garb, looking like a factory worker, bends to tie his shoes and waits till the street seems clear. He quickly gets into the side street right next to the barbed-wire fence of the factory and methodically cuts a hole and lets himself in. He then sprints quietly to the annex, where he knows ammunition is stored. He notices that there is a truck parked in front of the annex, with the cargo container locked. There is no driver. Hoon carefully places his garment bag under the cargo compartment of the truck and sprints back to the sidewalk through the hole. All of this took less than ten minutes!

Hoon walks back to the bus stop and waits for the last bus back to downtown to arrive at 9:55 p.m.

2155 hours
The bus arrives, half-empty. Hoon climbs on the bus and pays the driver. The bus leaves the stop headed east to downtown.

Boom! Boom! Boom! The sky in the back of the bus lights up as the factory explodes. The explosion below the truck caused the cargo to explode, which in turn caused the annex to explode! The stunned passengers try to look out the windows, but the driver drives on, determined to be home before the curfew.

"Hey, Comrade Moon, are you daydreaming?"

Hoon, startled, awakened from his reverie and responded, "No, Comrade Lee. I was just thinking about how we might support our Great Leader and assist our comrades in Vietnam."

"Yes, we must help our cause wherever there is a fight against the imperialist capitalists! But we must also liberate South Korea from the Park Chung Hee imperialist military regime! What you did in September was an exemplary demonstration of what we can do to cause confusion in South Korea!" responded Director Lee.

Hoon knew then that another glorious act of courage was in store for him—to kill Park Chung Hee, the dictator of South Korea and an ex-officer of the Japanese Imperial Army, which fought the guerilla forces of the Great Leader, Kim Il-Sung. Secretly, he also knew that there was another, more personal mission.

41

OF FATHERS AND MENTORS

1963, Seoul (37.5 N Parallel, 127 E Longitude)
Bo
Third Year of Medical School

The first two years' medical-school curriculum consisted of basic sciences. Among the second-year courses, Bo was especially entranced with physiology. Among other reasons, the physiology professor, Dr. Hong, was an enthusiastic teacher, who brought the subject matter to life by posing a question in the beginning of his lecture. "How does the heart know how much blood to pump? How does it know when the brain needs it more rather than the muscles or vice versa?"

Bo found these questions challenging. He also discovered that the technique of asking some fundamental questions at the beginning and finding the answers to the questions enhanced interest and mastery. He adopted the technique as his own.

He found that all of medicine was based on the principles of physiology, which was asking the tautological question, "Why does a living thing live?" The wisdom of the body. How life-forms have developed, through eons of evolution, a system that is so delicately balanced but so toughly constructed that living is the natural state of its being rather than the permanent stability of the nonliving. He found that as long as he understood the impingement of a disease on the basic physiologic principles underlying the organ system, the diagnosis and treatment of the disease could be easily deduced. If you knew physiology, you already knew most of pathology and clinical medicine.

Thus, Bo found the third year of medical school, consisting mostly of physical diagnosis, pharmacology, and clinical medicine, easy. He enjoyed the actual hands-on experience with patients. There, he could integrate his knowledge of the basic principles governing the body with his knowledge and interest in psychiatry, how the mind and behavior worked with the body.

Bo's interest in psychiatry deepened with the atmosphere of repression and anxiety in the larger milieu. Park Chung Hee, the military dictator, called for a presidential election in October, which was obviously going to be rigged as was Syngman Rhee's. Though there were credible opposition candidates, the outcome was clear from the beginning. The election was marred by an act of sabotage by presumed North Korean agents in September when a bomb exploded in a munitions factory in the suburbs of Seoul, causing several deaths and injuries. If the North Koreans wanted to cause chaos and instability in South Korea, however, this act of terrorism had the opposite effect by elevating South Koreans' anxiety and fear of the North Korean threat and increasing support for Park's anti-Communism.

Could authoritarian personalities be treated with psychotherapy? Could psychiatry be applied to the whole society and liberate individual initiative and creativity?

Psychiatry was a part of the clinical curriculum in the third year. The psychiatry professor, Dr. Yum, was aware of Bo's interest in psychiatry. Bo had hoped to be close to Dr. Yum as he took his course—he wanted to learn to become a psychiatrist, after all. However, Bo felt that Dr. Yum kept him at a distance. Bo learned that Dr. Yum was the only full professor in the Department of Psychiatry at Hyundai. Dr. Yum had the reputation of not allowing junior faculty to advance because he did not want to allow any potential rival to be in his department. "Does he see me already as a potential rival?" wondered Bo, but he dismissed the thought as ludicrous. A third-year medical student, a rival to the full professor and chairman of the department? Nonsense.

1974, New Haven, Connecticut (41 N Parallel, 73 W Longitude)
Psychoanalytic Couch

"Ja, vy ist it nonsense?" asks Dr. Lowmann.

"Because, Dr. Lowmann, how could I be a threat to him? I wasn't even a doctor yet. How could I threaten him? He was a big professor, and the chair of the department, to boot!"

"Ja, but how about now? Are you a docktor?" murmurs Dr. Lowmann.

"Of course, Herr Docktor Lowmann. Now I am a doctor... you know that...but you mean, am I a threat to Dr. Yum now? Hmmmm...I don't see how I can be. I am, in a way, ahead of him. I am an upcoming associate professor at world-renowned Yale University. I wouldn't covet his position; mine is better! I could, in fact, have his position if I wanted to go back to Korea. I'm sure the university would offer me full professorship plus the chairmanship if I asked them for it."

"So, there!" says Dr. Lowmann.

So, there, indeed. Does jealousy and rivalry know no boundaries of time, generation, and propriety? But, of course, that is the essence of the Oedipus complex. Jealousy across the boundaries of generations, of propriety! The son covets his father's wife, because he cannot possess her fully like his father, physically and sexually. And the father? Is he threatened by his son, just as the son is by his father?

Yes, many a time, come to think of it, I had made my teachers, and my father, feel impotent. I delighted in pointing out logical flaws in almost anything that my teachers and my father said. I delighted in embarrassing them, as long as I was on the safe grounds of logic. And how often did I feel that they were all jackasses?

And my dad. My dad, who was so dapper and, yes, so terrifying in his black police uniform! But he was always gentle and always so considerate of me. He had never been physically violent with me—never! He never hit me or slapped me, let alone spanked me! He always said, "Bo is a rational person. He will understand if we talk with him rationally." And I did. But then, many a time, I disagreed with him, and my mom, rationally (or according to what seemed rational to me at the moment). And I did what I wanted if they could not rationally persuade me to do what they wanted. And they accepted it. Even though there may have been times when they were right and I was wrong, they never forced me to do anything that I truly disagreed with. And they let me do anything that I truly believed in.

But I thought of my dad as a failure. A shell of the person that he could have been. I felt he was ineffectual, that he was more interested in being liked by others than in standing up for what he believed in! An ineffectual fool! I felt that he made the asinine mistake of joining the police force, when he should have continued his career in education. Like Dr. Kaiser. Dad could have been a Dr. Kaiser, respected by everyone. Come to think of it, Dr. Kaiser is like a dad to me, with his gentle, friendly demeanor.

Dr. Kaiser has brought me up in my career as an academic psychiatrist. He nurtured me in my research and in my clinical work. As my father had done earlier. Dad had nurtured my mind and my imagination with his fantastic and entertaining bedtime stories. And with his sweat and tears of humiliation, of being a policeman in a dictatorial regime, an object of hate by others, he had provided me with all the material things I needed, to be educated among the elite, to grow up proud, proud enough to feel ashamed of him.

Did my dad feel threatened by me? Perhaps. But if so, he never showed me that by being distant, remote, or uncaring, as Dr. Yum seemed to be.

Oh, Dad. It's me who was threatened. By you, for no rational reason! I, the would-be psychiatrist. And you understood. You believed in Pestalozzi, and you stood up for what you believed in! It was I who did not understand, who did not believe!

"Oedipus Redux," murmurs Dr. Lowmann.

42

THE LAST TRAIN TO AMERICA

May 1964, Seoul (37.5 N Parallel, 127 E Longitude)
Bo

Bo has been a senior in medical school for a couple of months already. The senior schedule was much more relaxed than that of the first three years of medical school, consisting mostly of clinical rotations to various wards. The seniors also had to study for the national licensing examination later that year. Unlike the entrance examinations, however, the licensing exam was something that most graduates of medical schools passed, and no one expected Bo to fail it. Then there was the ECFMG examination—the exam of the American Educational Council for Foreign Medical Graduates. This was an exam administered, on a voluntary basis, to all medical-school seniors and medical graduates who wished to have postgraduate training in the United States. The exam was set up by the American National Board of Medical Examiners and administered through the American embassy. Only physicians who passed the ECFMG were qualified to apply for postgraduate training in internships and residencies in the United States and participate in the American National Intern Matching Program.

Later, in the 1970s, another exam was set up for graduates of medical schools outside of the United States, the visa qualifying exam. Then, only physicians who passed both the ECFMG and the visa qualifying exam (which was essentially an English test) could receive training in the United States.

In 1964, both ECFMG and the licensing exams were scheduled for November, the ECFMG taking place two weeks before the licensing exam.

Bo felt at ease with himself. For one thing, he knew that he did not have to cram for the exams. He had been the top student at his medical school for three years straight. More importantly, he felt that he understood medicine, based on basic principles that he had mastered and continued to refine, apply, and modify. All he needed to do was to brush up on the existing knowledge base around the time of the exams.

Bo did want to train in the United States. But he knew that, first, he would have to serve in the army. The military regime insisted that all male Korean students serve in the armed forces after graduation from college, and Bo would be no exception. Three years of hard labor in a prison camp! He would not have minded serving in the army had Korea not been seized by the military junta. He had had no objection to protecting his country, especially the one for which Katie died and which he had helped to preserve through the April uprising. Then he would have been happy to risk death to protect his hard-won freedom. But, now, under the military regime, he felt that South Korea was little better than North Korea. The idea of donning the military uniform, even as a member of the medical corps, seemed pointless to Bo. No, if there was any chance he could avoid serving in the army, he would grab it. But there was no opportunity he could see of avoiding the inevitable. He had already registered for military duty when he turned eighteen and received a 1A classification, with deferment due to his being in college and in medical school. When he finished his medical school, he would no longer be eligible for any further deferment!

There was no summer vacation during the last two years of medical school. An apt preparation for physicianhood, thought Bo. At times, he wondered whether he should give up medicine altogether and be a poet or, more likely, a novelist. It seemed to Bo that the world of literature offered much more creativity and opportunities for flights of fancy than did medicine.

October 1964, Seoul, Korea

Special Bulletin to Medical Schools: The Ministry of Defense, in recognition of the need to have qualified specialists in the armed forces, will receive applications from senior medical students who wish to have specialist training overseas. Their military duty will be deferred until they have finished their specialist training overseas, not to exceed five years. Interested persons should apply within three weeks. Signed, Major General Chulwon Song, Chief of Staff.

Bo could not believe his eyes. Here was an opportunity to escape from Korea without first serving in the military. Never mind that you are supposed to come back and serve as a specialist. Such commitments were not even worth the paper they were written on. What was important was that you could leave! Bo found out that each medical school could recommend up to five students to have their military duty deferred for that purpose. The school, naturally, chose the candidates on the basis of their academic standing in class. Of course, Bo, Philmo, Bob, and Rabbit were selected. All they needed to do now was to pass the ECFMG exam and obtain a postgraduate training position in a hospital in the United States!

Hastily, Bo wrote to a number of hospitals in the United States to inquire about their postgraduate training programs. Postgraduate medical training then consisted of one year of general medical or rotating internship (rotations consisting of medicine, surgery, pediatrics, and obstetrics and gynecology), followed by three to five years of residency during which one receives specialized training in a particular specialty. Residency training in psychiatry or medicine takes three years after internship, while it may take up to five or six years in surgical subspecialties. He wanted to apply for a rotating internship, during which time he would apply to psychiatric residencies. This would give him at least several months in the United States before he decided on a residency. Being already in America, he would also be able to have personal interviews for the residency applications. He knew that, in order to be accepted by first-rate hospitals, personal interviews were a must.

Bo and his friends were comparing notes at the White Deer Tearoom.

Philmo said, "I think we should all try to go to the same city so that we can be together in America."

"Good idea. Why don't we go to New York, the capital of the world?" chimed in Rabbit.

"The Brooklyn College Hospital looks very promising. According to the book, it did accept a number of foreign medical graduates, as opposed to Columbia or Cornell, which accepted none," said Bob.

"Yeah, but I am interested in getting into a special combined research and medicine internship at Johns Hopkins, in Baltimore," said Bo. While he liked the idea of being in the same city, Bo had heard that Johns Hopkins was the best medical school in America, and he wanted to try his luck with the highly competitive program. "But I will rank Brooklyn College Hospital as my second choice," Bo said.

"My first choice is Cornell. But I will put Brooklyn College right after that," said Yulak.

December 1964

The exams came and went. Bo felt confident he did reasonably well on both the ECFMG and the licensing exams. In fact, he found out that he scored first in rank of all the candidates in Korea taking the ECFMG exam, with a scaled score of ninety. He was the third in rank on the licensing exam, the first two places going to two Seoul National graduates.

February 1965
Bo and his friends had agreed to meet at the White Deer Tearoom to share the results of the match and to discuss their plans.

Philmo was first to arrive. Then Yulak. Philmo said, "Brooklyn College Hospital, my first choice!"

"I got my second choice, the Brooklyn College Hospital!" said Yulak.

Bob arrived. He said, "I got my first choice, Brooklyn College Hospital!"

"Bravo!" said Yulak and Philmo in unison. "We are going to be together."

Bo came in. He said, "I got my second choice. Brooklyn College Hospital. How about you guys?"

"Bravo!" said the three others in unison.

Rabbit came in. He said, "I got my second choice. San Francisco General Hospital. How about you?"

There was silence. Finally, Bob said, "Yulak, Philmo, Bo, and I were all matched to Brooklyn College Hospital, in Brooklyn, New York. It looks like you will have to take overnight red-eye specials to New York to see us from San Francisco!"

"Gee, that's too bad. But I have a sister who lives in San Francisco, and my girlfriend was also matched to San Francisco. You see, she and I were in the match as a couple, and it looks like Brooklyn College Hospital didn't want one of us. But it's OK because she and I will be together in San Francisco, and I would much rather be with her than you boys!" said Rabbit.

Philmo said, "Great. At least we will all have someone we know on the West Coast!"

They all went to a beer hall that night and celebrated their new jobs, to begin July 1, 1965, in the United States of America. They were aware that their school days were coming to an end and a new phase of their lives was about to begin, as doctors in training, as beginning professionals, paid experts, however meager the salary might be, as opposed to students who pay tuition to learn.

Graduation Ceremony, Hyundai University

The medical students had two graduation ceremonies on the same day. Proudly wearing the black academic gown with the green hood, a universal symbol of medicine, the students first attended the university-wide graduation ceremony held in the amphitheater, complete with prayer and benediction and a rambling talk by the university president on the importance of idealism and faith among the youths. For most graduating youths, however, their idealism had been trampled by the military boots just as they began their college life, and what awaited them was the regimentation of military service and then incorporation into a gray regimented society. Except for the few fortunate medical students, including Bo. For them, fortune had smiled, and exciting careers and adventures awaited them across the ocean, in the land of promise, America!

The medical students then marched to their own building, where a special ceremony was conducted that included the actual handing out of the diplomas by the dean and the taking of the Hippocratic oath. Bo, being the first in class, received the diploma from the university president on behalf of his graduating medical-school class during the university ceremony. He was again the first to receive the diploma, this time handed out by the dean. Then, all other students were called by name, and each received his or her diploma from the dean, with a handshake.

Then, with the Hippocratic oath, they had now all become physicians. The realization of long-held dreams and aspirations, both the students' and their families'. Bo's parents were at the ceremonies, as was Claire and Cousin Soonkil, the thoracic surgeon. Even Uncle Chang was there with his wife. They all shook hands with each other, embraced each other, and congratulated each other. A day of glory for Bo and the Moon family.

Bo decided to spend the remaining several months before his departure to the United States in the Physiology Lab at Hyundai, helping and learning from Dr. Hong, the professor who had kindled his interest in basic questions and principles in medicine. He wanted to enjoy his last months before his clinical training in the lab, savoring the experiments and refreshing in his mind the basic principles of physiology and medicine that he knew would form the foundations of his clinical work with patients. Bo especially enjoyed the Sleep Lab, which was a part of the Physiology Lab. The Sleep Lab was a brand-new facility for patients with sleep-related disorders, including sleep apnea and insomnia, as well as for pure research into the physiology of sleep. The patients or subjects were attached to an electroencephalogram (EEG) machine through electrodes pasted on the scalp, and they slept while the technician observed the recording through the night. Bo volunteered to work as a Sleep Lab technician for the remainder of his time, until two weeks prior to his departure to America, even though it meant his spending almost every weeknight at the lab. Well, he did not have a particular girlfriend anyway.

At home, Bo, his parents, and Claire were now preparing in earnest for his upcoming departure. The Brooklyn College Hospital had agreed to advance Bo and his friends their one-way plane fares, to be repaid from their salaries. They would all fly on the same plane, a Japan Airlines flight from the Seoul Airport to Tokyo, and from Tokyo to Honolulu. Then, from Honolulu to San Francisco. There, Rabbit would deplane, to be met by his girlfriend, who would be there earlier than Rabbit, and his sister, who had lived there for a number of years. Bo, Philmo, Bob, and Yulak would then continue on to New York's Kennedy Airport on an overnight flight. Then, they would stay overnight at the Times Square YMCA Hotel and go to Brooklyn College Hospital the next day.

One Saturday evening, Bo's father asked Bo to come to the bird room, and he reached out and opened the drawer of his little writing desk. He took out a medium-length silver knife, with a jade handle with silver bolsters and a silver sheath.

"Bo, this is a knife that my own father gave me as I left for Seoul, to find my new life away from the province, to find my destiny. It has protected me from all evil forces. During the war, your mother kept it for me, and it protected you and your mother. Now, I give it to you as you start your own journey to a new land, to find your own destiny. Keep it always, and let it protect you from all evil. Stay safe. And fly!"

The Korean government allowed its citizens to take no more than one hundred dollars out of the country. Thus, each of them would have just one hundred dollars in their pockets when they left the country. That sum of money and one suitcase per person.

Bo wanted to stay overnight in Tokyo, to see the capital of the country that had played such an important role in the lives of his parents. Bo wondered if he and his friends might meet with some college students in Japan during their one-day stay in Tokyo. His friends agreed that it would be nice to see Tokyo and meet some students but did not know how to go about doing so. There had been practically no exchange between Korea and Japan for so long—they did not know of any student organizations or services. Bo decided to call Japan Airlines and inquire. Bo was pleasantly surprised to find, from the airline agent in Tokyo, that there was a social club of Japanese college students whose purpose was to meet Korean college students visiting Japan. The name of the club was Korea-Japan Student Exchange, KJSE for short. Bo was given the name of the president of the society to write to. The airline was also happy to arrange for their overnight accommodation in Japan at no extra charge.

Bo received a prompt reply from KJSE—they would be happy to meet with Bo and his friends and show them around Tokyo on June 28. They sent a phone number to call as soon as they arrived at the Hilton Hotel, where they would be staying in Tokyo, courtesy of Japan Airlines.

43

NOT FOR KIMCHI ALONE

June 1 (Tuesday), 1965, Seoul (37.5 N Parallel, 127 E Longitude)
Hoon

Itinerary for the week:

- Infiltrate.
- Dry run.
- Assassinate, assassinate.
- Melt away.

Hoon knew exactly what to do from the moment he checked into the cheap hotel in front of the Seoul Railroad Station, the same hotel he used two years ago when he blew up the factory on the outskirts of Seoul to disrupt the election. The election General Park Chung Hee won to become the dictatorial puppet of the American imperialists. Here he was, Moon Hoon, senior colonel of the KPA and a star of Covert Operations of DPRK Defense Committee, to finally achieve his burning ambition to assassinate Park Chung Hee!

Hoon, the genius of lone-wolf operations, the jackal of North Korea!

Infiltrating alone up to this point was a piece of cake, following the same routine as two years back—submarine to Kangwha Island in the dark of night, then ferry to Inchon, then train to Seoul. Hoon still marveled at how lax security was in South Korea: no one asked for travel papers or any kind of ID even at ferry crossings or train stations. He did have a fake ID in case it was needed, but other than that, absolutely no identification or potentially identifying items. Hoon had always worn the gold duck pendant necklace while he was in North Korea, but he left it at home with Myunghee when he was on a covert mission outside the country so that his identity could be concealed.

In DPRK, we do things differently, thought Hoon. We must protect our comrades from subversive influences such as persons with subversive ideas infiltrating from China or the Soviet Union. Since 1956 when Khrushchev started a campaign of de-Stalinization in the Soviet Union, subversive, liberal ideas started to contaminate elements of North Korean society, which threatened the undisputed leadership of Kim Il-Sung. Hoon had secretly placed bugs in the Soviet embassy in Pyongyang and was largely instrumental in uncovering the plot by those elements of the politburo who had ties with South Korea, China, and the Soviet Union to overthrow Kim Il-Sung in August 1956. A bloody purge followed, and the Great Leader Kim Il-Sung and the guerilla faction of the politburo who fought with him in Manchuria were now securely in power. And Hoon's father-in-law was an ex-guerilla politburo member! With the success of this mission, I might even be elevated to the politburo, Hoon daydreamed.

June 2 (Wednesday)
Dry Run
I remember the address as if it's seared in my brain—2413 Hwi-jo Dong, Seoul. Hoon opened the map of Seoul he picked up in the lobby of the hotel. Seoul had grown considerably since two years ago, but still the same bus route to Hwi-jo Dong! And it still stops running at 10:00 p.m. because of the curfew. I must arrive with the last bus and leave with the first bus at 4:30 a.m.

But for today, I must do a dry run of the assassination, my supreme ambition!

The assassination was planned for South Korean Memorial Day, June 6, which fell on a Sunday in 1965. President Park Chung Hee will be attending the ceremony, which will be held at the National Cemetery. Hoon made elaborate plans in Pyongyang regarding how to carry out this Kennedy-style assassination. He would hide behind a tombstone and shoot directly at Park while he was laying the wreath in front of the tomb of the unknown soldier. He had photos of the cemetery and knew exactly which tombstone he would hide behind. But he had to actually see it prior to executing the plans. He knew that he would have to spend the previous night in the cemetery, as it would be practically impossible to enter it on Memorial Day itself because of the tightened security.

I'll arrive there around 1630 hours and see when the shift changes. Hoon put on a nondescript gray cemetery worker's uniform he brought from Pyongyang and took the bus from the railroad station toward the cemetery, which was located in Dongjak Dong, in a southern suburb of Seoul south of the Han River. At this time of the afternoon, the bus was not very crowded, but still there were no seats, so he stood holding on to the hand bars. It took a good hour to get to the cemetery by bus, but there was a bus stop right in front of the cemetery. He was the only one to get off at the stop. The gate of the cemetery was open, and there was a sentry post. Behind the gate, he could see a treelined road leading to the cemetery and associated buildings.

1700 hours
Several uniforms began to appear on the road from the buildings, and they were headed toward the gate. Now more uniforms, just like Hoon's, and they were milling out of the gate toward the bus stop; some were crossing the street. Hoon nonchalantly walked toward the gate, tied his shoelaces, and started walking back toward the buildings; now there were a few workers coming into the gate,

probably the night shift. Good, thought Hoon, there are night-shift workers, though fewer in number. I would not look too conspicuous if seen outside. He scanned the cemetery and identified the area where he would be hiding, but it seemed the tombstone that he had in mind seemed to be missing. I'll have to investigate! He hid himself behind a tree outside a building and waited for the sun to go down.

2030 hours
The sun was finally down, and darkness enveloped the cemetery. Hoon lowered himself into a crouch and moved swiftly to the area in question. There was a tombstone, but it was lying horizontally on the ground, and before it was a freshly dug hole in the ground, apparently for a casket to be lowered. Even better, Hoon thought. If necessary, I could bury myself here with a breathing straw while they are looking for the assassin! He quickly moved away from the area toward the building, gradually stretched himself erect, and sauntered down the road toward the gate. There were two uniformed guards in the sentry post, talking to each other, without even glancing at Hoon as he walked out the gate. A bus came in a few minutes, and Hoon was headed back to his hotel.

2230 hours
I'll infiltrate into the cemetery Saturday night, stay either in the hole or behind the tombstone if the hole is filled and the stone in place, and wait for the ceremony. I'll be wearing my green camouflage, which will blend in with the grass. Once I kill Park Chung Hee, I'll blend into the crowd of panicked people in my nondescript worker's uniform, which I'll wear under the camouflage, and melt away, walking to the next bus stop, not the one in front, and then the train, then the ferry, Kangwha Island, the submarine, and a hero's welcome in DPRK. How proud Myunghee and Chulgi will be!

But tomorrow, a dry run of another kind...Justice to Suk and Yunhee. I would also like to kill Bo, but I know that he spends the night at the Sleep Lab on weekdays. Perhaps it's better this way; he is not really to blame, is he? I also found out that Suk and Yunhee now have a daughter called Claire. I would not kill Claire—she's only twelve and really does not even know I exist—and thankfully, I know she sleeps in the far bedroom where she would not hear me killing her parents. In the back of his mind, he visualized Sunmi at Camp Lucky and the taut rope around her neck as she fell helplessly into the trapdoor. No, I do not want that to happen again. Claire just has the misfortune of having Suk and Yunhee as parents, perhaps just like I have the misfortune of having Suk as my father. Moon Keh-Hoon, a member of the Patricidal Society!

June 3 (Thursday)
1400 hours
Dry Run for Justice!
Hoon had a good lunch at the restaurant in front of the train station. Naing-myun, a buckwheat noodle dish that's typically Korean, North Korean actually, but they seem to make it tastier here, probably because they have more meat available—the American imperialists grow a lot of beef and sell it to South Korea. In fact, Hoon had a dish of *bulgogi*, marinated strips of beef freshly barbecued at tabletop, too. Might as well reward myself for the courageous deeds I'll perform!

He donned his nondescript, inconspicuous worker's uniform, and a tool case in which he kept his sharp steel dagger as well as the other necessary tools. He left his fake ID in the hotel, which he might need on Saturday but not today.

The bus ride to Hwi-jo Dong was as expected, a long ride in a pretty crowded bus, although the crowd thinned out and almost disappeared as it neared its destination toward the edge of Seoul.

Finally, Hoon got off the bus and walked toward the address, which was across railroad tracks, some ten minutes away from the bus stop. Hoon noticed the identical stucco houses in the neighborhood, all with small backyards, some with flower beds.

The address Hoon was looking for had a tall fence and a wooden gate, which was locked. He peeked inside the fence through a gap in the wooden panels and saw no one. Hoon looked around; there was no one on this residential street. He took out a small instrument from his pocket, inserted it into the keyhole, and pushed the gate open. He looked around the house and knocked on the door—he knew there would be no one at this time of day, as both Suk and Yunhee were out, Suk with his buddies and Yunhee now working in a clothing store. Claire was in school. As expected, no answer. He picked the lock and went in. Past the living room and kitchen, on the right was Bo's room/study, which seemed not to have been used much lately, then on the left the master bedroom where Suk and Yunhee slept, and then past the bathroom another bedroom where Claire slept. And past that room, another small room full of birds in cages and potted plants. OK, just as I expected! It would be easy to come in, take care of Suk and Yunhee, and hide myself till morning and take the bus before Claire wakes up. Now where to hide, preferably outside?

Hoon came out of the house, locking the door behind him, and went to the backyard. In the small backyard, he found something protruding from the ground, like a covered entrance. It was indeed a cover he could lift up, and he saw that there was a ladder going down to a small underground dirt room—yes, the storage room for kimchi, which also served as an air-raid shelter! There was a large earthen urn there against the wall, presumably containing kimchi. A perfect place to hide! I'll come here on the last bus arriving by 2220 hours, hide here till about 0200 hours, do my work, hide here again till 0400 hours, and take the first bus at 0430 hours!

June 4 (Friday), Underground Dirt Room
0200 hours
Assassinate 1

Hoon's gleaming radioactive dials on his watch pointed to the appointed hour of reckoning. Everything went according to plan. The underground room might have been claustrophobic during the day, but at this time of night, it provided a degree of warmth and coziness from the chill of night. He stole into this cave some four hours ago and turned off his pencil light that he had used cautiously to come down the ladder. Leaning against the dirt wall, Hoon's head was intoxicated with the prospect of finally meting out justice to Suk and Yunhee and could hardly keep pace with his beating heart. Now the time has come for action! He silently climbed up the ladder, opened the cover, and emerged into the backyard. There was faint moonlight from a thin sliver of a moon, shaped like a smiling mouth, enough to find his way to the front door of the house. He opened the door silently with the skeleton key he had tested yesterday during the dry run, and quickly passed through the foyer. He had noted, before entering, that the window of Bo's room on the right was dark, as he worked at the Sleep Lab on weeknights. He stealthily walked to the master-bedroom door and quietly opened the door.

The sound of drunken snoring greeted his ears—Suk, as usual, was sprawled on his twin bed loudly snoring, dead to the world. Yunhee was in the next bed; she was not snoring but sound asleep.

Hoon pulled out his gleaming steel dagger, the one he had brought specially for this occasion, the one that he had used to torture and kill countless counterrevolutionaries, the one that he had sharpened countless times just fantasizing about the day it would extinguish Suk's and Yunhee's last breaths!

Suk first, of course! Hoon raised the dagger high, aiming at the heart of Suk's supine, snoring body. The steel blade of the dagger gleamed in the faint moonlight.

June 4 (Friday), 8:00 p.m., Sleep Lab, Hyundai University Hospital
Bo

After a light supper at the hospital cafeteria, Bo entered the vestibule of the Sleep Lab, thinking, "I am going to miss coming here when I leave for America in three weeks."

"Hi, Dr. Moon," greeted Miss Lee, the nurse manager of the lab. Bo had often been called Dr. Moon even as a medical student, but now that he was really a doctor, he was thrilled to hear the nurse call him Dr. Moon. "Dr. Moon, it seems we have a rare evening when we have no subjects to study—the two patients scheduled tonight have canceled. I think you might as well go home and have a rare Friday night free!"

"Well, I guess this is a real treat," thought Bo as he took the bus home. "My parents and Claire will be surprised to see me on a weeknight, but then they'll probably be asleep by the time I get home."

In fact, when he let himself into the house at around half past nine, it was dark. He came into his room and saw that Yunhee had left a small tray of supper on his desk as she always did every night, knowing that Bo would not be home but just in case. Bo ate some of the food in the tray, though he had already eaten a light supper around six in the hospital. As he began to feel full in the stomach, suddenly he felt very tired—all those nights he stayed up in the lab seemed to be catching up all at once. He lay in his bed, fully clothed, and fell into a deep sleep.

The recording was going smoothly, as the patient was snoring in the cubicle. The slow rhythmic lines on the polygraph showed that she was in stage-four sleep until suddenly the lines began to speed up and become chaotic, with high-voltage, sharp waves, and the patient began to convulse! A seizure! Click!

Bo awakened suddenly—this must have been a dream, but I distinctly heard a click, as if the door was opening. He listened intently in the dark and seemed to hear muffled footsteps and then the door to his parents' bedroom opening. Bo got up and took the knife that Suk had given him, which he kept under the bed, silently pulled the blade off the sheath, and silently opened his bedroom door. In the dim moonlight coming through the window, he could see that a man was hovering above his father, who was fast asleep, drunk as usual, in bed. In his raised hand gleamed a dagger, just about to strike. Bo, without hesitation, lunged at the man, and instinctively, the man half turned toward Bo, with his dagger raised in his right hand. Bo plunged his silver knife with all his might into his half-turned chest. The dagger in the man's hand fell to the floor as he collapsed soundlessly like a limp rag doll. But the falling dagger made a thud, and Yunhee woke up and saw Bo still standing.

"Bo, what are you doing here on a Friday night? And what is the sound I heard?" She turned on the light, saw the man on the floor with a knife handle sticking out of the left side of his chest, and began to scream, but the scream froze in her mouth, and no sound actually came out. Bo, coming back to his senses, held his mother in his arms and said, "Mom, don't scream. This man tried to stab Dad, but I stabbed him first with the knife Dad gave me. I think he may be a robber."

Suk was awake by now, and he rolled the man on the floor on his back to see his face. "No, I am afraid he is no robber," said Suk.

"Bo, you saved my life, and probably your mom's, too. It's a long story, and I'll tell it to you later, but now we have to do something about the body; he is dead, as you can tell."

In fact, Bo had ascertained that the man was dead—no pulse, no breath. The knife had punctured his heart as it penetrated his left chest as he half turned toward the lunging Bo. Blood was oozing around the knife blade that was still lodged in his chest. A relatively young man, maybe in his late thirties, looking quite muscular, with a hard edge, seeming to have a bitter grin around the clenched teeth on his dead face. A somewhat familiar face. Have I seen this man before?

"Shouldn't we call the police?" Bo asked his father.

"No, I think we should just get rid of him. I know almost certainly that no one will miss him, because I am sure he is someone I know, from North Korea. An assassin, and I am sure I was not the only intended victim. I'll tell you the story after we have done what we have to do."

Yunhee just looked at Bo and Suk, speechless with fear, but nodded her assent to what Suk was saying.

"I think we should bury him in the kimchi basement," said Suk. Bo and Suk wrapped Hoon's body in a bedsheet and dragged it outside and lowered it into the kimchi basement in the backyard.

"Look, there is a little toolbox that's not ours here!" exclaimed Suk as he shone his flashlight around the dirt room. It contained an assortment of lock-picking tools and skeleton keys as well as a sheath for a dagger. "He must have hidden here before coming up to kill us!"

They dug a hole into the dirt floor using the shovel stored in there. When Bo pulled out the knife from the dead man's chest, a considerable amount of semicongealed blood poured out of the wound, soaking the fresh dirt in the hole. They searched the body and found some money, a pen light, and a skeleton key in the pocket but no wallet, no identification, no jewelry, nothing on his person. Two toes on his left foot were missing. Clean, surgical amputation, noticed Bo.

They covered the body with dirt and stepped on the dirt until the floor was even. Thus was the body of Senior Colonel Moon Hoon, KPA, the jackal of DPRK Covert Operations, buried in the same dirt basement in which he had awaited the moment to assassinate his own father.

Later, while Yunhee was busy quietly cleaning the floor of the blood, Suk and Bo went to Bo's room, where Suk told Bo about his dreams as a young man while he was in school in Seoul—about his first love, Ann Moon, and how he had to break up with Ann when his father died suddenly and he was forced to marry Min, a marriage for financial gain, arranged by his elder brother, who was now the head of the household. Suk told Bo about his half brother,

Hoon, and half sister, Kyung, and how Suk met Yunhee when they were both teachers and how he fell in love with Yunhee and eloped together to Manchuria to start a new life. He told Bo that he knew his first wife, Min, instilled anger in their children and that Hoon became a Communist and went to North Korea before the Korean War and Min died shortly after Hoon left for North Korea and Kyung disappeared during the war. Suk continued, "I recognized Hoon as soon as I saw his face—Bo, you may recognize the resemblance, too. Also, there was this little mole on the right side of the neck, which he had even as a baby.

"I assume that Hoon was in the North Korean military, probably a covert operator, and came here to assassinate someone important, as well as me. I do feel guilty that I didn't take better care of the children of my first marriage. I am sorry you had to be involved in this, Bo. I tried to protect you from the sins and complications of your parents."

"I think I am beginning to understand—not fully, of course, but that you and Mom had a tragic, complicated life even before I was born. Of course, parts of the story you already told me, but the part about your first love and how your brother forced your arranged marriage and about my half siblings I really did not know. It's a good thing that Claire is still asleep—I think we should keep everything between us and not burden Claire, especially now that I think this chapter may be closed, at least as far as my generation is concerned."

Finally but unfortunately, I am afraid, Bo thought. Did I hear her name correctly? My dad's first love, Ann Moon?—was she the lady whose wedding picture I had seen in Katie's living room? Katie's mom! Oh, what might have been had Katie lived!

June 6, South Korean Memorial Day, came and went without an incident. Park Chung Hee would remain president of South Korea and make himself an absolute dictator in 1972 with a constitutional amendment passed through a rigged referendum, only to be assassinated by his own CIA chief in October 1979.

June 7, 1965, Pyongyang, DPRK (39 N Parallel, 125.7 E Longitude) DPRK Covert Operations wondered what happened to their star operator, the jackal of KPA. Perhaps the South Korean CIA was better than they thought?

Over the next weeks and months of Hoon's absence, Myunghee and Chulgi missed him who had promised them that he would never be an absentee husband and father, as his own father had been.

Now and then, on a moonlit night, Myunghee would open the locked silver jewelry box she had in the dresser. There, she would take out the gold necklace with a gold pendant shaped like a duck, identical to the one she was wearing on her bosom, with the inscription in the back: "10.15.1957. Loyalty, Love, Happiness. Kim Il-Sung." Myunghee would kiss the duck in the bill and slowly put it back into the box, lock it, and put it back in the dresser.

44

LOVE REBORN

September 1967, White Plains, New York (41 N Parallel, 74 W Longitude)
Bo, Ginny

"By the authority vested in me by the state of New York, I now pronounce you husband and wife!" said Judge Hudson, solemnly but with a smile. Ginny was wearing a white lacy dress that really looked like a modern wedding gown. I kissed Ginny tenderly on her lips. Then we embraced hard and kissed passionately. We didn't care that the judge was watching, along with Bob. Ginny and I were now married. Bob, of the four musketeers of the White Deer days, was with us, as a "best person"—no one deserved that title more than Bob. Bob was also responsible for taking pictures of our wedding.

Ginny and I were married. Finally, after one full year of engagement, and after exactly 650 letters had been exchanged between us, we were officially and legally married, by no less than a judge in the state of New York. On this crisp autumn day, in beautiful, wooded, tranquil Westchester, New York.

But our wedding was still a secret, at least to Ginny's parents, until another wedding, exactly one month from our real wedding. Our arrangement was a compromise solution, between Ginny's need to mollify her parents by having a religious ceremony and our mutual desire to make our real wedding a nonreligious ceremony. Ginny, being of Italian descent, had been reared in the Catholic Church, although she had rebelled against its constrictions. She felt, however, that her parents would be too hurt if they could not participate in the ceremony held in a Catholic church.

I had suggested to Ginny, in all earnestness, that we should elope and bypass all ceremony. She felt that her parents should not be deprived of a wedding ceremony. Marrying an Asian man out of her religion was bad enough. Not even to have a wedding ceremony would be an insult to her parents. So, we would go through another ceremony, an abbreviated Catholic ceremony, reserved for mixed marriages between a Catholic and non-Catholic, so said the Catholic priest who interviewed Ginny and me. But to us, that ceremony was a paper-only ceremony. Our real wedding date was in September, in beautiful Westchester County.

Following the brief but poignant ceremony with the judge, who spoke briefly about the significance of love and of our union, of two people from opposite ends of the earth, Ginny, Bob, and I had lunch together in a local restaurant. Then, Bob went home to Brooklyn, and Ginny and I walked together through the beautiful woods of Westchester before we went to my apartment in the Bronx. In that little efficiency apartment, in the little folding bed, Ginny and I made love as man and wife on our wedding day. Our lovemaking was tender and passionate at the same time; we felt as though we were making love for the first time, although we had made love many times before, almost daily since I moved back to New York from Kansas City that summer. Because our love had stood the test of time, the test of separation, and the obstacles of differences of religion, race, customs, and prejudice, we felt our love to be fortified to meet the challenges of the future. Because we shared our minds and our bodies for a whole year before the wedding ceremony, we knew that the ceremony would be just a milestone, but not the beginning of a different relationship.

In fact, even after the marriage, for a whole month, we lived apart but made love daily. Ginny had obtained a job as a nurse at the Einstein Hospital where I worked as a resident. She came to my apartment early in the morning, climbed into my bed, and then made coffee and breakfast for me. In the evening, we would have dinner together at the hospital cafeteria, come back to my apartment, and make love again, and then she would go back to her apartment in Brooklyn. The first month of our married life was, to me, a wonderful honeymoon at home. Although I wished that we were living together and looked forward to living with Ginny in a month's time, our marriage by commuting provided our relationship an added dimension of preciousness.

Yes, our love was a form of love at first sight. We were both enormously attracted to each other at that Halloween party in Brooklyn during my first year in the United States. I was attracted to Ginny's youthfulness, wit, and, frankly, body and her enormous eyes magnified by the thick glasses. While she was too young to possess intellectual sophistication like Katie's, she had an all-American directness and intellectual honesty that was at once appealing and refreshing. In a way, she was a combination of Katie and, yes, Mirah, that student nurse who had reawakened the possibility of love.

Some marriages, they say, are made in heaven. And some are made in hell. I see, in my professional capacity, quite a few of the latter. Spouses who cannot live with each other but who cannot live without each other. Spouses who destroy each other until only empty shells of the individuals they used to be live in an empty shell that used to be a marriage.

My marriage to Ginny, I am happy to say, was made neither in heaven nor in hell, in spite of the love at first sight. Our marriage is made by Ginny and me, two individuals who have worked on it to continue to make it a success. This involved, initially, having weekly communication sessions, when we would talk about problems and issues we had with each other. Later communications have become more flexible, including verbal arguments and flare-ups. But when it came to serious matters, in spite of all the angry feelings and recriminations, we have been able to discuss feelings and come to an understanding, even though it was, at times, extremely difficult.

We have certain differences that may be irreconcilable. For example, Ginny is more expressive of emotions, while I am reticent in expressing emotions. She, like my dad, likes animals and plants. I, like my mom, do not like living things but prefer inanimate objects and machines. I like intellectual arguments; Ginny, like most American women, prefers not to argue intellectually. But, importantly, we both love mysteries. And we are both wonderful cooks.

We both like music and good movies. We enjoy sex. And we both respect personal space. No, our marriage is not the ideal marriage that I had dreamed about. We fight, we argue, and often we shout at each other. But we do not destroy each other. We are, individually, too strong for that. And we make up. No, ours is a manmade marriage. Sometimes, I wonder what life for me would have been like if fate had been different at certain crucial points in my life. What if Katie had not died? Would we be living together, married, now, here in America or in Korea? Both practicing medicine? These are unknowable, imponderable, and therefore impossible questions.

Soon, Ginny and I will be celebrating our forty-sixth wedding anniversary. Yes, our marriage has lasted almost half a century. A rather remarkable manmade edifice. For eighteen years of our marriage, Ginny and I were two individuals in partnership. Then Ginny, Ali, and I became a threesome, a family.

Ali often asked questions that were surprisingly precocious. For example, when he was about eight, he asked, "Dad, how did you get to marry Mom?"

"I met her as a student at a party. I fell in love with her because she was so intelligent and pretty."

"It's funny how you two came from the opposite ends of the earth and met and fell in love in one moment. I don't know whom I am going to marry yet, among my girlfriends," said Ali.

Indeed, he had a number of girlfriends at that age.

"Well, perhaps it's a bit too early to think about marrying any of them yet. You will know when you are ready," I said. I hope I am right. And I hope that, eventually, Ali will find a lasting and gratifying partnership. And I hope that he understands, when the time comes, that destiny will bring him his partner but that it is he who has to recognize her and build and maintain the partnership with her.

45

A RED ROSE FOR A VIRGIN QUEEN

October 1979, Northwood Cemetery, Virginia (38 N Parallel, 79 W Longitude)
Bo

Mom, I place this red rose on your coffin as it is lowered into your grave, the little hole in the ground, in this strange land, Virginia, United States of America. How fitting, Mom, that you should be buried in Virginia, because I think of you as a virgin, a mother who strove to be a perfect, virginal mother, unsoiled by life itself. But then, Mom, you were the strongest, the most determined of all of us. You were, in a way, too strong, too determined—I could never live up to your iron will, your self-sacrifice, your sense of commitment. I tried, but I could never be you.

Unlike Dad, I know that you don't like sympathies, that you don't like others to feel sorry for you. But I can't help it—I do feel sorry about your life. Had you been born in America rather than in Korea, or, even in Korea, had you been born twenty years later, your life would have been far more gratifying, both for yourself and for others. You had the intelligence, the strength, and the wherewithal to have been a wonderful professional. But because of the time and place in which you were cast, you had to be just a wife and mother. How frustrating it must have been for you not to be able to apply your strength, intelligence, and determination toward an ever-expanding horizon. Instead, you concentrated all on love for one son, an undeserving son. It was your destiny to be hurt by men whom you loved. Your own dad, your husband, and, finally, me. Yes, although you deny it, you know that it is true! But, Mom, destiny is something one creates for oneself. You know that, too.

Mom, as far as money was concerned, you were a miser. You saved and scrimped, but then you were generous in spending it on me. In a different sort of way, you were a miser in love. Unlike money, you had plenty of love, you were made of love, but it was hard for you to give it freely, to your husband, to your children. I knew you loved me deeply, and Claire, too. But it was so awkward for you to express your love, above all to Dad. Whom you loved first and most. Yes, it is true, Mom. Your first and greatest love was for Dad. You turned it toward me because he needed, demanded, a different aspect of love that you had the most trouble with—physical, sexual love. I remember how you cringed when I sometimes tried to put my head on your lap, just to get the soft feel of your body! Poor Mom, how different your life might have been, and thus all our lives, if you had been able to let go and enjoy carnal as well as spiritual love.

You embodied the finest, the most powerful, and thus the most frightening aspect of the human spirit—an iron will. Even in an attenuated form, I feel that iron will in my blood, and I feel proud, and also frightened. Mom, your nickname was apt, frighteningly apt: "Doer without Words." Even your exit from life was a product of your will. Mom, it was a mistake. And I am angry that you brought and used the Seconal that I had procured for myself, for my own exit. I should have thrown the bottle away when I left Korea. But I know that nothing could have stopped you. Mom, I loved you. I love you.

With this rose, I bid you good-bye. This rose whose stem is cleaned of thorns, but I see the thorns in my mind's eye and the strength they give to the beauty of the rose. I know you will be strong. Wherever you are!

For now, nehn-nehn goroito, Good night. Sleep well.

1989, Guilford, Connecticut (41.3 N Parallel, 72.3 W Longitude)
Bo

"I love that music!" says Ali.

The music cassette that Ali uses in his violin class is playing Dvořák's *Humoresque* through the car radio. Whenever we drive together, Ginny puts on the tape so that Ali will become familiar with the music.

"You know, Ali, my own mother liked it, too," I say. Yes, Mom liked the *Humoresque,* she knew how to play it on the piano, and she even danced to it. A long time ago. When I was about Ali's age or younger. Before Dad became a policeman. I now remember my mom, with her young face with a rare smile, dancing to the tune of *Humoresque*—"humorous." Mom, who lacked a sense of humor. Who was always serious. But maybe she did have a sense of humor, although it may have been buried under tons of emotional baggage.

Ginny says, "Ali, your grandma, your dad's mother, would have really loved you if she were alive today. She was such a loving person. She would have doted on you and given you everything you want!"

Yes.

46

NOT BEFORE THE CASKET CLOSES

Suk's letter to Bo, dated December 1979

Dear Bo,

When you read this letter, I will have joined your mother in heaven, as I will leave this in the safe-deposit box, to be opened only by you after my death. Once I write this letter, I will seal it, and then I will put it in the box. I will not rewrite it or otherwise do anything with it. I just want to share my thoughts with you about your mother's death by her own hands. I will be writing down my very jumbled thoughts at the death of your mother, my wife. Needless to say, I am certain you understand the pain and confusion I feel about the turn of events of the last several months. I have lost a most faithful, loving wife, a companion for life, through thick and thin. Your mother is the one woman I loved all my life, someone who gave me love, pleasure, dedication, courage, hope, and two wonderful children.

Ever since that night, just before you left, when you saved our lives, she was fearful that what was buried in the kimchi basement would be found out. She was afraid that KCIA agents or North Korean agents were spying on us whenever she saw a stranger on our street. We eventually filled the basement with dirt ourselves and made it into a flower bed. Then we moved to our new apartment on the other side of the city. When the government decided to raze the whole neighborhood to build the highway some ten years later, we were concerned that there may be digging and the truth would come out. Your mother was at her wit's end with worry. When they actually started digging the neighborhood, though, many skeletons were discovered throughout the area. It turned out that the whole area was a killing field during the Korean War! These were eventually reburied in the tomb of the unknown soldier in the National Cemetery, because no one could tell whether the skeletons belonged to our side or to the Communists. She should have been comforted that the worry of discovery was gone, but she continued to be fearful and suspicious.

Since her head injury about a year before we left Korea, she, in addition, became gradually more forgetful, confused, and at times quite rambling. Bo, you may have noticed that yourself, especially since about a year ago. Even in America, she at times became quite suspicious of everyone. She became afraid of burglars at night, would not sleep a wink, keeping vigil at the windows. She was especially suspicious of me, of my having an affair with a woman. She accused me of visiting with the Chinese woman who lives in the apartment one floor above us and yelled at her in the hallway, telling her not to seduce me. But behind all that irascible behavior that, I think, came with age and maybe the head injury, I could still see the loving and faithful woman whom I have always known.

Bo, as I have hinted at times, your mother, my wife, Yunhee, and I have a special relationship that goes beyond the realm of the common sexual and domestic relationship of man and wife. Our love was born out of impossibility, and we have overcome insurmountable obstacles to be, finally, man and wife. I have told you about our adventures in Manchuria and the perilous escape from the Red Army. And the reasons why I gave up a promising career in education to become a policeman, to protect you and my family from the jealousy and hate of the family of my first marriage, a forced, arranged marriage. In spite of the humiliation I felt from wearing the uniform hated by a majority of the people, I felt proud that I could do something to improve the health standards of the common people as the police officer in charge of health facilities, and, above all, I felt proud that I could protect you and your mother and provide you with shelter and sustenance. I am proud of what I have done, and I am sure that your mother will share in the same pride. In fact, she has done more than anyone else in educating you, making sure that you had the opportunities to achieve your full potential. Bo, it was because of your mother, and because of her alone, that you were eventually able to enter Seoul Middle School. Even though, initially, you thought you failed it by a single point, you did get in. But if she had not forced me to go to Pusan and enroll you in an elementary school that had the mock exams and special classes to prepare for the exam, there would have been no possibility that you would have gone to Seoul.

And I was, frankly, quite oblivious to the fact that you, in spite of your brilliant mind, did need the mundane preparation necessary to pass the entrance examination. I depended on your mother at critical times in our lives, in making decisions and in carrying them out. If your mother did not restrain me from declaring myself as a teacher in front of the Red Army, none of us would be alive today.

Your mother complained, of late, of my drinking. Bo, perhaps you do not know this, but I had stopped smoking since you left Korea. I vowed that I would never smoke again, something I enjoyed very much, until I saw you again. I kept my promise. When I came to this country, I could have taken it up again, but, by then, it became quite clear that smoking was no longer something one did with clear conscience, and besides, it was so expensive.

Drinking, on the other hand, is something that gives me solace. When I am feeling unhappy, resentful, and angry. And when I am feeling ashamed and humiliated. Unfortunately, these feelings have become a constant companion of mine, and my only escape has been through sake and beer. Especially since your mother's head injury. Since she changed from being the devoted, loving wife to a suspicious, resentful woman. I know that it's not her fault but probably her brain injury. But knowing that does not help the immediate situation, a house filled with hateful chill. Only alcohol provided some warmth to the chilly air.

Well, our life in America has been a continuation of the chill. I know that your mother wanted to stay with you, Bo, rather than with me. If it could be arranged, I would have welcomed it, hoping that she might have been happier. But I know that it would have caused a terrible strain to your life with Ginny, Bo, and you were wise not to consider the possibility and have us live in an apartment near Claire. Neither she nor I have the right to impinge on the lives of our children, other than to be cheering spectators of their success.

Well, I guess I have written more or less all I need to write to describe your mother's state of mind, especially since her accident, and how it differed from what it used to be. Except to say that I have always loved her, and, come what may, I still love her so. And how I miss her! How I miss her sweet little smile and her quiet ways. How I even miss her suspicions and accusations. Well, by the time you read this letter, I would have joined her in the afterlife, which I believe in fervently. And in that life, once again, all the ills, all the distortions, will be corrected, and we will be together, as one, in our very best, true selves.

My blessings, prayers, and best wishes are with you, my dearest Bo.

Suk

April 1984, Northwood Cemetery, Virginia (38 N Parallel, 79 W Longitude)

Bo

Dad died today of stomach cancer. He was seventy-four years old. The cancer was diagnosed about six months ago. The doctor said that, at his age, cancer progressed slowly, and conservative treatment was indicated rather than a debilitating operation. I discussed the choices with him. He wanted to have the noninvasive treatment. He said, "I have lived a full life. I want to die peacefully and rejoin your mother in the afterlife. "

Dad did not suffer much. Except for the last month or so. Then, he seemed to be delirious, and he barely recognized me when I visited him in the hospital. He seemed to be talking to his students as though he were a teacher again. Then he spoke something in Japanese. I wished I could understand Japanese. At times he talked as though he were a policeman. In his delirium, he must have relived those experiences in his life that were meaningful to him. Were they pleasant memories? Were they memories of his triumph, his success as a teacher and administrator for the Japanese Empire, the realm of the Rising Sun? Were they memories of his hated work for the police force, for the dictatorial government of Syngman Rhee?

Did he relive his first meeting with Mom, singing Handel's *Messiah* together? Or were his memories of abandoning Min, his first wife, and their two children? Did he relive the perilous escape from the Red Army, with Mom leading him out of the prison of a schoolhouse in the middle of the night? Or did he relive his resolve to find Mom and me again, throwing away his beloved Zippo lighter as a sacrifice to the gods? Did he relive the nightmare in which his son kills his son? Did you see the silver knife stuck in the chest of your firstborn son?

People have said you were not a decisive person. You wanted to please people too much. Well, Dad, I know that you wanted to please people, because you loved all living things, above all people. And all living things thrived under your care, your canaries, your houseplants, your students, and your children. And above all, you trusted people, you trusted me, even when I did not see things your way, even when I did not study, even when I almost failed exams. You trusted in my basic intelligence and integrity. Yes, you were decisive in your trust. As the name, Daisin, that you adopted when you returned to Korea declares, you were a man of Great Trust. You were decisive in loving and in trusting, however undeserving the objects of your love and trust might have been. You were courageous in your decision. You were courageous in your belief in Pestalozzi. You were courageous in your love for Mom and for me.

Dad, I remember so many things about your life from the stories you told me. How your youthful dreams were first crushed by your oldest brother and the arranged marriage and how your dreams of a new life in a new land, so near fulfillment, were blown away by the wind overnight with the defeat of Japan in World War II. And how you and Mom centered your lives around me, as the embodiment of all your lost dreams and aspirations. I am sorry, Dad, if I could not deliver on all your hopes about me. I know that you will agree with me that I have to live my life my own way, that I cannot structure my life to fulfill your dreams.

I wish you had written the autobiography you were going to write. I looked for it all over your apartment, in the safe-deposit box, everywhere, but I could not find it. You lived such a fantastic, tortuous, and tortured life. Maybe, Dad, someday, I will write down some of the stories you told me. When I am ready to write my own story. Because your story is a part of my story. As your genes are a part of me. And they will all be a part of my son, your grandson.

I am sorry, Dad, that you will not be alive to see the birth of your grandson. Yes, we know that it will be a son, because Ginny had amniocentesis, as well as an ultrasound examination of the fetus growing in her womb. If you lived just three more months, you would have seen your genes carried to another generation. I know that you and Mom would have enjoyed seeing the miracle of another birth, to carry on the name of Moon, originally of Kangwon Province, Korea. Through Manchuria, Seoul, Pusan, Kosung, Brooklyn, Kansas City, Bronx, and now New Haven, United States of America. The fruit of the love that was sewn, generations ago, in lands that did not know the existence of each other. Love that was nurtured by human hands, caring hands, your hands, Mom's hands in spite of her avowed dislike of living things, and Ginny's and mine.

Dad, you have always said not to sum up a person's life before the casket closes. Now, as I close your casket, I whisper to you,

"Your life was one of love, love in all its vagaries and vicissitudes." As I close your casket, I close an epoch of my life and usher in another with a new life waiting to be born.

47

A TOKYO INTERLUDE

June 27, 1965 Seoul (37.5 N Parallel, 127 E Longitude)
11:00 p.m.

Bo's last night in Korea. At eight o'clock tomorrow morning, Bo would be on JAL Flight 001, destination Tokyo. Bo, Claire, and their parents had an early dinner. The one suitcase was packed and in the hallway, ready to go. Yunhee had pressed Bo's suit, for the second time that day, and hung it up in the closet. The pockets were already filled with the necessary documents, passport, and a wallet containing one hundred dollars. Yunhee had sewn a hidden inside pocket on Bo's trousers and put in it a single hundred-dollar bill. An emergency fund. Just in case. The carry-on briefcase was also in the hallway, together with the suitcase. It contained Bo's important documents and a chest x-ray that he would have to show the immigration officials when he landed in Hawaii. Yes, all was ready. As they were all ready to retire to bed, Suk asked Bo to come into his bird room.

Bo sat in one of his dad's uncomfortable chairs in the bird room. Suk also sat in a metal chair that was often used as a footstool to reach the upper bird cages. Suk said, "Bo, I wanted to say a few things in private to you. First, I want you to know that I am proud of you and what you did and I am so relieved that you are leaving this country, which has become like a prison for so many young people.

Especially since what happened that night, which, of course, was totally unexpected.

"Your mom and I owe our lives to you and to your courage. And probably Claire's too. You saved the lives of your family, perhaps the first of many lives you will save. Of course, no one will ever know of this, other than your mom and me and yourself.

Try to forget! What you did was necessary, courageous, and good! Remember that I am here now to talk to you because of that. And Mom and Claire.

"I am glad that you will be going to America, the land of freedom, the land of opportunity. Above all, a land free of Korea's past. You will achieve in America what I tried to achieve in Manchuria, a clean slate to start anew. Expand your wings in the free, vast land! Fly, and do not look back! I know that your mother and Claire expect you to send for us eventually. I would like that. But don't feel that you have to bring any of us to America. America will be your new country, where your future will lie. As for me and your mother, whatever she may think, we had our own new land and our own adventure. Now we are part of Korea and part of your past. Do not feel obliged toward myself or your mother. If you can, do bring Claire to America, because I hope you will provide her with an opportunity for freedom that I have not been able to provide for her.

"As you know, Bo, you've been educated in the way that I believe in, absolute freedom and trust in the innate potential in you. At least at home. As long as I could sway your mother in my educational belief. Unlike you, Bo, Claire has been educated more in the traditional Korean ways, mainly because your mother felt that she should have more influence on her upbringing because she is a girl. And I let her do this, because, Bo, to be frank, I have been too tired to argue with her and have my way. Although I have always disagreed with her restrictive attitude toward Claire, I simply did not have the emotional energy, while I was in the police force, to make an issue of it. I was content with you being brought up the way I felt was right. Now I am too old and too tired to make any changes, but you may be able to help Claire by helping her go to America. Where even girls can be independent and free.

"Bo, I know that you love Claire very much. I also know that because of the difference in age, and because you have been so busy with medical school, you have not really had much opportunity to know her and be a part of her growing up. She has much growing up to do still, and I hope some of that can be done in a freer land, where she could achieve her full potential, America!

"As for me, wherever you go, a part of me goes with you. A part of me, my genes, my flesh and blood, makes a part of you and will explore with you a new world. And this time, Bo, we will be successful, and we will not come back. You will start a new family line of Moons in America. You will be the first of a long line of Moons in the new land, unburdened by an oppressive and unjust tradition. By simply being you, you will carry the best of our family's tradition that is in your blood—creativity, intelligence, strength, and the courage and wisdom to use your endowments well."

Monday, June 28, 1965, Tokyo, Japan (36 N Parallel, 140 E Longitude)
10:00 a.m.

Bo, Philmo, Bob, Yulak, and Rabbit checked into the Tokyo Hilton Hotel. Their rooms were not ready yet. While waiting in the lobby, Bo called the phone number given to him by the president of the Korea-Japan Student Exchange. A woman's voice answered, "*Hai!*"

Knowing that *hai* in Japanese meant *yes* or *hello,* Bo answered in English, "Hello. May I speak to Miss Midori Ito please?"

"This is Midori speaking," said the voice in fluent English.

"Hi, I am Bo Moon, from Korea. I was given your name by Mr. Harada, the president of the Korea-Japan Student Exchange. I understand that you and your friends are interested in meeting Korean students."

"Yes, I was expecting your call. I believe you are staying at the Hilton Hotel, in downtown? We will be there shortly, within an hour. Please wait in the lobby. You will have no problems in recognizing us; we are a bunch of college girls!"

While waiting in the lobby, Bo remembered the tearful farewell at the Kimpo Airport. Mom, Dad, and Claire, all weeping—tears of sorrow? tears of joy? Bo wept, too. His face smiling, his eyes blurry with tears, his heart too full of nameless emotion—a mixture of sadness, hope, joy, apprehension—every conceivable emotion seemed to be mixed in there. And their distillation was the pure elixir, teardrops. Purifying, obfuscating, consoling teardrops.

In thirty minutes, Bo and his friends were met by three young women. Midori wore a pink one-piece dress that flattered her slender but curvaceous figure. Her face was a long oval, with a creamy complexion that reminded Bo of a Japanese doll. She had long black hair that complemented her white skin. She introduced her friends, Reiko and Miyako. Reiko was a very petite girl who wore a well-tailored two-piece black suit. Miyako, on the other hand, was a rather stocky, buxom girl in a white blouse and blue skirt. She had a round face that also reminded Bo of a different kind of Japanese doll—the roly-poly one. They were all quite talkative and friendly.

The girls of KJSE took Bo and his friends to lunch. Bo found out that the girls were all senior students in the Department of Asian History at Tokyo University, the most prestigious university in Japan. They, and some other students, including the president, had formed the Korea-Japan Student Exchange as they were learning recent Japanese and Korean history. Most of the students in the society had some ties with Korea: either their parents had been in Korea, or they had one parent of Korean heritage. They were, however, not Koreans. Most ethnic Koreans in Japan belonged to an association of Koreans that was sympathetic to North rather than South Korea. Ethnic Koreans in Japan were not given Japanese citizenship, even though they may have been born in Japan and lived in Japan for all their lives. The KJSE students felt that the youths of

Korea and Japan should put their unfortunate histories behind and improve the future relationship between the two peoples through personal and cultural exchange.

As very few Korean students were able to leave the country to come to Japan, they started meeting Korean students in transit and providing opportunities for conversation. They had attempted to visit Korea many times, but the military government would not allow it. Of course, such a visit was out of the question during Syngman Rhee's regime!

The lunch was delicious. They ate sushi, which Bo had suggested, and which the KJSE members paid for, saying, "I know that you would like to be the gentlemen and pay for lunch. But we also know that the Korean government does not allow you to bring any more than one hundred dollars outside of the country. You need to save all your money till you get your first paycheck in America!"

Then, they took a walk around downtown Tokyo, the Ginza, and the Imperial Palace. The girls pointed out various buildings and sites of interest. Then they sat in a little tearoom and talked about their two countries. Philmo was impressed with the prosperity of Tokyo. Bo was impressed by the cleanness of the streets, considering how crowded they were. Yulak felt that the imperial palace and the Buddhist temples showed a characteristic style of architecture that symbolized the Japanese essence. Bob, on the other hand, was a bit disturbed by the aesthetically unpleasing, busy advertising signs on the streets of Ginza. Rabbit was impressed by how well-dressed women were.

The KJSE girls said they felt envious of them, for their journey to America. Very few Japanese students went abroad to study or to live. They felt the Korean doctors were lucky to have the opportunity and courageous to leave their native land to study abroad for years.

"Yes, you must feel the way my parents felt when they left Japan for Manchuria, where they tried to build a new country," said Midori.

"I didn't know that your parents were in Manchuria. So were my parents. I was, in fact, born in Manchuria," said Bo.

"What a coincidence. I was born in Manchuria, too. Where in Manchuria were you born? I was born in Daeduk, near Harbin," responded Midori.

"I was also born somewhere near Harbin, I think. I don't know the exact name of the city. You see, I have always told people I was born in Seoul, to reduce unnecessary complications, such as whether I was Chinese and so on," replied Bo.

"Yes, I can understand that. For all we know, though, our parents might have been neighbors. Anyway, we think that Korea and Japan should again become friendly neighbors, helping each other."

They all agreed. The world is too full of needless antagonisms and of old wounds that are allowed to keep on bleeding. Bo felt that the young people of the world, free from the emotional baggage of their parents, should build a new world, based on openness, freedom, and reason. Bo's beliefs were reinforced by his brief encounter with Midori and her friends, young people of Japan holding similar beliefs as his and acting on them. Yes, in a way, Bo thought, the KJSE was like his own MSS, except, perhaps, Midori was more courageous than he.

48

OU EST LA CHOO-CHOO?

October, 1978, New Haven, Connecticut (41 N Parallel, 73 W Longitude)
Bo

I decided that my analysis had come to a decision point—whether to confide in Dr. Lowmann my deepest secret, that I was a killer of my half brother. The fateful events of that night in June some fourteen years ago were mercifully forgotten in my memory much of the time, except when they reemerged in some fleeting nightmares of a struggle, with a silver knife flung in the air. My dad and mom never brought it up, and I never brought it up to my consciousness. But, lately, I began to feel that this withholding of fratricidal memory was a major obstacle in any further progression of psychoanalysis. Confiding in Dr. Lowmann, however, meant that I would place myself within his power, and maybe even risk being exposed or arrested, though I doubted very much there would be any extradition to Korea and prosecution for lack of any evidence. Certainly, the only witnesses, my dad and mom, would not testify against me. But what about the baby who died when I was about two years old? I had wondered if I had killed it…am I a monster who killed two of my siblings? Where would I stop?

Fortunately, however, I began to doubt if I really wanted to be a psychoanalyst. Would it not be better to let sleeping dogs lie for all concerned and allow them to move on into the future, rather than being bogged down with ominous memories?

What if the memories simply led to more pain without any hope of redemption and there were ways of wiping them clean through chemical or electronic means? Biological psychiatry was in ascendance, and dwelling in the past may simply mean being left behind! I made my decision.

Psychoanalytic Couch

"Yes, Dr. Lowmann, I know that this is my last session with you. Somehow, the analysis has been stagnant, as my desire to become a psychoanalyst has declined. It simply doesn't make much sense to continue this, something I really don't believe in. And the number of patients I have to see in analysis—that would preclude my doing any real research in biological psychiatry. Times are a-changing, Herr Docktor Lowmann. Analysis is dead."

"You mean, for you?" murmurs Dr. Lowmann.

"Yes, for me. And for you, too, as far as having me as a patient is concerned. But, I guess, in a way, I feel stagnant, too. Things have become too much of a routine for me. I do them well, but there is no sparkle, no real challenge!"

"You mean, like having a baby?"

"A baby? Sure, that would be challenging, but maybe too much so. Anyway, I don't think we will have any. Ginny and I want to live for ourselves and not repeat the mistakes of our parents. Ha, sounds like we are mistakes. Maybe we are. Anyway, we want to have fun, and we are having fun."

"Ja, then, why stagnant?"

"Maybe too much fun is boring. I don't know. Maybe I want something, but I don't know what it is. Maybe I already had a child—Claire, I mean. Maybe one is enough. Although she is really not mine."

"Maybe you wished she had been and do not like the fact that she is not..." murmurs Dr. Lowmann.

"Maybe. Maybe not. Dr. Lowmann, I don't think we are getting anywhere. With analysis or with my life. Perhaps I will come back when I am ready to lay a golden egg!"

"Good luck, Bo."

I get up from the couch, shake hands with Dr. Lowmann, and leave.

"Good-bye, Dr. Lowmann."

Oedipus the King blinds himself after finding out that he had killed his own father and married his own mother. Perhaps I had blinded myself of the fact that I had, in my fantasy, married my mother and Claire was my daughter. But then the witnessing of her delivery brought home the enormity of my fantasy, of the responsibility of having a child of one's own, born out of the agony of the mother, soiled between urine and feces. Perhaps I would have much preferred to give birth to an Athena, born out of the head, rather than from a woman's womb.

December 8, 1979, New Haven, Connecticut (41 N Parallel, 73 W Longitude)

My phone rings. I answer. It's Dr. Kaiser, chairman of the Department of Psychiatry. My heart leaps to my mouth. I knew that the Board of Permanent Officers was meeting today to consider my promotion to full professor. This was the last hurdle in academic medicine, to be promoted to full professor.

Upon the completion of my residency in psychiatry at the Einstein Hospital in New York, I had taken a two-year fellowship there. Then, Ginny and I decided that we wanted to leave the hustle and bustle of the city and applied for faculty positions at the University of Pennsylvania and at Yale, where Dr. Kaiser, the former chairman at Einstein, was now chairman.

The first time I met Dr. Kaiser was in 1967, in Kansas, where he had come to speak at the departmental grand rounds. He spoke about the "Mind-Body Problem and Psychosomatic Medicine," the relationship between the mind and the body and how they interacted in health and disease. Both a psychoanalyst and a neurobiologist, Dr. Kaiser impressed me as a true open-minded scientist who also had a heart. In spite of his short physical stature and soft voice, I felt that he was a true intellectual giant. I remember asking a couple of questions of him after his presentation and his taking pains to answer my questions thoroughly, taking very seriously rather elementary questions from a first-year resident.

Later that day, Dr. Graves, the chairman at Kansas, had introduced me to Dr. Kaiser and told him about my wish to return to New York. Dr. Graves said, "Bo thinks he wants to go back to the East Coast, primarily for personal reasons, because he is engaged to someone who lives in New York. But I think a more important reason might be that he is really a promising fellow and some research experience on the East Coast should do him wonders as a future academician!"

"Well, that's very nice. And personal reasons are important, too. We psychiatrists must understand our personal needs and satisfy them or come to terms with them, because without such understanding and reasonable fulfillment of our needs, we surely cannot understand others' needs or help them," said Dr. Kaiser.

Dr. Kaiser had asked me about some of my patients. He seemed to take particular interest in a patient whom I attempted to treat with hypnosis, which was a rather bold thing for a first-year resident to do. Dr. Kaiser told me that he had himself been interested in hypnosis and assured me that it was quite proper for me to use hypnosis with that patient. At the end of the interview, he told me that he would accept me to his program.

Dr. Kaiser had left Einstein to become chairman at Yale while I was still a fellow at Einstein. As a resident, I asked him to supervise me on a research project. He did. I found Dr. Kaiser to be a warm, supportive mentor as well as an incisive supervisor. My first research paper was completed just as he left New York. We sent the completed paper back and forth by mail for refinements and revisions. Finally, the paper appeared in a major psychiatric journal in both our names.

On a snowy November day in 1970, Ginny and I had driven to New Haven for an interview for a faculty position at Yale. Although we got stuck in the snow coming back to New York, I had felt a strong attraction to Yale, with its neo-Gothic buildings and student-centered activities, and to the artsy little shops and streets of New Haven. Above all, I felt comfortable with Dr. Kaiser. He was a boss I could work for. He was a man I wanted to be friends with.

In December of 1970, I received a call from Dr. Kaiser while I was in my office in New York. By then, I was offered a position at the University of Pennsylvania, but I really wanted to go to Yale. When I had spoken with Dr. Kaiser earlier, he was still not sure whether he could find the funding to create a position for me at Yale. There was a recession, and then President Nixon had imposed a federal budget freeze and was cutting all federal support of medical education.

"Bo, I am glad to tell you that if you want, I can offer you a position as assistant professor of psychiatry, beginning July 1971, to work in the Psychosomatic Medicine Service. If you like, you can think about this for a week or so?"

I was delirious with joy! Of course, I accepted. On the spot. And Ginny and I were bound to New Haven, Connecticut, the following year. Northeast from New York. New Haven, a university town, an industrial town. A pretty New England town.

My years as assistant professor were busy, rewarding, and frustrating. My research went reasonably well considering the heavy clinical and teaching demands. But I loved to teach. And I loved seeing patients! I felt I could really help patients, and they seemed to feel my commitment to help. Through the years, my responsibilities increased so that by 1973, I was running the Psychosomatic Medicine Service as director. I also applied for, and was accepted by, the Psychoanalytic Institute. To become a psychoanalyst, however, I had to have my own personal psychoanalysis with Dr. Lowmann.

As I had hoped, Dr. Kaiser became my friend and mentor at Yale. He was always gentle and considerate but intellectually astute and honest. We started collaborating in writing a book for medical students. We wrote a number of research papers together.

A major disappointment occurred in 1975. The department had put forward a proposal for my promotion to associate professor, but it was turned down by the dean's committee. Dr. Kaiser consoled me by saying, "You know that I think, and the whole department thinks, that you deserve the promotion. But the dean's committee is composed of 'gray eminences' who just think you are too young and that there is no reason why you should get this promotion ahead of schedule. Because, usually, one becomes associate professor here after five years. And you have been here only four years. Don't worry, Bo. Next year, there will be no problem."

In fact, I received the promotion to associate professor the following year. And now, after three years as associate professor, I was again up for promotion, again ahead of schedule, to full professor! This time, however, I would leave if I was not promoted. I feel I deserve the promotion, after two textbooks, more than fifty publications, and running a major service for seven years! And I was just appointed director of a major medical-student course. And, besides, I have an excellent offer from the University of California, San Francisco, to head up the Psychosomatic Medicine Service there as a full professor!

Finally, I hear Dr. Kaiser speaking on the phone, "Bo, the Board of Permanent Officers just met and approved your promotion to full professor unanimously. It has also noted that you were promoted ahead of time, at the age of thirty-eight, one of the youngest full professors as an MD in the history of Yale Medical School. Congratulations, Professor Bo!"

I made it! The top of the ladder. Full professor at Yale!

1983, Guilford, Connecticut

Ginny's pregnancy test came back positive. She is definitely pregnant. At the age of thirty-six, after sixteen years of marriage. Initially, Ginny and I did not want to have any children at all. We had felt that both our parents had sacrificed too much for their children, and we were not going to make the same mistake again. Besides, the world was overpopulated, and there was no compelling reason why we should have any children. We enjoyed ourselves without children. We traveled all over the world. We could go anywhere at our whim. Without a child, our combined salaries were sufficient to allow us to travel, to eat out in good restaurants whenever we wanted, to buy whatever we needed. We couldn't think of ourselves being tied down with a child.

Until Ginny's biological clock started running out. We realized that in a few years' time, it would be unsafe and unadvisable for Ginny to become pregnant at all. We wondered whether we should give having a child a try, after all. I felt rather ready for another adventure, and perhaps having a child might provide that. What would our child look like? Would he or she be more like me or Ginny? My mom or my dad or Ginny's?

Eventually, Ginny and I agreed on a gamble. Ginny would not use any birth control for the next two years. If she became pregnant, we would welcome the child. If she did not become pregnant in two years, we would not have a child. We would let destiny decide whether we would have an offspring. We would be content either way. At least we would have given our child a chance.

The die was cast. And destiny responded.

1982, Luxembourg Airport (50 N Parallel, 6.1 E Longitude)
Ginny and I have just landed in Luxembourg, via Icelandic Airlines. We took Icelandic because it had the lowest airfare between New York and Europe, the airport in Europe being in Luxembourg. We have train tickets from Luxembourg to Vienna, where our international medical convention is to be held. Our plane arrived late, and we have only one hour to go to the train station to catch the train. We have no idea where the train station is. We understood that there were shuttle buses between the airport and the train station. We do not see any. We flag a cab.

"Please take us to the train station," I say.

"Pardon, monsieur. No speak English."

"Umm, *ou est,* umm, Ginny, what is *train station* in French?"

"Umm, I know, but I can't think of it right now."

"Uh, driver, the train, t-r-a-i-n, station?"

"*Je ne comprehend pas, monsieur. Le treene?*"

Suddenly, I have an inspiration. I say, "*Monsieur, ou est la 'choo-choo'?*"

"*Ah, oui, Monsieur. Choo-choo—train! Le gare?*"

We arrive at the train station with time to spare. Yes, we will muddle through. We will make do, and we will come out OK.

1983, New Haven, Connecticut (41 N Parallel, 73 W Longitude)
The ultrasound exam of the fetus, a marvel of modern medicine, was impressive. Ginny and I could actually see the little head, body, and even penis of the little boy in Ginny's womb. The technician took a Polaroid picture of the fetus and gave it to us. They also performed an amniocentesis, to test for Down's syndrome. Ginny's relatively late age made it especially important that we test for Down's syndrome, as the incidence of the disease increases with increasing age of the mother. Fortunately, it was negative.

We had already decided that the baby, if it was a boy, would be named Ali. If it was a girl, I threatened to name her Alphabeth. Ginny wanted a boy, and I wanted a girl. So, either way, one of us would be happy.

Ginny decided on a regime of prenatal education, which included listening to classical music daily and doing yoga exercises. She and I also attended Lamaze classes. We were going to cover all bases. We had already decided that we would have only one child, if any. We were not going to spare any expense or necessities for our only child, Ali.

49

TOWARD SUNRISE

August 1989, Guilford, Connecticut (41.3 N Parallel, 72.3 W Longitude)

Claire and her daughter, thirteen-year-old Jean, just went back to Baltimore after visiting us for a week. Jean is taller than her mother at the age of thirteen. She has a beautiful chocolate complexion and a very pretty face, an elongated face compared with her mother's round face. Her father, Bill Jones, is an architect. And black. Yes, Claire married a black man. Another first in the Moon family. And, now, she is divorced. Legally. Another first in the Moon family. Claire is still on friendly terms with Bill. They simply could not maintain a marital relationship, which I know is quite common in a marriage between two artists. They are just too independent, too creative, to make the necessary accommodations needed in maintaining a marriage—a series of compromises and accommodations. Perhaps art is too free for that.

Jean is not only beautiful. She is also athletic, being a wonderful gymnast. She also plays the cello like a professional, and she is an honors student. An intelligent and mature girl. Jean and Ali got along very well together. Jean, an Afro Asian, and Ali, an Amerasian. How the Moons like to mix the blood. Or perhaps this particular branch of Moons, the New World kind. They are both beautiful children, both far better looking, stronger, and more talented than any of their parents. My dad's hope and prediction have come doubly true: both my sister Claire and I have started new bloodlines of the Moon family, which arose as a family of warriors in the Korean peninsula a long, forgotten time ago.

America has welcomed immigrants, those persons who left their homelands for a dream, of freedom, of opportunity, of tolerance, of fair competition. America has sustained itself through them, through the infusion of new blood, new ideas, and new energy. America is eternal because it renews itself, it is the magnet for youth, for youthful ideas, experiments, and daring. It is a universe where stars die and then are born again. Unlike the tired old countries of Europe and Asia, America is built on the premise of change, of renewal, always a country of the future, never of the past.

Claire was happy, too. Finally, she seems to feel at ease with herself as an independent human being. When she first came to America, Ginny and I could not believe our eyes—here was my sister, who was reared by my own parents, who seemed to have a value system diametrically opposed to mine, who seemed to have been sheltered to the point of nonexistence. She had practically no experience of living or of loving. She had fully expected me to support her and find a spouse for her. All she felt she had to do was paint, not for a living but for the sake of art itself.

It was a challenge for Ginny and me to try to persuade her that she had to find a means of becoming independent, of supporting herself, of feeling herself as a self-sufficient and self-reliant human being. She did find a job, but soon after she married and quit. It was not until she was divorced that she found a stable job, where she used her skills as a fine artist to a maximum. But now she seems to feel good about herself as a person, who is not only independent but also a good mother, providing an outstanding education for her daughter. Yes, Dad was right. She had to come to this country to grow fully. And blossom.

May 1990, Seoul, Korea (37.5 N Parallel, 127 E Longitude)
The twenty-fifth reunion of my medical-school class. Yes, I am back in Korea, after a quarter of a century. I've never been back to Korea since I flew away from the Seoul Airport on June 27, 1965.

I had vowed never to return to Korea unless and until the military regime was no longer in power. Finally, massive demonstrations by the Korean people just before the Seoul Olympics in 1988 forced a constitutional reform and free elections. Several years before, the tin-pot dictator, Park Chung Hee, had been assassinated by his own Central Intelligence Agency chief, and another general, Chun Doo Whan, had inherited power in Korea. Now, Chun Doo Whan was gone, secluding himself in a Buddhist temple to atone for his sins. Democracy was restored in Korea. Economically, Korea had made good use of the decades of peace and become a power rivaling that of Japan. Some say that the economic miracle of Korea owed itself to the authoritarian regime of Park Chung Hee. Many others believe that the Korean economic recovery was due to the initiative and energy of its people, in spite of, rather than due to, the authoritarian regime that had been in power.

Our meeting is at the Hilton Hotel, in Seoul, in the Kangnam section, south of the Han River. When I left Seoul for the United States, this section of Seoul did not exist. It was outside of city limits, with no human dwelling to speak of. Now, this is the thriving center of new Seoul. There used to be only one bridge across the Han River, where, at the beginning of the Korean War, thousands perished when the South Korean Army blew up the bridge prematurely to prevent the invading North Korean Army from crossing the river. Now there are more than forty bridges across the river! And the portion of the city south of the river is larger than that on the north side.

How things change in a quarter of a century! But my classmates have not changed all that much. Other than signs of age. Gray hair. It's funny. All my classmates who came to the United States seem to have grayer hair. Those who stayed in Korea have black hair but seem to behave older than those who had come to the States. I now realize that those who stayed in Korea have been dying their hair. But we from America act much younger than our black-haired counterparts! What an irony! Youth is defined by behavior, a self-definition, not by looks. I feel younger than any of my classmates, which, in fact, I am. But age and acting older are more respected in Korea. Would I trade my youthful behavior for more respect? Never on your life!

The reunion is a great success. It is fun seeing my old friends and rivals again. Although, unfortunately, not everyone who should have been are there. Philmo, who is now a professor of microbiology at an American Midwestern university, did not come. I spoke with him before I came. He was too busy with his work—and his six daughters! Yulak, who is a graduate of Seoul National University, rather than Hyundai, is, of course, not here. Bob is here. And so is Rabbit, whom I have not seen for a number of years. He seems to have gotten, if anything, younger during all these years. He is still the fun-loving, happy-go-lucky guy, if at times harebrained. It is refreshing to see him again. Bob is his usual serious self, although his seriousness has become rather mellow, and he surprised me and Ginny by buying us dinner at an expensive restaurant. He used to be so miserly! But then his wife, the daughter of our English-literature professor from the Hyundai days, may have relaxed his uptight personality. She, like her father, has a literary bent. Ali and Bob have become wonderful friends, perhaps because Bob misses his child, an only son like Ali, who is now in college, away from home.

We have two free days after the reunion to stay in Korea and do whatever we wish to do. For one day, we take a train ride to Pusan, which I described earlier. Then we hire a taxi and try to visit my old neighborhood in Hwi-jo Dong, where my father's home for the patriots used to be and where my half brother, whom I killed, had been buried.

The taxi driver winces when I tell him that we want to go to the Chongyang District. As we drive away from the downtown district and head for the eastern end of the city, I notice that it has become so big, so crowded, that I can hardly recognize any of the old landmarks. I ask the driver to get off the main highway and take the streets so that we can see the area better. I now recognize the train station at the Chongyang District, a rather regal but shabby building. I point it out to Ali and Ginny. But then we notice that the train station is full of women in various states of undress. Obviously a red-light district. This used to be a very respectable middle-class neighborhood before I left. We continue on the road for some time, but I do not see any familiar landmarks. I ask the driver to backtrack and drive again. No familiar sights. Not only the street but also the neighborhood in which I used to live is gone. There is a wide highway and an overpass where the neighborhood used to be. On the side roads are crowded, slum-like apartments and old run-down factories. I later check the map, to see that the whole neighborhood that I had called home is no longer there. The whole neighborhood had been demolished, to make room for the highways, the tall high-rise apartment buildings, and the now-decrepit factories. Gone, gone forever, was my old neighborhood and the house that I called home during my turbulent high-school and college days. Gone with the wind. Like a speck of dust!

I ask the driver to go to the National Cemetery across the river. It's not that I just had a patriotic urge to pay respects to those who perished during the war, but there was a small voice in my head saying that I should visit the tomb of the unknown, where at least the remains of one person are known to me—those of Keh-Hoon, my half brother, whom I killed that fateful night in June, just before I left Korea for a new life in America. Could I ever cleanse my hands of my brother's blood?

...Cain attacked his brother Abel and killed him. Then the LORD said to Cain, "Where is your brother Abel?" "I don't know," he replied. "Am I my brother's keeper?" The LORD said, "What have you done? Listen! Your brother's blood cries out to me from the ground. Now you are under a curse and driven from the ground, which opened its mouth to receive your brother's blood from your hand. When you work the ground, it will no longer yield its crops for you. You will be a restless wanderer on the earth. Cain said to the LORD, "My punishment is more than I can bear. Today you are driving me from the land, and I will be hidden from your presence; I will be a restless wanderer on the earth, and whoever finds me will kill me."

But the LORD said to him, "Not so; anyone who kills Cain will suffer vengeance seven times over." Then the LORD put a mark on Cain so that no one who found him would kill him. So Cain went out from the LORD's presence and lived in the land of Nod, east of Eden.—Genesis

Later, Ginny, Ali, and I explore Myungdong, the entertainment district. We look for the White Deer Tearoom, of which I had described to Ginny and Ali many times as one of the most important places of my youth. No more. The street is there, but where the White Deer Tearoom used to be, there is a clothing store. No more White Deer. With our White Deer days, the tearoom itself now exists only in our memories.

They say you cannot go home again. How true! Where home used to be, there are now strange people, who have made the place strange as well. Yes, home is where I live now.

Wherever it may be, east of Eden...

June 1984, Guilford, Connecticut (41.3 N Parallel, 72.3 W Longitude)

A postcard designed by Mrs. Martin Kaiser, an artist of renown:

Bo and Ginny Moon welcomed their son, Ali,
To our planet by the sun
On June 27, 1984.

A postcard received by Bo:

To Bo and Ginny,
Congratulations and best wishes
For the beginning of a new era in your lives.

Horatio Lowmann, MD

June 1984, Guilford, Connecticut
Da-da-da-da.
The opening bars of Beethoven's Fifth Symphony, sometimes called the *Destiny*. This has become the theme, the leitmotif of mine as I entered Ali's life. Whenever I came to his crib, I would sing, "Da-da-da-da!" and he would flash his characteristic wizened smile at me. From the beginning, Ali was very alert and bright, and he had a sense of humor. He smiled whenever he heard music and whenever he heard da-da-da-da. Yes, Ali was a gift of destiny. An unexpected but desired, planned but unanticipated, improbable but inevitable part of Ginny and me. It is so fitting that da-da-da-da should signify our relationship. The relationship, the love, between the father, Dada, and the son. The opening bars of the symphony that has been called *Destiny* as well as *Victory*.

June 28, 1965, 7:00 p.m., Tokyo, Japan (36 N Parallel, 140 E Longitude)
Bo
Japan Airlines Flight 007, from Tokyo to Honolulu, took off, eastbound, toward the morning.

They flew for many hours. But by crossing the international date line, they have gained a whole day, and it is as if they had just left the Tokyo Airport.

"We will be arriving at the Honolulu International Airport in fifteen minutes. Please make sure that your seat belts are fastened and seats are in an upright position," the loudspeaker announced. In fifteen minutes, they would be touching down on the soil of the United States of America.

Bo had hardly slept. The excitement of his adventure that had already begun in Japan by meeting the articulate and friendly women students from Tokyo University, who, through their brief contact, nevertheless instilled in each other the notion that much could be done to overcome prejudice and narrow-mindedness through personal contact and exchange of ideas, filled Bo's heart with hope. And soon he would be arriving in the land of freedom and of hope. The land of George Washington, Thomas Jefferson, Benjamin Franklin, and Abraham Lincoln! Of Edison, Bell, and Einstein! As he looked out the window, he saw the sun starting to rise above the watery horizon. They were finally flying toward sunrise!

10:00 a.m., Honolulu, Hawaii, United States of America (21.3 N Parallel, 157.8 W Longitude)
Among Bo's friends, Yulak deplaned first, followed by Philmo, Rabbit, Bob, and, finally, Bo. Going through immigration and customs was unexpectedly easy. With several hours to spare before boarding a United Airlines domestic flight to San Francisco, they decided to explore Honolulu. They walked out of the terminal into the brilliant sunlight of Hawaii. At first, they were dazed by the sunlight. Then they felt the fresh breeze from the Pacific Ocean. And

the smell of flowers all around. An attractive girl in a hula costume placed a lei around the neck of each deplaning passenger.

"Welcome to Hawaii, and welcome to America!"

Blue skies, a warm but fresh breeze, and the fragrance of flowers. And sunlight sparkling on the firmament. A journey begun by his father a quarter of a century ago had come to an end. Bo was home in America. This was another beginning.

50

EPILOGUE: PARALLEL TRACKS

From a newspaper clip on North Korea, New Haven, January 2012.

The current president of North Korea is a dead man. Kim Il-Sung died in 1994. "The Great Leader" is designated in the North Korean constitution as the country's "Eternal President." His birthday, April 15, is a public holiday in North Korea and is called the Day of the Sun.

Since the failed attempt at de-Stalinization in 1956, Kim Il-Sung purged all potential opponents, particularly the intellectuals with ties to South Korea, China, and the Soviet Union, and North Korea became an isolated, monolithic, and closed society. Gulags sprang up in remote mountainous parts of the country, to which were sent not only the dissidents but their blood relatives as well.

The initial governing spirit of egalitarian Marxist-Leninist Communism was replaced by a nationalistic and chauvinistic ideology invented by Kim, "juche," loosely translated as "self-sufficiency." Far from self-sufficient, the North Korean economy collapsed as the Soviet Union disintegrated and China opened up economically. Unable to sell their inferior products to these countries, and North Korean state-run farms unable to produce effectively, famine claimed the lives of hundreds of thousands of North Koreans.

North Korea became a hereditary dynasty unique in the Communist world. Kim Il-Sung, upon his death, was succeeded by his son, Kim Jong Il, who was, in turn, succeeded by his son, Kim Jong Un, in December 2011.

In the meantime, the South Korean economy, owing in large measure to the dictatorial but brilliant development-oriented economic policies of Park Chung Hee, grew by leaps and bounds, to become the fifteenth largest in GDP in the world. In 1998, South Korea rid itself of military dictatorship and became a modern democracy.

June 26, 2013
Obituary in *Hankook Daily News,* Seoul
Ms. Minja Moon Park, former CEO of Minsook Textile Ltd., died of natural causes on June 25, 2013, at the age of eighty-five. Born Keh-Kyung Moon in Kangwon Province, she is credited with having built the highly successful Minsook Textile Ltd., having risen from the lowly position of a sewing-machine operator in Pusan. She was instrumental in developing computerized silk manufacturing in Korea. She won many awards, including the Korean Businesswomen's Association Achievement Award (1975) and the Presidential Entrepreneur Award (1980). Her husband, Soo-il Park, whom she had married at age fifty, predeceased her in 2006. She is survived by her adopted daughter, Soo-Kyung Park, who is currently the CEO of Minsook Textile Ltd.

E-mail from Bob, October 2013

Dear Bo,

You may be surprised that I am writing from Shenyang, which used to be Mukden, in Manchuria. As you know, I am active in the American College of Cardiologists, which has a medical exchange program with the Chinese government. A group of American physicians and I have been touring northern China, giving seminars and discussing medicine. At the end of this tour, there was an opportunity to make an excursion to Manchuria, and I decided to take advantage of it as I know that there is a large Korean community in Manchuria and also because I was curious about your birthplace near there.

Well, there is, indeed, a very large Korean community here in Shenyang, as well as in surrounding cities. In fact, in many of these cities, you hardly hear any Chinese spoken. And they have excellent Korean food, including kimchi. Interestingly enough, the Koreans here are very interested in hearing about America and South Korea, rather than North Korea, in spite of their proximity to North Korea. The Chinese government has granted the Korean enclaves a measure of autonomy, so they have their own schools, churches, and so on. I can well imagine that, had your parents not moved back to Korea at the end of World War II, you might be among the Koreans I have just met here.

Manchuria is a truly vast land. Mostly plains but also mountains and forest and, now, very rapidly growing cities! And it is cold! Cold, vast, and windswept, with limitless blue skies. Some of the old buildings and houses in the cities are reminiscent of the old houses in Korea built by the Japanese. I am attaching a few pictures of Manchuria—you may want to visit here sometime soon. We are not getting any younger, you know.

Give my best to Ginny and Ali.

Fondly,
Bob

Yes, Ginny and I plan to visit Manchuria next year. We have traveled quite extensively, to Europe, Australia, South America, Egypt, Israel, Japan, Korea, and China, but have never visited the place of my birth, Manchuria. I rationalize this by saying that most of our travels were to attend professional meetings, which were usually held in major cities. I am still teaching at Yale, though I plan to wind down a little to do more writing. Ginny has gone on with her education, obtaining a doctorate in psychiatric nursing at Yale, and is now working as a consultant to an Alzheimer's facility. Ali has become a full-fledged musician.

Perhaps it is time for me to visit the place of my birth as a tourist, knowing that one can never go back home again.

January 1992, Snowbird, Utah, United States of America (40.5 N Parallel, 111.5 W Longitude)

"Smoke rises in the distant mountain," I whisper as I regard the majestic, snow-covered peaks of the Rockies. "Where is the smoke in the mountain, Dad?"

I look at Ali's happy red face at seven-and-a-half years old, with wonder and concern in his sparkling eyes. I say, "In the distance, there, do you see it? Maybe it's mist rather than smoke. Ali, those words—'s-moke rises in the dis-tant mount-ain'—were the first Korean words I learned, from my own dad, a long time ago."

"You have to teach me these words, too, Dad."

"Yes, of course, I will, Ali."

I almost said, "And I'll also tell you about a silver knife that my dad had given me," but I didn't.

I was in San Francisco attending a professional conference a few years earlier. I had taken the silver knife with me for a purpose. At the pier on the Embarcadero, I boarded a northbound ferry. It was twilight as the ferry glided over the calm indigo waters over the bay. As I stood on the port side of the deck, it was becoming quite chilly, and most people went inside the cabin. In a while, the picturesque San Quentin Prison came into view. Now I was quite alone on the deck. I lifted the canvas bag I was carrying and threw it overboard. The bag contained the silver knife and a sizable stone for weight. As important as it was in the destinies of the Moon family, I decided it had to go to make our next generation free. From its bloody memories. This northern area of the San Francisco Bay lies almost exactly on the thirty-eighth parallel that divides the two Koreas. The blue waters of the Pacific Ocean, oblivious to the artificial parallel lines, continuously flow and intermix with the waters of Korea, Manchuria, Japan, and America. Let the silver knife rest in peace in this body of water. As I looked back, the sky was red, as if drenched in blood.

"But now how about going down for a hearty breakfast? Your mom is waiting for us," I say to Ali.

"Sure thing, Dad. Let's go!"

The peaceful valley beneath is coming to life in the morning sun. A flock of birds is flying above, the sounds of engines breaking the morning silence as people start to drive up to the ski resort for the weekend. It snowed last night, and everything is covered with fresh white fluffy, downy snow.

Ali and I ski down, side by side, into the refreshing morning breeze. On impulse, I look back on the slope we came down and see our ski tracks on the pristine snow, parallel but intertwined.

The End

AUTHOR BIOGRAPHY

Psychiatrist and author Hoyle Leigh has written numerous short stories and professional books. His latest work, a historical novel, is informed by his experiences during the Korean War.

Leigh was born in Korea but now resides in the United States.

APPENDIX: BACKGROUND INFORMATION

Japan
The Division of Korean Peninsula at 38th Parallel
North Korea during 1945-1948
Korean War
North Korean Prison Camps
Brief Overview of Korean History to World War II
Recommended Books

Japan

Japan is the island nation southeast of the Korean peninsula. It had been a rather backward military dictatorship by Shoguns who ruled in the name of the emperor who was no more than a puppet. A number of enlightened leaders restored the emperor's power in 1868 (Meiji Restoration or Reform), and modeled itself after British parliamentary monarchy. Then Japan rapidly modernized and Westernized itself to become an imperial power. Japan acquired Taiwan after winning the first Sino-Japanese War in 1895, and following Japan's victory in Russo-Japanese War, Korea had become a Japanese protectorate in 1905 and was annexed to Japan in 1910. Japanese Empire expanded further as it sided with the victorious allies in WWI and obtained a number of formerly German Pacific Islands. Japanese military invaded Manchuria in 1931 and set up the puppet state of Manchukuo. In 1937, the second Sino-Japanese War broke out, with Japan occupying Shanghai and Nanking and large areas of eastern China as well as large parts of Indochina.

The Greater East Asia Co-Prosperity Sphere was a concept proclaimed by Japanese foreign minister Yosuke Matsuoka in 1940. Under this concept, with the slogan of "Asia for Asians," imperial Japan justified her expansion and domination of Manchuria, Taiwan, and other parts of Asia, including Western colonies such as the French Indochina, Burma, and later the Philippines.

The United States opposed Japan's expansion into China, and Japan responded by forging an alliance with Nazi Germany and fascist Italy in 1940.

With Japan's attack on Pearl Harbor, Dec 7, 1941, World War II broke out, which resulted in Japan's unconditional surrender on August 15, 1945 after the detonation of two atomic bombs in Hiroshima (Aug 6) and Nagasaki (Aug 9).

The Division of Korean Peninsula at 38th Parallel

In November 1943, Franklin Roosevelt, Winston Churchill and Chiang Kai-shek met at the Cairo Conference and agreed that Japan should lose all the territories it had conquered by force. In the declaration after this conference, Korea was mentioned for the first time. The three powers declared that they were, 'mindful of the enslavement of the people of Korea...determined that in due course Korea shall become free and independent.'

"At the Tehran Conference in November 1943 and the Yalta Conference in February 1945, the Soviet Union promised to join its allies in the Pacific War within three months of victory in Europe. On August 8, 1945, after three months to the day, the Soviet Union declared war on Japan. Soviet troops advanced rapidly, and the US government became anxious that they would occupy the whole of Korea. On August 10, 1945 two young officers—Dean Rusk and Charles Bonesteel—were assigned to define an American occupation zone. Working on extremely short notice and completely unprepared, they used a National Geographic map to decide on the 38th parallel. They chose it because it divided the country approximately in half but would place the capital Seoul under American control. No experts on Korea were consulted." (Wikipedia, https://en.wikipedia.org/wiki/Division_of_Korea. Accessed 10/11/2016.)

This division was meant to be temporary and was first intended to return a unified Korea back to its people after the United States, United Kingdom, Soviet Union, and Republic of China could arrange a single government.

In December 1945, a conference convened in Moscow to discuss the future of Korea. A 5-year trusteeship was discussed, and a joint Soviet-American commission was established. The commission met intermittently in Seoul but deadlocked over the issue of establishing a national government. In September 1947, with no solution in sight, the United States submitted the Korean question to the United Nations General Assembly.

Initial hopes for a unified, independent Korea quickly evaporated as the politics of the Cold War and opposition to the trusteeship plan from anti-communists resulted in the 1948 establishment of two separate nations with diametrically opposed political, economic, and social systems. On December 12, 1948, the General Assembly of the United Nations recognised the Republic of Korea as the sole legal government of Korea. In June 25, 1950 the Korean War broke out when North Korea breached the 38th parallel line to invade the South, ending any hope of a peaceful reunification for the time being. After the war, the 1954 Geneva conference failed to adopt a solution for a unified Korea. Beginning with Syngman Rhee, a series of oppressive autocratic governments took power in South Korea with American support and influence. The country eventually transitioned to become a market-oriented democracy in 1987 largely due to popular demand for reform, and its economy rapidly grew and became a developed economy by the 2000s. Due to Soviet Influence, North Korea established a communist government with a hereditary succession of leadership, with ties to China and the Soviet Union. Kim Il-sung became the supreme leader until his death in 1994, after which his son, Kim Jong-il took power. Kim Jong-il's son, Kim Jong-un, is the current leader, taking power after his father's death in 2011. After the Soviet Union's dissolution in 1991, the North Korean economy went on a path of steep decline, and it is currently heavily reliant on international food aid and trade with China.

(Excerpted from Wikipedia, accessed Aug 12, 2013)

North Korea during 1945-1948

In the aftermath of partition of Korea, Kim Il Sung had arrived in North Korea on August 22 after 26 years in exile in China and the Soviet Union. In September 1945, Kim was installed by the Soviets as head of the Provisional People's Committee. Kim established the Korean People's Army (KPA) formed from a cadre of guerrillas and former soldiers who had gained combat experience in battles against the Japanese and later Nationalist Chinese troops.

Although original plans called for all-Korean elections sponsored by the United Nations in 1948, Kim persuaded the Soviets not to allow the UN north of the 38th parallel. As a result, a month after the South was granted independence as the Republic of Korea, the Democratic People's Republic of Korea (DPRK) was proclaimed on September 9, with Kim as premier.

By 1949, North Korea was a full-fledged Communist dictatorship. All political power was monopolized by the Worker's Party of Korea (WPK). The establishment of a command economy followed. Most of the country's productive assets had been owned by the Japanese or by Koreans who had been collaborators. The nationalization of these assets in 1946 placed 70% of industry under state control. By 1949 this percentage had risen to 90%. Since then, virtually all manufacturing, finance and internal and external trade has been conducted by the state.

In agriculture, the government moved more slowly towards a command economy. The "land to the tiller" reform of 1946 redistributed the bulk of agricultural land to the poor and landless peasant population, effectively breaking the power of the landed class.(excerpted from Wikipedia, 2013)

Korean War
1950-1953

The Korean People's Army (KPA) of the Democratic Republic of Korea (DPRK) crossed the 38th parallel behind artillery fire at dawn on Sunday 25 June 1950. The KPA claimed that Republic of Korea Army (ROK Army) troops, under command of the régime of the "bandit traitor Syngman Rhee" had attacked first, and that they would arrest and execute Rhee. Within an hour, North Korean forces attacked all along the 38th parallel. The North Korean forces were a combined arms force including tanks supported by heavy artillery. The South Koreans did not have any tanks, anti-tank weapons, nor heavy artillery, that could stop such an attack. In addition, South Koreans deployed their outgunned forces piecemeal and were routed within the first few days. On 27 June, Rhee secretly evacuated from Seoul with government officials. On 28 June, at 2am, the South Korean Army blew up the highway bridge across the Han River in an attempt to stop the North Korean army. The bridge was detonated while 4,000 refugees were crossing the bridge, and hundreds were killed. Destroying the bridge also trapped many South Korean military units North of the Han River. In spite of such desperation, Seoul fell that same day. There were numerous massacres of civilians and atrocities throughout the Korean war. Both sides began killing civilians even during the first days of the war.

On 25 June 1950, the United Nations Security Council unanimously condemned the North Korean invasion of the Republic of Korea. The Soviet Union, a veto-wielding power, had boycotted the Council meetings since January 1950 The Security Council, on 27 June 1950, published Resolution 83 recommending member states provide military assistance to the Republic of Korea. On 27 June

President Truman ordered U.S. air and sea forces to help the South Korean régime.

By August, the KPA had pushed back the Republic of Korea (ROK) Army and the Eighth United States Army to the vicinity of Pusan, in southeast Korea. In their southward advance, the KPA purged the Republic of Korea's intelligentsia by killing civil servants and intellectuals. On 20 August, General MacArthur warned North Korean leader Kim Il Sung that he was responsible for the KPA's atrocities. By September, the UN Command controlled the Pusan perimeter, enclosing about 10% of Korea, in a line partially defined by the Nakdong River.

To relieve the Pusan Perimeter, General MacArthur launched an amphibious landing on September 15, 1950, at Inchon (now known as Incheon), well over 100 miles (160 km) behind the KPA lines. On 25 September, Seoul was recaptured by South Korean forces. American air raids caused heavy damage to the KPA, destroying most of its tanks and much of its artillery. North Korean troops in the south, instead of effectively withdrawing north, rapidly disintegrated, leaving Pyongyang vulnerable. During the general retreat only 25,000 to 30,000 of the initial 200,000 soldiers managed to rejoin the Northern KPA lines.

By October 1, 1950, the UN Command repelled the KPA northwards, past the 38th parallel; the ROK Army crossed after them, into North Korea. MacArthur made a statement demanding the KPA's unconditional surrender. Six days later, on October 7, with UN authorization, the UN Command forces followed the ROK forces northwards. The Eighth United States Army and the ROK Army drove up western Korea and captured Pyongyang, the North Korean capital, on October 19, 1950. At month's end, UN forces held 135,000 KPA prisoners of war. Chinese People's Volunteer Army (PVA) and the KPA launched their "Chinese New Year's Offensive" on New Year's Eve of 1950. Utilizing night attacks in which U.N. Command fighting positions were encircled and then assaulted by numerically superior troops who had the element of surprise, the attacks were accompanied by loud trumpets and gongs, which fulfilled the double purpose of facilitating tactical communication and mentally disorienting the enemy. UN forces initially had no familiarity with this tactic, and as a result some soldiers panicked, abandoning their weapons and retreating to the south. The Chinese New Year's Offensive overwhelmed UN forces, allowing the PVA and KPA to conquer Seoul for the second time on January 4, 1951. These setbacks prompted General MacArthur to consider using nuclear weapons against the Chinese or North Korean interiors, with the intention that radioactive fallout zones would interrupt the Chinese supply chains. However, upon the arrival of the charismatic General Ridgway, the esprit de corps of the bloodied Eighth Army immediately began to revive. In early February, South Korean army and police ran a systematic operation to destroy the guerrillas and their sympathizer citizens in Southern Korea, resulting in two massacres of Communists. On March 7, 1951, the U.N. forces launched Operation Ripper, expelling the PVA and the KPA from Seoul on March 14, 1951. This was the city's fourth conquest in a years' time, leaving it a ruin; the 1.5 million pre-war population was down to 200,000, and people were suffering from severe food shortages.

On 11 April 1951, Commander-in-Chief Truman relieved the controversial General MacArthur, the Supreme Commander in Korea. MacArthur believed that whether or not to use nuclear weapons should be his own decision, not the President's. MacArthur threatened to destroy China unless it surrendered.

General Ridgway was appointed Supreme Commander, Korea; he regrouped the UN forces for successful counterattacks, while General James Van Fleet assumed command of the U.S. Eighth Army. Further attacks slowly depleted the PVA and KPA force but the war reached a stalemate at what the UN called the "Line Kansas", just north of 38th Parallel, until the armistice of 1953.

For the remainder of the Korean War the UN Command and the PVA fought, but exchanged little territory; the stalemate held.

Large-scale bombing of North Korea continued, and protracted armistice negotiations began 10 July 1951 at Kaesong.

In 1952, the US elected a new president, and on November29, 1952, the president-elect, Dwight D. Eisenhower, went to Korea to learn what might end the Korean War. With the United Nations' acceptance of India's proposed Korean War armistice, the KPA, the PVA, and the UN Command ceased fire on July, 27, 1953 with the battle line approximately at the 38th parallel. Upon agreeing to the armistice, the belligerents established the Korean Demilitarized Zone (DMZ), which has since been patrolled by the KPA and ROKA, US, and Joint UN Commands.

(Excerpted from Wikepedia, accessed June Aug 11, 2013)

North Korean Prison Camps

The internment camps for people accused of political offences or denounced as politically unreliable are run by the State Security Department. Political prisoners are subject to guilt by association punishment. The parents, children, siblings, and sometimes even grandparents or grandchildren are sent to prison camps without any trial for the rest of their lives.

The internment camps are located in central and northeastern North Korea. They comprise many prison labor colonies in secluded mountain valleys, completely isolated from the outside world. The total number of prisoners is estimated to be 150,000 to 200,000 Yodok camp and Bukchang camp are separated into two sections. The prisoners are forced to perform hard and dangerous slave work with primitive means in mining and agriculture. The food rations are very small, so that the prisoners are constantly on the brink of starvation. In combination with the hard work this leads to huge numbers of prisoners dying. An estimated 40% of prisoners die from malnutrition. Moreover many prisoners are crippled from work accidents, frostbite or torture. There is a rigid punishment in the camp. Prisoners that work too slow or do not obey an order are beaten or tortured. In case of stealing food or attempting to escape, the prisoners are publicly executed.

Initially there were around twelve political prison camps, but some were merged or closed. Today there are six political prison camps in North Korea. Most of the camps are documented in testimonies of former prisoners and, for all of them, coordinates and satellite images are available.

Prisoners are subject to torture and inhumane treatment. Public and secret executions of prisoners, even children are commonplace. Infanticides (forced abortions and baby killings upon birth) also often occur. The mortality rate is very high, because many prisoners die of starvation, illnesses,[work accidents, or torture.

Lee Soon-ok gave detailed testimony on her treatment in the North Korean prison system to the United States House of Representatives in 2002. In her statement she said, "I testify that most of the 6,000 prisoners who were there when I arrived in 1987 had quietly perished under the harsh prison conditions by the time I was released in 1992." Many other former prisoners, including Kang Chol-hwan and Shin Dong-hyuk, gave detailed and consistent testimonies on the human rights crimes in North Korean prison camps.

According to the testimony of former camp guard Ahn Myong Chol of Camp 22, the guards are trained to treat the detainees as sub-human, and he gave an account of children in one of the camps who were fighting over who got to eat a kernel of corn retrieved from cow dung.

(Excerpted from Wikipedia, accessed Aug 11, 2013)

The description of Camp Lucky is loosely based on the Hoeryong concentration camp, though Camp Lucky as a prototype opened about a decade earlier.

Hoeryong concentration camp (or Haengyong concentration camp) is a political prison camp in North Korea. The official name is *Kwan-li-so* (penal labor colony*) No. 22.* The camp is a maximum security area, completely isolated from the outside world. Prisoners and their families are held in lifelong detention.

Camp 22 is located in Hoeryong county, North Hamgyong province, in northeast North Korea, near the border with China and Russia. It is situated in a large valley with many side valleys, surrounded by 400–700 m (1300–2300 ft) high mountains. The southwest gate of the camp is located around 7 km (4.3 mi) northeast of downtown Hoeryong, the main gate is located around 15 km (9.3 mi) southeast of Kaishantun, Jilin province of China. The western boundary of the camp runs parallel at a distance of 5–8 km (3–5 mi) from the Tumen river, which forms the border with China. The camp is not included in maps[6] and the North Korean government denies its existence.

The camp was founded around 1965 in Haengyong-ri and expanded into the areas of Chungbong-ri and Sawul-ri in the 1980s and 1990s.[1] The number of prisoners rose sharply in the 1990s, when three other prison camps in North Hamgyong province were closed and the prisoners were transferred to Camp 22. *Kwan-li-so No. 11 (Kyongsong)* was closed in 1989, *Kwan-li-so No. 12 (Onsong)* was closed in 1991 and *Kwan-li-so No. 13 (Changpyong)* in 1992.

Camp 22 is around 225 km^2 (87 sq mi) in area. It is surrounded by an inner 3300 volt electric fence and an outer barbed wire fence, with traps and hidden nails between the two fences. The camp is controlled by roughly 1,000 guards and 500–600 administrative agents. The guards are equipped with automatic rifles, hand grenades and trained dogs.

In the 1990s there were an estimated 50,000 prisoners in the camp. Prisoners are mostly people who criticized the government, people deemed politically unreliable (such as South Korean prisoners of war, Christians, returnees from Japan)[16] or purged senior party members.[17] Based on the guilt by association principle they are often imprisoned together with the whole family including children and the elderly.[12] All prisoners are detained until they die and prisoners are never released.

There is a secret execution site in Sugol Valley, at the edge of the camp.

Conditions in the camp

Former guard Ahn Myong-chol describes the conditions in the camp as harsh and life-threatening. He recalls the shock he felt upon his first arrival at the camp, where he likened the prisoners to walking skeletons, dwarfs, and cripples in rags. Ahn estimates that about 30% of the prisoners have deformities, such as torn off ears, smashed eyes, crooked noses, and faces covered with cuts and scars resulting from beatings and other mistreatment. Around 2,000 prisoners he says have missing limbs, but even prisoners who need crutches to walk must still work. Prisoners get 180 g (6.3 oz) of corn per meal (two times a day), with almost no vegetables and no meat. The only meat in their diets is from rats, snakes or frogs that they catch. Ahn estimates that 1,500–2,000 people die of malnutrition there every year, mostly children. Despite these deaths, the inmate population remains constant, suggesting that around 1,500–2,000 new inmates arrive each year. Children get only very basic education. From six years on they get work assigned, such as picking vegetables, peeling corn or drying rice, but they receive very little food, only 180 g (6.3 oz) in total per day. Therefore many children die before the age of ten years. Old people have to work to their death. Seriously ill prisoners are quarantined, abandoned, and left to die.

Single prisoners live in bunkhouses with 100 people in one room. As a reward for good work, families are often allowed to live together in a single room of a small house without running water.[1] But the houses are in poor condition; the walls are made from mud and have a lot of cracks. All prisoners have to use dirty and crowded communal toilets.

Prisoners have to do hard physical labor in agriculture, mining and factories from 5:00 am to 8:00 pm (7:00 pm in winter), followed by ideological re-education and self-criticism sessions. New Year's Day is the only holiday for prisoners. The mines are not equipped with safety measures and according to Ahn prisoners were killed almost every day. They have to use primitive tools, such as shovels and picks, and are forced to work to exhaustion. When there was a fire or a tunnel collapsed, prisoners were abandoned inside and left to die. Kwon Hyuk reported that corpses are simply loaded into cargo coaches together with the coal to be burnt in a melting furnace. The coal is supplied to Chongjin Power Plant, Chongjin Steel Mill and Kimchaek Steel Mill, while the food is supplied to the State Security Agency or sold in Pyongyang and other parts of the country.

Human rights violations

Ahn explained how the camp guards are taught that prisoners are factionalists and class enemies that have to be destroyed like weeds down to their roots. They are instructed to regard the prisoners as slaves and not treat them as human beings. Based on this the guards may at any time kill any prisoner who does not obey their orders. Kwon reported that as a security officer he could decide whether to kill a prisoner or punish him in other ways, if he violated a rule. He admitted that once he ordered the execution of 31 people from five families in a collective punishment, because one member of a family tried to escape.

In the 1980s public executions took place approximately once a week according to Kwon. However Ahn reported that in the 1990s they were replaced by secret executions, as the security guards feared riots from the assembled crowd. He had to go to the secret execution site a number of times and there he saw disfigured and crushed bodies.

In case of serious violations of camp rules, the prisoners are subject to a process of investigation, which produced human rights violations, such as reduced meals, torture, beating and sexual harassment. In Haengyong-ri there is a detention center to punish prisoners. Because of the harsh treatment, many prisoners die in detention and even more are crippled when leaving the detention building.

Ahn and Kwon reported about the following torture methods used in Camp 22:

Water torture: The prisoner has to stand on his toes in a tank filled with water to his nose for 24 hours

Hanging torture: The prisoner is stripped and hung upside down from the ceiling to be violently beaten

Box-room-torture: The prisoner is detained in a very small solitary cell, where he could hardly sit, but not stand or lie, for three days or a week.

Kneeling-torture: The prisoner has to kneel down with a wooden bar inserted near his knee hollows to stop blood circulation. After a week the prisoner cannot walk and many die some months later

Pigeon torture: The prisoner is tied to the wall with both hands at a height of 60 cm (2 ft) and must crouch for many hours.

There are beatings every day, if prisoners do not bow quickly or deeply enough before the guards, if they do not work hard enough or do not obey quickly enough. It is a frequent practice for guards to use prisoners as martial arts targets. Rape and sexual violence are very common in the camp, as female prisoners know they may be easily killed if they resist the demands of the security officers.

Ahn reported about hundreds of prisoners each year being taken away for several "major construction projects",] such as secret tunnels, military bases or nuclear facilities in remote areas None of these prisoners ever returned to the camp. Ahn is convinced that they were secretly killed after finishing the construction work to keep the secrecy of these projects.

Human experimentation

Kwon reported about human experimentation carried out in Haengyong-ri. He described a sealed glass chamber, 3.5 m (11 ft) wide, 3 m (9.8 ft) long and 2.2 m (7.2 ft) high, where he witnessed a family with two children dying from being test subjects for a suffocating gas. Ahn explained how inexperienced medical officers of Chungbong-ri hospital practiced their surgery techniques on prisoners. He heard numerous accounts of unnecessary operations and medical flaws, killing or permanently crippling prisoners.

Reports on mass starvation and closure

Satellite images from late 2012 showed the detention center and some of the guard towers being razed, but all other structures appeared operational. It was reported that 27,000 prisoners died of starvation within a short time and the surviving 3,000 prisoners were relocated to Hwasong concentration camp between March and June 2012. It was further reported that the camp was shut down in June, security guards removed traces of detention facilities until August and then miners from Kungsim mine and farmers from Saebyol and Undok were moved into the area.According to another report the authorities decided to close the camp to cover its tracks after a defection.

Former guards/prisoners (witnesses)

Ahn Myong-chol (1990 – 1994 in Camp 22) was a prison guard and driver in the camp. In 1987 he was a prison guard in Kwan-li-so No. 11 (Kyongsong) and 1987 – 1990 in Kwan-li-so No. 13 (Changpyong).

Kwon Hyok (1987 – 1990 in Camp 22) was a security officer in the camp. He defected six years later, when he worked as a military attaché in Beijing.

No former prisoner from the camp is known to have escaped from North Korea

(from http://en.wikipedia.org/wiki/Hoeryong_concentration_camp, accessed 8/28/2013)

Brief Overview of Korean History to World War II

The earliest known Korean pottery dates back to around 8000 BC,[4] and evidence of Mesolithic Pit-Comb Ware culture or Yungimun Pottery is found throughout the peninsula. An example of a Yungimun-era site is in Jeju-do. Jeulmun or Comb-pattern Pottery is found after 7000 BC, and pottery with comb-patterns over the whole vessel is found concentrated at sites in west-central Korea, where a number of settlements such as Amsa-dong existed.

Written history dates back to a **Three Kingdom Period** beginning with Gogureyo (37 BCE), Baekje (18 BCE) and Silla (57 BCE). In 660 CE, Silla attacked, aided by Chinese Tang forces, conquered Baekje. In 668, Silla and Tang forces conquered Gogureyo.

Goryeo Kingdom (918-1392)

Goryeo was founded in 918 and became the ruling dynasty of Korea by 936. "Goryeo" was named as Wang Geon deemed the nation as a successor of Goguryeo.[. The dynasty lasted until 1392, and it is the source of the English name "Korea."

During this period laws were codified, and a civil service system was introduced. Buddhism flourished, and spread throughout the peninsula. The development of celadon pottery flourished in the 12th and 13th century. The publication of Tripitaka Koreana onto 81,258 wooden blocks[75] and the invention of movable-metal-type printing press attest to Goryeo's cultural achievements.

In 1231 the Mongols began their campaigns against Korea and after 25 years of struggle, Goryeo relented by signing a treaty with the Mongols. For the following 80 years Goryeo survived as a tributary ally of the Mongol-ruled Yuan Dynasty in China.

In the 1350s, the Yuan Dynasty declined rapidly due to internal struggles, enabling King Gongmin to reform the Goryeo government. Gongmin had various problems that needed to be dealt with, including the removal of pro-Mongol aristocrats and military officials, the question of land holding, and quelling the growing animosity between the Buddhists and Confucian scholars. The Goryeo dynasty would last until 1392

Joseon (Yi) Dynasty (1392-1897)

In 1392, the general Yi Seong-gye, later known as Taejo, toppled the Goryeo Dynasty in a coup d'etat and established the Joseon Dynasty (1392–1897), named in honor of the ancient kingdom Gojoseon[and based on idealistic Confucianism-based ideology.

Taejo moved the capital to Hanyang (modern-day Seoul) and built Gyeongbokgung palace. In 1394 he adopted Neo-Confucianism as the country's official religion, and pursued the creation of a strong bureaucratic state. His son and grandson,King Taejong and King Sejong the Great, implemented numerous administrative, social, and economical reforms and established royal authority in the early years of the dynasty.

Internal conflicts within the royal court, civil unrest and other political struggles plagued the nation in the years that followed, worsened by the Japanese invasion of Korea between 1592 and 1598. Toyotomi Hideyoshi marshalled his forces and tried to invade the Asian continent through Korea, but was eventually repelled by Korean Army and Navy, and assistance from Ming China. This war also saw the rise of the career of Admiral Yi Sun-sin with the "turtle ship"

As Joseon was striving to rebuild itself after the war, it suffered from the invasions by the Manchu in 1627 and 1636. Different views regarding foreign policy divided the royal court, and ascensions to the throne during that period were decided after much political conflict and struggle.

A period of peace followed in the 18th century during the years of King Yeongjo and King Jeongjo, who led a new renaissance of the Joseon dynasty, with fundamental reforms to ease the political tension between the Confucian scholars, who held high positions.

However, corruption in government and social unrest prevailed in the years thereafter, causing numerous civil uprisings and revolts. The government made sweeping reforms in the late 19th century, but adhered to a strict isolationist policy, earning Joseon the nickname "Hermit Kingdom". The policy had been established primarily for protection against Western imperialism, but before long Joseon was forced to open trade, beginning an era leading into Japanese colonial rule.

Joseon's culture was based on the philosophy of Neo-Confucianism, which emphasizes morality, righteousness, and practical ethics. Wide interest in scholarly study resulted in the establishment of private academies and educational institutions. Many documents were written about history, geography, medicine, and Confucian principles. The arts flourished in painting, calligraphy, music, dance, and ceramics.

The most notable cultural event of this era is the promulgation of the Korean alphabet Hangul by King Sejong the Great in 1446. This period also saw various other cultural, scientific and technological advances.[

During Joseon, a social hierarchy system existed that greatly affected Korea's social development. The king and the royal family were atop the hereditary system, with the next tier being a class of civil or military officials and land owners known as yangban, who worked for the government and lived off the efforts of tenant farmers and slaves.

A middle class, jungin, were technical specialists such as scribes, medical officers, technicians in science-related fields, artists and musicians. Commoners, i.e. peasants, constituted the largest class in Joseon. They had obligations to pay taxes, provide labor, and serve in the military. By paying land taxes to the state, they were allowed to cultivate land and farm. The lowest class included tenant farmers, slaves, entertainers, craftsmen, prostitutes, laborers, shamans, vagabonds, outcasts, and criminals. Although slave status was hereditary, they could be sold or freed at officially set prices, and the mistreatment of slaves was forbidden.

This yangban focused system started to change in the late 17th century as political, economic and social changes came into place.

By the 19th century, new commercial groups emerged, and the active social mobility caused the yangban class to expand, resulting in the weakening of the old class system. The Joseon government ordered the freedom of government slaves in 1801. The class system of Joseon was completely banned in 1894.

Foreign Invasions

Joseon dealt with a pair of Japanese invasions from 1592 to 1598 (Imjin War or the Seven Years war). Prior to the war, Korea sent two ambassadors to scout for signs of Japan's intentions of invading Korea. However, they came back with 2 different reports, and while the politicians split into sides, little proactive measures were taken.

This conflict brought prominence to Admiral Yi Sun-sin as he contributed to eventually repelling the Japanese forces with the innovative use of his invention, the turtle ship, a massive, yet swift, ramming/cannon ship fitted with iron spikes and, according to some sources, an iron-plated deck[The use of the hwacha was also highly effective in repelling the Japanese invaders from the land.

Subsequently, Korea was invaded by the Manchus in 1627 and again in 1636, after which the Joseon dynasty recognized the suzerainty of the Qing Empire. Though the Koreans respected their traditional subservient position to China, there was persistent Ming loyalty and disdain for the Manchus.

During the 19th century, Joseon tried to control foreign influence by closing the borders to all nations but China. In 1853 the USS South America, an American gunboat, visited Busan for 10 days and had amiable contact with local officials. Several Americans shipwrecked on Korea in 1855 and 1865 were also treated well and sent to China for repatriation. The Joseon court was aware of the foreign invasions and treaties involving Qing China, as well as the First and Second Opium Wars, and followed a cautious policy of slow exchange with the West.

In 1866, reacting to greater numbers of Korean converts to Catholicism despite several waves of persecutions, the Joseon court clamped down on them, massacring French Catholic missionaries and Korean converts alike. Later in the year France invaded and occupied portions of Ganghwa Island. The Korean army lost heavily, but the French abandoned the island.

The General Sherman, an American-owned armed merchant marine sidewheel schooner, attempted to open Korea to trade in 1866. After an initial miscommunication, the ship sailed upriver and became stranded near Pyongyang. After being ordered to leave by the Korean officials, the American crewmen killed four Korean inhabitants, kidnapped a military officer and engaged in sporadic fighting that continued for four days. After two efforts to destroy the ship failed, she was finally set aflame by Korean fireships laden with explosives. This incident is celebrated by the DPRK as a precursor to the later USS Pueblo incident.

In response, the United States confronted Korea militarily in 1871, killing 243 Koreans in Ganghwa island before withdrawing. This incident is called the Sinmiyangyo in Korea. Five years later, the reclusive Korea signed a trade treaty with Japan, and in 1882 signed a treaty with the United States, ending centuries of isolationism.

In 1885, United Kingdom occupied Geomun Island, and withdrew in 1887.

Conflict between the conservative court and a reforming faction led to the Gapsin Coup in 1884. The reformers sought to reform Koreans institutionalized social inequality, by proclaiming social equality and the elimination of the privileges of the yangban class. The reformers were backed by Japan, and were thwarted by the arrival of Qing troops, invited by the conservative Queen Min. The Chinese troops departed but the leading general Yuan Shikai remained in Korea from 1885-1894 as Resident, directing Korean affairs.

After a rapidly modernizing Japan forced Korea to open its ports in 1876, it successfully challenged the Qing Empire in the Sino-Japanese War (1894–1895). In 1895, the Japanese were involved in the murder of Queen Min, who had sought Russian help, and the Russians were forced to retreat from Korea for the time.

As a result of the Sino-Japanese War (1894–1895), the 1895 Treaty of Shimonoseki was concluded between China and Japan. It stipulated the abolition of traditional relationships Korea had with China, the latter of which recognised the complete independence of Joseon and repudiated the former's political influence over the latter.

Russian influence was strong in the Empire until being defeated by Japan in the Russo-Japanese War (1904–1905). Korea effectively became a protected state of Japan on 17 November 1905, the 1905 Protectorate Treaty having been promulgated without Emperor Gojong's required seal or commission.

Following the signing of the treaty, many intellectuals and scholars set up various organizations and associations, embarking on movements for independence. In 1907, Gojong was forced to abdicate after Japan learned that he sent secret envoys to the Second Hague Conventions to protest against the protectorate treaty, leading to the accession of Gojong's son, Emperor Sunjong. In 1909, independence activist An Jung-geun assassinated Itō Hirobumi, the Resident-General of Korea, for Ito's intrusions on the Korean politics. This prompted the Japanese to ban all political organisations and proceed with plans for annexation.

Japanese Rule (1910-1945)

In 1910 Japan effectively annexed Korea by the Japan–Korea Annexation Treaty, which along with all other prior treaties between Korea and Japan was confirmed to be null and void in 1965. While Japan asserts that the treaty was concluded legally, this argument is generally not accepted in Korea because it was not signed by the Emperor of Korea as required and violated international convention on external pressures regarding treaties. Korea was controlled by Japan under a Governor-General of

Korea until Japan's unconditional surrender to the Allied Forces on 15 August 1945, with de jure sovereignty deemed to have passed from the Joseon Dynasty to the Provisional Government of the Republic of Korea.

After the annexation, Japan set out to repress Korean traditions and culture, develop and implement policies primarily for the Japanese benefit. European-styled transport and communication networks were established across the nation in order to extract the resources and labor; these networks were mostly destroyed later during the Korean War. The banking system was consolidated and the Korean currency abolished. The Japanese removed the Joseon hierarchy, destroyed much of the Gyeongbokgung palace and replaced it with the Government office building.

After Emperor Gojong died in January 1919, with rumors of poisoning, independence rallies against Japanese invaders took place nationwide on 1 March 1919 (the March 1st Movement). This movement was suppressed by force and about 7,000 were killed by Japanese soldiers and police. An estimated 2 million people took part in peaceful, pro-liberation rallies, although Japanese records claim participation of less than half million. This movement was partly inspired by United States President Woodrow Wilson's speech of 1919, declaring support for right of self-determination and an end to colonial rule for Europeans. No comment was made by Wilson on Korean independence, perhaps as a pro-Japan faction in the USA sought trade inroads into China through the Korean peninsula.

The Provisional Government of the Republic of Korea was established in Shanghai, China, in the aftermath of March 1 Movement, which coordinated the Liberation effort and resistance against Japanese control. Some of the achievements of the Provisional Government include the Battle of Chingshanli of 1920 and the ambush of Japanese Military Leadership in China in 1932. The Provisional Government is considered to be the de jure government of the Korean people between 1919 and 1948, and its legitimacy is enshrined in the preamble to the constitution of the Republic of Korea.[110]

Continued anti-Japanese uprisings, such as the nationwide uprising of students in November 1929, led to the strengthening of military rule in 1931. After the outbreaks of the Sino-Japanese War in 1937 and World War II Japan attempted to exterminate Korea as a nation. The continuance of Korean culture itself began to be illegal. Worship at Japanese Shinto shrines was made compulsory. The school curriculum was radically modified to eliminate teaching in the Korean language and history. The Korean language was banned, Koreans were forced to adopt Japanese names, and newspapers were prohibited from publishing in Korean. Numerous Korean cultural artifacts were destroyed or taken to Japan. According to an investigation by the South Korean government, 75,311 cultural assets were taken from Korea.

Some Koreans left the Korean peninsula to Manchuria. Koreans in Manchuria formed resistance groups known as Dongnipgun (Liberation Army); they would travel in and out of the Sino-Korean border, fighting guerrilla warfare with Japanese forces. Some of them would group together in the 1940s as the Korean Liberation Army, which took part in allied action in China and parts of South East Asia. Tens of thousands of Koreans also joined the Peoples Liberation Army and the National Revolutionary Army.

During World War II, Koreans at home were forced to support the Japanese war effort. Tens of thousands of men were conscripted into Japan's military. Around 200,000 girls and women, some from Korea, were engaged in sexual services, with the euphemism "comfort women". Previous Korean "comfort women" are still protesting against the Japanese Government for compensation of their sufferings

Christianity

Protestant missionary efforts in Asia were nowhere more successful than in Korea. American Presbyterians and Methodists arrived in the 1880s and were well received. In the days Korea was under Japanese control, Christianity became in part an expression of nationalism in opposition to the Japan's efforts to promote the

Japanese language and the Shinto religion. In 1914 out of 16 million people, there were 86,000 Protestants and 79,000 Catholics; by 1934 the numbers were 168,000 and 147,000. Presbyterian missionaries were especially successful. Harmonizing with traditional practices became an issue. The Protestants developed a substitute for Confucian ancestral rites by merging Confucian-based and Christian death and funerary rituals.

Recommended Books

Korea: The Politics of the Vortex
Gregory Henderson
Hardcover: 495 pages
Publisher: Harvard University Press; 1st edition (October 1968)

Escape from Camp 14
Blaine Harden
Paperback: 224 pages
Publisher: Penguin Books; Reprint edition (March 26, 2013)

Crisis in North Korea: The Failure of De-Stalinization, 1956
Andrei N. Lankov
Paperback: 274 pages
Publisher: University of Hawaii Press (June 2007)

The Real North Korea
Andrei N. Lankov
Hardcover: 304 pages
Publisher: Oxford University Press, USA (April 2013)

The Korean War
Bruce Cummings
Paperback: 320 pages
Publisher: Modern Library; Reprint edition (July 12, 2011)

The Forgotten War
Clay Blair
Paperback: 1136 pages
Publisher: Anchor; First Anchor Book Edition edition (January 24, 1989)

The Way Out (Fiction)
Meg Choi (Song-hae Kim)
Paperback: 344 pages
Publisher: CreateSpace Independent Publishing Platform (December 14, 2012)

www.ingramcontent.com/pod-product-compliance
Lightning Source LLC
Chambersburg PA
CBHW060530310726
48982CB00002B/486

* 9 7 8 0 9 9 9 2 4 8 4 0 9 *